Apocalyptic God

Y.F. Valentine

Cemi Books Publishing

South Jordan, UT

Thank you to everyone who contributed to the creation of this book.

First, thank you, Daldalezz, for creating the fantastic art. You truly brought Apollo and Dafnie to life. Thanks to my excellent editor, Jeannine T, it means the world to me you love my story.

Last, I thank my family, who supported me on this wild ride, and my husband, Leo. Babe, I borrowed your pompous personality to create Apollo.

Chapter 1

Provocation - Ancient Times

At the foot of the temple's stairs, bathed in dried blood and guts, Apollo admired his lavish palace.

He had accomplished the unthinkable. The terrible python accosting his family for years lay dead. As the lord of these lands, he and his loved ones could live in peace—no more hiding, running, or fearing for their lives. Like a fleeting memory, danger would no longer knock at their door.

Now, his head fogged with lightheadedness and relief—confusing emotions warred in his chest. The monster standing in his way to glory was now rotting away in the fields. But at what cost?

"I'm... ready for..."

As he wavered, a surge of doubt swept over him, questioning his future. But everything changed in the batting of an eye—certainty sending cold shockwaves throughout his body.

"Everyone to follow me. I answer to no one but Zeus. I'm a man. The crowned prince of Olympus. The rightful king of these domains." Ogling at a reflective metal, he cringed at the sight of his appearance. "Disgusting!"

He moaned in satisfaction as his servants disrobed him. They rid him of the soiled vestments of his youth and prepared him to emerge as a man. His attendants picked rotting gunk and muck from his body.

Afterward, he waded deep into the warm pool and sat by a bench near a waterspout. Peace washed over him as he steeped in the fragrant water.

"My mother will live like a queen. Leto, mother of Zeus' first-born son, will rise above all others. And I... want... her, my huntress, my sweet nymph, a befitting bride. We'll rear warriors, artists, and scholars," he murmured, already with someone in mind—a beautiful naiad. Apollo couldn't deny his lust for the young woman. He wanted to woo the immortal beauty tonight and make her his wife.

But first, he wished to purify his body. "This will be a nightmare to clean." Grime and gore clung to his skin and robes as a frown marred his elegant face.

The insufferable goddess pestered Zeus about killing the elemental beast. Rather than waiting for him to look presentable, his stepmother demanded that he stand trial, no matter what.

Hera, the jealous instigator, had caused the whole tragedy to begin with. He'd just reacted. He'd killed the python in self-defense. Instead, he puffed up his chest, ready to receive his punishment. Other than being Leto's son, he'd done nothing wrong.

He protected Delphi and its lands—the regions he cared about. He didn't care about his father or the conflicted look on Zeus's face as he stood his hearing.

"To live and celebrate the python's death. Honor the beast, tormentor of your family," his father hollered over his shoulder as he left the hall. Disappointed, Hera followed behind her husband.

After returning to the palace, he winced at the man staring back from the mirror. Furiously scratching his dirty flesh, he jogged to the ample bathing pool by the master room. A shiver ran through his body as he admired the crystal water. He sighed in defeat, knowing that the pollution on his physique would poison the bath.

He used the assortment of soaps and oils on the ledge, taking his time cleaning. Grimacing, he cleaned the remnants of his battle with much care. The rancid muck clung to him like a second skin. He scrubbed himself until he flushed from the rough treatment and abrasion.

Soon, the revolting liquid offended him. Only after a thorough washing did he make it to his chambers and prepare for the day. Standing straighter than usual, he selected his attire for the festivities—a funerary service to honor the wretched beast and to celebrate his superiority.

His helpers chose each garment to enhance his commanding presence. As always, he looked impressive. Certainly, today, he picked the sun to give him the natural halo he deserved. He aimed for gallantry and desirable appearances.

The sheer billowing curtains let in a light breeze, stroking Apollo's perfect hair. He admired the sunrise on the horizon, allowing his servants to style him for the day. He aspired to look divine for his subjects. The Pythian Games would become a grand celebration—more monumental than the ordinary Olympics.

His magnificent legacy! As he stepped out into the forest, he radiated confidence. The gentle sunlight tinted his features, creating a splendid aura that made him extraordinarily handsome.

Once outside, he spotted a small gathering at the temple, now his home, reading his chariot. With his chin held high, Apollo wore a stern look on his face. Judging by the goosebumps on his skin, he sensed the admiration from those around him. It reaffirmed his belief. He embodied royal splendor amidst the simple yet lush greenery.

"Today, I honor the beast and proclaim the Pythian games. Henceforth, Delphi will hold artistic and athletic events to crown champions in the fourth cycle of the seasons. Both men and women can partake," he said as he mounted his chariot and called to those close to him. "Now spread the word. There is a new benevolent master."

He scanned as everyone ran in every direction to obey his command. "My realm! This banishment is what I want—to become the lord over these regions."

The thrilling awareness of pleasure radiated across his body. He took to the skies to survey his grounds. Speechless, he looked at the vastness and splendor of his country. After a while, he steered his golden chariot into the mountainous woodland to kick off his procession. His eyes swept over the lush green canopy of the forest, marveling at its beauty. His chest swelled with fondness when he admired his new fertile domains.

"I love this place better than any other! I want to begin anew and plant my roots in these beautiful lands. Start a family with that lovely naiad—she stole my heart," he murmured, a confession meant for him alone. His thoughts raced with affection for the nymph huntress. He plucked a leaf from a nearby branch to admire its loveliness while listening to Nuthatch's melodic tune.

The fresh air, a mix of dew and musk, saturated his consciousness. He closed his eyes to appreciate the wood aromas invading his senses—a blend he'd cherished since childhood. Nirvana mixed with unbound jubilation, only found in the embrace of the antique towering trees.

The mortals and woodland spirits pranced and jigged around in contagious celebration. The forest provided a treasured hunting scene, and his heart brimmed with appreciation. His ears perked at the hushed conversations. It created a harmonized melody with the gentle rustling of leaves.

The festive gathering, which painted a tapestry of unity and reverence woven into the very material of his ancient woods, swept across Apollo's gaze. He smiled graciously, knowing that his realm would become prosperous—a commitment he would never break to his people.

News of his kill spread like an uncontrollable blaze. The excited buzz celebrating his punishment amused him the most. The whispers floating here and there tickled like a butterfly fluttering its wings by his ears, enjoying all the attention like a deviant child. He beamed at the thought of pissing Hera once again—too easy for him to pick on his stepmother. His very existence proved to be a thorn in her side.

The sun god also thirsted to glimpse at the conflicted look in his father's eyes, wondering what to do with him. Apollo enjoyed every second of his antics and felt like screaming with delirious delight. A wicked mask settled on his debonair attitude.

"Apollo, the hero and king of these lands! It sounds magnificent," he murmured, feeling euphoric and like he belonged at the zenith of the world. His desire to bask in the spotlight exhilarated him, filling his head with romantic ideas of grandeur. All eyes landed on him as he rode with his chariot through the crowd with arms wide open.

Once at the clearing, he caught sight of a satyr playing an aulos. The male agitated the onlookers with his joyful and energetic tunes. "Oh, a fellow music lover, how charming! He'll be perfect for announcing my arrival to the mob." He dismounted his carriage to continue his glorious procession on foot. "Satyr, my disciple, I pick you to announce your mighty lord's coming."

Delighted, the woodland creature preached to the congregation in great earnestness. "Lo! Apollo, the imposing god of the sun and melody, arrived victorious, manifesting divine potency and virility to all present. His resplendent ringlets rivaled the sunbeams while his gaze reflected the boundless heavens.

The performer pranced and pirouetted as he continued his speech, "Wrapped in the sun's affectionate embrace, the noble god's conquest over the nightmare plaguing these parts, the horrible python lies now defeated. His quiver, once brimming with a thousand arrows, is now empty. The accomplishment is testimony to his might. His greatest feat is the fierce battle he waged for us, his people, and to safeguard and claim his rightful domain."

The male vociferous tone carried through the clearing, boasting with a melodious voice. Apollo's verbal improvisation was on point, impressing the snobbish princely god. "Behold our lord, part ways, and let him through."

The crowd's earsplitting roar overwhelmed all other sounds. With his head held proud, he puffed his chest and continued promenading. Slowly and steadily, he walked through the lush trail. Cocky beyond belief, Apollo called upon his power to cast an even, luminous glow around him. He looked like the sun. Utterly marvelous.

Unknown to the new king, greed became his undoing. In a drunken high brought only by vanity, he laughed without restraint, a tone that carried nothing but selfishness. His baritone voice resonated like thunder, electrifying everyone close enough to listen. The euphoria enveloped him as he coaxed his magic to manifest and enhance his celestial presence even more.

Aroused by his enchantment, he flicked his golden mane enticingly. His pompous gait mesmerized even the tiniest of creatures in the forest. He was a show-stopping sight, grabbing his lyre from his bag and plucking at its strings.

Time to perform!

Time to sing!

His songs, the royal honey for all his subjects, enticed the birds to serenade his eulogies. The ethereal melodies inspired his admirers to dance in his wake. Even the trees swayed in reverence as Apollo continued his musical promenade, an interlude of artistry.

"Hark thee, an important decree! On this day, the inaugural games of the Pythian Games!" he shouted once he reached an expansive clearing. His gaze landed upon the multitude with a commanding presence. He raised his hand, and the crowd went silent. He savored the crowd's exhilaration.

"Athletes from faraway realms, we celebrate your prowess to pay tribute to all who seek fame. In various competitions of might and wits, we all partake. If so, be willing without discrimination. Games of many disciplines bound. Allow the spirit of harmony and glory to unite us all. The winners shall receive a myriad of blessings. And the heavens will etch and inscribe our names in the annals of history. Embrace and take victory for thyself." He boasted. "Let the tournament begin! Compete in my honor and be triumphant," he said, his thundering voice traveling through the area.

And so, the Panhellenic Games began. The Delphian amphitheater hosted a busy schedule of lyrical and theatrical contests, while the athletic matches took place on an expansive field.

By midday, the events barreled ahead in full swing. After his musical performance, a graceful faun presented Apollo with a beautifully crafted wreath woven from oak leaves, brambles, and golden acorns—a crown befitting the handsome god.

A lively mob of attendees soon surrounded him. Drunken with anticipation and yearning, their eyes glazed with want. With shimmering eyes, some hoped to capture Apollo's fancy. As clear as day, the swarm wanted to bask in his charm. His allure came as a gift many coveted—even for a day.

Apollo was born to be admired and favored. He enjoyed being the center of attention.

He couldn't help but acknowledge an attractive young man standing amidst the gathering. With short, vibrant reddish-brown hair and his beauty pleasing—impersonating temptation—he pulled away from the crown to stand before the beautiful man. Apollo drew the lad close in a gentle hold, wrapping his muscular arms around his waist. Possessiveness washed over his senses.

Their lips met for a kiss that sent pleasant tremors over his entire body. It also ignited an unquenchable fire from the pit of the stomach, spreading up to his head. Their bodies intertwined like vines in need of an anchor. Each touch and embrace fueled his sexual cravings with an insatiable hunger.

Tender at first, the youthful male's hesitant touches drove Apollo frantic with starvation. "Too gentle, my love," he whispered, capturing an earlobe to tease. Encouraged, the lad grew bolder and braver. His musky scent and savory lips incited him wild with lust. He wanted to lose himself in the arms of his young admirer.

The deity of light and the sun sighed with want while he ground his excited shaft against the man's leg. His kisses became more demanding as time flew by. Every caress oozed with desire —his ecstatic appetite.

They idolized each other until they reached the delightful pinnacle of earnest release, both spent and enjoying the afterglow of their union. Apollo yearned for him now. Indeed, his head swelled with better plans for the night—with no one around.

He wanted the man.

He craved his beloved huntress as well.

Together!

However, he ought to part and find her first. For now!

He sighed in dismay as he released the captivating man. "I must leave you as I'm needed elsewhere. But stay by my side, my dear," he whispered to the dumbfounded lad. He claimed the precious man's lips one last time before parting reluctantly.

Still reeling from the euphoria, Apollo made his way to the stage, bowing low at the applause. He wanted to sing, praise, and love. "I shall grace you all with my songs of power and devotion. Melodies of adventure and lust will fill your ears and inspire you. All ought to delight. All rejoice. Enjoy my subjects. Relish aplenty!" Dancing his way toward the crowd, he continued his presumptuous parade.

Amidst the contestants, mischief waited patiently. Eros threaded his bow with a skill unmatched by anyone. His fluid release of his arrow caught Apollo's attention. Consumed by his ego, Apollo dismissed it as beneath his mighty dignity. Witnessing a childlike god joyfully indulging in a task intended for heroes was preposterous. The imp tried to understand a weapon designed for men like him, the crown prince and son of Zeus. Worthy warriors deserved to wield a noble armament, not Eros.

"Alas, audacious lad! Tis I, the lord and master of the bow and arrow. Why do you handle arms meant for men? Tis I who strikes true at savage beasts. Such an instrument befits only a man like myself. Tis I who beats down his foes. Not long past, I conquered the python, its belly spanning vast acres, with many of my arrows."

His arrogance and disdain permeated every word as he carried on with his ill-meaning judgment.

"Is it not your mastery to ignite smoldering passion?"

A smug smile spread across Apollo's full lips before he continued. "Your trade meant to torch love flames is your game. Rather than trying to own my glories, pursue your own elsewhere. I forbid your kind from employing such noble weaponry."

His tone seethed with impudence. His voice cut through the air like a sharp blade, leaving bitter tension between the two celestial beings—a foolish mistake.

"Oh, Phoebus Apollo! God of foresight and light, you will meet your plight. It's your destiny."

Enticing his hips and parading his youthful body, Eros bowed to the prince in a feigned ovation. "My bow, a faithful and formidable power, shall assail you down where you stand. The might of gods surpasses mortal kin. My glories are divine. In grace, my brilliance outshines your current feeble feat. Tell me, my dearest opponent, whose glory shines brighter, mine or thee?"

Eros fluttered his wings in annoyance before he turned to leave. "Though your radiance embodies the sun's eternal flame, my bow will strike true in love's unending game. Your heart belongs to me, and I will curse it," the mischievous divinity of love finished as he flew away.

Apollo paid no heed to Eros's overly patronizing banter—the scorn didn't merit his attention. The god of passion held little sway over the majestic being. The master of the hunt didn't bother with petty individuals. In the end, Eros's words meant nothing to the patron of many blessed skills.

The deity of light didn't feel threatened by the frivolous god of desire. He exuded an aura of invincibility and dominance—he viewed Eros as an inconsequential immortal. Besides, the Olympian god's confidence brimmed with power and unrivaled prestige that knew no bounds in the realm of the mighty deities.

Short of mind and having forgotten about the incident, he took delight in the grandiosity of his games. His cherishing subjects celebrated his athletic prowess by taking part in various events and indulging aplenty. The sun's rays bathed him in glory, and everyone loved him. He lived in a trance of devotion—an all-too-consuming, debilitating haze—blissfully unaware of the consequences his hubris brought upon himself, dooming his life forever.

The deity continued celebrating for the rest of the afternoon, ignorant to the spiteful eyes that followed his every move—a gaze seething with malice and contempt. The blond supreme being enjoyed his admirers' lascivious attention in abundance as he let down his guard, oblivious to the predator on the hunt for his blood.

He danced, sang, and engaged in sensual activities with anyone seeking his attention. "Oh, my beloved devotees, make my day! I'm delighted, and nothing can ruin my day," he murmured, lightheaded and joyful as his flawless day resumed. Nothing could go wrong.

$$***$$

The cunning yet brutish deity of love crafted a plan. Spite simmered inside Eros's malicious heart to teach the mighty sun divinity a lesson. Galled by Apollo's arrogance, he wanted nothing more than revenge. He considered ways to plot the perfect punishment for most of the day. As the games continued into the late afternoon, Eros recognized the beautiful naiad nymph, Daphne, attracting the looks of many men. She danced and frolicked with her sisters and maiden hunters.

Daphne's arrival silenced the chatter as all eyes gravitated toward her. Her sun-kissed complexion emanated a natural glow, bewitching the spectators. Within her deep, expressive eyes, a blend of wisdom and sentiment played, hinting at a profound depth.

Tresses of dark chestnut tumbled around her countenance, entwined and decorated with delicate silk strips. Her hair was a work of art—a masterpiece weaved of hair and ribbon.

At the heart of the festivity, Daphne embodied elegance, effortlessly capturing attention and admiration. Beside her, a redheaded nymph exuded unwavering devotion and fidelity, adding a layer of enchantment to the tableau.

While hunting out in the woods and hard to miss, Daphne's captivating beauty dazzled Eros. Her hair would dance behind her as she ran through the forest. Her wild beauty added to her tantalizing mystique. Many men wanted her untamable personality, but none could have her. Daphne wished to hunt and honor her maidenhood.

Daphne was a devoted follower of Artemis, the sister of the proud Apollo. The nymph chose a life of celibacy. "Oh, the blessed odds," Eros murmured—a vicious confession graced by a smile.

Like the goddess of the hunt, she cherished the woods more than anything else. She only hoped to remain pure and unbound by the confines of marriage. She adamantly rejected being owned by any man, steadfast in her refusal to be confined.

Eros often overheard Peneus pleading with his daughter Daphne to wed a man and bless him with a strapping son-in-law. The river god wanted many grandchildren, but the nymph dismissed his plea as a foolish wish. Matrimony was out of the question for the woman. The idea didn't appeal to her, and she embraced her freedom above all else.

Once, Eros heard a defeated Peneus curse at his daughter's beauty. The minor god foretold a day would come when a man would pursue her like a ravenous predator. As a man, the nymph's father knew the longing to sink one's teeth into a woman's flawless skin. He feared a man would come and subject her by force if she did not marry a man, not by will.

Peneus wanted a vigorous man who would protect her. Daphne dismissed her father's outrageous wishes. Like Artemis, she loved her freedom and didn't need a man.

Then Eros recognized Apollo's fleeting glances toward the

group of maiden hunters where Daphne stood. The prince's hawklike gaze followed the naiad hunter. His curiosity brightened his face. Daphne's palpable excitement led her to the contests and took her place among the other participants. Joy, barely withheld, overshadowed the elegance on her face when she joined the challenges.

Apollo's sly manners showed through like a clear sky. At first, he feigned interest in the competitions. But then the lusty prince couldn't stop spying on the gorgeous nymph. Enthralled by the beating music, Apollo danced with a hypnotic groove. He showered his attention on the ravishing man clinging to his arm. Cautiously, Apollo navigated the euphoric crowd. Eros noted the prince's demeanor, which hinted at desire. Hidden under the veil of constraint, Apollo struggled to conceal his urgent lust for Daphne.

Eros's eagle eyes watched the exquisite maiden hunter walk to the shooting range. "So charming! 'Tis perfection!" Eros murmured with vile intent. He followed as the woman produced her silver bow from thin air and notched an arrow in a fluid motion without a moment's pause.

The nymph embodied instinctual accuracy. Anxious onlookers quieted for a moment, captivated by her effortless confidence and skill. The fluidity of her movement held an artistry as she released a projectile. With uncanny precision, a single arrow hit the center mark—a sight to behold.

Thunderous cheers echoed throughout the multitude with infectious joy. But when Eros turned toward Apollo, he noted the god looked beyond proud at the display of the beautiful hunter.

"My love's arrows shall pierce even the most divine of hearts; thus, Apollo's vanity will bring his demise. May my golden arrow lodge deep within his chest. Let my arrow of lead strike the soul of the indomitable yet lovely Daphne," Eros whispered as he flew to the shady peak of Mount Parnassus to carry out his plan.

As he sat perched on the mountain's ledge, he waited until the opportune moment to execute his most devilish plans. At that point, Apollo admired the festive Daphne again. Eros pulled out two arrows, one sharp from gold and the other blunt with lead.

At once, Eros caught the shy attraction in Apollo's eyes as the sun god stopped in his tracks. Daphne turned to face the prince, noticing him. The two exchanged a glance that seemed to last in time. Then Daphne smiled and looked willing to reciprocate the god's feelings. Apollo looked bashful, about to make his move.

Chapter 2

Maiden Hunter

Like any other day, the morning bore a renewing magical freshness. Dew and the thick scent of musk mingled in the atmosphere. The sun's beams filtered through the dense canopy of the ancient trees, mingling with the dust fairies to create an enchanting scenery.

Daphne woke at dawn and stretched on her bed for a few lazy moments. She only wanted to enjoy the last lingering sleep because she deserved the tiny break after staying late with her sisters. They'd run through the forest, stargazing and admiring the full moon.

As soon as she jumped out of her cot, the warm sunrays danced over her face, making her frown, trying to shield her eyes from the intense brightness. She stumbled toward the bramble-framed window, closing the leafy curtains to block the blinding light. "Oh, bless the gods, yet another beautiful day," she murmured as she stretched with the lazy demeanor of a mountain cat.

With a smile, she climbed the ancient oak she called home, a gift from her mother, Gaia, which she appreciated.

The tree stood tall like a guardian. Its thick trunk and rough bark scraped her bare hands and feet as she descended. After she reached the ground, she buried her toes in the grass. The silky dirt and coarse turf rooted her to the moment.

After a wink of time, she strolled toward the tranquil lagoon near her forest house. The gentle scent of wildflowers wafted through the air as she approached the beach, its surface shimmering with the reflections of the clear skies.

Once by the pond, Daphne sighed in pleasure. A shiver ran down her spine when she dipped her foot in the icy lake. Water lapped her skin, awakening her senses with a caress like a lover's. A refreshing and divine thrill came as she scooped some of the liquid, allowing the droplets to cascade over her hair and face, restoring her.

She cherished her morning ritual, which connected her to her element. She took her time swimming in the pool, enjoying the revitalizing sensation that washed over her. Daphne knew her father sent his love and blessings.

Upon finishing her bath, she looked up, only to find a bird of prey soaring above her as if keeping a close eye on her whereabouts. Daphne's curiosity sparked tenfold, and she wondered why the animal needed to breach her domain.

Forest creatures knew better than to intrude on her small dominion without permission. As the hawk circled closer, she craved the twinge-like prickle of protectiveness. Her hunter instinct came to life as she prepared to defend her territory, her home.

Wrapping a soft drying cloth around herself, enjoying the silky fabric against her skin, she followed the hawk's path through the gaps of the tall trees. With each step she took, her bare feet sank into the rich soil, savoring the magic that lingered in the ground as she pulled on her powers to find out what the birds needed from her.

At first, the roots of the majestic woods wanted to mingle with the very essence of her spirit. The enchantment grounded her, filling her mind with peace. Nature cautioned her to be careful and discover the hawk's true intentions.

"I must always be prudent. The woodland is dangerous, and this hawk threatens my honor. Its master is keeping a close eye on me. This nonsense needs to stop!" she mumbled as the wind played with the loose strands of her hair. The leaves rustled their answer around the forest, agreeing with her.

Her frustration boiled over as the creature continued to circle her. Angered by the intrusion, she put all her irritation behind her threat. "Reconsider, you naughty bird, if you're here to spy on me! Tell your master I'll marry no man."

Her direct and harsh tone reflected her internal conflict. She wanted her wishes respected, but a man's cravings came before hers. "Oh, my dear! The master of that fowl desires you in ways beyond your comprehension. He wields great power and can be very persuasive when determined," a woman spoke from above her. "I know this because that hawk's owner is my brother."

Finally, she realized Artemis, looking strong and beautiful as always, lurked. She jumped from the tree she perched on and landed next to her. Her regal countenance and gaze commanded obedience.

Daphne bowed out of respect. The cloth hardly covered her bare body, and the wetness of her skin made the fabric stick in places. Upon realizing this, she dried herself as best as she could. Her cheeks became hot with embarrassment.

The holiness looked amused by her random display of shyness. They had enjoyed each other's company many blessed times—intimate nights that she cherished for eternity. Still, she somehow felt shy around Artemis. "Dear goddess! I didn't expect your arrival. It's a great honor to be in your presence. What do I owe the pleasure of your visit?" she asked, sitting by the woman's feet and breathing in the sweet scent of lavender and fresh spring water.

Artemis patted her head as Daphne sat by her. Daphne rejoiced at the attention, hoping their encounter would end in each other's arms. Looking up at the imposing goodness, she sensed something was off. "I wish to ask you a question. Why do you want to be one of my hunters? I already have plenty of followers. You are beautiful and can marry. I can see you having mighty sons and daughters that could make any man proud and be the envy of all the other gods."

A gasp caught in her throat when she saw Artemis pitied her. "Your beauty is boundless and a fierce warrior. Why would you give up such a future for a life of eternal maidenhood?" the huntress asked her with tenderness.

She studied the divinity closely. *Is the noble goddess testing me? She must be. I need to show her my unbreakable devotion to her,* Daphne thought, sighing in defeat while glaring at the other woman.

"Your concerns are understandable, but I..." She collected her thoughts to plead her case. "I wish to be a hunter like you, content to give up marriage and motherhood," she pleaded, embracing the woman's shapely leg nearest her. "To me, all I want is strength and independence. I want to prove that I am more than my beauty. I want respect as a warrior." Daphne paused, a shy smile gracing her lips. "I want to be by your side. Free! I hunger for you and live for you. I'll bow to no man. Just you, my lovely goddess."

"You want to be independent, you say? The very essence of your devotion binds you to me. I see no difference if you marry a man," Artemis rebuked with a loveliest of smiles.

Daphne stood, ignoring that her wrap had become undone, leaving her naked before Artemis as she tapped on her chest with her fist. Desperation drowned her as she tried to plead her case. "True, but there is a distinction. I do this because it's what I yearn for. But if I listened to my father, I would have to subject myself to a man's whims. I don't want that. I want to be with you until I'm no more."

"But... what if that man offers you power along with the world? What if that man cherishes you like his equal? What if he showers you with many blessings? And... what if you become his muse to his art?" Artemis asked, caressing Daphne's soft and plump cheek. The goddess leaned in and kissed her. A gentle touch of their lips calmed her frayed nerves. Little by little, the turmoil raging inside her died. It was like magic.

Daphne clung to the other woman as if her life depended on it. When they parted, she missed the other woman's luscious nectar. She wanted more. "You're strong and have given me sanctuary. I want to be like you."

Looking unamused, Artemis stepped back to scan her as if gathering her thoughts. Picking the cloth from the ground, she secured it around Daphne. "Have you broken your fast, my lovely water nymph?"

Looking unamused, Artemis stepped back to scan Daphne as if gathering her thoughts. Picking the cloth from the ground, she secured it around Daphne. "Have you broken your fast, my lovely water nymph?"

"No!" she countered, a bit forcefully for her liking, knowing better than to be impetuous. "But... have you eaten anything yet?"

"I haven't, so let's eat and talk in peace."

Artemis led her to the tree house. Like a cat, she quickly climbed the tree branches as Daphne followed suit.

In a hurry, Daphne went to her room and searched for her chest in the corner. She found a simple but very practical knee-length hunting tunic. Excitement coursed through her veins, quickening her pulse as she got ready.

The goddess, looking beautiful, came to visit. Warmth embraced her the moment she entered the kitchen. Soon, a delicious aroma assaulted her senses, paralyzing her mid-step. She stared as Artemis threw herbs and root vegetables into the cauldron.

Horrified, she rushed to the hearth to take charge of the cooking. "Oh, no! It's not proper. Something so mundane is not befitting your station." Daphne's desperate cry startled Artemis. Creatures scurried away in fright as Artemis moved close to the woman. She jostled Daphne to the nearby table chair as she checked their food. "You are my guest. I just... I just needed to get dressed, my lady. This looks lovely and hearty. I'm eager to try it."

As she approached the fire, the pot's contents bubbled. An enticing aroma wafted from the pot, making Daphne's mouth water. The breakfast looked delicious, and she couldn't wait to enjoy their meal.

Artemis smiled as she stared at her. "You know, the master of that hawk from earlier, while bathing, taught me how to make that stew. He's kind-hearted and doing his best to become a doting husband. He's also a talented cook and cares for others, even though he sometimes doesn't show it. My brother can be charming when trying to impress a potential lover. But now... he's like a mountain lion in heat, looking for his mate." She drawled as she grabbed a couple of bowls and spoons from the open shelf close to the wellspring. "He's been watching his lioness for a while. He wants you all to himself."

Daphne moved away from Artemis as if the goddess carried a plague. She didn't like the way the other woman talked. It made her uncomfortable. "Too bad for him. I won't reciprocate." She filled their dishes and set them on the table. Before sitting for her meal, she fetched the basket with day-old bread, which would pair well with their stew. "You're devoted to your maidenhood, and I want the same. So why are you pushing this issue?"

"It's because I treasure my baby brother. He..." Artemis paused as if looking for the right words. "His smile alone can melt icy hearts, and my heart is no exception. Although insufferable with his cocky personality, he can be a sweetheart. He killed the python to avenge our mother and prove his worth as a man... just for you. Today, he intends to win your favor. He's determined to do so. Besides, he's been bugging me with questions about you." She rolled her eyes in frustration.

Discouraged, Daphne sat and ate in silence, thinking.

The lad liked to roam and hunt in her forest. His shiny golden hair intermingled like a vine with the greenery. His pale skin, a stark contrast against the dark bark of the trees, created a fascinating synthesis. He mixed with nature and somehow made it work.

She cursed her beauty, which attracted too much attention. "Why are you pushing this issue? Are you punishing me?"

"No! I'm not disciplining you, my lovely hunter. Even though I adore you, I see greater love in my baby brother's eyes. I hate to admit this, but he loves you—borderline obsessive. I'm surprised he's acting shy around you. He's bombastic on many days, but he's a blushing mess with you. I wouldn't mind seeing you return his affections. You have my permission." Artemis picked at her food before staring at her point-blank. "I'm encouraging it."

Mulling over Artemis's proposal, Daphne remained silent for the rest of their meal. Her mood soured, already dreading the conversation. As she finished breaking her fast, Daphne spotted the goddess fidgeting with a flower from a nearby branch. "Why do you want me to become his lover when I can be yours?" she asked, honesty dripping from her words.

Artemis reached out to kiss her forehead, like a mother kissing her child. "Oh, my fearless huntress! I adore you over the other maidens. But my devotion to freedom, nature, and the moonlit nights is far greater than my affection for another being," she said in a sweet and balmy tone.

Daphne looked away, dejected. "I understand." In vain, she hoped Artemis would reciprocate her affections. But it seemed she was a short-lived fling.

"Do not despair, my dear. You are special to me and have a piece of my heart. We have a task. My brother asked for hog and venison for the festivities. Will you help me?" Artemis asked, looking like the moon on a cloudless night as she left.

Staring at Artemis's empty spot, Daphne couldn't contain her sadness as a tear rolled down her plump cheek. A water sprite approached her to kiss the droplet away before turning away to tidy her place.

"I'll always aid you... and be by your side." She tried to hide her emotions from the other woman. Shaking her head and clearing her troubling thoughts, she gathered her equipment and rejoined Artemis at the base of her tree house.

Laughter echoed around the wood as she spotted the goddess climbing a tree and hopping from one branch to another. "Try to keep up," Artemis warned as she set off into a run.

Daphne cleared her mind to push down the slight sting of rejection in her chest as she ventured deeper into the forest. Jumping from one limb to another, she followed Artemis.

Soon, they reached an ample and fertile clearing. Not waiting a second longer, Artemis let loose a few arrows. Her movements were fluid, like that of a dancer. Daphne watched in admiration as the goddess. Inspiration washed over her as she aimed and released multiple projectiles, and before long, they had gathered plenty of game for a feast that could last several days.

"I think this should do. You can get ready for the celebration. My servants clean and prepare these for the festivities," Artemis said, leaving without looking back.

She felt an all-consuming emptiness take hold of her chest. While trekking back to her house, she stared into the distance. She slowly returned to her little cottage in the tree, enjoying the peaceful forest. Being enveloped by nature had helped calm her thoughts, making her feel at ease even after a crushing rejection. As she approached her home, Daphne decided not to join the others, feeling indisposed.

After cleaning her weapons, Daphne lounged in her hammock overlooking the mountains, trying to find peace from her racing mind. Emotions warred in her chest as tears came too close to the surface. "I don't like strangers. I want to be left alone."

Her tired muscles screamed in pain as she stared at the roof. Rest eluded her.

The rustling of leaves warned her of visitors. "Daphne, I know you're hiding. I caught wind of what happened…"

The melodious voice of one of her hunter sisters, Ismini, came from below. "Are you coming to celebrate the new lord of Delphi?"

Daphne's heart fell apart. "Ismini, I don't feel like celebrating."

"Forget about Artemis! You have me. Besides, her brother honors the python with many competitions. He's also handsome and searching for a wife. Rumor says he worships you." Her twinkling and sweet laughter turned into music to Daphne's ears. "You lucky nymph."

"We are supposed to remain chaste, like our goddess, Ismini," Daphne replied, glad Ismini existed in her life. "Besides, you're my sweetheart. I shall never part ways with you."

"Oh, we still do. I cherish every second we spend together. But that doesn't mean we can't enjoy the company of Artemis's brother. He's quite the sight." Ismini giggled before she continued. "I would renounce my vows for someone like him."

Daphne rose from her hammock, heading toward her balcony and leaning on its railing. "Didn't you vow to remain a maiden, Ismini?" she asked, intrigued.

As expected, the python killer became the subject of

everyone's conversations, which fascinated Daphne. She needed to meet the lad who lingered in the shadows, watching her.

Leaping into motion, she spotted Ismini's pout and smiled. She wanted to face the man and the hawk's owner. "All right! You cherish your free will, but I need to bathe first."

"Hey-ho!" Ismini shouted in excitement. "I'll be waiting and bring only your best."

With a huge grin, she went to her modest chambers. Going about her trunks, she detected a package pinned with a golden arrow by a corner. "This is not mine."

She took hesitant steps toward the unfamiliar box. After undoing its decorative knots, she found dried fruits, nuts, silky robes, and embroidered ribbons.

"When did this... oh, by Olympus! Someone invaded my home, my sanctuary!" Her hands shook with realization. "This is exquisite. This mysterious man is declaring his love..." A numbing fog settled over her head as she examined the bag. "But... do I want to accept his love and return his feelings?" An infectious smile played on her lips as resolve fixated on her heart. "Maybe... I should take my chances, listen to the goddess, and allow her brother's courtship. We'll become a family of expert hunters to live in the wild and rear a new generation of cunning warriors." She smiled. The idea held the sweetness of a young flower.

With her new robes packed, she sprinted to the cave to bathe with her sisters. Her core burst with love, thinking of Ismini and the hunter who wanted her as a lover. Once at the cavernous spring, she shuffled to the other nymphs but moved to a secluded spot with Ismini. She wanted some privacy.

Engulfed in her lover's embrace, Daphne stared deep into Ismini's azure gaze. Her red curls shone against the sun. Daphne reached out to caress her lover. Her golden-brown complexion contrasted with the other woman's pale skin—a beautiful opposition.

She felt her lover's hand become bolder, exploring every surface of her body. Heart racing, she deepened their kiss as Ismini's hands became brazen in their exploration. A thrill coursed through her veins when her sweet lover found her clit and caressed her with the gentlest of touch.

Daphne wrapped her leg around Ismini in a moment of pure bliss to give her better access to her achy center. On her part, Daphne's gracious hands explored the other naiad's body until she found that spot that made Ismini blush beautifully and reddened at the attention.

She ran her finger along Ismini's bundle of nerves. Before a gentle finger, and then another, slid into her welcoming canal. Lost in her euphoria, Daphne surrendered to her lover's desires and reciprocated, sliding her wet fingers between her folds and inserting two fingers into her swollen core.

"Mmmm, Daphne, more!" Ismini whispered in her ear, sending shivers all over Daphne's body. "My forever lover."

Daphne savored her fast-approaching pinnacle—about to crash and overwhelm her senses. And by the gentle flutters of Ismini's dewy slit, she could tell her lover inched closer to her surrender. "Ahhh, Ismini! I love... you!"

Ismini brushed her lips against the delicate curve of her ear. "I love you, too! But... I'm close... don't stop!" Her whisper sent a thrilling warmth cascading down Daphne's spine, and the soft kiss that met the tender skin of Daphne's earlobe created an electrifying sensation.

Like a crashing wave on a stormy day, Daphne found her

release. Ismini joined her in her own euphoric relief. A lyrical moan floated to Daphne's ears a few seconds later. Her afterglow tinted her cheeks a lovely shade of rosy red. Her light blue eyes, unfocused, held a wetness of satisfaction.

Daphne felt a heaviness in her chest, striving to burst free and let her emotions loose. "Artemis suggested I marry her brother. I don't know what to think," she confessed, vulnerable but respecting the goddess' desire.

"I wonder—is she playing Cupid?" Ismini asked in jest, but then regret marred her pretty face. She looked disheartened. "It's an honor to be the goddess' sister-in-law." Suddenly, a pleasant smile shone, looking as if she was trying to hide her true feelings. "Let's get you ready. I see he sent expensive presents. I hope you won't forget about me."

Daphne smiled, knowing Ismini would always be by her side. "You'll always be my sweet lover, Ismini!" She approached the other woman and planted a passionate kiss. "Tonight, we shall admire the stars in each other's arms."

After their bath, they prepared for their day in their finest robes. Daphne loved her friend's handy work with her looks. Ismini went to great lengths to make her look beyond beautiful for the day.

On her part, she made sure Ismini looked her best for the day. They walked hand in hand, greeted with competition and merriment as they arrived at the games. She partook in the celebrations by dancing and proving her skills as an expert archer.

During her break, she saw him—the hero in the flesh, her handsome secret admirer. His woven blonde hair shone like the sun. The exquisite robes hugged his well-sculpted body, accentuating his power.

She forgave his past misdeeds as her knees lost their strength. Her heart fluttered to life, beating faster as she regarded him. He showered his admirers with his attention until their eyes met. She flushed and turned away, feeling shy. When she dared to look at him, she caught his furious blush, which tinted an attractive shade of red from his neck to the tip of his ears. "Maybe being with a man wouldn't be so bad," she whispered as they exchanged fleeting looks.

His handsome smile made her wonder if he desired her. She found his adorable shyness endearing, and it charmed her to reconsider her vow. Daphne sat at a crossroads. Her mouth salivated at his juicy personality. And wildness seeped from him like a warm blanket. An enticing man!

She wanted to run to him and savor his lush lips and admit she yearned to become one with him. For the first time, she longed to know how a man would feel inside her. Delving tenderly into her dewy center, she thought, sending a pleasant shiver through her body.

Chapter 3

Chase

"Oh, how lovely this day is!" Eros reached back for two very distinct arrows. "On this audacious day, I, master of love and archery, seize this opportunity to impart a priceless lesson to Apollo, Zeus's first-born son." He ducked and lunged in preparation to execute his plan. The marvelous day carried the warmth of triumph, and even the heavens celebrated the sun god.

But... the lava of hostility moved elevated from his stomach, about to break free from the confines of his body. Great apathy buried inside his gentle contours. His celebrated beauty paled when his grudge reared front and center. "With unwavering precision, I draw back my bow, ready to release the arrow that carries the power of my skill and the wisdom of my words. As the projectile soared through the air, its message echoed in the depths of Apollo's being, forever etching this profound teaching moment into the annals of myth and legend," Eros proclaimed to the heavens as he deftly notched both arrows and released them in succession.

He let them fly to their intended targets, aiming for the hearts of Apollo and Daphne. "I hate that motherfucker!" Venom seethed from his sweet, plump lips as a wicked smile morphed his features. "He ought to be cautious around me from now on. I 'll never forget. I'll never forgive."

The golden dart struck Apollo deep within his marrow, sending a feverish and uncontrollable passion through his veins. Consumed by an insatiable hunger, Apollo yearned to devour the nymph hunting his dreams, Daphne. Her ethereal beauty and enchanting spirit captivated him beyond comprehension. His infatuation, a borderline obsession, kept him up at night. His body burned with desire, preventing him from acting with reason.

Every fiber in his center craved to make her his, to bask in the radiance of her presence and shower her with his love by any means necessary. He wanted to have her bend to his will and, worse, even have her against her will. Sweat trickled down his face while his hair clung to his damp forehead.

He struggled to catch his breath as the air grew thicker with the essence of his raging lust. "I want her so fucking much. She's mine!" A shaky inhale and exhale failed to provide relief as an inferno consumed him, starting in his loins and clouding his judgment.

Unexpectedly, something nefarious lodged in Daphne's heart. The sensation assaulted her senses, defiling her free will like a poisonous splinter, spreading its malice all over her, clouding her awareness. Her soul battered like a drum about to implode at any second. Her body trembled, making her head spin. And then, disgust washed over her frame as Daphne scowled at the handsome man. "My predator!" she murmured as the man stared back at her with a vicious hunger that almost made her faint.

Her heart rate increased, and her breathing came in short, constricting gasps. She could understand why her skin crawled at the sight of the man. Daphne could not bear to be in his presence any longer. She wanted to vanish from his view. "My foe!" Daphne shouted. Curious eyes darted to where she stood.

The man's azure eyes held a fire that ignited her, and she felt like a deer when a wolf got ready to attack. She glared into the hero's hungry eyes, holding her ground, but his slow approach put her on edge. Her breath caught as his wildcat agility granted him the advantage, as he avoided anyone who got in his way.

Daphne's father's ominous warning would soon come true. Every fiber of her being screamed. Her heart pounded in her ears, drumming the start of her demise. Clearly, Peneus' warnings echoed in her head, their weight sinking deep into her soul.

Her worst nightmare reared its ugly face. It stared down at her, challenging her into defiance. She ran before the god gave chase with might greater than hers. He caught her, claiming her as his most sumptuous prize. Adrenaline coursed through her veins—Daphne's uncontrollable need to bolt sent shivers throughout her frame.

Fear gripped her as her body froze. Yet resolve burned in

Daphne's eyes. The clutches of impending doom, eager to capture her, threatened to consume her entire existence. Daphne realized too late she needed to escape. Without sparing a second thought, Daphne sprinted at full speed with incredible might, heedless of her destination.

But the blond man looked hell-bent on making her his. If the man captured her, there would be no escaping his cage. Now more than ever, she wished for the warm embrace of freedom to flee into the sanctuary of her beloved forest.

Without a doubt, he would take her against her will—his frenzied eyes showed her as much. Her senses prickled with danger, putting her on edge, ready to fight, as her brain yelled, *Be alert and... RUN!* Her psyche screamed at her as her body grew cold.

Thus began a relentless pursuit. Frantically, Daphne sought a haven, while Apollo, consumed by his desires, pursued her like a fierce animal.

His chest constricted with need. A burning sensation engulfed his loins. His raw emotions stumbled with his erratic actions. It became apparent that Apollo's thoughts fell apart with pain, an all-consuming, hard-to-resist sense of longing.

His powerful legs moved on their own accord when the lass of his desire appeared. She soared further away from him. As she fled from his grasp, he lost control of his mind and body. He didn't understand why, but when his delicate maiden sprinted away, he reacted in kind.

Apollo dashed without understanding why he acted this way. His usual calm and methodical disposition succumbed to his impulses. He behaved out of character when a vicious need sank its teeth into his neck. It injected its poison of irreverence.

"Wait, my precious nymph! I heard you're Peneus's daughter.

Please! I beg of you! I'm not your enemy," the sun god shouted after the beautiful fairy, running as fast as his feet could manage.

But the gorgeous naiad didn't listen as her sprint remained determined. Her exposed refusal colored a clear picture—not to let a man catch or tame her. She looked ready to fight for her freedom above all else. As a free spirit, Daphne fled from him like a scared hare. The sight filled his soul with both yearning and sadness.

Daphne dashed through the woods, her pace teasing his desire. His heart pounded with relentless appetite, pursuing her, as the look of fear and desperation painted her innocent yet lovely features. Apollo ran even faster. He yearned to touch the woman that fanned the inferno raging inside his chest with every step she took.

Amidst the chaos and confusion, Eros's sweet smile—a wicked mask—made Apollo's blood boil over. His gut told him Eros was behind this debacle. He lunged headfirst into the other man's deception.

This bastard is trying to teach me a lesson. Just wait until I get my hands on him. I, the great Phoebean god, will put him in his place. But first... I need to have her. He thought as anger morphed into desire when a sliver of her skin peeked from under her shawl, covering the deep V of the front of her robe. His mouth salivated when a gust of wind blew the woman's skirt to reveal a shapely leg. *Oh, for the love of Olympus! I crave to have those pleasing legs wrapped around my waist as I take her.* The thought overtook any rational thinking as he continued the chase. "Nymph, Wait! Daphne! Stop, my precious one..." he cried, worried she would injure herself trying to elude him.

"Sun lord, Look! She'll get hurt! It's best if you didn't let her escape. Make haste!" Eros shouted as he glanced over his shoulder. The wings of the god of lust flapped as he came down from Parnassus to track Apollo.

"By the gods' blood! He instigated this, but..." he mumbled.

A sudden movement ahead of him distracted his reflections. The ribbons that tied Daphne's hair caught on a tree and loosened her luscious mane, trailing behind like a curtain of silken threads.

"This is how a sheep runs from the wolf, a deer from the mountain lion, and a dove with fluttering wings flees from the eagle. Everything flies from its foes, but love drives me to pursue you. Pity me. Please cease your flight, my dearest one!" Apollo begged the naiad to stop running, to avoid the chase, and to let him worship her.

Her defiant eyes told him to halt, but he couldn't. Concern welled inside him as the nymph ran through the forest—careless of danger. Horror seeped through his veins as Daphne tripped over a few times but recovered to continue her escape. Thin branches battered her delicate skin, making him wince at the angry welts forming on her beautiful golden-brown countenance.

"I am afraid you might fall headlong, or thorns will scar your legs and cause you grief. These are rough places you run through. Slow down, I ask you. Check your flight, and I, too, will stop," Apollo called to her, desperation driving him.

"At least inquire whom you have charmed, I beg you!" Daphne glanced over her shoulder. Her wise eyes gauged her pursuer's progress. Much too late, he realized that her sure steps took her further into the depths of the woods, to the dangerous parts of the forest. She appeared filled with an intense willpower to outrun Apollo and to escape his clutches.

When he tried to reach her, having gotten close to catching her, Daphne's determination seemed to spark to life with renewed resolve and resiliency. She continued her flight. Unmindful of the stinging branches lashing against her skin, oblivious to the thorns that tore her garments to shreds, she ran.

Concern took root deep within Apollo's gut. However, the challenge of capturing fleeting beauty spurred him on. "I am no mountain man, shepherd, or rough guardian of the herds and flocks. Rash girl, you do not know. You cannot realize whom you are running from. It makes sense, so you run," Apollo said, worried. Desire, kindled by the glimpses of her tempting skin, stirred his passion even more. He ran faster.

"Indeed, mighty sun god! Impress her. She will love your wooing without a doubt. Oh, blessed lord of these lands! Captivate her and pique her curiosity to uncover your identity. Take her as your woman. Now," Eros provoked the other man.

Tricked, Apollo continued his ill-fated chase. Despite his brain screaming to quit this foolishness, Eros's goading propelled him. "I am Apollo. Delphi and its territories are mine. Claros, Tenedos, and Patara have acknowledged me as their sovereign. Zeus is my father, the king of gods. I'm the crown prince of Olympus. People can see the past, present, and future through me. Strings sound in harmony with my songs. My aim is certain, but a true arrow wounded my heart." The ruler realized his mistake, but his body refused his command to stop, and he kept up the pursuit. His desire burned him asunder, swallowing his logic.

"The entire world calls me the bringer of aid. Medicine is my invention. My power is in herbs. But any herb cannot cure this love nor heal their lord!"

Daphne seemed to slow her pace, exhausted and breathless. "Stay away from me and let me be. I wish to be free and not bound by any man, especially not you," she pleaded as she tripped and almost fell.

A smug-looking Eros enjoyed the misfortune unfurl.

Apollo captured the already weary beauty. Her dampened brow glistened from the exertion of her run. *She's tired. Now is my chance,* he thought. His mouth salivated at the idea. Once he caught up to her, his motion tumbled them both to the ground. He twisted mid-fall to prevent Daphne from hitting the ground hard. Their tumble—a minor triumph—got him closer to victory. She struggled to escape Apollo's grip, but he tightened his hold on his beloved. "Just like a wild creature from the forest, trying to free yourself from the hand of a skilled hunter. My beautiful doe, please don't fight me, and let this be," he whispered, his breath hot against her neck.

Trapped! She could go nowhere but to escape into a realm of euphoria—with him in the lead.

No matter what he did to control her, her thrashing didn't stop. Worse, the friction between them, the heat of their bodies, and the sweet scent of the naiad inflamed his desire. Closing his eyes, the magnetism of his passion surfaced too close to the surface. He pressed his erection to her leg to find some release. "Can you not see the love in my eyes for you? You will be the queen of these lands and my heart," he begged as he licked the shell of her ear.

Apollo knew he must have looked pathetic when Eros's vicious laugh floated his way. The god of romance mocked him as lust diminished him. All traces of rational thought eluded him. Like a feral animal, mindless ardor drove him. Eros planted a terrible impulse to drive him frantic. As his eyes watered, it dawned on Apollo that Eros had orchestrated his downfall. His inevitable doom shrouded him like a cloudy day.

"Now I will leave the two of you alone," Eros boasted, malice seething from his tone as he flew away. "Apollo, it looks like you have your hands full. I don't wish to interrupt any longer. Enjoy!"

Daphne's eyes shone with defiance when she escaped his clutches. Apollo felt the instant void in his arms the moment she broke free. The unfortunate accident that followed left him gasping for air. The exquisite tunic, a gift he gave her to show her his love while she slept, rested, ruined, frayed like his chances of being with her as his mate. Instead, her innocent body lay exposed to his lustful appetite. Much too late, her sculpted and delicious form displayed to his enjoyment. She tried in vain to cover herself. Apollo's mouth salivated at the sight as he caught her ankle and pulled her close.

Mmm! She has luscious curves in all the right places. I will write songs inspired by Daphne's beauty. He mused as he reached for her, wanting to explore every hill and valley of her figure. *She's perfect and all I've ever wanted. I want to hide her... She's MINE!* His mental somersaults encouraged him, a delirious rambling.

But the more he sought to have her, the more she resisted. "No! All males are vile. Our dear goddess Artemis says so. Men only want one thing from us—to rut like animals. I'll never be yours!" Daphne cried as she untangled from his grasp to distance herself from him. "Oh, Mother Gaia! Oh, Father Peneus! I beg you... please help me!" Daphne begged her parents for aid. "If your streams and earth have divine powers, change me, destroy this beauty that pleases too well, especially the one giving chase."

Daphne's words echoed through the woods. Apollo sensed the grove turning eerily quiet. Even the wind went still. A chill snuffed his passion and replaced it with dread. Her request reached her mother and father. Heartbroken, Apollo crumbled as Gaia and Peneus answered their daughter's plea. Horror settled in as she took root in the ground. The skin of her feet transformed into bark and crept up her body.

"No, no, no, my precious nymph, my wife. Stay by my side! NO!" Apollo screamed, horrified at the sight as his beloved metamorphosed before him.

Helplessness burrowed deep within his heart. "Please do not beg for something such as this. I shall forever cherish and treasure your company. I crave your companionship as equals and the opportunity to spend our time together. Your presence brings me immense joy. Let's build beautiful memories. Be... be happy!" Apollo begged. He reached out to the naiad, the love of his life. But her skin turned into bark anywhere he touched. She spurned him, shattering his heart with her disdain. He tried ripping the bark, hoping that would stop her metamorphosis, but Daphne shrieked in pain. He watched in horror as blood dripped from plant-woman wounds—her mutation incomplete.

Dumbstruck and cold.

When he looked down at his wet hands, terror drowned him as blood trickled from the pieces he ripped from his darling during his desperate frenzy. "NOOOOO!" Apollo bellowed as tears clouded his vision, streaking down his dirt-stained, chiseled cheeks.

He lost his hold on sanity as his sweet and beloved nymph chose death. Her life essence dissipated before his eyes. As Apollo embraced his paramour, he sensed her heart quivering beneath the new bark. He held the branches—love seeping through his pores—their limbs resembling shapely arms. His heart crushed as his lips pressed against the trunk, but even the wood recoiled from his kisses. Still, she remained distant, resisting his advances even in her humanoid tree form.

Distraught, Apollo crumbled as Daphne completed her transformation until only a beautiful slender tree endured. Dread turned his blood cold, and his mind went blank. They could never be together. His heart bled at the idea of not being with his huntress. "Since you cannot be my bride, you must be my tree! Laurel, you will adorn my hair, and I will fashion my lyre and quiver from you. You will go with the Roman generals. When joyful voices praise their triumph as the Capitol admires their long processions."

Closing his eyes, he stood with unstable legs. "You will stand outside Augustus's doorposts as a faithful guardian and watch over the oak crown between them. And just as my head with its uncropped hair is always young, you will also wear the beauty of undying leaves," He muttered, gasping in pain and with a raw voice. His emotions waded close to the surface, about to shatter his soundness. He barely held on to his composure.

Apollo's plump tears streamed down his dirt-stained face, bestowing many blessings upon the tree's roots. The laurel inclined her fresh branches, swaying her leafy dome in consent. Leaves and limbs showered in approval. With devastating finality, she accepted him, but at a cost.

Deflated, he lay at the base of his beloved tree for hours, ignoring the celebrations in his and the python's honor. Grief and longing for his dead lover made his heart slump heavily. Tenderly, he ran his fingers over the formed bark, feeling her presence. The tree's life force carried the soul of the woman he once loved.

He woke from his stupor, drained. The day grew late as the sun dipped on the horizon. Numbly, he chose a few loose brambles to create a wreath for himself. Apollo didn't forget to build a second crown for the true victor of such a petty game.

Now, he ought to atone for a preventable tragedy. The memory would hunt him for the rest of his life. Hopelessness shrouded him like a blanket on a hot day. Bullying Eros evolved into an irritable splinter at his side. If only he combated the urge to listen to his pride or to resist it. He shouldn't have ridiculed the winged man. All would have been well, and Daphne would have willingly become his bride. Her eyes told him as much before Eros struck them with lies. "Why did I mock someone like him? Foolish of me to think that way..."

He beat his chest, chastising his ridiculous endeavor. "Oh, blessed Olympus! Why?" Regret weighed his consciousness as he realized it was too late to mend his wrongdoings. An all-consuming numbness settled in his heart, leaving a solemn lump in its place. Stupidity sucked out of him all traces of joy. Apollo felt weak and yearned to be alone.

As he stood, a scattering of fallen branches distracted him—precious remnants of his tussle with his beloved nymph. Selecting a few sturdy ones, he carried his heavy load to the bustling clearing, where the joyful festivities continued unabated in contrast to his troubled mind.

"Oh, dear Apollo! You look like a man who just battled a beast," Eros joked, pointing at Apollo's state. "Look at your tattered tunic and your hair. Also, you are all covered in dirt. Did you take a tumble?" The god of love laughed at Apollo's condition in front of those present.

Apollo checked his rumpled look, his outward appearance mirroring the unrest within his heart. However, he remained indifferent to his disheveled shape and Eros's taunting. Apollo wanted to be left alone. "You, Eros! Your aim was true. Thus, I declare thee the victor in archery."

Apollo placed the rudimentary laurel wreath from his sacred plant on Eros's head. It gave the god of amour a graceful touch of triumph. Apollo found Eros's smug smile irritating, but Apollo ignored him. "Deliver this piece of wood to Hermes. I want his flawless craftsmanship to create a new lyre and a quiver for me," Apollo said as he stared at the lumber with love. "This material is precious to me. Handle it with care. By the way, faun, what is your name?"

"Fernhoof, Your Highness, my name is Fernhoof."

He yearned for quiet and solitude. Without waiting for further response, Apollo turned, ready to leave the festivities and retire to his palace. "Thank you, Fernhoof. You are kind."

When he turned, a redheaded beauty with sky-like eyes scampered through the crowd. Desperation painted on lovely features as a cry threatened to break free.

"Daphne, oh, my sweet love. Where have you disappeared? Please answer me. Where have you gone?"

The young maiden naiad broke down as despair sketched a picture of anguish.

A devouring sadness dampened his reality while isolation plagued his existence. Without his precious nymph, emptiness settled deep in his entrails. Salty rivulets trickled down his cheek, followed by a second and a third. Apollo's tears flooded once more. He yearned for solitude. His heart pounded uncontrollably as a painful squeeze grew in intensity with each heartbeat. He ran. The crowd turned into a distant blur that wouldn't bother him for the night.

Chapter 4

Dafnie - Present Time

The homey aroma of damp soil, the sweet fragrance of pine, and the peppery smell of transplanted laurel leaves—the air carried this mix of tantalizing scents. After traveling far and wide for a while, exploring countless destinations, she found her home. Nothing in the world could compare to the natural perfumes of Phoebus Groove. She was an avid rock climber and runner, but nothing compared to the town. It offered everything she wanted. Best of all, her element surrounded her.

She gracefully navigated the winding trails buried deep in the forest surrounding the quaint town. Tranquility settled innermost within her bones in a motherly embrace. With each breath, a sense of belonging washed through her soul. Dafnie didn't stumble over during her careless jog. The jutting roots and the overgrown brushes didn't concern her. Her body knew what to do—jumping and veering over any obstacles. It came so naturally to her. More than capable, she cruised through the wood with ease. For some odd reason, it whispered to her its secrets and dangers.

Through the gaps of the towering trees, the sun's golden rays peeked through, casting soft shadows around her. She immersed herself in the serene beauty of her surroundings. Leaves rustling i n the gentle wind hummed a ballad of serenity. Lastly, the melodic chirping of birds completed the harmonious symphony of natural lyrics. Each footfall blended effortlessly with the rhythm of the music. The evergreen forest throbbed as if dancing with the tune. It appeared the wilderness rejoiced to have Dafnie's company.

With her favorite upbeat pop songs oozing through her earphones, the energizing melodies intertwined with the sounds of the environment, creating a unique and vibrant soundtrack to her run. The song fueled her introverted spirit, adding an extra spring to her step and amplifying her joy. Her footsteps drummed with the uplifting tunes as she became lost in the moment. Phoebus Groove's breathtaking beauty elevated her to pure solitary bliss. She immersed herself in the harmonious bond with nature and music as time drifted ahead.

In the outdoors, a sense of release melted away her concerns. The place relieved her of her frequent stormy days. The soothing pause urged her mind to detox and disconnect. There was a magical communion between her and the wilderness, an energizing break to delve into within. The minute she stepped into the thick of the forest, her worries evaporated. Her daily life didn't matter. Comfort flowed over her like a blaming embrace, taking away her troubles. The sun's warmth heated her skin, delivering a profound sense of serenity and bliss, like a kiss from a loved one.

The winding route took Dafnie to her favorite spot in the

woods. She continued through the thickets, immersed in the moment's magic. She focused on the trail stretching before her. It invited her to run deeper into the forest. At that moment, nature beckoned to her. For Dafnie, her invigorating daily runs developed into a beloved custom, a soulful connection to the surrounding world.

Suddenly, an overwhelming sense assaulted her, similar to the time of her parents' death. The sentiment always started this way. She was an outsider—no mistake about it—unable to fit in with others. From a tender young age, her kookiness didn't quite click with normal standards. Throughout her life, a nagging sensation on the back of her neck warned her something important was amiss. Genuine friendships eluded her, and her place in her life remained unclear.

At some point, she took a chance and changed. Although an innate loner, she yearned for the company as loneliness weighed her down. She fought against the unsettling void in her chest, ready for a change. Despite her yearning for stability, Dafnie started the endless pursuit of the right partner. To make matters miserable, men seemed to avoid her. About to give up on finding someone, a kind man showed up and swept her off her feet.

Happiness only lasted for a blink when things spiraled into heartbreak.

Everything sounded fine between them one moment and stormy the next. The fuzzy events escaped Dafnie's understanding. Her then-boyfriend betrayed her by rekindling a relationship with his ex-girlfriend. Even worse, he insulted her by calling her naïve and inexperienced. Worst of all, his heartlessness knew no bounds. With his shame out the window, he humiliated her in front of the other woman. A wave of smallness washed over her, driving her into a cruel circle of self-doubt. All because of the jackass, Dafnie grew more isolated. Being around others always made her feel anxious and conscious. Like an ugly duckling, she shuffled through life unseen.

Thus, isolation became a part of her. Despite her profound yearning for a loving connection with a significant other, she gave up on finding her other half. Instead, she prioritized her education and, later, her career.

But carrying the weight of her age—tender twenty-eight years of life—she wished for more. More than once, she daydreamed about the perfect companion—a partner to whisk her to a grand adventure. She wanted to share her life with someone who would not cause her harm.

One day, Dafnie's psychologist surprised her by switching things during their session. Her doctor pushed her to settle on childhood memories—the movements she cherished with all her heart. The period provided a different sort of comfort. It helped her talk through certain buried emotions. Like a floodgate, her feelings came rushing out. Her physician listened to her as she cried and talked about her past—an unusual occurrence. Relationships no longer frightened her.

After the meditation, relief snuggled in her mind. The sadness clinging to her shoulders dissipated, and her load became lighter. She turned a new leaf, determined to try harder. Slowly but surely, she opened up to others and broadened her social circle. It started with conversations here and there. Soon, she pursued a hobby she enjoyed instead of a numbing task.

Running shifted her routine, and the forest trails welcomed her without expectations. Her daily jogs offered sanctuary—an incredible healing balm from her otherwise overwhelming life.

Also, she sensed a deepening bond with nature growing with each passing day. Its essence and wisdom seeped into her very being, becoming one with her.

A profound sense of peace embraced her. Amidst the gentle rustling of leaves and the melodious songs of birds, Dafnie found solace in her life—away from relentless pressures and expectations from ordinary life. In the tranquil oasis of Phoebus Groove, time froze. It allowed her to appreciate the morning's serenity and beauty. Like any other day, Dafnie continued her run toward her preferred spot, the creek, where she would mediate and center.

At first, her morning seemed like any other—habitual. But this time, an unsettling air clung like an intense headache. "Today seems like it doesn't fit, off even." Dafnie stopped in her tracks and turned to check her surroundings.

A sudden movement by a nearby tree caught her attention. A hawk perched on a branch fixed its sharp gaze on her, studying her.

"Today seems like it doesn't fit—it's off, even." Dafnie stopped in her tracks and turned around to check her surroundings. A sudden movement by a nearby tree caught her attention. A hawk perched on a branch fixed its sharp gaze on her, studying her. "You naughty hawk, you scared me. Are you here to spy on me?" She inched closer to look at the bird better. "You seem to have a master, judging by your tag and bells."

It was odd to see a hawk in the area. Hawks preferred high-elevation fields and plains with strong wind currents. Dafnie couldn't resist the charm of seeing a magnificent animal in her proximity, surveying its surroundings. "I guess a brief break is in order. You silly thing are too handsome not to admire."

Joy surged through her body with a tingling sensation. A warm thrill spread from her cheeks to her ears. The sight captivated her as she admired the glorious creature. Enjoying the occasion, Dafnie committed the image to memory. Her heart rejoiced, and she savored the fleeting connection that grounded her for the whole day. "Thank you for your time, you gorgeous bird," she said before resuming her jog.

The previous weeks had punched her in the gut with too much work. People kept changing her project deadlines for no reason. Her work drained her most days. But once at the creek, peace settled deep in her belly. A cleansing inhale washed her worries away.

As the team's senior software engineer, she shouldered many responsibilities, but she'd reached her limit. She felt restless and on the verge of losing control of herself. The time she spent outdoors granted Dafnie a respite from her life's relentless demands.

Taking a deep breath, Dafnie forgot about her problems and immersed herself in the tranquil embrace of nature. A refreshing warmth overpowered her, banishing any negative emotions from her existence.

The light cloud of mist billowing from the stream caressed her skin. Its soothing effect carried away the stress and plaguing worries invading her mind. With eyes closed, she opened up to her surroundings and found solace in the musical rush of the water. "No more challenges, just the present," she reflected and began breathing exercises. Soon, calm washed over her the moment she cleared her thoughts.

And she reached for her spiritual center. "Balance. Nature. Love. Forgiveness," Dafnie started her mantra as her body relaxed. "A hike and a garden. Crops and bees. Butterfly wings fluttering." She continued as childhood memories flooded back to her, bringing peace. After a few minutes of relaxing and remembering the best of her life, Dafnie stood from her spot to trek back home, her mood lighter.

Still perched on a tree near the stream, the hawk remained still. Its penetrating gaze fixed on Dafnie and piqued her curiosity. She wondered what drove the creature to this area and to be fixated on her.

It seemed unusual for a predatory bird to display such behavior, but Dafnie ignored it. With many pressing tasks for her to care for, thoughts of the animal jumped to the back of her mind. Instead, she focused on her run back home. Her playlist resumed at full blast as usual. The music's beat quickly immersed Dafnie in her little heaven and shut out any outside distractions.

As Dafnie neared her house, she saw the Lewis load a moving truck parked in their driveway. Since Dafnie had moved to town, the couple had become her loving neighbors. With open hearts, their warm greetings filled a void in her, putting her at ease—her anxiety all but forgotten. It didn't take her long to realize the hardships they'd faced. They longed for a family that would never come.

Elaine and her husband had bought the house to raise kids. But as years passed, they realized that family would never be. They yearned for a family, and she missed having her parents around. So, a lovely relationship started between them. Mrs. Lewis checked up on her almost daily while she spent time with them on the weekends. They had formed a family of their own. The elderly couple radiated love that reverberated with Dafnie—a treasured connection.

Seeing them packing filled her with dread. Her hands shook,

and breathing came in quick puffs. *Calm down!* She chanted over and over in her head. "Morning, Mr. and Mrs. Lewis! Are you redecorating your house this year?" Dafnie asked as unrest gave her the jitters when she passed the truck. She smiled and waved at the couple.

Elaine looked away from the box she fussed about, returned the greeting, and looked excited. A sparkle in the other woman's eye brightened her attractive features. "Oh, good morning to you too, my darling girl!" This was the greeting from the older woman as she closed the flaps of the small box she carried. "No, we're moving to our cabin for good. Our house caught someone's attention, and they paid good money for it." Mrs. Lewis paused, playing with her hands, feeling awkward and fidgety.

"They bought the house furnished. We're getting some personal things, like our wedding pictures and family heirlooms, before leaving..."

"What?" Dafnie said, dumbfounded, words spilling out unfettered. Stunned, she couldn't believe the unfolding news—her breath hiccupped by the surprise. "Now, who will I talk to about decoration tips and... and life? You know I'm messy and can't decorate or organize a house. I'm even messier with my affairs. I think I'll be in a bind, Mrs. Lewis." Dafnie stared blankly at the other woman, wondering why she word-vomited her thoughts instead of pausing.

Mrs. Lewis stared at her for a few minutes before reacting with love. "Hahaha! No worries, honey! You have my number. You can always call me. I'll always be there for you."

"I'm sorry, Mrs. Lewis! That came out so wrong. I-I..."

Mrs. Lewis smiled at Dafnie as she hugged her. The grappling tension melted as she returned to the embrace, breathing in Elaine's floral perfume, which reminded her of her mother. "Oh, no worries, my darling! All too sudden, even for us," Elaine said as she gazed back at her with tenderness. "If you need us, our doors are always open."

Dafnie beamed, relieved someone to rely upon. Movement from the driveway distracted her when Mr. Lewis peeked around the truck with a gentle smile.

After adjusting a few boxes in the back of their vehicle, he joined his wife, planting a sloppy kiss on his wife's pump cheek. "The missus holds a soft spot for you. Trust me! She'll worry about you aplenty. So, expect her to call you now and then to make sure you're all right. You're like a daughter to her, Dafnie."

Dafnie grinned ear to ear, although melancholy wanted to settle and take root in her heart. *Once again, alone with no one to fall back to. Why?* The thought fluttered in her head as she tried to push aside her loneliness.

Solitude was a constant companion of hers, one that refused to leave her alone. Happiness swelled her heart at the couple for starting a new chapter in their lives, but deep down, the hollowness of loneliness embittered her mood.

Forcing down an acrid lump of misery, she breathed the renewing scents of pine to find her center. A calming pressure wrapped her mind as her heart swelled with happiness at the couple's new chapter in life.

Her heart swelled with happiness at the couple's new chapter in life. Yet the urge to spend more time with them overwhelmed her. They'd helped her in every way, including healing her heart. "You're very kind, Mr. and Mrs. Lewis. You mean a lot to me. It feels like I've taken more than what I've given, and I appreciate it. Thanks for everything. And... Mrs. Lewis..."

"Oh, my sweet girl, you mustn't thank me. If anything, I should thank you. You have given me something I never considered I would have."

Understanding bubbled over as Dafnie nodded, recognizing the familiar ache. Then—with fidgety fingers—playful curiosity toyed with her good sense. "So... who's my new neighbor?"

"Oh, Bob, do you remember? I can't seem to recall. The only thing I remember is that his last name is uncommon," Mrs. Lewis asked as she handed her box to her husband.

"It's Mr. Delphoes. I believe he's in the music industry," Mr. Lewis said, taking the box from his wife to the car. "His representative mentioned he's a sought-after composer and songwriter looking for a peaceful place away from the city. He asked a lot about the neighborhood."

"Interesting! It seems we'll have a celebrity in our midst. I hope we don't get strangers lurking about because of him." Dafnie said as she grabbed one of Elaine's suitcases and placed it inside the couple's vehicle.

"I don't think it should be any problem, honey. The man said Mr. Delphoes keeps a low profile, and very few people know his most recent whereabouts."

"Oh! That's comforting to hear..." Nervously, Dafnie fidgeted with her hands—debating whether to press for more information. Her eyes sparkled with curiosity, but she restrained herself from asking too many questions. "When should the new neighbor arrive?"

"We plan to be out by this afternoon. Your neighbor wanted to move in as soon as possible." Mrs. Lewis gave her a sad look before hugging her one last time. "I believe his representative is handling everything. The house needs to be cleaned and ready to move in by tomorrow evening. So, the new owner should be here by tomorrow night at the earliest."

Abruptly, Dafnie got light-headed. "Wow, Mr. and Mrs. Lewis, that... was quick," she started, her voice trailing off as it broke with emotion. You didn't waste time deciding on this new chapter of your lives." Her anxiety bubbled up inside her as she panted. This is not a proper... goodbye."

Concern painted Elaine's face as she approached Dafnie. "Yes, the current owner moved fast. Mr. Delphoes's assistant came to our house unannounced this past Wednesday with an offer we couldn't refuse. Bob and I decided we needed to part ways with the house. It's time to start anew and enjoy retirement. But look at me, my child. Take a deep breath and calm down."

Accepting Elaine's gentle touch, Dafnie tried hard to focus and center her emotions. *Breathe! Balance. Nature. Love. Forgiveness...* she pondered as she took a few cleansing breaths, giving Elaine a weak smile. "I know you have many plans, but I'm glad for you." Dafnie looked around, looking for an escape— an excuse—to avoid an upsetting conversation. "I better let you get back to your packing. You've plenty to do, and I bet you will have a long drive ahead. But..." She paused, trying to figure out what to say next. "Before you leave, please come to my house to say goodbye. Treats for your trip will be ready for you and your husband." Dafnie embraced Mrs. Lewis as if holding on to a lifeline. "I'll miss you!"

"I'll miss you too, my sweet girl. Now you're making me worried. Are you sure you'll be fine?"

Dafnie's vision blurred as her eyes watered, and tears threatened to spill unceremoniously. "Sure… I'll be okay. Just…"

"This isn't a proper goodbye… I'll call you tonight after we check into our hotel. I may ask you to send a care package. I love to gorge on your delicious treats. Are you baking those fantastic chocolate chip and cranberry cookies I love?" Mrs. Lewis said, her eyes sparkling.

"Of course! I'll also include the recipe for whenever you want to have a treat."

"Thanks so much, honey. I don't have the patience to bake; you know that."

Dafnie felt much better after Elaine's lighthearted comment. "Now, I'll not bother you anymore and let you pack." Mrs. Lewis and Dafnie hugged for a long time after they said their goodbyes. At first, Dafnie held on to their embrace but let go of the other woman to let her finish packing.

Her imagination ran wild, and she wondered how life would be with Elaine and Bod and what kind of person her new neighbor, Mr. Delphoes, would be. Uncertainty filled the air as Dafnie entered her home. In their close-knit community, she didn't doubt their paths would cross.

She eagerly awaited that moment to extend a friendly gesture, striking the delicate balance between being neighborly and respecting boundaries.

However, amidst her excitement, a tinge of melancholy lingered in Dafnie's heart as she looked out her kitchen window. Her esteemed, longtime neighbors continued their packing as they prepared to leave.

The neighborhood would feel their absence. Essential pillars of the community, their eyes always brightened when helping others. They effortlessly integrated into everyone's daily lives—especially hers. Their presence burrowed deep in Dafnie's heart. Like fresh air, her relationship with Elaine and Bod bloomed into something vital. Her mundane routine developed into a refreshing mantel of solace with their ever-present company.

"This sucks!" Her breathless whisper sounded vulnerable. Heartbroken, she gathered the ingredients for her breakfast and the baked treats for Mrs. Lewis. Dafnie couldn't help but feel a pang of sadness invade her conscience. She baked one last reminder of love before parting ways. As she baked the simple sweet, she moved about the kitchen to prepare her morning meal.

But soon, curiosity got the best of her as she put the cookies in the oven.

Would the new neighbor be young or old? she pondered as she wiped away a few crumbs from the kitchen counter. "*By the sound of it, Mr. Delphoes is quite the personality in the music industry. Someone with a wealth of experience... unlike me. Plain and inexperienced old me.*

Like a tide, a horrible thought crossed her mind. "For sure, I'll bother him. People like him don't entertain someone like me. But..." Interest made her all jittery and impatient. "What would he be like?" These and many more questions danced in her mind as she pulled the baking sheet from the oven. While cooling the treats, deep in thought, she gnarled on her bottom lip—worried and hurt.

Without realizing it, her morning had become a blur of movements. Like a well-practiced routine, it readied her for yet another hectic workday. She predicted another dull day of meetings and some work. After she finished breakfast and prepared for her job, Dafnie's thoughts hastily turned to work. Once at her home office, looming deadlines and mounting responsibilities consumed her. The idea of juggling multiple tasks burdened her mind while she dealt with the loss of two dear friends.

"Focus, Dafnie! You need to focus. Balance. Nature. Love. Forgiveness."

Apprehension weighed her down as her hands shook from her nerves. "Take it easy! You got this." Dafnie closed her eyes, finding her center, before facing her day. She started the daily meeting with a fast click and clank of her keyboard.

"Morning, everyone! Let's start today's stand-up by taking turns discussing our progress and any concerns we may have. I'll start by saying that I persuaded the sponsors to postpone any new feature requests until the current phase is complete."

The keyboard clicking filtered through the call as she typed a few things to focus on later that day. "Convincing the client was hard. Despite their stubbornness, they eventually changed their mind after clarifying their doubts. We agreed that any unplanned demands could delay the project, and that's a win for our team. Once we release the project's ongoing features, we'll focus on iterating through these planned enhancements and release them as we finish them. Now, the floor is open for your work updates. Matt, can we start with your update first?"

Dafnie resumed her day without further surprises—a calm and typical day.

Chapter 5

The Movers

"Damn it! I can't believe it. Today, of all days, work took an annoying turn of events. When are they going to understand they need basic functionality first?" In a fit of irritation, she jabbed at an innocent tomato. The thick clumps of the fleshy fruit lay wasted in a juicy mess. Then her lettuce became her next chopping victim on the block—and frustration.

"Why do they keep pushing for those features? It's beyond me! Their lack of focus on what should be important is... argh! It seems they want bells and whistles before the product even works." She sputtered to the empty room. An unsettling lump lodged in her throat. She stared at her slashed dinner preparations, mulling over the day. "Strange woman! Why do you talk to yourself? You and the quirk you can't outgrow..." Others cringed at the peculiar trait of her monologues, though they comforted her.

"I already miss Elaine and Bob. I'm glad we got together.

They were serious when they mentioned they wanted to leave and left right after lunch. I hope they make it to their new place soon." She spotted some activity next door as she went around the kitchen to prepare supper. "What's going on?" she sighed, moving the sheer curtain aside to have a better look.

She glanced out the window and discovered the early evening still hung low on the horizon, the beautiful orange hue of twilight tinting the sky. Then, her eyes caught a fleeting movement inside the house. The person didn't bother to turn on the lights, making it impossible to identify the occupant.

"Did he arrive already? That was quick..." As she looked at the driveway, she spotted the garage door open and a few boxes sitting in it. "How interesting! Elaine and Bob just left right after noon."

Her new neighbor seemed keen to move, but the change happened too fast for her liking. "I'm not sure if that's you, Mr. Delphoes, but you're moving too fast. I wonder why you want a fresh start here. We're in the middle of nowhere. There's nothing here. But... welcome to the neighborhood," she mumbled, walking away from the kitchen window and assembling her butchered ingredients into a half-decent meal.

She couldn't blame him. The town was idyllic—a dream. And that was the main reason she rushed to Phoebus Groove—a slice of heaven, hard to pass when the troubled mind demanded peace. Above all else, she strived to manage a peaceful and cozy existence. Although it took her months to move in, the wait was worth it. "Why are you moving in such a hurry, Mr. Delphoes?" she wondered, like a mystery she wanted to unravel. "What are you escaping from?"

By now, the cleaning company attracted an ever-growing

audience. With dinner in hand, she looked out the living room window. People crowded on the street to check the commotion. They scanned the goings-on at the vacant house.

Then, a white van pulled up at the new neighbor's home. "This is really going down. Way too quick and drastic for comfort." She recognized the man who exited the truck, looking all business and with no game. "Mmmm, I remember using their services before..." It didn't surprise her one bit that Mr. Delphoes would hire them. It only made sense to employ a local company and build relationships. "Smart one, sir! Quite an olive branch offering to the community."

Having nothing better to do, amused by the unfolding events, she lounged by the window. Absent-mindedly, she slowly lifted her fork to her mouth, following the cleaning around. "I don't get why I find this so... enjoyable, but here I am." Confusion settled in her mind as she spied on her neighbor's affair. Without a spare moment of reflection, she munched on her dinner, staring at people going about their work—or peeping like her. "It looks as if Mr. Delphoes will move in by tomorrow, then..."

The early evening colors changed from orange to black as the sun dipped on the horizon. The dark, empty house next door gave Dafnie the chills as her skin broke out in goosebumps. Once vibrant with laughter and activity, it now stood eerily silent.

The faint sound of a door closing fluttered through her open window. Soon after, she overheard the roaring of an engine. She followed the sedan as it sped away down the road.

A gut-wrenching knot formed in the pit of her stomach as she peered at the muted house. Absence thickened the air with emptiness. With her neighbors gone, the oppressive lack of their presence came like a clear day, as if silence had the sudden urge to scream.

She stared at the empty house, devoid of its usual energy. The flavor of loneliness crept into her mouth, leaving a bitter aftertaste. Her chest tightened as her breathing came in short bursts. Sensing the tendrils of anxiety creep from the back of her head, Dafnie looked around for an outlet. "No, no, nooo! What can I do? I need to find something quick... I... can't... too... stuffy..."

She turned one way and the other. Cold sweat trickled from the back of her neck. Frantically, she headed to the closest bathroom to splash water on her face. "I need to find something to... distract me." Her breath puffed as she stared at the pale woman in the mirror. "My... I can't breathe."

Her heart shattered as she recalled Elaine waving goodbye as her car sped away. The crushing moment left her numb until that moment. Her eyes stung—on the verge of tears threatening to spill uncontrollably. Then her eyes landed on the view outside, beyond her neighbor's empty driveway.

The forest was her sanctuary. She ran—a hazy dash—to the brook as fast as her legs managed without faltering. Just like in her life before moving to town, overwhelming loneliness invaded her soul, and panic electrified her nerve endings. Rivulets gushed out and cascaded down her face without restraint. As silence enveloped her, she wondered why she was alone—again.

Breathe, Dafnie, fucking breathe. She told herself as she sat in her spot by the creek. The landscape became dark in the blink of an eye, but she didn't care. She needed to center. "Balance... nature... love..." She relaxed, thinking of her favorite things. *Hike. Crops. Butterfly wings.* A sigh escaped her lips as she remained still, listening to the night. She closed her eyes and took in a refreshing inhale. "Please, calm! You'll be fine... everything... will..." Her eyes skimmed around, searching for an anchor. Perched on a nearby tree, the hawk from earlier fixed its gaze on her.

✳✳✳

Dafnie stirred as the sun rose early Saturday. Its soft, warm rays illuminated the subdued room in the morning hours. After her eventful evening, she stretched and went about her usual dawn ritual.

This time, her run took her further into the woods—a longer break away from pressure. Her footsteps echoed through the quiet trails, a rhythmic sound. She found the much-needed harmony as she immersed herself in the tranquil space. The chirping and gentle rustling of the leaves awakened her and made her whole again.

This is heaven, and I love it all... above anything else! The ponderous little voice rejoiced at the freeing awareness that embraced her. Belonging draped her as she delved deeper into the forest. However, she struggled to describe it, always welcoming.

Home greeted her with open arms. In nature's embrace, she encountered peace from her monotonous life. That morning, she pushed her limits—what her body allowed. With her breath slightly labored, she trekked her way back to her house. A wave of rejuvenation spurred her on.

Just as Dafnie returned from the trail, a sleek black truck pulled in front of Mr. Delphoes's residence. The vehicle howled in a low rumble as it came to a halt. Behind it, a luxury sedan followed, its gentle roar announcing its impending arrival. Its surroundings reflected on its polished surface.

A sophisticated-looking man drove the expensive car. His hands gripped the leather-clad steering wheel with casual confidence. Extravagance and money defined this man with shame.

An elderly gentleman dressed in an elegant suit rode as the passenger. With a distinguished air, the older man focused on talking over his shoulder and writing in a notebook.

Dafnie couldn't help but glimpse at the truck's side with " Delphoes *Music Enterprises"* etched in shimmering gold. Her interest peaked as she watched the events unfold. She couldn't fight the temptation to slow her pace and watch the process as she ran past them.

Once inside her house, she rushed to the closest window facing the commotion. A small crowd of townspeople gathered to witness the event. The crew of professionals, all well-garbed, grouped around the truck expectantly.

She gawked as the two men from the sedan approached the team, preoccupied by their exchange. The driver, dressed in a tailored suit, strode toward the waiting vehicle. The tip-tap of his polished shoes reminded her of a well-tuned clock.

Meanwhile, the older man chatted with the man overseeing the move. Dafnie found it entertaining to listen to the animated conversation between the two. Once done, the two went their separate ways. As the other man addressed his company, the man remained engrossed in his notes.

When the gate opened, it revealed an impressive array of instruments. Soft padding protected the precious cargo while the crew patiently waited for further instructions. The younger man spoke with urgency. His determined voice carried great confidence. "We must put all these instruments in place before Mr. Delphoes arrives tonight. Pretty soon, another truck is coming with his belongings. We need to hurry, so let's get moving."

The movers wasted no time. They sprung into a blur of motions, getting to work in rapid succession. Someone leaped into action and removed the padded blankets, revealing various instruments.

She watched the aged man hurrying to several men about to handle the truck's precious cargo. Dafnie strained her ears but couldn't catch what the mature man said. She picked a flurry of hand gestures towards each instrument. Amidst the mishmash of words, two words stood out—"living room."

"It makes sense..." she whispered as her words trailed off. She knew the house's layout by heart. The grand room, designed for entertaining large groups, had ample space—a great place to display such treasured artifacts.

Given the multitude of instruments and the opulence, entertainment revolved around Mr. Delphoes's life. The fact became all too obvious, like the brightest summer day. By appearance alone, he'd woven himself into the music industry. Indeed, his possessions confirmed his accomplishments. Everything screamed unquestionable success.

When the older man finished his directions, the crew sprang into action. First, they offloaded a stunning Steinway & Sons baby grand piano. Even with her untrained eye, the magnificent piece of furniture left her in shock. As the group hauled the precious cargo indoors, the instrument's polished walnut twinkled under the sun. The mature man, an instrument expert by his looks, instructed the men to move the piano inside the house.

Casually thrown over his shoulder, the man carried a backpack stuffed beyond its capabilities. She glimpsed concern on his face before producing a measuring tape from his bag. He measured the entryway while looking at his notebook. His meticulous nature shone as he jotted his notes.

"Never seen a piano being moved... It's no wonder Mr. Delphoes picked him for the job," she mumbled, brushing away a stray lock of hair, fascinated by the event.

Ultimately, the crew managed their tasks problem-free, maneuvering the piece into the house. The older man disappeared inside with an excited bounce to his step. Another man carrying a toolbox followed right behind. Soon enough, the noise of a drill and metal clanking filled the air as repairs and assembly started.

After the monumental move, the team unloaded several string instruments. It turned into a parade of violins, violas, and cellos trailed by a train of guitars. Before long, a second truck arrived with more people and things. Although fascinating, intruding on someone else's affairs made her queasy.

"Time to continue with my day. Prying on others' business is not a respectable trait. Remember what your mother taught you."

Soon, a delicate but rhythmic knock came from the door, interrupting her thoughts. "Danielle! I should have expected this..." she murmured, apprehensive about the visit.

Upon opening the door, Danielle's warm, infectious smile greeted her. The other woman's enthusiasm always surprised her. "Hi, Dafnie! It's been a long time since we saw each other," the woman said with a seductive drawl. She figured the other woman craved some good gossip.

"Yeah! Last December, during Lewis's Christmas party," Dafnie said, moving to the side to allow the other woman in.

"Oh, yeah! I'll miss it, as it was a classy celebration. But... with our new local celebrity, holidays will get even fancier. How have you been?" Danielle asked, excited.

"I've been fine, I guess. How about you?" She asked, knowing the purpose of the unexpected visit. Ignoring her question, Danielle barged in, settling on a sofa by the window. She made herself at home while spying on the chaotic activity next door.

"I'm eager to meet our mysterious neighbor. I wonder what he's like?" The other woman propped up her breast as if preparing to devour a decadent dessert.

"Did you know the man is a prominent musician and producer? Before leaving, Mrs. Lewis told me his last name was Mr. Delphoes. So, I Googled him, you know... and discovered he's famous worldwide. His list of clients is quite impressive."

Her eyes sparkled with possibilities. "However, there aren't many pictures of him online. It's almost like he's a homebody or something. Not a single picture of his face! One thing is for sure: No one can hide. He appears marvelous. And yummy! My mouth just waters at the thought of meeting him."

"Well... it looks like you'll get your chance."

"I'm preparing a welcome basket. That way, I can meet him in person. See if I get lucky, and we can hit it off, you know?" Danielle finished with a peppy attitude.

Her behavior did not surprise Dafnie one bit. With her enchanting beauty, the other woman had the flair to make anyone weak in the knees. However, the other women preferred guys with power and money. Her demeanor shifted from cordial to sultry vixen, radiating sensuality. Recognized as the town mingler,

Danielle rejected anybody who didn't measure up to her lofty expectations.

"Well... Danielle, I trust you're ready to impress him with full force. He'll be delighted to have such a fun neighbor like you," she said, her tone oozing sarcasm.

"Yeah, I'm very confident he'll like me," Danielle said, standing from the sofa and heading for the door.

Mistaking Dafnie's comment, the woman took it as a sign to go after Mr. Delphoes. Dafnie couldn't help but shake her head and sigh in frustration. She hoped Mr. Delphoes would see past Danielle's seduction—but who knew? The last thing they needed was another small-town-lovers' spat—another uncomfortable petty squabble.

"Good luck with that one, Mr. Delphoes! Danielle is on the prowl," Dafnie muttered as she locked the door and headed to her office for the rest of the day.

Chapter 6

In the weeks prior, Apollo felt barren of sympathy for anyone. He showed no compassion to mortals and immortals alike. His character was opposite to his usual bigger-than-life self. The lingering dread of his last visit to Olympus haunted him longer than expected.

Worse! Zeus's volatile ploys weighed on his heart until he stopped caring. The encounter left him devoid of emotions and unable to connect with others, as if under a curse.

But Friday night proved to be nothing short of magical. When he opened the door, he couldn't believe his luck. Adonis remained, looking alluring. Adonis' presence was like a soothing balm and eased Apollo's troubled thoughts. Like magic, everything changed the moment his long-time lover appeared before him.

His mental fog cleared. The troubles that had weighed him down lifted with sudden force—like a gust fluffing his feathers and priming him for the flight of his life. Indeed, the unexpected rendezvous transformed into the climax of his day. The other man's seduction dribbled from his gaze like nectar while he was a bee hungry for sustenance. Restraining himself any longer became an impossibility for him.

He stood there, dumbfounded beyond comprehension. The surprise rooted him in place, and his brain refused to function. "What... are you doing here?"

"I missed you!"

"But what about…?" He trailed off, lost for words and mind stumbling for a reason.

"Aphrodite? My consort understands my heart is as free as the wind. Besides, I covet your company. You visited Olympus recently but stormed off. Did you neglect your promise to visit?"

A profound longing settled deep within Apollo's soul. As their eyes locked, their eternal connection blossomed once again.

"Oh, my dear beloved, for that, I must atone. What do you wish me to do?"

"Well... for starters, you can kiss me. Next, we can think of your punishment," Adonis said with a playful tone as expectation brightened his eyes.

"What if we forget? I earned my penalty..." Apollo teased as he reached for a soft yet lovely lock of hair.

"Then we forget. Now, I'm hungry for those lush lips." The hunger in Adonis' words ignited Apollo's fire.

With no other encouragement, Apollo pulled his handsome lover into a possessive embrace, refusing to let go of his lifeline. And left no doubt of his craving for an unforgettable night. Thus, he passionately kissed the other man, pinning Adonis's hands above his head in a greedy move driven by passion.

An unhurried dance of their mouths as they savored their sweet affection until both stood breathlessly. Before long, Apollo and the god of desire tumbled into bed, enveloped in a worshiping hug.

"I fucking want you, Ado! I need you now."

"What are you waiting for? I'm right here!" His boyfriend's whisper floated to him, embracing him in devotion and stirring his ardor to new heights.

Done with their conversation, having all the approval he required, his bold hands explored every corner of his lover's physique unrestrained. They tossed aside their clothes and tried to find the comfort of one another's overheated skin. Words grew redundant as they ascended into their passionate affair.

Despite their time apart, he knew his beloved Adonis well. And the beautiful immortal understood his heart in return.

He took a moment to reminisce. Each encounter carried recollections of their desires that remained ever etched in their minds, an enduring reminder of their deep attachment. As their touches turned more knowing, their desire heightened, and the kiss left lingering want. Forever ardent, they filled their escapades with delight.

Clear as day, like two puzzle pieces fitting perfectly together, their unrivaled chemistry blossomed. Ordained by the fates themselves, an ethereal their devotion.

A match meant to be.

Lost in their arms, Apollo explored his lover's tender lips until his feverish body demanded more.

His demanding kisses drove him to delve lower, moving away from their heated mouth down to a sculptured chest. Not bulky like his own, but well defined after years of training in the art of war.

He captured a pink nipple, compelled into teasing the gorgeous man. Suckling on one of Adonis's peaks, his fingers played with the other, wringing out cries of pleasure from his partner.

Not wanting to wait any long, Apollo wished more than anything to witness his love in the throes of euphoria. Leaving a trail of fluttery kisses, he dipped down until he found the source of his current infatuation—his mate's elegant cock. Without delay, he took his companion's pulsating rod deep within the confines of his mouth.

Soon, the room filled with Adonis's moans as he swayed his hips in harmony with his bobbing.

"My love, I can't wait any longer... I want you now, mmm!" his mate moaned, handing him a small vial.

Thrilled beyond measure, he unstopped the bottle and poured a delicious amount of the lubricant on his lover's rosebud. "Just give me a few moments, my dear! You're not ready," he whispered, placing gentle kisses on the other man's groin and tights.

Adonis wiggled in delight, a brief resistance later as he caressed the delicate spot that disarmed the other man. "We've done this many times... Please, hurry!"

"Shh! Don't be so impatient. I promise we'll feel good soon. Let's not rush this." Apollo's vow mingled with Adonis's panting, echoing throughout the room as he inserted a second and third finger into his lover's bliss.

"Mmm! I can't wait."

In a flurry of motion, Adonis pushed him to his back and reached between them to massage Apollo's erection, standing proud and ready. His lover wanted to take control, and he allowed it with open arms and an excited staff. With slow and methodical movement, his partner lowered himself on him until fully seated.

Their heavy breathing flooded the room with intense passion, followed by the light slapping of skin as Adonis moved. Apollo, on his part, met his lover's thrusts as he admired the pink flush that crept from Adonis's chest all the way to the ears. Rapidly, their reality became overrated as they reached higher toward euphoria.

"Hold me close! I-I can't..." Adonis whispered as he tried to catch his breath.

"Shhh! I got you, my dear!"

Apollo promised as he pulled his lover in for a kiss that drove them overboard into a world of ecstasy. They remained tangled in each other's arms as the night stretched, seeming never to end.

Until... they succumbed to exhaustion after hours of enthusiastic fever.

As Apollo opened his eyes, a satisfied sigh escaped his lips. Dust particles danced with the rays filtering through the heavy drapery of the hotel room. The sun glowed high in the sky in the early dawn. A quiet morning teasing reminded me of the previous night.

Two's faint yet tranquil inhale and exhale rhythmic breathing —their soft breath—was the only sound breaking the silence in the room. Intent on waking the room's occupants, the warm light drifted over to the bed. The playful beam interrupted Apollo's serene slumber.

The sight of his lover greeted him, spooned against his tender squeeze. His possessive arm tightened, holding the other man in a loving embrace. *My gorgeous partner, you fill my night with pure fantasy. An unforgettable encounter. I admit I'm eager to uncover the purpose of your stay.* A sigh of contentment escaped his lips.

He couldn't help but smile as he watched Adonis's peaceful sleep, his chest rising and falling with each breath. He snuggled closer as the other man shifted in his arms. The tempting scent of his lover ignited his desire once more prior to parting ways. He ought to leave. A long and tiresome journey awaited him for the rest of the day, and he fancied to find the reason for his partner's visit.

The unwanted separation didn't go unnoticed as Adonis stirred awake. His lips brushed against his lover's brow before he begrudgingly untangled their limbs and headed to the shower. While he got ready in the bathroom, he heard shuffling around as he finished showering. A soft towel hugged his waist, and the sight of Adonis folding their clothes into neat piles greeted him.

Proud as ever, Adonis looked up from his handiwork and winked at him. However, his jaw dropped when a cloud of steam billowed from the room. "Oh, for fuck's sake, you're giving me the butterflies. Your aura is spellbinding. Are you doing it on purpose?"

"No..."

The saucy denial aroused Adonis's skepticism, which marred his features, as his words hit the mark of understanding on the man as he admitted his intentions. For the time being, Apollo's capricious nature remained hidden. "Yes, you know I like to show off my good looks. It's part of who I am."

He moved with feline grace as he reached out to the heartthrob lounging on the bed. His fingers gently glided down the soft contours of Adonis's cheeks, reaching the man's ear—hovering with expectation. An impish smile played on his mouth, pulling his sweetheart closer and joining their lips into a passionate lock. Great yearning filled his heart with the affectionate act. "Good morning, my Ado! Does anyone besides your consort know you're here?"

The murmur forced a visible shudder through Adonis's frame when he pulled away for a fleeting breath, turning to magma, the blood pulsating through his body before placing a gentle kiss on Adonis' sensitive spot on his neck. "No one thinks I'm with you. I covered my tracks well. And please... don't worry about my mate, she understands. I wanted to spend the night with you. You need me."

The mighty god prince chuckled as he kissed his lover once more. "I must admit, your visit was a pleasant surprise. It pleased me very much. Though..." He trailed off, walking away to look out the window. He stared at the horizon, to the young radian pink morning sun. He didn't want to continue the conversation.

"Apollo, you're acting like the world lost its luster. You used to be excited to live among humans. What happened?"

Apollo turned to his bag and pulled out a fresh change of clothes, avoiding the question. "Why don't you freshen up? I'll get room service, so we can chitchat for a bit. I take it you still have coffee, right?"

Sighing, Adonis headed to the bathroom to get ready. "I hate secrets and hope we can chat."

"I promise I won't hide anything from you." He picked up the receiver to order food before the start of their day.

First, he donned dark jeans and a light blue button-up shirt.

He looked in the mirror to ensure everything looked in place. Then, he completed his look with an expensive wristwatch and leather shoes, which gave him a hint of elegance while toning down the appeal of his appearance. He lounged at the table by the window, pulling out his phone to catch up on work emails and the news as they waited.

Their food arrived before Adonis finished his shower. It didn't surprise him a bit. The other man enjoyed taking his time grooming. He tipped an excited-looking server and knocked on the bathroom door. "Food is here, and it's getting cold."

"I'll be out soon. I'm starved!" Adonis called out as he grabbed a plate and sat at the table. He placed his phone within reach and scrolled through the entertainment feed to catch up. As expected, all his work topped the charts. He smirked, pleased he still got it after many years of absence.

"That's one nasty habit, my lord! I find it rude to have a phone on the table during meals," the handsome immortal whined, emerging from the bathroom with a puff of steam, not bothering to cover up. Dripping and looking hot, troubling Apollo as he adjusted his overenthusiastic erection.

He headed to his pile of discarded garments and frowned. "I hate wearing the exact thing twice in a row, but I must admit, I wanted to see you so badly. Packing was not on my list of priorities—not even close ..."

"You can wear some of my things. We're about the same size as if cut from the exact cloth." He shoved a bite into his mouth and chewed his food with greed.

"Your clothes are too casual for me. I like to look expensive."

"Mmm... to each their own. I'm thrilled you came here, but something is bothering you—it's written all over your face." The callous pause thickened their surroundings as Apollo glared at the other man. "Why are you here?" He asked, curious about Adonis' unexpected visit.

Nonchalant and very much unaffected, Adonis seized a fresh pair of underwear from his bag, accustomed to his mood swings.

Next, Adonis finished getting dressed in the tailored suit he wore the night before, undoing the top buttons of his shirt and ditching the tie. It gave him an air of casual elegance only Adonis could manage with ease. He grabbed his breakfast and sat across from him. "I'm here to give you a warning."

"A warning… and that would be?"

"Recently, you've been trying hard to please your father. I don't particularly enjoy saying this, but he's losing his mind. He acts paranoid as power slips from his tight grip."

"My father is power-hungry to the point of insanity. I'm confused about whether I should adore him or hate him. The man is lackluster, and I… despise it…"

Apollo's narrowed eyes and curled lip spoke volumes.

I need to fucking calm down. Let nothing or anyone affect you. Anger simmered in his gut, making its way to Apollo's throat. At first, it impaired his speaking ability, but his neck muscles relaxed as the minutes passed.

"On the flip side…" Adonis drawled, fingers drumming on the table. "Hera's influence strengthens daily."

"I'm aware. Anyway…" He paused, looking out the window before he continued. "I'll not interfere with her plans."

"Do you think she's planning something?"

"I know she's planning something for sure, Ado. After all these years, I admire her."

"You... admire her?" Adonis asked, his questioning gaze landing on Apollo, gauging him.

"Yes. Her ambition is commendable. Besides, we have been getting along for a while, believe it or not." Apollo's statement cut through the air like a knife.

Adonis looked at him with suspicion shining deep in his wise eyes. But as he sipped his drink, he frowned and scrunched his nose, displeased about something, before spitting the contents into the cup. "I refuse to subject my delicate palate to another mouthful of this crap. I've grown accustomed to your herbal blends, and this drink is sickening."

The reaction brought a booming laugh from Apollo as Adonis pushed the drink away.

"The Last time you were in Olympus, you and Zeus met to talk about something important... and in private," Adonis said, hunting for answers.

Certain the other man was in the hunt for information, Apollo chose his next words carefully. "You said so yourself. My audience with Zeus happened behind closed doors." His drawled seethed with disdain at the memory. "In private." The pause that followed carried the weight of accusation. "How did you come about this information?"

"People talk... and Olympus guards no secrets. Our penchant for gossip when bored is too great. Information is the only thing we live for. We lost our way... unlike you. You keep busy in the human world."

"I see..."

Hot coals of anger started spreading within him, but he snuffed them out when Adonis graced him with a sad smile. Still, tiny traces of embers troubled him, making him restless. "I was looking for you. But then... you looked pissed, storming off like a hellion when you came out of your father's chambers. What did you talk about?" Adonis changed the subject to something juicier.

"He wanted my help to rectify the mortal realm. We're losing influence over the mortals, and he wants to restore our standing as lords. It's not worth the effort, but I'm considering his proposal," Apollo said, reflecting on his actions.

He resisted the urge to ignore his father's words, sensing a deep obligation to respect his father's desires. When looking into his future, he became puzzled by the vision. And he wanted to know more. "Are you positive? Listening to your father is risky."

"He asked, and I'll deliver. I hope my work pleases him. Although pondering on my track record of exploits, I could piss him off yet again. Besides, I received a premonition. I need to do this."

"A vision? Well, Zeus seems out of sorts, so if you want to follow this vision, be careful." Adonis took a few bites of his food before he continued. "You know how he feels when cornered. On another news, Eros has been..."

"Don't... mention that motherfucker's name in my presence, Ado. He's the reason I've lost so much. He's on my shit list."

"I'm sorry."

"You'd better be... It wouldn't surprise me if he stirs trouble again, putting me in a difficult situation." He pushed away his food, losing his appetite, and batting their exchange devolved to the subject of the one immortal hell-bent on making his life a misery. He sighed to calm his anger before smiling, not wanting to continue their conversation. I must leave. My trip is still long and tiresome. I want to get to my new home and get some rest, but... I expect we'll see each other soon. At my place?"

"I hope so, too. Our duties keep us busy. Despite that... I miss you very much."

"Me too, and we can always fix that. Right, my sweet Ado?" With a charming smile, he grabbed his leather duffle bag and sauntered to the door. "Shall we go now?"

"Indeed."

He and Adonis walked side by side to the lobby; the pair attracted everyone's attention. Apollo's casual look, which contrasted with Adonis's expensive appearance, made them stand out. Aware that he looked majestic, Apollo held his head high with century-old, conditioned ease.

The two gods went to the hotel receiving area, where he dropped off the room key and headed to the exit. Before facing Adonis, Apollo fished out his dark aviator sunglasses from his bag. He reached out to his lover and drew him close for a kiss that lasted several minutes. Reluctant to let go of his paramour, he allowed a fraction of the distance when he spotted people gawking. He paid no heed to their curiosity; he didn't give a damn. "I guess this is where we part ways."

"Take care, Mr. Delphoes! Until next time. And Apollo... please be careful with our kind. Many envy your power and influence. I always fear for your well-being."

Adonis walked toward his ride, swaying his hips back and forth, stealing the attention of passersby.

Apollo tried to digest the warning and waited for the other man to drive away. He dumped his bag in his car and headed to the coffee shop across the street. As soon as he entered the quaint shop, all conversation stopped at once—an all-too-familiar circumstance.

The barista smiled radiantly at him. "Welcome to Beans Oasis! What can I get for you today?" The woman's flirtatious manner, batting her eyelashes and all, didn't surprise him. He affected many people in similar ways.

Having seen the events of the day, he met his fate head-on. "I want an iced tea matcha latte. For the boss, Mr. D, he would like a cappuccino. Hold the cream." He flashed a devilish smile capable of melting anyone's heart, intending to escape the situation.

"Coming up, sir!" The younger woman slipped around the small area to prepare his order.

Like in his vision, the woman scribbled on the cup for the latter, excited. Afterward, she moved to make the espresso drink. Before long, the woman beamed at him with both drinks in hand. She batted her eyelashes, looking hopeful. The fates determined he needed to break her heart and reject her attempts.

"Here, dear! I believe this is your favorite, right?" He winked at the young woman while handing her the sweeter of the two cups. For a few heartbeats, she looked dazed as the gears of her comprehension spun in tandem with her confused thoughts. He turned with head held high, taking his bitter cappuccino—not before stashing a big tip in a nearby jar.

"But..." she started, standing there with a pale face and a drink in hand.

"Sorry, sweetheart! I need to get going."

Ignoring the woman's complaint, he left the shop and headed toward his car. Once buckled and ready to go, the roar of his vehicle reverberated down the street. Steering the supercar out of its spot. He punched the address to his new house prior to driving away. "Fuck! This trip will take most of the day... but I fucking dig this car so much that I don't mind. Besides... the scenery pleases me."

The scenery took his breath away with its majestic beauty. He always appeared at peace driving—long drives were his preferred medicine. The outdoors always beckoned him to reach out, and he was glad he did.

After spending the entire day confined in his vehicle, he seemed delighted as he reached Phoebus Grove's town. The sky was blood-orange when he entered the neighborhood he now called home. As his property came into view, he felt a heavy weight lift from his chest. *I'm where I belong—peace! Quiet! And no fucking court protocols. At last, I can be myself and not walk on eggshells—not that I care about breaking a few rotten eggs along the way,* he thought as he sighed in contentment, approaching his new place. The moving crew was about to leave, having finished their work for the day.

The roaring sound of his supercar disrupted the neighborhood's quaint streets. A crowd outside, enjoying the early evening, shifted toward the source of the commotion as his shiny black luxury sports car turned onto his house's driveway.

It seemed his home had been the center of focus. Now... he'd show them the main course. He slid the door open and exited the vehicle with curious eyes following him. Apollo felt their eyes burrowing on his back as he revealed his tall and powerful build for everyone to see and admire. He grew accustomed to the attention his muscular form and flowing golden hair commanded and exuded a captivating presence.

His eyes remained hidden behind his dark sunglasses, but his chiseled features spoke volumes of unrivaled attractiveness.

Unashamed of his magnetic appeal, he flaunted it with shameless zeal.

He appreciated the flurry of activity at his new home. Satisfied by the view, a gentle smile tugged at the corners of his mouth when things fell into place. Apollo walked toward the movers, ignoring his neighbors' curious looks as they stopped to survey his noteworthy arrival.

He turned his attention to the sound of a door closing, followed by heavy footsteps. He caught sight of the back of a young woman jogging in the opposite direction, donned in warm workout clothes and a cap. An inexplicable urge to chase her crossed his mind, but he denied himself and dismissed the thought as foolish. Before she vanished into the forest, he trailed the woman's swift movements.

A drop of sweat trickled from his nape all the way down his back. Goosebumps covered his body, putting his nerves on edge. Bitter nausea consumed his focus as his mouth salivated but grew dry at once. He had never experienced such a repulsive response.

Each sway of the woman's hips tempted his legs to move—to claim her.

The woods would be an enjoyable place to find a cherished partner. Coax her into intimacy until we're both satiated and drunken with lust. Then... I will not stop there... His wayward, fiery thoughts became more vivid and intense, imagining her body writhing and undulating with need. With a light sheen of sweat covering her flushed copper skin. A low growl bubbled up from deep within his chest and...

Shaking his head, wondering about the unexpected—all-consuming—allure.

Fuck, that came out of nowhere! He adjusted himself, careful not to get caught in the act. He whirled toward the crew and nodded in approval.

Now that he'd arrived, he took charge of the moving team and his instruments and moved to the older man. With a gesture of respect for the other man, he reached out his hand to greet him.

"Mr. Cappetti, I take it all went well?"

"Yes, Mr. Delphoes. Everything should be ready for you, sir. John left to buy you some groceries. We'll be out of your hair soon." The mature man rummaged through his bag before giving a level look at his boss.

"Thank you for all this. I appreciate it. You did such an excellent job taking care of my wonderful instruments. Your devotion doesn't go unnoticed."

"What a wonderful place, Mr. Delphoes! You'll find lots of peace. I'm looking forward to your next masterpiece. Maybe a concerto or a symphony?"

"I promise I'll create a symphony that the masses will swoon over."

He chuckled as he took a deep breath, filling his lungs with the crisp air of his surroundings as he walked inside. The stately house exceeded his expectations with a classic architectural structure. Yet it radiated a welcoming aura.

Home! He thought, walking in and heading straight to the living room, which housed all the beloved instruments he'd collected throughout the years. He moved toward his cherished baby grand piano and caressed its keys, love swelling in his chest. A profound awareness of unadulterated serenity washed over him—much like a lover's comforting embrace in a moment of weakness.

He now had a place in which he could create, where his music could thrive undisturbed. A place to live in peace… away from his Delphic throne.

He then focused on his beautiful concert harp, remembering when he composed some of his best works. The thought of composing once again sparked impressionable excitement and motivation within him. "Well, Father! The world must fall silent. Only the worthy ought to celebrate the lyrics of my melodies. The brave will learn to worship you again. I trust you'll be content," he whispered, followed by a handsome and devilish smile.

Chapter 7

Climb

As the sun peeked over the horizon, casting a warm tint into the room, Dafnie quickly rose from her sleep like any other day. The bright melody of chirping birds outside her window greeted her. The little creatures busied themselves with their morning routines. Smiling, she stretched, snuggling into the soft blankets before rising from the bed.

She trudged to the bathroom, shuffling along the velvety carpet. As soon as she reached the room, the cold tiles welcomed her bare feet. She trembled at the sensation, which gave her goosebumps and jolted her awake. Sighing, she headed to the shower and turned the water on, letting it run for a few seconds before stepping into the spacious stall. She sighed in relief. "This is heaven."

The gentle sound of running water filled the room as she gathered her things, preparing for her usual morning ritual. She indulged in a quick wash, enjoying the refreshing cascade to awaken her senses and invigorate her mind.

Once she'd finished in the bathroom, Dafnie changed into comfortable workout clothes. She tightly braided her sometimes unruly curly hair and covered her head with a beanie to avoid her mane from getting caught in the ropes or in the way.

She also checked and packed her climbing gear—along with some snacks—before leaving the house. Her heart beat with anticipation, a sensation that only intensified as she stepped outside. The sun's gentle glow illuminated Dafnie's performance bicycle. Her preferred mode of transportation, parked on the side of her driveway, twinkled and sparkled under the bright light. With swift and practiced ease, she mounted her bike, enjoying the familiar crease of the seat beneath her. Pushing forward, she rode away, glancing at the house next door.

The center of the town's gossip, Mr. Delphoes's home, shimmered in the morning glow like a mirage in a barren desert.

"Weird!" She rubbed her eyes, and she moved toward the house. But she stopped. A shiver ran through her body, alerting her of potential danger. The feathery hair by her nape stood on ends as she watched the house in question come in and out of focus.

An oppressive cloud settled over her mind, sending warning alarm signals racing through her and colliding with a painful slam on every nerve ending in her body. The tingling sensation overwhelmed her as she took one step back... and then another. Not wanting to dwell on the stifling emotion, she mounted her bike and rode away, looking for sanctuary.

The gentle *clinking* sound resonating around her comforted her. Joined by the sound, the chain emitted a soft hum. The neighborhood's enveloping tranquility pillowed the soul like a warm embrace, only broken by the click of her bike.

She rode through the quiet streets, taking in the familiar sights of her neighborhood: the dew-kissed grass, the golden hues of the rising sun, the line of towering trees on the horizon, and the silent houses. They all created a serene atmosphere, which she cherished.

Finally, she reached as far as possible with her bicycle. The woods closed in with their untouched limbs, and the rocky path made maneuvering around challenging. Fishing out her locks, she trusted the sturdy post to keep a silent guard on her bike.

The trailhead became crowded with hikers and climbers who met every Sunday at dawn for a fun and thrilling gathering. She grabbed her gear. She greeted a few of the climbers as she passed by them to start her hike to the spot they planned to hike. "Morning, everyone!"

"Oh, morning, Dafnie! How's work?" the group leader asked as he moved around and talked to various people.

"It's a relentless menace, to be honest. Super busy but surviving. Can't complain, though."

The guy laughed in understanding before turning away. "Glad we have Sundays to de-stress and reset, right?"

"That's correct!" she smiled, pleased to connect with passionate outdoor people like herself. During the walk, she cleared her mind, embraced the calm energy from within, and harmonized her thoughts.

"I'd hate your job. It sounds stressful."

"I got used to it, I guess, but about today's climb, this one is challenging. We must be careful with the smooth slopes. They're slippery this time of the year."

"Yeah… that's why those with solid climbing experience will lead. That means you'll be leading today."

"I don't mind…"

"Hey, I heard you got a new neighbor," an excited Thomas interrupted her as she was about to wrap up her plans. "And…" the young man teased as he wiggled his brows. "He moved in last night, stealing every woman's heart when he arrived. The whole town is abuzz with the news. Have you met them yet?" His cheeky comment oozed with innocent interest.

"No, I haven't. I believe he arrived when I left for my evening run. I didn't pay attention," she stated, rolling her eyes as she walked toward him.

"So… Do you know who he is?"

"Well, sort of… the Lewises said his name is Mr. Delphoes, I believe? It sounds like he's very involved in music. I even learned he's well connected from Danielle."

"Is he married?"

"Not sure. I haven't met the guy. He's probably single, judging by the items he brought and his sports car. His things screamed 'classy bachelor with wildly extravagant preferences.' I left the house because I grew tired of all the commotion. I only glimpsed him."

Thomas couldn't hold his excitement. "Nice! I may go visit you to check out the car, then."

"No, not you too…" she complained.

"Oh boy, your neighbor Danielle must be on the prowl then…"

"Yeah, she came by my house yesterday, spying on the house and workers. She prepared a welcome basket for him. It's good that she didn't stay long, though. She can be sweet but gets carried away when she's after a guy." Dafnie rolled her eyes, feigning hurt. "When I moved to town, she did nothing like that for me. I'm hurt. I didn't get one of her infamous welcome baskets reserved for single guys."

Thomas gave her one of his signature laughs, which could brighten a room without effort. "Well, I hope your new neighbor can handle her then, or maybe he'll bask in the attention," he joked.

They both laughed as they reached their planned destination at the base of a challenging cliff. "Let's focus on our climb for now. By the way, how's your girlfriend? I found out she's opening her online shop." Dafnie's eyes sparkled with curiosity.

"Yeah, she took the plunge and quit her job. She's pursued her hobby of jewelry making as a career. Man, she's a talented metalsmith who's created some awesome stuff."

"Really? That's amazing that she's doing this. She's been wanting to pursue her hobby for a long time."

"Yep, that's right, and what I told her! A few weeks ago, she got a massive order from an anonymous customer and is working around the clock to fulfill it. It's the main reason she isn't here. She's too busy." He beamed at her, in tune with his inner goofiness mixed in with affection.

"That's great to hear! I'm glad that she found something she loves. Happy for the two of you." She unpacked her climbing gear.

Their friends arrived soon after Dafnie and her friend reached the cliff base. Their faces glowed with excitement, eager to conquer the towering rock formation. They exchanged warm greetings and prepared for their workout. Today, Dafnie was to pair with Thomas.

With careful attention to detail, Dafnie readied and inspected her and Thomas' gear. She examined their carabiners, shoes, and harnesses. Everything seemed in order before she began her day with a full-hearted drive.

Remembering past phone accidents while ascending, she securely stowed it in her bag. Long ago, she learned to commit to memory the beauty of her surroundings and embrace the thrill and difficulty of the exercise without distractions.

Determined, she readied her mind to tackle her challenge—the face of a challenging cliff. A quiet intensity surrounded her. All her fellow climbers recognized and respected her commitment and skills. Her body flowed with fluidity, her movements methodical and rhythmical. She climbed with such ease and confidence and made for the activity. Her many climbs bled with a fearless dedication to her craft. Every rope knot she tied and every piece of gear she calibrated showed her dedication and commitment to her craft.

That day's climb challenged their experience. A sheer cliff face demanded physical and mental strength, but instead of daunting Dafnie, the challenge seemed to invigorate her. She thrived on the adrenaline of heights, the required focus, and the satisfaction of winning over her limitations. Her life hung on the line. "Hey, Thomas! Are you ready?"

"Yes, ma'am!" he said, excited about their climb and the invigorating workout.

"This is going to be a tough one. You need to focus and stretch beforehand. Also, make sure you secure the anchors well. Okay?"

"Will do!" Her daily climbing partner became determined with his stretches to limber himself up.

With a nod, Dafnie warmed up with her friend for their ascent. Dafnie regarded her hands while applying some chalk. Despite years of climbing, weathered calluses didn't tarnish her palms and fingers as they should have. She couldn't help but find it odd that her hands remained soft, with a delicacy beyond comprehension—petite little appendages, smooth like a flower's petals.

As the group started their ascent, Dafnie led the way with Thomas, both setting a steady pace. Her concentration stood like an unbreakable perception, her eyes scanning the surface, planning the next move and hold. The world around her seemed to fade into insignificance as she moved higher, losing herself in the climb's rhythm.

As she inched to the top, the view grew more spectacular. The world below became smaller as they climbed higher, and the view from above took her breath away. A cool breeze caressed her skin like a lover's caress, and the early morning sun warmed her back like a trusty friend. The burn in her muscles coursed through her body like a flash flood, along with the sweat on her brow and the thrill of the ascent.

She couldn't help but flash a triumphant smile as she reached the summit. The breeze swayed the few strands of hair that had come loose as she stood by the ledge, waiting for Thomas to finish the rest of his climb.

When her friend reached the top, she helped him over the ridge. Thomas slumped on the ground, breathing hard, as he pulled the tube from his hydration bag for a much-needed drink.

Sitting on the edge, she enjoyed the sense of accomplishment. She looked around—the sight of the sun having risen, casting a golden glow on her surroundings. Dafnie experienced profound contentment when nature embraced her during such moments. Amid the otherwise bleak reality, she found solace in the wilderness, harmonizing with nature with every breath she took.

"Shit!" Thomas said, catching his breath and looking worse for wear. "You sure can climb. You're a machine. Are you even tired?"

She laughed at his reaction. People always thought of her as weak, but they soon changed their minds when they saw her go up a wall. "I'm a little tired," she said.

"I have a hard time believing that. You sit there, looking like nothing. Are you even human? Do you even breathe air? Man... I'm light-headed now. Phew-eee!"

"Well, I've been doing this for quite a while. My mom and dad always took me cross-country, with climbing as our favorite thing to do."

"I remember your stories when you went hiking as a kid. Where are they? You should bring them along."

Dafnie turned cold at the mention of her mother and father. Chatting about her parents still left a sour tang in her mouth. After so many years, talking about them stunned her, a haze settling on her brain. People assumed her family still lived for some odd reason, but she ignored the pit that opened inside. "Unfortunately, they're gone," she said, trying not to sound heartbroken.

"I didn't know, Dafnie. I'm so sorry for your loss..."

Her eyes stung a little as she remembered the day she got the call about her parents' accident. As she looked back, the oppressive weight of grief crushed her heart. "You're fine, Thomas. I don't talk about it with others. I was eighteen and starting college

—a rough year for me..." Numbness washed over her senses, her brain running on autopilot. She tried to remember that time of her life. Forever lost and a dark cloud that refused to let her go—all a big blurb. "But I'm okay now. That entire week passed by in a blur. I recall very little from that time other than feeling empty."

"How did it happen?"

After mulling it over, she caved in. "A car accident." She turned to her friend, gave him a big smile, and tried to change the subject. "Are you recovered? Because we must find our way down." Dafnie's laughter echoed through the quiet summit when Thomas complained about being too tired to climb down. She needed the distraction. The last thing she wanted was to go down a dark, stifling road when doing something dangerous.

Chapter 8

Morning

As the morning sun appeared over the horizon, clarity shone over the landscape. The neighborhood just past Phoebus Groove came to life with activity at a slow and steady pace. Birds began their routine, a frolicking chorus, flying and diving for food. The rustling of leaves replaced the evening stillness as creatures jumped from one tree to another.

The sound of doors opening and closing as kids ran outside to meet their friends. They rushed about, excited and ready to go on their Sunday adventures. Parents called out to their children, instructing them not to stay out too late. The neighborhood became alive as the sun bid its welcome to the day.

When Apollo blinked, the bright rays blinded him. He smiled at finding a quiet place that reminded him of his palace on the outskirts of Mount Olympus. "I'm going to doze off for a bit. Signing that new artist was a bitch, and Ado's zeal on Friday left me exhausted," he purred, a smile playing on his lips. His eyes fluttered shut as the weight of his laziness weighed them down. After his long but enjoyable drive, he sighed and slept until late. "Mmm! A lazy day sounds like it's in the works. This hardworking god needs some rest. I deserve it. When did I sleep in last?" he murmured as his body succumbed to rest once more.

Living in the city stifled him. He couldn't spread his wings and create art. The unbearable noise of the masses muddled his brain and hampered his creativity. The never-ending rush hour took a toll on him. Exhausted, he had reached his limit with the loud disruptions.

Then, his business took a turn he didn't plan for. The small recording studio he set up a few years back—one of his various pastimes—skyrocketed. He expected the popularity but not the fast growth he'd experienced. People starved for his musical creations, and he complied to fulfill their wishes.

Artists from all over the world flocked to his studio and begged to record with him. Many sought his mentorship, drawn to his knowledge. Satisfied by the clamoring for his guidance, he wanted to teach them to forge a new troupe of muses.

Because he is the lord and master of music, he desired mortals to worship him more than they did his father. Not even the fires from hell would bend his will to rule and guide.

But success came with a chaotic schedule and overworking, so even a god experienced weariness. The meetings, the travel, the recordings, and the auditions for new talent kept him on his toes. On top of his busy work life, chaos ruled his personal life with his melody.

For him, hits and classical tunes would stand the test of time. The compositions spouted out of him like water, captivating everyone's hearts. As for his love life, he never deprived himself of a lover. Blessed by his mighty presence, a beautiful man or woman clung to his side. Someone always held his fascination for a short time before he lost interest and shifted to another person—another creative influence.

But now life would be so much different and peaceful. The quiet community's charm captivated his heart from the very beginning. Nothing compared to nature, not even the city. Apollo itched for the forest's natural allure but yearned for a place as far away from Olympus. He moved because of the calmness surrounding the neighborhood amid the evergreen woods. He'd played a crucial role in founding the town and was glad to be back. Pleased to be at home and proud that Phoebus Groove grew into a quaint western town.

The stunning scenery surprised him as he journeyed to his new home. For some odd reason, his pleasant drive the day before made him whole again. As he lay in bed, he daydreamed for the rest of the morning and remembered the rolling hills and vibrant wildflowers.

He settled into his fluffy pillows to inhale the calming scent of lavender infused on his pillow. Just as he was about to drift off to sleep, a scraping noise came from his bedroom window. "Seems like it won't be a lazy day after all. Daedalion, is that you?" he complained as the bird tilted its head, giving a sympathetic squawk.

Groaning, Apollo opened his eyes and shifted on the bed. He caught sight of a splendid hawk perched on the windowsill. Its feathers glistened with a mix of vibrant fall colors, reflecting the beauty of nature itself. He smiled at the memories they shared. Since his youth, Apollo's faithful companion had fearlessly weathered every obstacle and challenge by Apollo's side. His worries lifted from his shoulders as he watched the fowl tilt its head one way or another. Its jerky movements carried a hypnotic charm.

The expensive sheets worthy of a prince concealed his nakedness. Woven by master artisans from the plain of Olympus, the bedsheets tangled around his lower body, covering his sculpted hips. His legs, pillars of powerful elegance dusted with golden wispy hair, lengthened before him.

When he raised his arms above his head, the sinewy muscles of his abdomen rippled beneath the warm glimmer. He stretched to his full length and beyond the confines of his bed. He was an impressive height, towering over many. The gentle rays highlighted every curve and contour on his frame. He exuded strength that seemed to blend with the stillness of the morning.

He peeled back the soft covers, feeling the sun's warmth caressing his impeccable silhouette. The golden rays emphasized each line and curve of his body as if worshiping him for existing. His chiseled features, perfected by his heritage, made him a living sculpture—a masterpiece crafted by divine hands.

"Good morning, Helios! Feast your eyes if you wish, as I know you're watching," he said, conceited.

"I already know how you look. You like to flaunt how perfect you are. Now get dressed, you bastard," Helios's whisper fluttered through a bright glimmer, conveying its master's message.

Apollo smiled at the other god's annoyance.

"Good morning, Helios! Feast your eyes if you wish, as I know you're watching," he said, conceited.

"I already know how you look. You like to flaunt how perfect you are. Now get dressed, you bastard," Helios's whisper fluttered through a bright glimmer, conveying its master's message.

Apollo smiled at the other god's annoyance, displaying more

of himself to the other immortal. Helios scoffed as he dared to flaunt his manliness instead. His chest, a landscape of hardened muscle, rose and fell with each steady breath he took. His brawny arms flexed at the slightest move. With veins etched elegantly against his skin like a roadmap of power and strength. Every inch of him attested to Apollo's raw and unfettered virility. His natural scent is a blend of musk and pine—a subtle hint of his great affinity for the wilderness. His refined, unforgettable, and royal features were only associated with perfection and power.

Aware of the spectacle, he presented it to his companion and Helios. He ran a lazy hand through his messy hair, his fingers tangling in the golden strands, still holding an elegant curl untouched by the tossing and turning of sleep. His sleepy, azure gaze, half-hidden under heavy lids and thick lashes, scanned the room. The sunlight created a halo around his form, trying to find his discarded dark-blue silk robe and pants.

Awash in the golden embrace of the morning, he created a remarkable sight. He stood as a sight of raw perfection, fierce character, and unimaginable allure. Even in his proud nakedness, his grace seemed to remain unaffected, as though his bare form stood as the most natural state of being.

He hastily donned his robe and pants before going to the window, where his loyal companion still patiently waited. "My friend! Thank you so much for the visit. I'm thrilled you found this place to your liking. It shall be our new home from now on. We'll make splendid memories here, I'm certain." He reached out to the window latch with a light chuckle.

Daedalion stared back, his piercing eye glistening with intelligence as he seemed to understand every word he said. The bird's loyalty shone through its intelligent stare. As Apollo opened the window, Daedalion flew inside with familiarity and ease. He went straight to the wooden perch he kept for the hawk and pruned its feathers. Apollo and the hawk built their bond on trust and shared experiences.

Unlike the rumors, he didn't subject the animal to anything. Their bond became an instant connection that had happened when he saved Daedalion from death. Although he busied himself with his business and the recent move, Apollo didn't want to neglect his feathery friend. "I suppose sleeping in is out of the question for today. You ruined my plans."

He stared and waited as his friend finished grooming. "Are you hungry, my friend?" he asked as he walked toward the door, not waiting for an answering squawk. The hawk was more than capable of hunting for its favorite foods, but Apollo loved to dote on his longtime friend. He wanted to share a special treat he'd been saving for the bird for some time.

Meanwhile, he headed toward the staircase without glancing behind. Daedalion's graceful flight drew it to perch upon its master's shoulder. A sense of great unease washed over him. He sensed something would happen today that he would dread.

He experienced a wave of visions of a woman coming to visit today, intent on dating him and something he refused to entertain. Ever. He could make out the face of the woman, but the events leading up to the meeting jumbled when he tried to see what happened before their meeting.

The image remained blurry in his mind's eye. From his sight, the woman was attractive but not his type. He refused to indulge the woman, a social climber. He refused to entertain the challenge and her charms. Apollo's task didn't involve a woman like her.

As he entered the kitchen, he prepared a unique blend of seeds and berries for Daedalion, adding some ambrosia. His companion had wandered the mortal realm for a long time. Apollo believed he deserved a morsel of the food of the gods. Besides, the bird had earned its immortality.

After caring for Daedalion's well-being, Apollo went to the espresso machine and brewed a cappuccino for himself. He took a sip, savoring the milky bitter flavor he loved and craved most of the time. Standing by the kitchen counter, he recognized a familiar uneasiness settled at the corner of his vision—unable to shake it off.

"Shit, a premonition!" Something serious beyond his control lay afoot, and it seemed unstoppable. Though did he dare stop it in favor of his plans? No—he didn't want to, and he needed to let it be.

Shaking his head, he went to his living room to enjoy his drink. On his way to his sofa, he caressed the keys to his piano before sitting and picking up the book from the previous night. He always loved to begin his day with a bit of reading. As he settled into the comfort of his sofa, he immersed himself in the intricacies of the historical events depicted in the book. His fingers glided over the pages, tracing the text as he absorbed the historian's perspective.

Daedalion's soft squawks filled the room, setting the stage for a normal day. The rustling of pages and the sound of his antique grandfather clock created a symphony of tranquility that lulled him into serene relaxation.

The distant sound of a bicycle passing on the street jarred him from his peaceful reading. He glanced out the window. His gaze turned contemplative when he glimpsed a woman passing by, wearing a hoodie that covered most of her face.

Her workout clothes clung nicely to her form. It revealed attractive curves in a petite form topped by beautiful, sun-kissed skin peeking here and there. Despite her disheveled appearance and the obvious signs of fatigue reflected in her slumped posture, she looked stunning. The woman seemed to exude energy and stamina. Her aura seemed familiar, but he couldn't figure out why.

Apollo followed her every move. She expertly dismounted her bicycle, impressively balancing on one leg while riding the last few yards to her house. Then she disappeared into her home, parking her bike inside the garage.

He couldn't help but admire her wild spirit and perfect body. The sight stirred something within him once more. Just like the previous evening, when he'd first spotted her, he'd had a visceral reaction to her presence. Just as she disappeared into her house, the commotion in his heart eased. Thus, he returned to his book.

But his mind wandered elsewhere this time—to the woman who lived next door. The time to get ready and start his day began. He itched to play his piano. With a last sip of his cappuccino, he closed the book and went to his room. He dressed for the day—to impress and melt whoever's heart would come to his door and end things in heartbreak.

"Mmmm. My neighbor seems to be a wild beauty. Like my sweet laurel..." he muttered with a hint of sadness. Not knowing why, memories of Daphne came to him.

Chapter 9

Music in the Air

"Not a chance," Dafnie murmured as she opened the garage door and moved about her modest vehicle. Deep within, unease stirred as she refused to use her car around town.

"I'll only drive that coffin on wheels only... when necessary," she acknowledged, walking past her vehicle inside the house. Anxiety muddled her head while sitting behind the wheel. As an exercise of pure strength, she drove only when needed and as a last resort. After her parents' accident, she relied on other means of moving around town.

She hung her bicycle on its rack and fetched the cleaning rags. Dafne cleaned and prepared her bike for her next ride. Satisfied with her work, she went inside her house to care for herself. After she closed the garage door behind her, the creaking gate echoed through the house.

When she entered her clean home, she couldn't ignore her

nasty smell. "Argh! This is hideous," she said, sniffing her clothes. "I hate when I smell this bad."

She couldn't help but wrinkle her nose at the lingering odor of adventure that clung to her clothes and hair. Proof—quite obvious—she went all out during her routine. "I'm done with this nasty stench," she sighed in surrender. "No matter how exciting a climb can be, I need a thorough clean. Ohhhh! The comforting embrace of the hot spray washing away that grit and grime I accumulated all morning long," she said aloud as she sighed in relief.

She placed her climbing shoes in a bucket by the door. This allowed the dirt to soften throughout the day, making it easier to wash off later. For a second, she considered getting all the cleaning out of the way, but she changed her mind. The temptation to tidy herself played with her motives.

Thinking of the warmth cascading over her proved too appealing. The relief to her tired body called on to her. She cherished the untamed beauty of nature but soon parted ways with the unpleasant yet inevitable foul aftermath.

Before retiring, she did one last check. She examined her worn and dirt-streaked gear, making a mental note to get new gear. The ropes and carabiners had reached the end of their lives and needed to be replaced. After she typed a message on her phone, she stored her stuff in a storage cabinet.

After testing and putting away her equipment, she stopped by the laundry room. Once there, she undressed and started the machine to wash her dirty clothes. Prior to donning her robe, she checked the tiny cuts on her arms and hands. Thanks to some very sharp rocks, she received the injuries while reaching for a rock when distracted. Although minor, the sting became a familiar yet annoying pain—a bothersome reminder she needed to pay better attention to her surroundings.

With the well-stocked first aid kit in her washing room, she fetched the disinfectant and bandages to treat her wounds. She rigorously cleaned and disinfected the cuts. After cleaning her scrapes and feeling satisfied with her work, she did one of the spare terry robes in the laundry room and headed to the master bedroom.

More tired than usual, Dafnie padded her way to the bathroom. The soft, welcoming embrace of the plush carpet against her feet helped ease some of the fatigue as she laboriously trekked to her room. Once inside, she headed to the bathroom without a second to spare.

Carefree, she hung her robe and turned on the shower, letting it warm up. She sighed in relief when she jumped into the shower and let the tepid water ease her sore muscles. Under the hot shower's downpour, she deliberately scrubbed every speck of dirt clinging to her body. The warm spray embraced her from the moment she stepped inside. The dirt washed off her skin like a soothing symphony, balmy in her mind and melting away the fatigue. A heavy sigh escaped her lips as she allowed herself a long bask in the comforting embrace of the steam-filled rain.

After her thorough all-out cleanse, she dressed in comfortable clothes. Simple leggings and a loose-fitting tunic top made of soft cotton completed her look, wrapping herself in homey comfort. Next, she reapplied medicated ointment and bandaged her scrapes before heading to the kitchen. She was ravenous.

Before leaving the house, she'd gulped on a shake and munched on a protein bar. Now back home, she starved for a better, more substantial meal. From the kitchen, she listened to the hum of the washing machine filling the quiet house as she pulled ingredients from her fridge.

With each passing minute, her hunger intensified. Thus, Dafnie prepared a modest yet nourishing breakfast to start her day well. Lost in thought, she absentmindedly stared as her food finished cooking, jabbing at the food here and there.

Her mind drifted away from her when she suddenly picked up a song from the outside. A tune she never heard before. "Oh, is that…?"

The chiming sound of a piano carried a hypnotic magic that transported her to a place of harmony. She found her center of gravity didn't elude her. It reached out like a lost little sparkle, tentative and scared. For the first time in a long time, she reached out to find comfort—though she was also frightened and hesitant.

Belonging...

Dafnie paused in her tracks as realization dawned on her. "Mr. Delphoes, nice to meet you through your music! Are you gracing us with your talents this morning?" She closed her eyes to appreciate better the melody trickling through the open pane.

"It's a thing of beauty," Dafnie whispered as she sat at her small but cozy dining table, ready to enjoy the unique ambiance of her meal.

A gentle breeze came through the window, carrying a piano's enchanting sway. Delicate notes swirled in the air, composing a mesmerizing tune that gracefully drifted through the neighborhood, sweetening her fare. The harmonious music flowed with an eloquence that mesmerized her. It was a distracting impression that added an extra magic touch to her day.

With her fork halfway to her mouth, Dafnie found herself

hypnotized. Her attention veered away from her brunch and toward the beautiful serenade—out of place in the calm morning. Adding a touch of harmony to her day and the promise of something new to look forward to.

The piece appeared gentle yet stirring, like a warm breeze over a calm sea, exuding an aura of serenity and awakening. It was a slow piece. Lulling her mind to imagine the player's devotion. The notes lingered in the air, each one purposefully played and beautifully resonating. Transported to a different world, Dafnie couldn't help but smile as she closed her eyes.

The tune, as fluid as the morning dew, stoked each note, trickling into the next in a seamless cascade of sound. The delicate harmonies painted an ethereal and grounding auditory landscape. Its ebbs and flows seemed like ocean waves, with a hypnotic dance of sound and silence.

Enticing music graced the air with exquisite serenity, wrapping her in a comforting, intimate blanket. The enigmatic allure of the distant piano was like a siren call, pulling her toward the source of the call, echoing with mysticism.

Captivating sounds, which could only be described as magical, interrupted the peaceful morning surroundings. From the house, the center of attention the previous day, the sweet notes of the keyboard permeated the otherwise impassive neighborhood with its melodic beauty.

As the last bite of her food disappeared, Dafnie remained seated at the table, her ears keen on the entrancing tune still coasting on the breeze. The compelling notes of the piano continued to fill her home, wrapping her in a cocoon of gentle sound as if the music talked to her.

She let the melodies soak into her being. The rhythm almost

matched the beat of her heart. The music drifted a balm to her tired and bruised body, easing her tiredness. She sighed in contentment, finding her mind at peace. When the last strains of the alluring melody faded, a sudden sharp knock sounded at her front door.

With a start, the noise pulled Dafnie back to reality. Dejected, she rose from her chair, her brow furrowed in mild annoyance. She didn't expect anyone but suspected the visitor would be a pesky encounter at best.

As she neared the door, the knock became more urgent. Taking a deep breath, she opened the door and met one overly excited Danielle standing by her doorstep. Garbed in a flowing yet very revealing summer dress, the woman radiated pure charm. Excitement sparkled in her eyes, prowling for the perfect man.

Her peppy neighbor styled herself with flawless makeup. It was clear from her garments that she dressed to impress and seduce. Her eyes twinkled with trepidation with her artfully arranged wavy hair against her ocean-blue eyes. The woman held a gigantic basket, too oversized for anyone to lug around. "Woohoo! Hey, neighbor!" the woman screeched. "This is heavy but needs doing."

Sizing the other woman, Dafnie hesitated before saying anything, curious to know what she wanted. "Oh, hey there, Danielle! What's going on?"

"Dafnie, you won't believe it, but I've got a lot of goodies for our new neighbor," Danielle cried, barging into the house without waiting for an invitation. "Many locals pitched in to help make this beautiful basket for Mr. Delphoes," she said, unable to contain her excitement. "Do you have anything for it? I know you baked some of those amazing cookies for Mrs. Lewis. You always make extras, right?"

Danielle's eyes bore a mischievous gleam behind her question. Far from being neighborly, her intentions carried dusky vanity. A wide smile spread across her face, adding to her radiant charm. Standing in front of her stood a femme fatale, ready to make her move on a man she didn't know.

"Yes, as a matter of fact! I made them between Friday and yesterday. Made more than plenty to go around." She smiled, having understood Danielle's plan from the beginning. "I'll grab them for you."

The other woman followed Danielle into the inviting kitchen, where the aroma of freshly baked goods filled the air. Danielle's eyes shone with temptation as she watched her reach for the golden-brown snacks on the countertop. "You are a dangerous woman, Dafnie."

"Why is that?"

"Your treats are my weakness. It smells divine here. How did you learn to bake?"

Dafnie swallowed hard, remembering days past. "My mom taught me," she said, looking out the window. She could still hear the piano from next door.

"Oh, I'm sorry! I didn't mean to bring that up..."

"It's okay!" Dafnie forced a smile before she continued. "I have two types of treats you can add to your basket," she said as she reached for the breadbox and avoided the subject of her mother. "There's brownie and mocha chocolate chip cookies. They're still fresh, and there is plenty to go around. They'll go to waste if I don't give them away."

"Perfect! I'll take them both! I knew you would come through for me." As she stared at the sweets on the counter, Danielle's eyes widened in excitement. "I'm positive our new neighbor will enjoy them. Thank you. You are a lifesaver. However, can I have some for myself?"

"Sure—I have more than enough."

"Yay! Now I need to work extra hard in the next few weeks to burn off the calories." She stuffed some treats into the basket and some in her purse, looking thrilled with the goodies. Dafnie couldn't help but giggle at Danielle's energy, amused by her attitude. With a confident nod, the blonde vixen waved goodbye to Dafnie. Her heels clicked on the sidewalk as she approached Mr. Delphoes's house.

Dafnie quietly closed the door and headed to the window facing the home in question. She waited for the events to unfold. From her vantage point, she saw the other woman knock on their neighbor's door with an exaggerated flair. The bombshell blonde fixed her perfect hair and pushed up her breasts.

Seconds later, a handsome, tall man opened the door—their new neighbor, Mr. Delphoes.

Chapter 10

Melodic Visitor

Apollo found himself lost in his world of melody inside the house. He sat at his new baby grand piano. His fingers danced over the keys with well-practiced grace, a tender precision that seemed almost instinctual as he reached the last notes of the piece. Apollo's fingers lingered on the piano keys, letting the notes ring out in the quiet room. The last strains of Debussy's *Clair de Lune* hung in the air. An emotional echo of the music filled the space. Enigma enveloped him as he came down from his artistic high.

His morning preference for playing Debussy became a daily ritual for decades. He understood the composer's music like his own. The magical tinkles offered respite to his weariness, a calming essence that centered on his otherwise dull existence. It created a serene energy that clutched him, influencing the course of his day.

As he opened his eyes and raised his hands from the keys,

Apollo's heart pounded, drumming inside his chest as the song's resonance gradually faded, leaving a profound, reverberating silence. A sense of placid tranquility washed over him.

He always found the piece's subtleties to touch his soul and be beautiful. Its gentle ebbs and flows echoed the rhythm of his heartbeat—of nirvana inspired by purity. A contented sigh escaped his lips as he lifted his fingers from the keys. He clicked with the melody, connecting with the music, the emotions it evoked, and the peace it brought to his being.

Completing the tune enveloped him in an affectionate cocoon. The moment remained an intimate instance shared in time. Apollo wavered with emotion, touched and honored by the composition. True to his routine, he played the piece from memory. After all, he manipulated the circumstances and influenced the composer when he lived among humans during the composer's time. To him, living amid mortals had become an escape.

Sometimes, he left his palace in Olympus to dwell on the human plane. Crucially, he ensured his cherished art remained alive and thriving—not lost. He needed an outlet to cope with his most annoying condition, immortality.

Music connected him to another plane of reality. He basked in the joy of creating something beautiful. His hands and heart constructed something meaningful. A true testament to the transformative power of music, he lost himself in the melodies that reached his soul's center. Apollo leaned back, closing his eyes and basking in the piece's afterglow, the sweet notes still playing in his mind.

Then, something stirred inside Apollo's chest. An encroaching urge to play something livelier burrowed in his chest. The time for the woman to show up at his doorstep approached fast. The inevitable and unexpected visit of a woman who brought with her bad news. He needed something to cheer and calm him. "Well, Rachmaninoff, *Piano Concerto No. 3,* it shall be," he whispered as he caressed the keys again.

Apollo's fingers flew over the keys, bringing to life the concerto's energetic and passionate notes. The music filled the room, chasing away any lingering melancholy from the earlier piece. As he played, his mind focused on the confrontation about to happen and poured his impending frustration onto the instrument, closing his eyes.

As he started, his fingers danced over the keys with agility and precision, coaxing a symphony of wistful sound from the instrument. The rawness of the emotions for which Rachmaninoff's renowned compositions resonated in each chord.

The rhythm drifted undisturbed across the air. The lingering sounds permeated every nook and cranny of the quiet neighborhood. Turning the mundane and ordinary into something spectacular. He felt powerful, and his hypnotic influence would reach far. The piano's melody, a captivating amalgamation of harmonies, drove Apollo to clasp at the musical notes dancing through the air. He used his magic to paint a harmonious picture of resolve. The sweet notes of the concerto filled the air with mysticism that only music could create.

A scene.

One moment.

A testament to his artistic magic's power.

How flexible the heart could be with its influence.

Rachmaninoff's music continued flowing from the depths of

Apollo's soul, weaving a melody that would burrow in the memories of those enraptured by the harmony.

Apollo timed his performance as he reached the concert's end. With increasing intensity, he poured his entire energy into the final crescendo, bringing the intense melodic finale to a satisfying and powerful conclusion. After a few heartbeats of silence, he opened his eyes when he heard someone knocking at the door.

Apollo, filled with exasperation and defeat, released a sigh of frustration. He regarded his once-prized gift of prophecy and foresight as more of a burden than a blessing. He prepared by playing the piano for the encounter. However, he didn't look forward to mental gymnastics later on. "Argh! Why won't these types of women leave me alone? I want a bit of peace today."

The thought of what lay ahead filled him with dread. "I hate this already," he grumbled but maintained his composure and tried to be polite. Despite his efforts, he couldn't help but feel uneasy.

His new neighbor waited outside his door. He understood that ignoring her was out of the question. She appeared in his visions, haunting his thoughts. Their meeting carried a purpose, a reason for happening.

Mindful of his part in fate's plan, he needed to address her and the situation. And confront the prophecy that persisted and forced him to meet this person. Avoiding their encounter would only bring complications. They would meet, and he would learn about the purpose of their meeting and her role in his life.

He sighed as he stood from the piano bench and headed toward the door, steeling himself for the inevitable confrontation. As Apollo reached for the doorknob, he couldn't help but wonder about the chaos this new neighbor might bring into his life. He knew the woman would accost him, but she would give up in a few days—something he didn't look forward to, but he had already devised a strategy. Apollo realized the interaction would be brief but have a purpose, even if unclear. So, he bit down on a toxic remark threatening to hurl from his lips.

Today, he would receive something important from the woman. Now, as for the problem, he remained clueless about this life-changing gift that awaited him. He straightened, eager to learn what fate harbored for him. Even if that part of his vision turned chaotic, a blurry and messy disappointment, he would face it head-on.

Here goes nothing, Apollo thought bitterly to himself as he turned the knob of his heavy front door to open the door. As he swung open the door, Apollo's eyes fell upon a woman with elegantly styled blonde hair and mesmerizing blue eyes. The woman's features radiate great confidence and determination. She wore a stylish outfit that hugged her curves, accentuating her beauty.

"Good afternoon, Mr. Delphoes," she greeted him, her voice brimming with enthusiasm. "Welcome to the neighborhood! My name is Danielle, and I'm your neighbor from across the street. We're all eager to meet you and count you in as one of us."

"Hello, Ms. Danielle." He tried to hide his disinterest but failed to act the part. It didn't matter if she spotted his discomfort —the woman seemed unstoppable. "Pleased to meet you. I'm excited to be here and be part of this wonderful community." He left out the part "to become acquainted" on purpose. "And please, it's Apollo, if you don't mind. What brings you here, ma'am?" he asked, placing great emphasis on the honorific. He wanted his message to come across loud and clear.

"Oh, no need to be so formal. Call me Danielle, Apollo..."

Danielle purred, batting her lashes, her voice laced with a hint of flirtation. She smiled and extended her hand for a handshake while handing over the colossal basket, which Apollo reluctantly accepted.

This woman is so dense, he thought. His desire to be alone escalated by the second as she continued her flirtatious tango. Everyone reacted that way around him. He regarded himself as a man of distinct elegance and charm. His casual style highlighted his tall stature and sharp features, a testament to his godlike nature to always look flawless. Wearing a simple button-down shirt and jeans proved enough to impress and make him stand out, no matter what. This posed a problem as it drew unwanted attention. Current case in point: Danielle.

In his eternal existence, he'd once reveled in the adoration of countless suitors. He'd even taken advantage of his impressive looks to get anything he wanted. He'd become the perfect tool to accomplish everything he desired by charm alone. However, after enduring millennia of this behavior, he'd become disgusted by the treatment. The novelty of the attitude grew old, leaving him unsatisfied beyond measure.

"Nice to meet you, Danielle," Apollo's voice came across even. He didn't crave to experiment with the woman. "What can I help you with, if you don't mind me asking?"

"I've brought this small gift, a generous expression of appreciation from your neighbors. Inside, you'll find homemade goodies and presents from our community."

Danielle's warm smile displayed perfect teeth as she handed Apollo his welcome present. For some odd reason, he found himself pushed back in time. Shoved back to the days when humans would bring him offerings in order to gain his favor. But he put behind the old ways. "Thank you, Danielle, for the thoughtfulness. It's a lovely gesture." He didn't want to encourage the woman. So, he trod with care.

"You're most welcome. Now, as for my gift... I'm here to make you lunch," she said, pride leaking from her lips.

Taken aback, Apollo watched as she moved to a porch chair with a heavy Dutch oven, a bouquet, and two pink boxes.

When Danielle picked up her things, she went inside his house without hesitating. Her boldness took him aback. She was a stranger with a warm demeanor, acting as longtime friends with no understanding between them.

He pieced together her intentions and realized why she insisted on making lunch. She was on the prowl, trying to get him to warm up to her, and he would have none of it. "Ms. Danielle, wait... I'm trying to relax today. Last week was... pretty hectic for me. The only thing I wish for is for some peace before I'm needed at work on Monday." Apollo tried to keep his frustration in check and placed his welcome present on the console table by the entrance. "Next week, I have a lot of work to do. I just want to relax."

"Oh, no worries. I'll be on my way as soon as I finish putting this in the oven. Just a few minutes, and I'll be out of your hair and on my way." Danielle gave him a quick wink before disappearing into the kitchen. He followed as she carried the heavy pot to the kitchen, unsettled by her pretentious attitude. "Come on, Apollo. Don't be a killjoy. Let's get to know each other."

Resignation marred his features, and he sighed in defeat. "Well... have you lived here for a long time?" he asked, trying to be sociable. He propped himself by the kitchen entrance while crossing his arms in a defensive stance.

"I've been living here for almost ten years. Love the place and the people here," Danielle said as she punched in the temperature.

"I see. Well, it seems like a charming community." He tried to be polite but lost his battle with patience.

"It's a great place indeed. But let's talk more about you, Apollo. What do you like to do for fun? Do you have any hobbies or interests?"

"Music is my passion. I also like to compose. Few know this, but I like to hunt, too," he answered as his eyes scanned the items the woman left on the counter.

"I see. I heard a beautiful song coming from your house this morning," Danielle complimented with a seductive smile.

The sun god ignored her comment as his eyes landed on the two pink boxes next to the flowers. He walked over and inspected a box. After opening the delicate container, he spotted some mouthwatering chocolate chip cookies. "My favorite!" he whispered, craving something sweet. He helped himself to a cookie and took a bite. "These are fantastic," he said with his mouth full. "Are they from a shop in town?"

"Oh no, my darling! They're from your next-door neighbor, Dafnie. Her infamous treats are a hit around town. Sometimes, when schools have a bake sale, they ask her to make those for them." A chuckle escaped her, refusing to be contained.

"I see. Well, they are delicious..." he said, caught in a trance. His skin prickled with an unfamiliar sensation.

"I know it. Dafnie is a loner but a fantastic person," she said, setting the dish in the oven. "Okay! This will be ready to eat after the timer goes off. You want to return to your quiet day, so I'll leave for now. But we need to have a date."

"Thank you, Danielle. I appreciate it, but please don't go through this trouble again. I have a personal assistant who takes good care of me." A genuine smile graced his handsome features while dodging the subject of dating anyone.

"Oh, it's no problem at all. We're neighbors, and we should help each other out." Her warmth dribbled from her lips as she rubbed his arm. Apollo raised an eyebrow, uncomfortable with the gesture.

He stepped aside, avoiding his visitor. Not wasting any more time, he escorted Danielle to the porch. As they waved goodbye, Apollo felt a pull from deep within. Compelled to look at the house next door. He spotted the silhouette of a female behind a sheer curtain staring at him.

For some bizarre reason, the impulse to go to her place rose from inside a forgotten corner of his being. A piece of him left him in a void when she moved away. He shook his head, dismissing the thought. *Foolish to become soft and lust after a woman. I need to stay on course. On track with my plans,* he considered as he turned toward Danielle.

"Thank you again, Danielle. Have a good day," he said, closing the door behind him. Apollo sighed and walked toward the window, looking at the neighbor's home. A sudden, uncommon restlessness flowed over him. He couldn't shake off the idea he needed to get to the mysterious lady, to chase her.

"Now... with my harp to wash away the poor taste of that visit," he muttered as he headed toward the precious instrument.

He'd learned nothing from the woman. Other than receiving fantastic treats, fate's plan was still a mystery.

Chapter 11

Before the Chaos

Three weeks have passed since Apollo settled into his new place.

Home never seemed so tempting and fulfilling. He lived in many places, but none were this welcoming. With ease, he adapted to a comfortable routine, focusing on his art and music. To a degree, leaving the hustle and bustle of the city supplied him with much-needed relief. The previous evening, he received a crucial package. It arrived in time for his plan to be put into motion.

He picked up his cell phone to dial his assistant's number. His fingers danced across the screen. As he brought the phone to his ear, he couldn't help but accept the weight of the moment, the gravity of the task at hand. His plan slipped to its final stages.

"John, it's me!"

He began, his voice steady and severe, reflecting his determination. His room appeared to quiet down as if holding its breath in anticipation.

"I received the special package we discussed. We need to deliver its content. I want the new owners to get these soon."

His tone carried an urgency that rang throughout the room. The walls seemed to close in with the news. Silence met him on the other side of the line. John knew well about his plans. The other man objected, but he refused to listen to reason. He moved past anything that came across as rational.

"Last night, I received an important collection of jewelry. A local jeweler crafted them. She's poured her heart and soul into these pieces, showing her exceptional talent and skill. They're honestly works of art. I want you to come over to handle the deliveries. These gifts must go out today."

"All right, sir! I'll be at the house in about half an hour."

His assistant sounded bitter. He understood the other man's anger, but everything fell into place according to his plan—he was under control, like always.

"Thank you. I'll be waiting."

He closed his eyes before hanging. Stress sat heavy in the pit of his stomach and constricting his chest. His head swooned with lightheadedness as the gravity of the situation invaded his thoughts.

"At least the house seems at peace. Like it agrees with my plans."

His murmur interrupted the tranquility of the room. Otherwise, silence seemed to vanish as he went through the motions of preparing for the busy day ahead.

Apollo couldn't help but pace around the living room. Restless. His eyes drew to the scenery outside his window. The vibrant colors of the blooming flowers and the gentle sway of the trees provided a momentary distraction, but his mind grew impatient.

"I need to imbue these pieces with their blessing before John gets here," he reflected, his voice filled with reverence.

"The new owners, including the jeweler and her family, must receive them by the weekend. She's in a relationship, and her boyfriend should get one. I may be a jerk, but not heartless. These will protect them."

His thoughts raced with ideas of what to do, but a brief pause rooted him on the spot—making him hesitate. He detected the piece he ordered at the last moment.

Indeed, the exquisite yet delicate necklace with an intricate laurel wreath pendant and a green sapphire pleased him. He felt a peculiar connection with the enigmatic woman next door, which made finding the right gift even more important.

He experienced a surge of determination and excitement as he handled the necklace with the gentle care he reserved for those he deemed worthy of his affection.

"Stange, I'm acting this odd for a woman I have yet to meet."

His neighbor lived alone, seldom venturing beyond her home except for her daily workouts. Danielle was a frequent visitor, the only person coming in and out of the house. No one else came or went.

A recluse.

No matter how hard he tried, he couldn't shake off the interest bubbling inside him. The baffling attraction ate at his mind toward the woman. Danielle mentioned her name was Dafnie. A curious series of events. Something about Dafnie intrigued him. Strangely, an allure to her took deep roots.

He failed countless times to examine her future. Whenever

he tried to use his powers of foresight on Dafnie, he captured a glimpse of a murky vision. For the second time in his life, his capabilities wavered.

Long ago...

His powers first failed with Daphne...

Shaking his head, he continued with the blessing. He cleared his mind, imbued the jewelry with his divine power, and channelled his energy and intention into the sacred act.

With each piece, a sense of satisfaction flowed over him, knowing the precious gift would bring protection to their owners with powerful blessings that would keep their wearers safe from harm.

He last endowed the green sapphire wreath pendant. The exquisite ornament, with its blue gem at its heart, still fascinated him.

A special blessing that deserved his time—a gift not meant for a customer or a friend. A token of longing for his enigmatic neighbor with whom he found an inexplicable connection.

As he held the charm, an inexplicable emotion moved him. He sensed a mystical pull toward its future owner. Apollo glanced over to the empty window of his neighbor's house—a deep yearning to meet her.

"I'll make sure she receives this," he promised himself.

Holding the necklace, he allowed his divine energy to flow into it. The energy pulsated right from under his fingers, his power seeping into the Delicate jewel, intertwining with its essence.

A serene glow filled the room, and a gentle hum vibrated through it, resonating with his intent. With keen focus, he poured his goodwill and desires into the ritual. Not a stray thought interrupted the process. The air seemed to thicken with the sheer power of his concentration.

Suddenly, a vision flashed before his eyes—brief and indistinct, like a fragment of a dream. He witnessed a woman holding the pendant. Even though he didn't see a clear picture of her, the woman glowed with inner light.

He could only make out her tawny skin, which carried warmth like the sun-kissed earth. She exuded an unparalleled, exotic radiance. Even though he couldn't distinguish her features, the woman looked safe, content, and... happy.

The vision melted away as quickly as it appeared, leaving him with a comfort spreading in his chest. The vision's meaning was unclear, but peace lodged within him after it ended. It reassured him that his pendant would bring guidance and become a beacon of protection to its intended owner, his neighbor.

His mind wandered to how often he admired her from afar. From a distance, he could tell she exuded beauty. Her curvy figure moved with tempting grace, only found on Naiads and Artemis' maiden hunter. Her rear left him feeling hungry and hypnotized. The light swayed from her hip pendulum with each step.

It reminded him of a particular nymph, his first love, who once ran away after he professed his love to her. He sighed, acknowledging the need to let go of the past and let bygones be bygones.

This woman was not his lost lover.

He looked at the necklace, glistening under the soft light of the table lamp. Pleased beyond imagination for the first time in a while, his heart swelled with fortitude. A critical time to set his plans into motion and deliver the artifacts.

After Apollo worked his magic, weaving his desire into pieces. He chanted in the ancient language of the Titans and placed a protective spell on the jewelry. No one could steal these from their owners.

After blessing the pendant, he went to his desk, pulled out his ink and quill, and a monogrammed postcard to write a letter for his enigmatic and enticing neighbor.

To my elusive lady,

I hope this note finds you well. You might find it strange to receive this present from someone you've yet to meet. Without further ado, I'll get to introductions by taking the lead.

I am Mr. Delphoes. The man causing all the commotion and who bought the house from Mr. and Mrs. Lewis. We haven't met yet, but I hope we can change that very soon. I've seen you like to keep to yourself, but time is overdue for a gesture of neighborliness on my part.

Thank you for the delicious treats you made when I first arrived. Their mouth-watering sweetness brought joy to my heart, and I can't stop thinking about them. I count on you sharing more of those delightful morsels with me! Maybe over dinner?

Now, moving on to the primary purpose of this note...

I've included a small gift—a pendant, an item that will bring protection and strength. With humble desire, I offer a token of friendship and goodwill that I hope you'll accept. It holds many blessings, and I desire to safeguard its wearer—you!

Please accept this small keepsake. I want you to know you have a friend next door. I look forward to the day we can meet face-to-face. Until then, stay safe and take care. I would feel honored if you wore this pendant—always.

Warm Regards,

~ Mr. Delphoes

Apollo concluded the note, ensuring every word conveyed his thoughts and emotions. He finished his letter by adding his flourishing and elegant signature as a last addition. Then he placed it in a small linen envelope.

Pulling a lighter and a wax stick from his drawer, he placed the stick over the flame until the tip melted. He then dripped a few drops of the warm wax onto the back of the envelope before pressing his ancient signet ring into it, leaving behind his intricate house crest, a hawk framed with a laurel wreath.

He carefully put the pendant back into its wooden box and placed the note on top. Peace washed over him, knowing his neighbor would be out of harm's way, safe from his self-serving actions. After tying an elaborate bow, he placed the present inside the desk drawer.

Shortly after, the front door opened. Apollo's assistant, John, arrived sooner than expected. He picked up a bracelet and walked over to John.

"I want you to wear this at all times," he said as he clasped the bracelet around John's wrist.

John looked down at the bracelet. The man admired its intricate design before looking up in askance. A slight tingle coursed through his body as soon as the trinket touched John's skin. The protection spell worked, and his assistant was now safe from harm.

"Thank you, sir, but I still don't understand why we are doing this and why I have to wear this bracelet all the time," John said, looking up at him with a confused expression.

He painted a knowing smile. "It's for your protection. Just trust me on this one."

John nodded, understanding shining in his eyes.

"I have printed the shipping label and some instructions for you. After packing these, please drop them off at the post office. Please pay for expedited delivery and hand-deliver the ones from town."

He pointed to the pile of shipping material and jewelry boxes on his desk.

John nodded again. "I'll take care of it right away, sir."

"In the meantime, you can use my office to finish the packaging and head out. The day is still young, but we can't waste our time," he said as he grabbed the present from his drawer and headed toward the door. "I have some business to take care of, but I'll return in a few minutes."

As he left the house, he grabbed the box with the wreath pendant. He couldn't help but feel a sense of relief, knowing that the precious pendant would soon be in the hands of its rightful owner.

Since moving to his new home, a pull dragged him toward his secretive neighbor. Destiny insists he only captured glimpses of her from afar, but something prevented their fateful meeting. He needed to find out why. In the next few days, he would send Daedalion to Olympus to spy for him.

As he stepped onto the porch, a sudden demand bubbled from within to ring her doorbell. He craved to meet the woman who bewitched him. *One of these days, we'll meet, but now is not the right time,* he thought.

His affairs demanded his attention. He could not waste any more of his precious time. Also, the timing was everything. So he waited.

With a graceful flow, he placed the box in front of her door, knowing full well that the doorbell camera would alert her to his presence.

He snatched one last look at his neighbor's house before returning to his own to finish his duties as the god that would bring suffering to all. With lots to do still. And no time to waste.

From behind a tree, Hera watched as her stepson sauntered away to his house.

"Right where I need you, my dear son. You're helping my cause, unbeknownst to you."

The queen walked to the innocent-looking box, waiting to be claimed by its adorable owner. She flipped her wrist, and a sudden swish of magic wrapped the box. The container refused to obey her command at first.

"Apollo's powers grow stronger. As planned! Now, I need to ensure she's ready. All be for naught if her powers manifest before it's time."

Green and purple magic crept into the center stone. The sun god's magic prevented hers from coexisting inside the stone. But a stroke of luck blessed her when his powers allowed the intrusion, as she willed her goodwill to its owner.

"The only thing left is patience as my plan sets into motion."

Chapter 12

Pendant

Dafnie coded away, engrossed in her work and the loud music. Her finger flew over the keyboard. The world outside of her cocoon didn't exist then. She worked on some last-minute changes her manager wanted to be released in their next software update.

She hoped to impress their sponsors, so they selected her to do the job. Despite the challenges, her team kept moving along with their project at a slow but steady pace.

The recent requests, to an extent, were practical but lugged insignificant risks to their timeline.

Hard to pass on! A win for us, but... we'll need to haul ass and work extra hours. She considered their gains, going down her list of pros and cons. "Fuck it! They need to wait and plan better."

Upbeat music blasted from her earphones when her phone buzzed with a message. It startled her, setting her heart racing for no reason. Curious, she paused her task, ending her sprint, and picked up her device to look at the notification.

Her home security system alerted her to recent activity by her front door. Intrigued, Dafnie opened the app to check what was going on. No one, not even Danielle, would dare interrupt her during work hours.

The screen came to life, revealing the view from her door camera. Surprisingly, she saw a tall man with flowing blonde hair turning away from her door. She didn't open the application in time to see his face as he walked away.

The way he stood, with his head held high and shoulders squared, commanded the authority to captivate anyone's attention. His dominant presence left no room to doubt his impressive power. Most important, his mysterious actions intrigued her. Inquisitive by nature, intrigue ate at her willpower.

"Why is this man here?" she murmured, wondering about the purpose of the visit.

Dafnie rewound the footage to when the man came into view. She watched the towering figure enter the frame, clutching a little wooden box.

He climbed the porch two steps at a time, reaching her door with relative ease. He crouched to place the parcel by her door. Before leaving, he smiled at the camera and turned, walking back toward the other house.

After a brief video glitch, his appearance left her with even more questions.

Who is this man? Why did he leave a package for me? Dafnie thought, puzzled by the man's actions and the item by her door.

She stood from her desk to check out the guy lurking by her door—her suspicion in full-blown overdrive. When she reached the room facing where the man took off, she regarded the blond man entering the house next door.

Mr. Delphoes, is that you? And... what are you up to? What's in that box? Dafnie's thoughts raced with doubts.

She walked towards the window overlooking the house in question. Fixated by his behavior, she became captivated by his actions. She encountered the imposing man roaming the house as if preparing for something important.

Occasionally, she got glimpses of his elegant features when he wandered about the house. One time, he faced her home and stared at where she stood. Stunned, she stepped back, scared he spotted her snooping on him. But he spun away and strode away.

"Fuck! Did he spot me?!"

She griped, caught gawking at her neighbor. She blushed and yelped in embarrassment. Perplexed, she turned away, crossing the fine line of privacy. An unwelcome intruder in someone else's world.

But a new emotion replaced her discomfort in seconds. She couldn't resist the pull of curiosity, her mind racing with questions about the intriguing box the handsome and enigmatic Mr. Delphoes left behind.

Driven by confusion, she rushed to the door to find a lovely carved wooden container with a neat bow.

As she reached for the gift, her fingers brushed against an envelope hidden beneath the knot. Upon closer inspection, she pulled out a note in beautiful handwriting.

"To my elusive lady," she started reading, shocked he regarded her in such a manner.

"Why does he think I'm elusive when he could have rung the bell and talked to me? Instead, he walked away."

She complained as she continued scanning the letter and found that he wanted to meet her soon.

"Did he not make the first move because he thinks I like to be alone and wants me to make the first step? He's acting weird. He only needed to wait for me to come to the door. I would have answered."

She looked up from the message to stare at her front door once she read about the gift.

A pendant that will bring strength. Ahh! That's interesting. He also assumes I need protection. She mused, concern leaving a vile aftertaste in her mouth.

Mr. Delphoes overdid it with his show of appreciation. But deep inside, the thought of someone thinking of her moved her.

As she finished reading the heartfelt letter, she couldn't help but appreciate her neighbor's gesture. His remarks resonated with her because of their incredible sincerity. While she absorbed herself in the note's content, familiarity washed over her.

"It's impossible! I feel like I know him... but how?!"

A sudden cloud of disorientation muddled her perception of reality.

Yes! You know him from way... back—from another time.

Swooning, the little voice in her head. Like another being crawling inside her to leave its mark.

"That's impossible. A man like him is hard to forget. I would have definitely remembered him."

Dafnie scanned the note one last time, double-checking for any missed details.

"A friend next door! That's nice of him."

Dafnie stared as she opened the box, revealing a delicate necklace—a wreath pendant with a beautiful center green sapphire.

Such an expensive and lovely memento took her aback. Standing by her door, overwhelmed and at a loss for words—disarmed by the thoughtful surprise.

It was odd to receive a keepsake from a stranger. Her mind went into overdrive, and she thought of a way to repay the man.

"This gift is too much! How many batches of cookies do I need to bake to pay back this lavish present?"

She questioned whether to accept the exquisite treasure. Opening the box, she pulled out the delicate pendant and marveled at its impeccable craftsmanship. A simple yet elegant piece that didn't command attention but admiration. The memento, though imperfect, carried an unexplainable perfection, clueing her into a man of great thoughtfulness.

She fastened the necklace around her neck—an unconscious action—and an unfamiliar yet pleasant sensation overcame her. The charm tingled against her skin, seeming to hum with quiet energy.

For some unknown reason, she couldn't bear removing the jewelry—ever. Wearing it compelled her to cherish the delicate piece, and she was very grateful to her giver.

Overwhelmed by the wish to do something special for the man, anxiety flowed through her body. Dafnie wouldn't rest until she wrote a letter to the man of the hour. Eager to reciprocate the kind gesture, she dashed to her office to retrieve her stationery. She also hoped he would wait for her to open the door the next time he came.

Dear Mr. Delphoes,

I hope this note finds you well. With genuine gratitude and sincerity, thank you for the elegant gift you placed on my doorstep.

Your thoughtfulness took me aback. Shocking even. With its exquisite pendant, the necklace is stunning and an extraordinary item.

Still...

I seem undeserving of a splendid piece, but I appreciate your kindness. Not every day does one receive this beautiful keepsake with significant meaning. Your generosity brought joy to my challenging day.

I look forward to returning this goodwill, as I must reciprocate such a token with something of equal value. You mentioned you loved my treats. I hope you don't mind and tire of them, as I plan to repay your favor with sweetness.

Thank you again for your thoughtfulness. I say this from the bottom of my heart.

Sincerely,

~ Dafnie

Dafnie put the note in an envelope and a spool of decorative ribbon before heading to the kitchen. Once there, she walked to the bread storage to get some leftover cookies she baked for the local school fundraiser.

She placed the sweets in a spare tin. She then wrapped a bow around the container to make it look attractive. Dafnie grabbed a roll of Washi tape from a drawer nearby to attach the message to the pack.

She set the box on the counter to admire her work. However, her treats paled compared to her pendant, content with the gift. With a broad smile, she slipped to her neighbor's house with the small present.

Upon reaching Mr. Delphoes' door, nervousness overcame her —unsure what to do next. Hesitating for a few seconds, she left the goodies before the door. Then, as if something told her to run away from the place, she ran away from the man's house.

The sudden change in her mood left her puzzled and disoriented. A pull and push warred within her—a force swaying in different directions. She couldn't shake the feeling that something was off.

As she went inside her house, quietly closing the door, she slumped on the floor, breathing hard. She closed her eyes and started meditating to soothe her frayed nerves.

Standing up, she took a deep breath to relax before making her way to the kitchen. By then, dinner rounded the corner, and hunger occupied her thoughts.

She whipped up something quick but nourishing. With her meal ready, she settled into the living room, prepared to enjoy a movie. She tried to take her mind off her mixed feelings at Mr. Delphoes' house.

She decided on a drama to help her take her mind off work and her strange emotions. At that instant, she was unconcerned about her choice. The show helped her pass the time, to an extent —a stress reliever more than anything.

For the second time that evening, Dafnie's phone vibrated. This time, an emergency text from the local authorities buzzed, advising everyone to stay indoors.

News of an outbreak flooded her feed, one horrifying news after another. Every channel reported the increasing number of cases and the affected areas. The virus's rapid mutation puzzled doctors and scientists.

Despite experimenting with various treatments, none proved helpful against it—a fruitless effort. Like a hydra, it weakened at first, but then the virus would counter like an injured animal.

The disease spread at an unprecedented rate, and the experts urged people to exercise extreme caution during this recent crisis. Her fingers curled around the pendant as she read the messages, an out-of-character unconscious act.

Chapter 13

Preparation

Her employers emailed after the crisis text, addressing concerns about the crisis. They recognized the situation's consequences and allowed their members to prepare. As remote employees, Dafnie's team considered themselves fortunate to work around their schedule—whenever suitable.

However, her manager emphasized the need for a plan for everyone's safety. Faced with the situation's urgency, she organized a meeting.

"As you can see, we have another emergency on our hands. These are trying times, and we must do our best." Her throat felt raspy and dry, answering every question from her group. "Do we have anything else we want to discuss?"

"But... this means we can take time off to prepare? We have this important deadline, but we are getting crickets from our sponsors."

"Julie, that's a valid concern! To address your concerns, I emailed the managers for more updates. I advised them to move our dates to a later date. If you experience any problems, please contact me first. Now, take the day off and get ready for lockdown. It's okay if you can't work tomorrow. Are there any more questions?"

She dismissed the group when everyone shook their heads.

"Well... that concludes our meeting. Please stay safe!" And just like that, she disconnected and set up her phone to receive all her notifications. Not wanting to dwell on the gnarling thought creeping in. It distracted her as she paced around her office, worrying about the next steps.

Anxiety came out of nowhere, rising like wildfire and wreaking havoc in its wake. "I ought to get more supplies. There's still so much I'm missing. And... I'm by myself... no one..." A swoon of panic assaulted her as the room started spinning.

Like a network stream that encountered a glitch, the events on the TV played in her mind on repeat, overloading her stress and making it hard to think. Debilitating fear rooted her in place as images of being trapped consumed her.

She hated feeling cornered.

As the gravity of the situation sank in, her focus shifted into overdrive. Despite feeling overwhelmed by the impending quarantine, she ought to move. Thoughts and ideas on how to endure it and tackle all the unexpected 'what-ifs' now engulfed her.

"It's so confusing when my body does this..." She found it odd that her body reacted this way. One minute, she would lose her sense of panic, followed by an adrenaline rush that shifted her into survival mode. "Better get moving. Staying put does me no good."

With her knees unstable and hands shaking, she methodically inspected her pantry and scanned the shelves lined with artfully arranged jars, cans, and boxes. After plenty of deep breaths, she crafted a strategy, considering every scenario, from stockpiling essentials to creating a daily plan. She moved around the house and wrote anything necessary, checking for vital things.

She diligently reviewed her kit, verifying that it held everything for an extended period. She emailed friends to stay in touch and strategize during the lockdown. The past taught her the importance of remaining flexible and prepared for a prolonged stay home—alone.

"I must... think of something else."

Looking out the window, she smiled at her raised beds, brimming with a healthy bounty—and confidence.

Every year, her bountiful garden supplied her with fresh produce and essential ingredients. She planned to collect as many seeds as possible to secure a rich harvest this time. By designing her yard, she aimed to extend her growing season in the face of necessity. Admitting to being prepared, she added the purchase of more material to support a steady food supply when in need and to give away.

She spent her entire morning organizing all aspects of her life —laser-focused. As usual, she took notes to arrange her affairs on her to-do checklist for quite some time. Preparing for an extended lockdown, she wrote the required precautions in case of an emergency. She weathered earlier crises. Her obsession with prepping busted her mind. Even better, she chose books and shows this time to entertain her and ease her stress and anxiety.

She made some last-minute adjustments as she finished her

shopping list and gathered her purse. Then, perking her ears at the knock, she went to find out who arrived.

Looking distressed, Danielle's eyes filled with worry while her hands trembled.

"Hey, Dafnie! I can't believe we're on another lockdown."

Her neighbor showed her the latest news about the crisis.

"I hope we still have time to prepare and that we're not too late," she stepped outside, concerned.

"True! I'm worried about my parents. They live far from here. This confinement is freaking me out, like last time. You understand... there's no denying I'm a wreck—my life is so hopeless." With a troubled look, the other woman, her only friend, shared with her. "Last time, I went through hell checking up on them."

"You mentioned they are in a secluded area?"

"Yeah... I know they will be safe, but I worry about them."

She moved away from the door and showed the other woman to the sofa closest to the foyer. Danielle sat on the couch and went to the kitchen to boil water for tea. She often invited the other woman to make her feel at ease, and the least she could do.

"You don't have to fear for them. They'll be all fine, and I have an idea."

✻✻✻

Dafnie brought an assortment of herbs to choose from.

"Why don't you move in with them until the lockdown is over? You can help them with anything they may require. I suggest you decide today so you can leave by tomorrow at the latest. I'll check your house while you're away."

"Really?! You would do that for me?"

"Of course!" She reassured the other woman. "We're neighbors and friends, okay? We need to look out for each other during times like these." Danielle's eyes welled with tears as she accepted Dafnie's offer, grateful for such a thoughtful neighbor.

"My parents have a homestead that provides them with food needs, but they're also old. I believe a guy helps them out, but he can up and leave. They would be defenseless…" Her voice trailed off. "I'm sorry! I'm here talking about myself and acting selfish. Shit! I only think of me and dismiss others!"

"Don't worry about it. Now, let's focus on what's important— your loved ones. The best action would be to make it to your parent's house as soon as possible. We never accept what may happen. And I'll take care of getting your house ready for your return when the lockdown ends," she said, a hint of urgency in her tone.

"Okay! Thank you so much. I appreciate that. I've already started packing to be with them promptly." Emotion dripped from the woman's lips.

"No problem at all," she acknowledged, saddened by thoughts of her past while gathering her courage. Memories of her time with her mother and father flickered through her eyes. Her heart bled at the thought of them. They may have been a small family, but love gushed like a waterfall during the rainy season in the West.

"Yes, I know you would. Your mom and dad are so lucky to have you. Oh… I forgot…"

Danielle realized something and started bouncing from one foot to another. "I'm so sorry! You lost your parents in that accident. I remember now... You're so strong. How did you carry on after something like that?! I would have been a mess."

"Who told you I'm not a mess?! If you haven't caught on... I'm a loner, and... you don't have to apologize. It happened long ago, and I've learned to live with it. I miss them daily, but they want me to move on," Dafnie's voice holding a gentle yet firm tone. "Now, you must focus on getting on your journey."

"You, ummm... Your neighbor enjoys glancing at your house whenever he's outside. A dreamy grin always appears on his lips when he stares your way. Undoubtedly, he's uninterested in any woman. He's got this charm that seems to lighten up a room wherever he goes, but he carries great yearning about himself."

A sorrowful smile marred her stunning features as she moved to a chair.

"I think you can talk to him and find out. You two might have a lot in common and hit it off... He seems like your type. I can already picture you with him. You look cute together if you ever meet. Could be the start of something special."

Dafnie considered it but soon dismissed the idea. She glanced at the window, watching her neighbor's house's silhouette in the morning light. She sighed in defeat, convinced she lived alone for the rest of her life. Men were not into her, or so she thought. After their note exchange, Mr. Delphoes and she never crossed paths. Apart from their impromptu exchange the previous evening, none of them made a move.

Dismissing the idea, Dafnie smiled at Danielle. "Or... maybe he's curious about the neighbor who keeps to herself and socializes when forced to. I'm a hermit, don't forget that."

"You are not! Even though you keep to yourself, you like having company. The fact you opened your home to me says a lot.

Otherwise, you wouldn't open the door to me," Danielle said, laughing as she walked out and headed toward her house. "I'll call you. That way, we can track each other and make sure we're doing fine. Deal?"

"Deal! Now, you need to leave. Traffic will be a nightmare the longer you stay. Your parents need you."

"I'm moving. Don't you see?"

Danielle ran inside her house, waving goodbye. For the rest of the morning, Dafnie texted some last-minute notes before she left town. She at once received a response. "I'm about to take off. Please... take care, hon."

She smiled at the message before responding, "Be careful and take great care of your family. I will keep in touch."

"I will. And thanks! I will call you as often as I can. Consider what I said! Knock on your neighbor's door and reach out to him. He's a hottie," Danielle rebutted, a bit too excited for her liking.

She chuckled at the remark. "I will only if you get on the road now."

"Awesome!" Danielle's uncomplicated response came as loud and clear—a straightforward acknowledgment. She listened to the opening and closing of a trunk, followed by someone getting in a car and starting their engine. Walking toward the front window, she stared as Danielle drove away.

Despite not being close, she found it pleasant to interact with the other woman sometimes. She appreciated Danielle's friendly side when she didn't bother trying to impress a potential love interest. Enjoyed their conversations became the sort of pastime during quiet afternoons.

Men were always at the forefront of their conversation, but

they talked about their past at other times. Often, their exchanges were about experiences. Being a patient listener, she allowed Danielle to talk about herself and her exploits.

Dafnie turned her head to glance at the clock and realized noon was almost upon them. Before revving the engine, she closed her eyes and took a few breaths.

After her parents' accident, she hated driving and only used the vehicle when necessary. Once calm, she started her car and went to the store. She pre-ordered her things to make the outing quick.

By late afternoon, she stowed her stockpiles, reading to stay indoors. While sorting through her supplies, her pendant and the small intricate laurel tattoo on her wrist interacted. The artifacts feed off their powers. A faint glow emanated from the charm and the tattoo, but she was too busy to pay attention to trivial things. Dafnie continued with her day without seeing the strange behavior.

Later that day, as darkness claimed the day, spreading its dark tendrils over the skies, the community became uncannily silent. People marched, dragging their feet, into their homes. Some prepared for dinner, while others got ready to binge on their favorite shows. Concerned individuals turned their concentration to the news broadcast detailing the imminent lockdown scheduled to begin at midnight that evening.

Chapter 14

Visions

Unease settled like a gray cloud on Apollo, making him restless. For the first time in his life, nervousness consumed him. For some strange reason—bewilderment replaced his natural confidence. He looked around the living room to find dirty dishes and discarded notebooks scattered around, getting in his way.

"Shit! This is ridiculous. I'm not this way when I'm about to carry out my plans in the past. What's different this time?"

Leaving over, he reached for a ripped piece of paper shoved inside a cup. He didn't remember how it got there. Only remembering his actions blurring into one another as if moving through a thick fog.

"What's this? I don't..."

He stopped...

Shock coursed through him as he internalized the note's contents.

I want to meet you, my elusive neighbor.

Why do you hide from me? Why am I this attracted to you?!

I don't understand this emotion growing inside my heart, but I desire to be by your side, to spread your delicious body on my bed, and have my way with you. Fuck you until your world is just me. And...

Dread came like cold water being dumped on his head as he continued reading his lovesick, detailed rambling. Until his eyes focused on a phrase that gave him pause—his heart skipping a beat.

To cage and shield you from the world, a place where no lead arrow can reach its target—your heart.

"What the fuck?! When did I fucking write this?"

His grave whisper carried an odd ring around the room, leaving a void in his chest. With shaky fingers, he called forth a spark of fire and turned the note to ash. While dumping the mess, realization struck him. For the past few days, he would back out —lose control of his body during his trances.

Then, a light tap and the jingle of keys warned him of John's arrival. He headed towards the door to greet the man, leaving his mess behind and forgotten.

"John," he said as he began going about his home office, gathering some sheet music he discarded earlier and moving it to a corner on his desk.

"I want to discuss the packages we sent out three days ago. I trust they have reached their respective owners." His voice echoed around the room as he rearranged the papers in a neat pile and sat on his leather seat.

His assistant nodded and cleared his throat before responding.

"Yes, sir. We deliver every single package with signatures—if you need those. I reviewed your emails, and some appreciate the thoughtful gift. What should we do with those messages?"

"Good... Please send them a message telling them I'm honored for their friendship."

He sank into his chair, absorbed in deep thoughts. Music formed in his mind as he tried to relax.

Apollo admired the exquisitely written note from his neighbor sitting at his desk. Tenderly caressing the cardstock with the gentleness of a lover. He picked up the letter and read its content for the hundredth time, feeling a sense of inexplicable yearning. He couldn't figure out why he held off that way, but something seemed off. Unable to conceive any reasonable justifications, he questioned his behavior countless times.

Despite searching for logical answers, none were clear and forthcoming. Up to this point, he caught fleeting glimpses of his next-door neighbor's enigmatic beauty now and then. The circumstance aggravated as if something prevented them from meeting until the right moment.

Three days ago, Apollo received an alert that someone lurked by the front door. The anticipation built from within—an excitement to glimpse and admire his neighbor's, the mystery woman's, face.

At last, I will catch the woman who haunts my dreams.

He remembered thinking—a memory that to this day haunted him—as he stared at the notification. Hands trembling, he opened the security app to examine the clip. Apollo's excitement was at an all-time high at the thought of gazing at the woman's face. Unfortunately, the camera malfunctioned when her face came into view.

He lost count of the times he rewound the footage. A part of the video glitched, blurring the delicate features of his obsession —corrupted beyond repair. Despite replaying the feed in multiple instances, he couldn't find any answers. Frustrated, he hurled the phone into his yard.

Apollo suffered an inexplicable, magnetic attraction toward her as if the universe conspired to unite them while keeping them apart.

"So fucking annoying! Why am I not allowed to gaze at her lovely face?"

His arguments kept playing in his head, ideas rushing around, unable to stop the flow. Her presence captivated him, every gesture etching itself into his memory. A sense from within that meeting her would be gratifying, igniting a passionate love that would consume him. He hoped he wouldn't fuck things up once they met.

His days shushed like an eternity pulled on its threads as he yearned to approach her. But the timing never seemed right, teasing him with moments that slipped through his fingers and prevented him from coming to her house to meet. His desire grew by the day. An obsessive compulsion swamped him as images of her consumed his waking hours and invaded his dreams.

"John?"

"Yes, Mr. Delphoes?" his assistant asked, awaiting further instructions.

He held firm, ready for this moment for years, and now that the time was almost here, he wanted everything to go as planned. He didn't want any loose ends messing up his plans. "Make sure you're all set for the event I'm about to unleash."

"Sir? I don't understand," his aide answered, looking confused.

He couldn't blame the other man for his confusion and smiled. Knowing all would fall into place soon enough, he approached his friend and touched his forehead. Time to follow through with his goals.

"I bestow upon you the miracle of foresight and good fortune. Also, I confer on you the gift to recall all your past and the wisdom to use those memories to your advantage. Last, you shall comprehend my identity and my motivations."

John stood frozen in time; his breath caught in his throat as Apollo withdrew his hand from his temple. A profound sense of clarity washed over him as a gentle wave of realization broke through his consciousness. At that moment, a surge of purpose coursed through his veins. He asked what it all meant, but then his mind remembered his mission and his pivotal role in Apollo's schemes.

All of his past lives came rushing back to him. He recalled the time he crossed paths with the deity without fail. The handsome sun god gave him the gift of foresight in each lifetime.

His face lit up with acknowledgment when memories of previous experiences overwhelmed his perception—a borderline painful experience. Images of accompanying his boss on various journeys.

Every single success and failure yielded worldwide consequences.

Apollo possessed the power to manipulate human history with ease. But this time, their encounter seemed different, as if he played with fire and was ready to go to war for himself and his ideals. Stunned, John looked at his employer and old-time ally.

The sun god smiled, content with his decision, as he approached the front door. "Long time no see, my friend! Once again, I am glad to have your back."

"Sir!" He called out to his mentor, yet the man strode ahead without glancing back. "Please, Apollo! What's all this? I don't follow. I'm overwhelmed."

"Remember, John, everything I do carries a purpose. Visions will come to you, and you must decide on an outcome. Trust your instincts and understand that what I give is a gift, not a curse," Apollo's voice echoed through John's mind as he scanned him and walked away. "I hate to witness your suffering once more, like in your previous lives."

Blinked in confusion, John shook his head, trying to process what happened. He experienced an intense connection with Apollo—one of entanglement in some grand scheme of things set up by destiny themselves. "Like in my prior life, sir?" He mumbled before a flash of memories came rushing over, remembering the events that led to his demise. "I died because of my skill of sight. Folks guessed I was under the influence of the devil."

Apollo explained with a disheartened look, doing his best not to come across as a jerk.

"That's right. People refused to acknowledge your gift as a blessing, and you got punished. Too late when I came to rescue you," he said in a saddened-laced tone, pausing and gathering his wits.

"Make sure you're ready for what I'm about to do. You'll need to help others survive. Trust your instincts and guide people to safety. Remember that you have something precious—many will follow. And to answer your question, yes, we have met all of them in your past lives."

John furrowed his brows in confusion. "Sir, may I ask what the purpose of those packages is?"

"Please. I think we're beyond formalities. You can call me by my name," Apollo replied, his expression serious.

"I'm sorry! It appears odd..."

"You don't have to apologize."

Apollo flashed a charming smile at the other man. John's face turned red, so bright it gave him an adorable glow. He could but wonder about the indecent images floating around the other man's head of many shared encounters left in the past. They shared a romantic history in John's former life. However, John had already formed a deep connection with someone else in this life.

"It's time for my last act, undeniable catastrophe. I'm making sure everything is ready for my apocalypse."

"But... why? Why do you want to end the world?"

Apollo's eyes softened, and he sighed, deciding to be vague about his response. "It's necessary. A new beginning cannot happen without ending what's old and broken. You're not aware of this, but conflict is brewing among gods. I'm fucking tired of all their bullshit."

John could sense the weight of Apollo's words as if the very air around him grew heavy with their significance. His eyes widened in shock, reflecting the awe and trepidation that flooded his mind. A portal to the future opened before him.

Drawing him into a vivid dream that unfolded like a tapestry of events.

In this sight, John envisioned a woman standing beside Apollo, shrouded in an enigmatic veil of mystery and power. Her presence radiated with a brilliant glow. Her eyes sparkled with otherworldly wisdom while her every movement exuded an aura of ancient knowledge. Together, they glanced at the world crumbling around them like a delicate mantel unraveled at its seams.

But then, the vision shifted as if the threads of fate were being rewoven with soothing precision. John watched with quick breaths as Apollo and the mysterious woman embarked on separate paths, traversing insurmountable trials. Yet their unwavering determination and belief in their purpose propelled them forward.

Their ways converged like two rivers joining forces to create a single and powerful flow. Eventually, John witnessed the birth of twins and the renewal of the world, which was tranquil and harmonious—a land where everything was right and where individuals turned the scars of the past into symbols of resilience and growth.

The sheer magnitude of the picture overwhelmed John.

What did it mean? What role did he play in this grand plan? Questions swirled in his reason like a storm, but one thing became obvious: He needed to depend on Apollo's plans. He believed this vision held the key to a beautiful future.

And so, with a heart filled with hope and a spirit ready to embrace destiny, John took a deep breath and committed himself to the journey ahead.

John's mind still reeled from the vision when Apollo spoke again.

"Trust yourself and your abilities, no matter what you learn. You have a vital role to play here, John. You'll save many."

Chapter 15

Mysterious Plant

Hence, Apollo prepared himself for the next phase of his strategy that evening. A sense of urgency consumed him. The air around him felt oppressive to the point of suffocation. The virus unleashed upon the world spread as expected. He needed his plan to go without complications. He insisted on being precise about his execution.

Wasting no time, he went about the house gathering his weapons. The hunting knife that Hephaestus beautifully crafted for him a few centuries back. The blade would remain sharp, never dulling, no matter what it cut through.

Out of habit, he inspected the edge. With a satisfied nod, he sheathed the weapon and strapped the leather sheath to his thigh. Apollo then headed to his office with determined strides. Once he arrived at his desk, he conjured a golden key, causing a magical keyhole to materialize in the lower right drawer.

The small lock faintly gleamed as he opened the

compartment. Rushing to get things going, he scanned the inside, and the items he searched for came into full view. He reached for the embroidered pouch and emptied it onto the desk's tabletop. The oversized pods glistened, their waxy surface reflecting the lamp's light.

His ocean-colored blue eyes glowed with an unnatural divine radiance. Brilliant specks appeared on his irises as he called forth his powers and surveyed the husks before him. The intensity of his gaze matched the fiery determination within him, fueled by a profound sense of purpose.

He raised his hands, his fingers dancing as if strumming an ethereal harp with a symphony of anticipation. As he started the enchantment, a chant formed on his lips with a sing-song quality to it.

Closing his eyes, Apollo had visions of what would happen next. The seeds, once sown, would give rise to thick and twisted tendrils that entwined themselves with the surrounding nature. A burst of pollen would fill the air with every flowering plant, carried away by the gentle wind.

With its invisible grasp, the spores would sow within its intended victims, those afflicted by the virus. The vicious nightmare about to unfold would spare no one. Both humans and animals would transform into sinister monsters.

After finishing his enchantment, he gathered the seeds and placed them inside the bag. He then thought of the areas he singled out. Apollo handpicked several locations with large gatherings, teeming with life and energy. Plenty of spots where his plant would thrive. A mist of spores scattered with the gentle breeze like an unstoppable force of nature. The plant needed infected individuals to feed its curse.

"All will go according to my plan," he muttered. He already imagined the vines growing, covering everything in sight. Only a matter of time before the pollen spread, and his next phase would begin. He grinned, his lips curling into a wicked smile. This would be his masterpiece, his magnum opus, and started the grand finale. He only hoped that the results would please his father.

Now or never, his plot hatched into motion.

A surge of excitement engulfed his awareness. In a flash of light, he closed his eyes and teleported to his first location, New York City's Central Park. Gazing at his surroundings, the few unsuspecting park goes didn't regard his presence. In fact, invisibility shrouded his every step as he walked through the trail and admired those around him. People searching for relief from the confines of their homes, finding solace in nature.

"My people, I'm sorry for your destruction. I helped you rise. Now, I must bring your demise."

He reached into the pouch, and with a flick of his wrist, Apollo scattered some of his pods in an open field. Using his power of persuasion, he coerced the Anemoi to create a gust of wind to spread the seed in all directions.

The moment the seeds touched the dirt, the creepers sprouted, growing at an alarming rate. Apollo's eagle gaze followed as the vines intertwined, creating a tangled web of plants and a cocoon in the center.

A few seconds later, a thick cloud of pollen appeared from the pupa, drifting into the air and dispersing, advancing the unsuspecting city. After he finished his work in New York, he moved to his next location, Shinjuku Gyoen National Garden, in Tokyo.

Like before, with a snap of his finger and a flash of light, he materialized in a secluded park. He looked around, and the vibrant hues of the place greeted him. The blossoms swayed in the breeze as the masters of the winds announced their presence to him.

With meticulous care, Apollo started his process again, spreading his seeds and tending to the vines that spread through the city oasis. Fueled by his touch, the limbs flourished, their tendrils reaching out and releasing another cloud of pollen. The wind carried the pollen, dancing through the atmosphere as it headed toward the unsuspecting city dwellers.

As swiftly as he appeared, he vanished in the blink of an eye. Moments later, he materialized in a different location, the air crackling with the surrounding energy. Without setbacks or concern, another area close to a bustling metropolis teeming with people going about their daily lives.

As he moved from one place to another, his actions unfolded unnoticed by mortals, blissfully unaware of the invisible deity among them. He repeated the same process in Paris, Buenos Aires, Delhi, and Kinshasa.

"I'm sorry, my delightful world. I helped you and your people grow and thrive. But now it's time to respect my father's wishes, this once, and reset." Legs heavy like lead, he dragged his feet around to each location, a shadow among a blur of faceless mortals—unseen and undisturbed—going about their day unsuspecting.

Apollo's hand delved into his pocket, fingers closing around a handful of pods. He felt the husks pulsating with power. With graceful precision, he spread the seeds across the ground. Each time he sowed his plant, the vines grew right after. His absent gaze shined as the sprouts proliferated and intertwined with their surroundings.

Compared to anything in existence, the wicked and stunning blossom would grow in the center of the chaotic mass of sturdy limbs. Afterward, the inevitable cloud of pollen would rush to the surrounding areas and beyond with the help of the wind gods that sided with his cause.

"May you bring what I desire, my dearest creation!"

From the corner of his eyes, a tiny little bud opened, releasing a pink puffy cloud. A man closest to him coughed once, then twice, before continuing on his way.

"It begins!"

Apollo smiled as his form shimmered and disappeared.

✳✳✳

After finishing his work, he vanished one last time, reappearing in his house. About to relax, a blinding flash disturbed his mood. The unexpected guest came to give him an earful. The atmosphere thickened with expectation.

"I think you are going too far, my sweet little brother," a firm yet gentle voice spoke from the shadows.

"Artemis, can you please stop with the pet names?!" He complained, spotting a wicked smile spreading across her face. "You realize I hate them."

"Really! You love to use them on your favorites. Your lovers dig that nonsense from you."

He rolled his eyes at his sister's teasing. "Anyway, what brings you here?"

He turned to face his twin, unblocking his weapon and putting down the embroidered sack on the kitchen counter.

"You know very well what I'm here for. Your actions are causing chaos and destruction. What are you trying to achieve with this?"

"This is necessary, dear sister. This planet needs to be cleansed, made pure again," he argued, his face writhing in disgust.

"With something this important, you don't impose your decree on your own, Apollo. You lack the authority to claim ownership of something like this," she countered with unwavering resolve.

"Why can't I pass judgment? Do you see our father stopping me? Wake up, Artemis! He's the one that asked me to do this. Besides, we are the masters of this world. We do whatever the hell we want. Am I wrong?!"

Vexation poisoned his veins as a sneer disfigured his handsome appearance.

"Because you're not the only god in charge of Earth, Apollo. You have no right to play with people's lives and destroy them as you deem fit."

Anger busted from the seams of her patience as she sighed, exasperated.

"Fine, if you want to stop me, then try. I want you to know this! I'll not back down. I hope my intentions are clear. This land must be reborn, and I'll do whatever it takes to make that happen."

His tone commanded obedience with a finality trained to diminish anyone beneath him.

She remained silent for a moment before she spoke again. "I know you're hurting, my dear brother. You've experienced denial in many things, especially in love, which made you cynical, but

I'll do what's necessary to stop you. Their time of unlimited kno-wledge is almost upon them. I'll defend the mortals and this planet," she declared.

"And how are you going to carry out your plan, Artemis? Are you willing to take risks and do what needs to be done to protect them? Because they are more concerned about gossiping and bic-kering amongst each other than working together," he countered.

"I treasure everything about this world, even if it means go-ing against you, my brother. They need more time to do better with guidance," she replied with steely determination.

He glared at his sister for a few more moments before responding. "Their time is over, and the world they know will be reset. My ploy is already in motion."

Before disappearing into the shadows, Artemis shrouded her message in mystery. She said, "I have also planned to fight this, Apollo. I'm part of something beautiful that will fix everything. You'll see..."

He admired her resolve with a frown. Puzzlement undid his

What's up her sleeve? His bitter thoughts consumed him, rott-ing at his confidence.

With resolve, he settled his mind up to force his agenda through. No matter the consequences. His chest puffed with ambition to exercise his will, even willing to give up his immortal life for his goal.

With a smug smile, he turned and walked to his living room, confident in his power and the success of his plan. He sat on a chair by a window.

The mortal world would soon be reborn, whether the gods or mortals wanted the change. His plan marched on—unstoppable and without resistance. The end was near, and Apollo would be the harbinger of it all. Those most deserving will inherit a paradise and find salvation. At the same time, those who destroy this precious land will perish.

The gods loved to toy with the lives of mortals and the less fortunate. Immortality compelled them to turn unhinged. But for the first time, his game of life and death would transform everything forever.

Alas, no turning back from his actions now. The end inched closer, with more to come.

Just as he prepared to shower, a fluttering of movement caught his attention at his neighbor's house.

He approached the window and looked out. He marveled at the woman's silhouette moving around the house. At that moment, Apollo couldn't help but feel a tinge of regret and sadness about what he was doing.

Why am I feeling this strange attachment to a woman I haven't met? It makes little sense. He thought, nibbling on his nail—a habit he never outgrew since his youth.

Suddenly, Artemis's words echoed in his mind. "Too many precious experiences slipped through my fingers too many times. Of course, I'm fucking bitter! Denial turned me into an asshole."

With each step he took around the living room, his musings grew troubled, and the wall bore witness to his rambling.

"A group moves against me... and my plans. And... things will change. What does it mean?"

He shook his head, trying to clear his thoughts. No time for distractions—urgency propelling his inclination. With a wave of his hand, he created an invisible barrier around his house, ensuring that no one trespassed or exited his territory without his consent. With one last glance over to the house next door, he seductively touched his lips, whispering a silent apology to the woman.

"Forgive me, my dear. But this is necessary for the greater good of this beautiful world. This is my domain, and I must protect it by destroying it," Apollo said with a hint of regret before turning away from the window.

He understood his actions would bring suffering but needed to move forward as planned. His father wanted this. Henceforth, time for him to continue with his plan.

To lead it to the end, no matter what obstacles may come his way.

Chapter 16

"Danielle, I'm glad you arrived at your family's home. In hindsight... leaving when you did was the right choice. I heard from the morning news they're not allowing people on the road anymore unless it's for emergencies or to pick up supplies."

"Yeah... in certain cities, crime rates have reached record highs, and authorities warn against going outside. My parents live in the middle of nowhere, but you are all alone there," Danielle said, expressing her concerns. "I should have urged you to come with me. What was I thinking?"

She wondered the same, but they didn't think the situation could grow out of hand. Despite that, she remained optimistic about her present circumstances—nothing else to make things any better.

"Don't worry about me. I'm sure I'll manage." Dafnie tried to reassure the other woman. "The town seems to be quieter than usual. I've spotted people packing up and leaving, and only a handful of us seem to be around."

"Is my house okay?" Danielle asked, worried.

"It looks fine from where I stand. I popped by your place this morning. I did some cleaning. Dust collected over the days."

"Thanks so much, Dafnie. I'm grateful for your help. It's overwhelming to process everything unfolding. I'm at a loss for words..."

"I know it's a lot to take in, but we must stay positive and be prepared for whatever comes next."

She tried to calm the other woman, although a sliver of doubt stirred an uneasiness that frayed her nerves.

"I'm still going to insist... Why don't you come over to my parents' house? I know... it can be troublesome. Annoying people around me became a sort of specialty of mine, especially with men. But staying all by yourself gives me the heebie-jeebies. Something might happen to you, leaving you unprotected. Are you still going on your runs every day? It's dangerous, and you must put your well-being as a top priority."

Danielle's tone held a hint of uncertainty.

"Not anymore. I did at first, but when I learned about everything happening worldwide, I quit running through the trails for some time. I even stopped going outside unless it's to buy groceries," she added.

"Well, I'm going to leave you now, but call me if you need help, okay?" The other woman asked, her voice sounding hesitant.

"Thanks, Danielle. I will. Take care and stay safe!"

"Wait, Dafnie! Please come over." Danielle approached her conspiratory. "Have you said hello to Mr. Delphoes yet? The two of you must hook up."

She didn't know how to respond but went with the first thing that came to her mind. "We haven't met, and I don't think he'll like me. Anyway... you seemed to bond with the man helping your parents?" she asked as a diversion.

"Well... That guy and I have been hitting it off quite well, if I say so myself."

The other woman's laugh trickled over the receiver, humoring her.

"Besides... the heartthrob next door is very much available. Your treats found their way to his heart already. I got slapped in the face by his gorgeous presence. And, oh... don't get me started with his scent—divine! He was all spice and masculinity. I'm getting wet just thinking about it."

Embarrassed, she blushed and changed the subject. "I'll try. Danielle, I've got to go. My dinner is burning."

"Okay! But please consider what I've said. Maybe the two of you could come to my parents' house. That way, we can stay safe together, but I'll leave you. I know you're cooking. Take care."

"Bye, and call me!"

"I will, and the same goes for you..."

An overwhelming emotion spread from the middle of her chest to the rest of her body—close to buckling her knees. She hung up before her anxiety crashed upon her. The relief stuck as soon as she ended the conversation.

After she placed her phone on the charging station, she returned to the stove, the rich aroma of a hearty stew wafting through her kitchen. She stirred in some fresh tomato, the wooden spoon scraping against the bottom of the pot as she mixed the ingredients. The rhythmic motion was almost therapeutic, a welcome distraction from her troubled mind.

With caution, she added her long-perfected homemade pasta to the bubbling water. The gurgling sound echoed through the space, breaking with the whistle of silence. After cooking her simple meal, she headed to the living room to turn up some mindless entertainment while she ate.

At least, someone she knew lived far away from trouble—secure. But she couldn't help but regard the unease and dread eating at her wits. Dafnie's hunch worried for the worst yet to come. Something new and terrifying happened every day that put everybody on edge.

She couldn't shake off the nagging impression that maybe, just maybe, they were being judged and tested. She clung to the hope that her friends were out of harm's way.

After taking a few bites of her food, she reached for the remote and switched on the television for some news. The anchor's voice filled the room, his tone somber as he reported the escalating chaos worldwide because of the virus. Images flashed across the screen. In some towns, people scrambled for supplies in supermarkets. Heated disagreements escalated into physical confrontations, and law enforcement struggled to keep order.

The correspondent continued painting a grim picture as the death toll rose higher each day.

"There's been a recent development. A bizarre type of vegetation appeared out of nowhere, spreading throughout the major cities. All attempts to eliminate this threat have proven unsuccessful. Discovered a few hours ago but appears to have multiplied. We urge everyone to avoid contact with the plant, and if you see one, please report it to your local authorities."

The news anchor announced to his audience, his voice filled

with urgency. Trepidation painted a clear picture on his face—
the situation was out of control.

Dafnie felt a chill creep up her spine as she sighed in unrest
and desperation. The overwhelming rush of panic flung her on
edge. Her heart raced with concern. Had she done enough to prepare for something like this? Never in her wildest dreams had
she ever thought something like this would happen to her. But
now reality sank like a bolder in her mind. She needed to be ready for whatever came next.

A commotion unfolded outside, drawing her attention.
When she approached her window, she recognized several neighbors shoving their belongings into their cars. Some drove without
a care for other's safety, endangering those confused by the chaos,
while others cried and pleaded with their families to hurry and
leave.

Swallowing hard, she realized she was still holding on to her
fork, forgetting the once delicious dinner and losing her appetite
in the face of the disaster. The news segment shifted to a guest,
who made his announcement with a grave expression.

"We have an urgent update. The authorities have confirmed
reports of a recent development in our current situation. The virus mutated, and it's become more dangerous. This pandemic
might be worse than earlier ones," the health official warned, her
voice echoing through her living room. Her heart pounded in
her chest as she sat back on the sofa, her mind racing with worry
and uncertainty as she absorbed the disturbing news.

"Experts advise everyone to stay indoors and avoid contact

with others at all costs. We're facing an emergency, and our government urges its citizens not to stress as they work on finding a solution to this crisis. In the meantime, again, we urge our audience not to go anywhere," the commentator delivered in a stern and severe monologue.

She couldn't believe her ears. The newscaster continued to caution people about the situation. She knew she needed to remain calm and follow instructions, but panic got the best of her. She went to the kitchen and tried calling Danielle, hoping to pick up, but soon got a busy signal.

Shit! I need to do something, she thought as she gawked at her phone.

Communication was down. Dafnie's heart sank, fear and uncertainty gripping her. She couldn't help but think the worst-case scenario was becoming a reality so fast. What if the world ceased to continue? She panicked as grim thoughts plagued her.

Her head became foggy with self-doubt, blocking her from thinking straight. She ran to her room as the report played in the background. Desperation constricted her lungs, and her breaths came in laborious bursts. The news continued to deliver more disturbing developments, adding to her panic.

I need to pack and move to safety. I should have listened to Danielle.

The chant drummed in her head as she entered her closet. With great urgency, she fetched a light travel bag and extracted comfortable clothes, perfect for her cross-country. She only packed the essentials in case she needed to ditch her car.

Next, she lacked a first-aid kit for emergencies.

Shit, I haven't thought of everything that could go wrong. I'm so screwed. I'm not ready for this.

Her thoughts thumped around her head as her breath hiked in tempo.

Her brain raced a thousand miles per hour, making her feel woozy. She sought refuge, a sanctuary to ensure her safety. She ought to...

"Holy fuck! What the hell is he doing? Is he mad? Doesn't he understand there is an emergency? That... that people are dying. Why does he look relaxed and happy? Does he even care?!" she whispered as she looked out the window facing her neighbor's house.

Her head spun out of control. She sat on the bed, rocking back and forth, trying to figure out what to do.

"No, no, no! Not now..."

Her brain fog invaded her consciousness as she curled into a ball until everything went black, and she passed out. Losing her battle with her emotions.

✳✳✳

Apollo enjoyed a blissful soak in his hot tub on an early summer evening.

Oblivious—with every intention and purpose—to the world crumbling around him. He sipped his finest wine while popping a few pieces of cheese and berries, marveling at the salty-sweet flavors.

He reached Elysium on Earth.

"Perfect! Just Perfect!

His silent companion pecked at its feathers, grooming them like any typical day.

Apollo laughed. Smugness oozing from him, darkening his otherwise bright aura.

"Silence would swallow the screams, fights, and chaos. But afterward, harmony would reign absolute and undisturbed. Tonight, I celebrate!"

He whispered as he downed his drink to have another glass.

Nyx was the only god who survived eternity unscathed. Since the beginning of time, her mental fortitude helped her to be loved and...

Feared!

In the realm of endless glittering nights and pure blackness, she reigned from the shadows. Since the first time she opened her eyes, knowledge flowed like a glacier river through her. This also meant she knew a great deal about the future, like this moment. The knowledge slid into her mind the moment she came to be.

And so...

Gentle and patient, she bid her time.

Waiting.

Ready to strike at any moment.

"Now is my time. I have the right allies, the right people to rule this world."

Her hypnotic whisper floated through the air, spreading a cloud of golden dust around and away from her. Extending black tendrils of darkness all over Earth to shroud her slow procession away from her realm. As she ventured away from her starry throne to a simple house in Phoebus Groove.

Rarely did she venture outside her domain, but today was an exception.

As she arrived at her destination, a room that embraced nature whole with a beautiful woman slumped in a heap.

"Oh, dear! She fainted... I can't have that. She needs a good night's rest."

Dark magic extended from her fingertips as Dafnie floated mere inches from her bed.

"Now time will stop for you... as you sleep away the tragic end of the world. But when you wake, fulfill your destiny, you must. Influence the god who holds sway over these lands—the one capable of ruling—yet has no interest in doing so. Make him take responsibility for your sake and the sake of others."

Chapter 17

The Day After

As dawn broke, the first rays of sunlight streamed through the gaps in the curtains, illuminating the room in a soft glow. A new day, but not the same world that Dafnie knew.

With a sudden jolt, Dafnie's heart raced as she bolted upright in bed, her body covered in a cold sweat. Her eyes widened with fear as she struggled to shake off the remnants of a haunting nightmare that consumed her rest.

Amid overwhelming despair, she sought refuge in sleep, seeking solace from the exhausting and unfolding events that drained her emotions.

Depleted!

Every fiber in her screeched with dread, burdened by worries and uncertainty ahead. The numbness in her finger spread within her as anxiety grabbed hold of her—an infection contaminating her soul.

As the morning light filtered through the curtains, Dafnie's mind remained shrouded in a thick fog. She searched for a glimmer of optimism to guide her through the day. But hope slipped through her fingers as memories fluttered back.

She lay on her bed, listening to the strange whistle of quietness outside. Then she realized this was not a nightmare but her new reality.

The distant echoes of the news anchor's voice replayed in her head.

The sight of Mr. Delphoes enjoying his soak, sipping on his wine, oblivious to the chaos. His image haunted her in the oppressive serenity that shrouded her.

Silence…

The house was silent.

She remembered leaving her TV on, and now there was no sound. In a frantic haze, she made it to the room, greeted with unnerving stillness. The screen showed a simple, however terrifying, message.

"Emergency Broadcast System."

She snatched the remote with trembling hands and switched the channel.

"Emergency Broadcast System."

She tried another station yet again.

"Emergency Broadcast System."

Nothing…

As she turned off the dreadful display, the room stood still, enveloped by an uncanny quiet ringing. Her skin prickled with dread as she came to terms with the situation.

This is only temporary. Things will get better and go back to normal, right?! She thought as numbness took residence in her psyche.

Hope slipped away as she stared at the empty streets outside her window. A fat tear rolled down her delicate face.

Once again, an oppressive influence overwhelmed her. A heavy weight pressed upon her chest as it had on the day she received the devastating news of her parents' tragic accident.

The sterile scent of the hospital, which faded from memory at some point, returned with vicious strength, engulfing her senses and triggering haunting memories. The atmosphere shifted, becoming something suffocating, wrapping around her with a relentless grip, making it difficult to breathe and reminding her she was alone.

Alone...

She went to her office and started her computer. Her hands quivered as the monitor came to life, and she tapped on the keys. The team's communication app loaded first, cluttered with notifications.

Her colleagues' messages bombarded her screen. As she scrolled down the long chat list, the conversations became more terrifying than the last.

"Family members infected. I need to take time off to care for them."

"Death toll rising."

"Quarantine measures in effect."

"No cure found yet?! What the fuck is going on?"

"I'm scared..."

"Please send some backup... My family is sick."

"I'm hearing weird noises..."

"HELP!!!!!!..."

Dafnie's spirit crushed as she read the latest texts, each puncturing her fragile hope as she frantically wrote an email to every-one in her company:

"Is anybody here?"

Like a mindless being, she keyed the quick question. Her fingers swiped across the screen before sending another message. No thought behind her actions, only instinct.

And then she waited...

Tick... Tock...

Her clock declared as minutes turned into hours, waiting for a response that never came.

But none came.

"I'm trying to find any survivors. Is anyone still around?"

Please... answer...

She pondered, her mind doing flips and circling the plead like a quiet prayer.

"Do we stay home, or do we need to evacuate?"

Her frantic finger tapped on the screen, knowing quite well no one would respond to her message.

"Respond, I beg you!"

Beaten, Dafnie did her best to compose her frayed nerves and sat in her office. Her heart filled with fear and uncertainty about the world outside. She wondered about many things.

What happened? How did this crisis escalate this fast?

Left behind! A wave of isolation passed over her as a slump loaded her mind with no one to turn to for support. She faced this new reality alone, and she needed to think fast. Delaying any longer would only make the situation worse.

With a deep breath, Dafnie steeled her nerves and pushed away from her desk. She ought to find out if there was anyone st-ill in town.

Am I late for help? Am I all by myself? I'm fucked, if that's the case. The nagging thoughts delivered an all-consuming chill that closed up her throat.

Before venturing around the neighborhood, she had good mental and physical stamina to prepare for the unexpected.

She hesitated, unsure about the condition of the streets. The possibility of being stranded, with no escape, sent her heart racing.

"Relying on my car can lead to trouble."

Chewing on her nail, her lips move in their own accord, mumbling her troubled mind.

Unaware of the potential dangers ahead, a quick glance out her window did little to inspire confidence in the current conditions.

Dafnie changed into hiking boots and packed a backpack with essential items. As she stood in front of her door, taking a deep breath as she stepped beyond her door, she realized she wanted protection.

She went to the basement, where she kept her old high school stuff, and searched for her old baseball bat for self-defense. It had only been a few minutes before she ran to the garage to get the rest of her equipment.

Once there, she grabbed a rope and carabiners in case she needed to use them. Dafnie then shoved her weapon into an ample pocket of her backpack. She then lowered her bike from its rack and inspected its tires and brakes as she headed out.

Satisfied with her gear, she approached the door on the side of her house. She opened it and peeked outside, her heart racing as she took in her surroundings.

There was no one around—not a single soul in sight. The streets lay in eerie silence. The chaotic debris contrasted with the deafening absence of human presence.

Residents fled in a rush.

"Damn it, not good! I got left behind."

Before she could stop it, a soft whisper slipped from her lips —her biggest fears confirmed.

One hesitant step.

Followed by another.

As she crept away from the safety of her home to venture into ruin.

Abandoned cars left wide open. As far as her gaze stretched, suitcases and clothes littered the ground before her. The scattered wreckage everywhere was a testament to the commotion that cast an air of desolation. As Dafnie stood on her spot, disbelief washed over her. The once idyllic street, with its charming houses and manicured lawns, now resembled a scene from a war zone.

She drew a deep breath, summoning her courage before venturing into the world beyond her garage. Every click of her bike's wheels reverberated in the oppressive silence that enveloped her. Her natural agility supported her in navigating the maze of deserted cars and debris. Her primary goal was to blend into her surroundings while circling obstacles.

After crossing the familiar streets for a few blocks, she reached the main street leading to town. Yet again, abandoned cars and trash cluttered the road. The residents left the places open and in disarray.

Nothing seemed to make sense to Dafnie. Phoebus Groove was a peaceful place, untouched by the chaos depicted in the news elsewhere.

But that was yesterday.

Now, the familial warmth was long gone. Now, disorder and confusion reign about.

How did things spiral out of control overnight?

As she pedaled into the city center, the streets became more crowded, with more ditched vehicles and at the mercy of the elements. More houses opened for anyone to enter, and more belongings scattered on the road.

The once captivating roads and homes now resembled a wartorn landscape. Dafnie couldn't help but wonder if anybody stayed behind. Mindful of her surroundings, she cycled farther away from the safety of her house toward town to find signs of life.

Upon reaching her destination, Dafnie's spirit crumbled as she took in the startling sight before her. The charming locale, adorned with vibrant storefronts, transformed into a hauntingly silent stage. The wind whispered through the deserted alleys, desolation whispering an uncanny welcome. Only the occasional creak of a swinging sign disturbed the silence. Goosebumps broke throughout Dafnie's body as she took in the view, surrounded by the ghostly remnants of their spirited community.

Once filled with bustling activity and wares, the abandoned stores and restaurants lay barren with decay and alarming stillness. The doors stood wide open, revealing the haunting vestiges of hasty departures.

Outside, another eerie scene unfurled—spreading tendrils of unrest.

The several booths set up for the local market, teeming with fresh produce and handmade crafts on a usual day, now lie in ruin. The canopies now lay torn and tattered, clinging to the skeletal frames. A disquieting, oppressing presence of annihilation consumed the air.

Turning around, looking for signs of life, she spotted a digital sign that flickered with a chilling message.

"STAY INSIDE. BE SAFE."

Dismounting her bike, her hands trembling as she leaned against a nearby lamppost for support. She scanned the chaos, her eyes stinging with the onset of tears. How did it come to this?

A day ago, laughter and chatter filled the streets, children played, and neighbors greeted one another. Now, the town was a ghost of its former self, a haunting silence that echoed the despair of its deserted inhabitants.

She hyperventilated at the view. She looked around her surroundings, desperate with her attempts. Until she spotted something strange. Nature had already reclaimed its territory.

Thick weeds pushed their way through the small cracks in the pavement, reclaiming the land that was once under human control. The booths toppled over showed early signs of being overgrown by vines and mold. The storefronts had an abandoned appearance, with moss and ivy creeping up their walls—a haunting, terrifying sight.

Anxiety and confusion swirled within her as she wondered what to do. She couldn't understand how a place filled with life now lay barren. A deserted wasteland that grew overnight.

How did a peaceful haven like Phoebus Groove turn into pandemonium?

The resounding question in her mind.

As Dafnie calmed down and grappled with the stark reality, she knew she had to press on to see if she found out if anyone was still in town.

Hiding.

Trying to survive.

She needed to find help.

As she mounted her bike, a peculiar shine from the inside of her wrist grabbed her attention. An unusual luminescent light was pulsating from under her clothes. She pulled the sleeve up, revealing the laurel tattoo from long ago. It pulsated with a faint glow as if it were alive.

The small ink grew in size and complexity, with intricate details reaching the crook of her elbow. She propped her bike against a nearby wall and then sat on the ground to stare at her arm in alarm.

What is happening to me? What does this mean? She thought to herself, fear creeping up her spine.

Dafnie was losing her grip on reality as she hyperventilated, hands becoming slippery.

"Am I hallucinating? Is this all a bad dream?" She muttered, trying to make sense of the bizarre situation.

Suddenly, the pulsating tattoo on her arm emanated a soothing warmth. Calm and clarity washed over her. She paused but realized she needed to concentrate on finding help and answers.

As her racing heart slowed, she rose and mustered all the strength to continue. She lingered around the area to steady the drumming in her chest. Her head whooshed about, dizziness gripping her body as her laborious breathing refused to settle. A deep Inhale and a steady exhale helped a little when her center wavered.

Her focus wobbled in and out, but with each cleansing breath, steadiness seeped in and spread about her. Then, a plan formed in her mind and put it into motion.

"I need to get back to my bike. I must survive this."

Staying strong guaranteed her survival despite the growing fear and uncertainty that drifted too close to the surface. Panic and anxiety wouldn't help her in this situation of life and death.

The urge to stay focused and act rational consumed her.

More than anything else, she needed to prevail, no matter what. With renewed determination, Dafnie pulled the bike toward her in a protective stance—a comforting shield. She swung her legs over the bike and pedaled with fresh resolve.

Her top priority—tenacity!

To secure as many supplies as possible.

For her survival and future.

Chapter 18

The Loot

Pedaling with determination, Dafnie steered her bike to the local hardware. The blue exterior, once vibrant and cheerful, looked faded and dull to a weather-beaten hue. Still surprised by the rapid deterioration of her surroundings, she squared her shoulders and pushed open the creaky door. The bell hanging at the top of the door jingled before tumbling to the floor.

She stopped in her tracks, her heart racing at the sudden loud noise. After a slight moment, she braved to continue further in the shop. A pang of nostalgia infected her, remembering when she came to the store a few weeks ago to buy more gardening supplies. Shaking the memories, she delved deeper into the hardware.

Once inside, she found the place in complete disarray. Shattered wood and toppled objects littered the floors. A chaotic scene charged the air with terror, and goosebumps prickled her skin. Her throat dried with dread.

People tried to survive no matter what.

The place's ghostly ambiance made her tremble in fear. Dust particles floated in the light and peered through the cracked windows. Items haphazardly strewn across the floor recited a story of struggle.

But as she ventured further into the store, she witnessed its pristine state—untouched. As she browsed through the aisles, she discovered some helpful stockpiles. She grabbed some flashlights, batteries, and a first-aid kit. As she stuffed her backpack with her provisions, she searched everywhere to make sure she missed nothing else she would need.

Dafnie skirted about the aisle where the fastenings and chains dangled from their hooks. Grim determination on her face as she maneuvered across the clutter. To secure her future livelihood, she must stock more supplies. Picking up heavy-duty padlocks and a couple of lengthy, lasting fetters, she weighed them in her hand, confirming their sturdiness. The cold metallic touch of the locks and links felt reassuring.

She snatched a few tools, handpicking a durable hammer with a comfortable grip, a multi-tool kit with various attachments, and a box of nails in assorted sizes to ensure she fortified any windows or old feeble doors at the grocery. On her way, she grabbed wooden planks in case she needed to board up any door or window.

As she finished strapping the supplies to her bike, she considered locking the hardware store for future excursions. Fear and determination drove her forward, directing her not to lose valuable resources to scavengers lurking nearby.

After searching the cluttered desk, she found the clunky chain with more keys than necessary. On her way out, she lowered the gates in front of the shop and locked the gate behind her.

Ready, Dafnie stepped onto the deserted street, placing the heavy backpack on the rack. Secured with the rest of her supplies, she shoved her things as she glanced around—on high alert. Then she climbed on her bike, her grip firm on the handles even though her slippery hands made it much harder to get a better hold. As she pedaled away from the hardware store, she couldn't help but feel a sense of accomplishment—even the small ones.

She took the first step toward survival in this desolate new world. Her journey was far from over, and the road ahead remained undecided. But at that moment, she seized the opportunity to tackle any challenge, even if her conviction refused to take part in it.

She ought to focus.

And above all, she must stay alive.

With that thought in mind, Dafnie pedaled on, her destination set for the nearest market. The sun loomed overhead, bathing the tranquil neighborhood in a radiant golden hue. Despite being noon, the light carried a muted quality to its luster, casting a hazy glow over everything.

As she rode along the winding streets, she couldn't help but detect more signs warning people to keep away. The closer she got to the grocery store, the more severe the messages became.

"Danger!"

"Stay out!"

Painted on a bakeshop door, a large red "X" marred the delicate yet faded paintings.

Dafnie took a deep breath, knowing some calculated risks

were necessary. She faced the unknown to secure more supplies—her life hinged on her bravery. She realized she needed to heed the warnings.

While she slept, passing like a storm, time fast-forwarded unchecked by logical comprehension.

The cacophony of her thoughts the previous night raced nonstop, crashing into her brain like an overused computer. The sour tang of worry lingered in her mouth—the mental load proving too much for her. Seeing Mr. Delphoes enjoying himself, ignorant of everything around him, sent her anxiety into overdrive.

She wondered about the handsome man's odd attitude. Could it be that after working in the music industry for many years, he developed nerves of steel out of necessity? She only imagined living a brutal life where one dismissed feelings in such a way. Worse! To ignore alarming news and act detached during an emergency.

Either he only possessed icy emotions or...

He didn't own a television and lived oblivious to reality on purpose.

Unlike him, her head stopped processing as pandemonium ensued all around her.

Upon waking, the lingering weight of her nightmare clung to her like a draining fog. Nevertheless, the sight of chaos that lay waste outside shattered all hope.

Dafnie's first thought was to scamper inside—safe. More than anything, she longed to remain in her bubble and out of harm's way.

With a deep breath, she pushed onward. She needed to secure more supplies before sunset, and the grocery store was her only choice. She couldn't let fear stop her from surviving.

With each pedal, a sense of determination grew from within, fueled by anticipation. To be quick and efficient, she hand-picked only the hard-to-find items before returning them to the safety of her cozy home.

As she arrived at the supermarket, her heart raced with excitement and dread. Her efforts could attract unwanted attention if anyone were spying on her. So she must be careful with her plans. But she also understood that securing supplies moved up on her list of survival essentials. With that thought, Dafnie made her way to the neighborhood market.

The first thing she did was secure all exits to withstand attacks and the elements. Having frequented the shop many times, she inspected each exit door with meticulous care to ensure her safety. She arrived at the office to get the spare keys, but luck disfavored her. She sighed, knowing to use the padlocks and chains from the hardware in her home.

After blocking all the doors, she directed her attention to the exposed windows. She spotted the security shutters and locked them to keep her loot safe.

After ensuring the store was secure, she took a moment to browse. The bare shelves, with only a few remaining cans and boxes scattered around, provided little confidence in stability. Dafnie's core sank at the looting, leaving very little behind and the pickings scarce.

She wasted no time and went to another place—just outside town—to explore the area a bit more. Her heart pounded as she rode her bike, hoping she secured another shop with more supplies.

As she arrived at her next location, she regarded the sunset on the horizon. She ran out of time and needed to hurry. Dafnie decided she would only look around and head back home as soon as she finished checking the site. She didn't want to be out after dark, especially during an uncertain time.

She discovered that despite the store's chaotic state, enough stockpiles remained for grabs. As she navigated through the aisles, careful with each step. The shattered glass and overturned shelves provided clear evidence of past struggles.

"I hope everyone I care about is okay?!"

The bustling shop now stood eerily silent, with Dafnie being the sole occupant. With trepidation, she realized she had the entire store to herself and started systematically surveying the corridors.

Once satisfied with her generous loot, she snatched the hardware tools to fortify the supermarket. She boarded up the exposed windows and reinforced the doors that appeared feeble.

Content with her work, she looked outside to find the sun dipping on the horizon, and darkness descended upon her. She understood the time to leave and landed sooner than expected. Loitering risked her life—she ran out of time.

Too late to accomplish anything else for the day. She only now hoped to make it back safely.

With her bike loaded with a few items, she packed them onto the rack. She set out on her journey back, knowing she needed to be careful on her way home. She pedaled as fast as possible, ignoring the eerie feeling that crept over her.

A warm sensation traveled up her arms as she pushed through the dimly lit streets. She stopped to look at her arm and saw that the pulsating tattoo seemed to glow brighter from under her cuff. When she pulled up her sleeve, she examined the design as it changed and grew.

The pattern became more intricate, weaving in and out, like a serpent coiling around her arm and moving past her elbow. The strange behavior made her stomach churn with unease.

A swoon of light-headedness overpowered her. Head spinning, disorientation settled in as terror invaded her mind. Suddenly, she heard a piercing noise as the night engulfed her, followed by many loud screeches before everything darkened.

Chapter 19

Fated Meeting

As Dafnie ventured deeper into the unlit streets, the town's landscape contorted and warped as the evening twilight enveloped her. The once charming buildings loomed over her like monstrous apparitions, casting grotesque elongated shadows, stretching and twisting across the concrete beneath her feet.

After the hideous noises from earlier, an eerie silence blanketing the town surrounded her, punctuated only by her ragged breaths and the rhythmic thump of her heart in her ears. The faint glow of her tattoo and the brilliant shimmering of the moonlight were the only sources of light illuminating the streetscape with an alien, ethereal hue.

Suddenly, a flash of movement caught her eye. She spun around, her senses heightened, her grip on the handlebars tightening. From the corner of her vision, she witnessed a flicker of something misshapen lurking in the shades. It darted and wove between the shadows, its form indistinct and shifting.

A primal fear seized Dafnie as she grappled with the unknown. A creature seemed to stalk her from afar. Every instinct screamed at her to return to her bike and pedal to escape the terror that lurked out of view and in the darkness.

The dark alleys appeared to have come alive as if reaching out for her, pulsating and squirming with an ominous life of their own. She stopped in her tracks, spotting more movement a few blocks away. This time, the figure of a woman wandering the street with an unstable gait.

"KYAH... KYAHHH.. KYAHHHHHH..."

A high-pitched grating screech, coming from the staggering woman, echoed through the block, followed by a second and then a third. As the hysteria-inducing noise continued, Dafnie's instinct warned her to duck behind an abandoned car. She peeked over the vehicle's window. People wobbling down to the unnatural woman responsible for the commotion put a pause on her motivation.

Dafnie scanned around, taking in their strange behavior. The figures stumbled toward that woman—acting with unnatural crudeness. Their uncoordinated movement sent them stumbling, and their eyes glazed over and unfocused.

A sickly green tint covered their skin, with pus-filled blisters seeping out. Their clothes, dirty and torn in places, offered the evidence of time—long pass. Razor-sharp fangs replaced what used to be normal teeth. These creatures lost all traces of their humanity, remnants of their former self obliterated.

"KYAH... KYAHHH.. KYAHHHHHH..."

The screeching pierced the air, growing more intense with each passing moment. Disbelief consumed her that hell unraveled before her—demons' frenzy oppressing by the seconds. The varmints blocked her way, and a paralyzing dread pin pricked her skin as she surveyed the area for a quick escape.

Paralyzed by the mounting horror, her heart pounded out of control, her chest constricting in pain as she tried to remain hidden from the lurking danger. The eerie silence amplified her fear, and every creaking sound seemed to echo through the air.

She knew there would be no way out if one of these things found her. The darkness weighed on her, and she fought to handle her trembling body, hoping to pass unnoticed in the shadows behind the car. She needed to get to her house fast.

Dafnie peered onto the dark street from her hiding spot, careful not to attract unwanted attention. Her heart pounded with dread, but her determination to stay alive propelled her forward. Her desperate gaze scanned the surroundings, searching for a way out of this treacherous predicament. Suddenly, a hint of hope caught her eye—a path opposite from the screaming and menacing creatures.

Risky move, for it might bring her face-to-face with the terrifying beasts. It also presented a direct way back to the safety of her home. With a deep breath, Dafnie steeled her nerves and prepared for the imminent danger, reminding herself that courage was often born out of necessity.

"KYAH... KYAHHH.. KYAHHHHHH..."

She gritted her teeth and focused on her escape route. The beasts seemed to creep about, but that didn't mean they would not give chase as soon as they spotted a victim to prey on. Thinking on her toes, she came up with a plan. She needed to be ready to ride fast.

With her heart racing and adrenaline pumping, she mounted her bike and prepared to bolt. She searched around, relieved that no obstacles were in her way. She took a deep breath and made a run for it.

"KYAH... KYAHHH.. KYAHHHHHHH..."

The screech came as she pedaled as hard as possible. Hope swarmed inside her as her street came into view.

"Just a few yards away."

Dafnie murmured as she tried to pedal faster, but her legs already felt heavy. Frustration stuck with her as she realized her body reached its limits.

Her heart pounded against her ribcage, the thumping echoing in her ears like a monstrous drum. She picked up the screeching sound of the creature in the distance. Terrified of being chased, she glanced behind her. Nothing gave chase to her—the coast was clear.

As she moved forward with a tentative stride, she slowed, mindful of each step. She scanned her surroundings, keen not to miss any dangers lurking in the shadows. The silence enveloped her, broken only by the faint rustling of leaves and the distant cry of a nocturnal animal.

The moon, visible through the thick canopy of trees, cast eerie silhouettes on the path ahead. Every fiber of her being was on high alert as she navigated the darkness with the utmost care, determined not to stumble upon anything unexpected.

"kyah... kyahhh.. kyahhhhhh..."

The screeches, loud and piercing moments earlier, faded into the distance. An all-too-consuming relief washed over her as she pedaled from the wretched noises—unscathed.

At least those horrible creatures didn't follow her. Comfort filled her heart as she hesitantly traversed the streets. She resisted the temptation to use a flashlight to light her way, as she did not want to attract any unwanted attention.

Instead, she used the moonlight to guide her.

Once Dafnie reached the edge of the town center, a deep sigh escaped her lips, letting the tension escape her body. She took a moment to catch her breath. She found a temporary respite in the relative calmness of her surroundings as she pedaled at a comfortable pace.

However, several miles to her house, taunting, as she glanced at the path ahead. With a lingering sense of caution, she reminded herself to conserve her strength in case another unexpected event unfolded on her way home.

As she put great distanced from the horrifying scenes in town, she allowed a glance at her wrist. Amidst the frantic search for safety, she neglected to conceal her tattoo—a minor oversight from the overwhelming chaos she fled from.

The elaborate ink seemed to dance as it took another shape. As Dafnie traced her fingers over the lines, a sudden jolt of energy propelled her onward. The sensation overpowered her reality, driving her to stop and take another look at the tattoo.

As she examined the design, it morphed before her eyes. She spotted the pattern that blanketed her arm as she removed her hoodie. The tattoo evolved beyond comprehension, becoming more complex and intricate as she admired its new design.

Interest, making her forget to stay quiet. "What does this all mean? Is this thing warning me that the night is not over? That something bad will happen?"

In the meantime, she kept riding at a comfortable speed. Safety was her top priority, and getting answers to what happened to the community moved to the back burner of her mind.

"I will make it. I need to... focus!" She whispered with resolve as she rode on.

With a determined look, she picked up her pace without exerting herself and reached her neighborhood a few minutes later.

She scanned the area, and an all-too-consuming, eerie quietness swallowed the atmosphere—too quiet for comfort. Left with no other choice but to continue to safety.

Feeling uneasy, she got off her bike and walked for the rest of the way—her home was not too far. The number of abandoned cars and debris littered everywhere made it tough to move and stay alert.

Better to slow her pace than be sorry. Even if her journey back took longer because of potential threats, she needed to be ready for an attack or an ambush.

As Dafnie drove through the neighborhood's streets, traveling faster than ever. However, no matter how hard she pedaled, her surroundings moved slower than usual. Her heart sank as utter darkness enveloped the area, leaving her at the mercy of the disturbing silhouettes.

An eerie sight she wished to leave behind. The once familiar neighborhood transformed into a haunting abyss.

The devastation seemed beyond surreal at night. Time played a wicked trick on her by keeping her out of the loop of events—unconscious on her bed—oblivious to the chaos unfolding all around her.

As Dafnie approached her house, an unsettling movement in the shadows distracted her. Her heart pounded in her chest as her eyes darted to her destination, trying to find the source of the disturbance. She tried to remain calm, but her body prepared for the potential threat to attack, each muscle tensing in anticipation.

The sounds of the night appeared magnified. Each rustle of leaves, every creak of branches, and flutter of wings echoed in her ears. The silhouette of her house loomed in the darkness. Its once welcoming facade now seemed oppressive and foreboding as she spotted movement close to her home on her way to safety.

She squinted, trying to make out the figures twisting grotesquely by her house. She couldn't tell if they were limbs swaying in the wind or animals moving about. But as she moved closer, the shapes appeared to take on a more human-like form.

Dafnie's eyes widened in shock, and she realized the menacing shadows stalked her place. Torn between finding a safe hiding spot or confronting the mysterious beings head-on.

"Ack... Ack... Scccrrrrr... Shriiiiiiiiiik!"

As if sensing her dilemma, a creature let out an ear-piercing shriek, causing her to flinch. She ducked behind a car as the beast turned her way. Her tattoo glowed with insistent brightness, reacting to its presence.

She grabbed her bat and hugged it against her chest like a shield. With her heart thumping hard in her ribcage, she braced herself for a potential attack. But to her surprise, the creature snarled and veered away. Dafnie needed to be quick and find a safe place to spend the night.

"Skreeeeeech!"

Startled by the creature's cry, Dafnie's instinct kicked in. She shifted her attention toward the source, only to see it retreat in the opposite direction. Dafnie's eyes darted around the vicinity, and she spotted a soft glow emanating from the second floor of Mr. Delphoes' house. As she focused, the silhouette of an individual reading a book caught her eye.

An idea took shape. She left her things behind and only took her weapon, ready to defend herself. She would try to recover them later, but now she needed to run fast. Without hesitation, she bolted toward her porch.

But she didn't count on the creatures still near her house.

"Scrrr... Sccrrr... Scccrrrrrr!"

The beast screeched as it dashed for her. Its bloodlust drove it into a frenzy.

Change of plan! She thought as she clenched her hand around her bat, set to fight, and ran towards Mr. Delphoes' house.

Hope surged within her, and she headed for her neighbor's house, running up the front steps to the door. She knocked on his door, debating if he would let her in. As she waited for a response, panic rose from her core as the creature's footsteps drew closer.

"PLEASE HELP! I NEED HELP!"

She screamed with all her might, grasping at faith that aid stood on the other side of the door.

Left with no choice, she readied her weapon and ran to the yard to meet the creature. Dafnie prepared to swing her bat with all her might, not caring if she would harm the monster. She only cared about surviving.

As she reached the front, the varmint was gaining on her. A wicked-looking clawed hand stretched out to her, ready to snatch her. Without missing a beat, she swung with all her might.

THWACK!

The solid sound came as it contacted the creature's head, lunging at her. The fiend let out a brief howl of pain before falling to the ground, unmoving. She abruptly heard low growls coming from behind her. As she spun to face her next threat, a projectile flew true, straight to its target, hitting the beast square in the fore-head and causing it to collapse with a thud.

Dafnie focused on the projectile's trajectory. On the balcony, Mr. Delphoes stood—crossbow in hand—looking attractive and ready to go to war.

Fuck! I need to focus and not think about how good he looks... The thought sneaked through her defenses.

Without hesitation, she sprinted towards her savior's house, leaving no second to spare. As the shadows unveiled more creatu-res in pursuit, her savior released yet another arrow, narrowly missing Dafnie's face and striking its intended mark.

"Quick, inside!" Mr. Delphoes urged, reaching for the knob.

As she entered the house, her neighbor followed and locked the door. Once safe, she surrendered to exhaustion and collapsed onto the floor. Her eyes remained fixed on the door, which emit-ted a subtle glow along its edges—as if sealing them inside. Blocking all nightmares out and safety indoors.

Relaxing coldness descended over her brain as hope escaped her. The chaos of the night took its toll on her body as she blac-ked out.

Chapter 20

The Encounter

Wearing a calm expression, Apollo immersed himself in a fascinating book, seeking solace and tranquility before retiring for the evening. With each passing page, the night unfolded without incident, offering respite from the chaotic life he now lived in. The well-crafted poetic prose contrasted with the world outside.

But... his focus eluded him since the start of all this mayhem.

"This is absurd! By now, they should have turned to dust. What went wrong? Everything was perfect when I planned this..."

The loudness of the evenings made him recognize he needed to reconsider his plan a bit more. Despite his initial hypothesis, the creatures thrived, growing stronger each day.

"Scrrr... Sccrrr... Scccrrrrrr!"

A creature screeched in the dead of night, shattering the silence into a million pieces.

"Here we go again. I'm tired of those noises. So annoying!"

Apollo mumbled under his breath, his frustration swimming close to his face as he placed his book down.

He headed downstairs to start on his enchantment for the evening. The ritual's sole purpose was to ward off the lurking monsters and drown out the screeching that threatened to disturb his peace. Midway down the stairs, someone banged on his door.

"PLEASE HELP! I NEED HELP!"

A woman screamed, banging on his door, begging he would let her in.

Had she, with a sharp gaze, glimpsed him moving about the room? Had she seen him sitting by the window and drove her way to his house? And why did a foolish woman venture out at a dangerous time?

Impossible!

Annoyed by the daily nighttime ruckus, he cast a spell to conceal himself from monsters and mortals.

But... I'm invisible to the world... and to her?!

He preferred to enjoy evenings in peace and without interruptions. With his perimeter, ordinary humans, bound by the limitations of their beliefs, lost their ability to sense his presence.

No way she spotted me that far away. Not after I activated the barrier. So, how was she able to see me?

He swiftly moved to the entrance, heart pounding with concern for the woman fighting for her life. With irate steps, he wasted no time as he closed the distance toward the front door. His eyes locked onto his weapon by the tall side table positioned nearby for easy access during emergencies—a steadfast ally in times of peril.

As he reached out, his fingers brushed against the smooth surface of the stock, guiding his hand to the weapon's foregrip. The icy quality of the crossbow's wood and steel welcomed his hand. The familiar weight evoked the essence of a seasoned hunter.

With practiced precision, his nimble hands loaded a bolt into the waiting barrel, the metallic click echoing in the silence—primed to unleash its fury. Apollo steeled himself for the onslaught that awaited beyond the threshold.

With a firm pull, he swung the door open and set his hawk eyes on the scene unfolding in his front yard.

He spotted a woman engaged in a deadly dance, bat at the ready, and ran to confront a creature giving chase. The woman got into position without skipping a beat and twisted mid-step to deliver a mighty hit—a whack containing all her strength.

THWACK!

The resounding thud of her crude weapon echoed loud and clear as it struck the beast on the head.

She is extraordinary! His heart pounded hard against his chest with the force of an out-of-control mallet—The ear-splitting percussive rhythm overwhelming as he admired her athletic body move with precision and grace.

Like a seasoned hunter running through the woods.

My Daphne... is alive! But! How?

But danger still loomed beyond. He needed to concentrate and dispose of the foul, wretched soul attacking the daring nymph, ensuring it remained down. He readied his weapon with great agility and aligned his sight with another target. With unwavering focus and determination, he pressed the trigger.

The bolt traveled true to its intended mark, making a loud

thud. Missing the woman's face by a few inches as she spun to face her next prey.

Upon spotting the fallen creature, the woman shifted her attention to scan her surroundings. She turned her gaze to where the arrow came from, giving her rescuer a full view of her features, and for a split second, their eyes met. Apollo stood on his balcony, crossbow in hand, shaken to the core.

Without hesitation, the woman dashed in his direction—to her savior. A truth he craved to embrace with all his might.

However, he lacked the comprehension to process the reality that unfolded before his eyes. Contrasting their shared distant memory of long ago when she fled from him.

Oh, he truly wanted her!

Touch her.

Hug her.

Take in her sent.

Shower her with kisses.

And take her all night, for eternity.

But not meant to be... yet! More unfortunate souls in pursuit announced themselves from the shadows. He released another arrow, missing the woman and striking another monster.

"Quick, inside!" he shouted as he stepped aside, reaching for the door—intending to lock her inside.

As soon as the woman entered his house, safe and sound, he followed right behind. Just as he shut the door and replaced the seals, he heard a creature shriek in agony as they walked onto his porch. Apollo listened for the things to scurry away in discomfort, warning the waiting hoard on the street.

The enchantment's soft glow glistened in the dimly lit room, casting a sheen reflection on the walls as it set into place. The magical barrier shimmered into existence with a gentle hum, enveloping his home in a warm embrace of protection. Its ethereal light danced across the room, bringing a sense of tranquility and security and restoring peace to his hidden world.

Then, her alluring, sweet scent overwhelmed his faculties, stopping him in his tracks and losing his concentration.

He turned toward the woman, taking every rise and fall of her chest and a thin, wet sheen on her skin. But his heart dropped when she collapsed onto the floor. Looking exhausted, her eyes remained fixed on the door as if making sure nothing would barge in. Only after she recognized she was out of harm's way. Her eyes blinked closed, blacking out for good.

Apollo lifted her in his arms and carried her to the nearby couch. He set her down with much care, providing gentle comfort and brushing her hair away.

He exclaimed as he nudged her shoulder. "Daphne! Wake up, my love. Shine those pretty eyes at me. Please!"

The woman's eyes fluttered open before bolting upright. In a state of panic, she scanned her surroundings until she realized where she was, but her fear persisted. Dumbfounded, she stared at him, her eyes widening with shock and disorientation.

"T-the neck... a-are you.. my new neighbor?"

Her stammering made her teeth clatter. A disheartening glance swept over her as she tried to make sense of her situation.

He only nodded in response, his heart racing with mixed emotions. The woman sitting next to him was Daphne, who captured his soul many millennia back—like a skilled hunter captures its prey. The love that slipped through his fingers. And now she sat right before him.

"Ahem... You are correct. I'm Mr. Delphoes, although I moved in a few weeks back. You're at my house. I overheard your cry for help, and after seeing those things were chasing after you, I rescued you," Apollo explained, trying to keep his voice steady as he brushed off a stray hair.

"Are you sure?" She sounded incredulous.

"I'm certain... What is your name, my darling?" His deep tone became hypnotic as he weaved his magic to make his nymph feel at ease.

"Dafnie... Valencia." Cautious of her environment, she looked out the window, confused.

"Mmmm... well, Dafnie! You don't need to worry. We're safe here. I gave them a good scare."

He reassured with an unwavering stare, delivering a white lie for her sake.

She nodded, her gaze uncertain and stance awkward. Clear the unfamiliar surroundings caused her considerable discomfort.

The stunning woman, the mirage of his past, bobbed her head, still looking unsteady and out of place. She sighed in relief as she locked eyes and smiled at him. "Thank you, Mr. Delphoes." Another sigh escaped her luscious lips as she calmed.

"Please call me Apollo," he replied with a smile of his own, a sense of familiarity and rightness in her presence. "Now! Judging by your appearance, you've been out all day. Why?!"

"I panicked and did something stupid instead of knocking on your door for help."

A predatory smirk crept to his face, imagining an encounter never meant to be.

"The shower is available if you so desire. May I suggest some rest, too? It seems you were out all day. I'll make us some tea as you freshen up. I'm guessing you're familiar with the layout of my house?"

Dafnie nodded her answer.

"Great, make yourself at home. You can use my bathroom. I'm afraid the guest rooms are not ready. The towels are in the linen closet. You can find something to wear. However, they will not fit you. But take any that looks comfy and works in the meantime. The washer and dryer are available if you need to use them." Apollo's imagination ran amok and at an all-time high—hopeful he would be lucky to have his lover this time.

She hesitated for a moment before nodding in agreement. Cautious of his intentions, the woman shifted to a comfortable position.

Yes, my love! Be careful of me. I'm not that noble. His mind worked overtime on ways to keep her by his side—and chambers —for eternity.

"We should try to stay in one place. These mutated monsters materialized in just over a week. It's..."

"A week?" Her breath became labored as she looked about, ready to bolt. "Those things appeared... a week ago? But... that's impossible. It's been only a night..."

Apollo's eyes widened in surprise. He felt his heart skip a beat and scrutinized the tempting woman. He saw the sincerity in her eyes.

"Interesting... You had a troubled day, and I suggest freshening up. After washing, join me for some tea. It'll do you some good." His mind was racing with plans for the evening.

Dafnie nodded again as she disappeared up the stairs. He wanted to follow her and devour her, but he knew better. If he chased after her, she would reject him and retreat into an unpenetrable cell. So, he paused until the running water assured him his nymph showered before turning to dinner preparation.

While he lingered for the water to boil, he couldn't help but think about the strange twist of events.

What a cruel fate?! To bring my beloved from the dead.

But somehow, she was back in his life, and he would do anything to make sure she stayed by his side this time. Apollo smiled as he reached for his unique blend of herbs into an infuser, knowing his life would change forever. He hoped Dafnie would trust him enough to stay with him and allow him to love her.

Then, as if realizing something, he remembered Artemis's words from the last time they met, before she disappeared.

"Oh, my dear sister! You told me you made plans to stop me from wrecking this world. Was this your plan all along? To disarm me this way?"

He lost his patience when his sister appeared, brushing her hair away. She smirked, rolled her eyes, and turned to walk away.

She's playing hard to get. He reached the end of his ropes, screaming his demand. "Artemis, answer me!"

"Oh, my beloved brother, you do not know half of it. We follow a much-worthy leader." She withheld something vital from him, teasing him for being none the wiser. "And, no... I only execute and obey orders."

"Why? What are you up to?" He demanded.

"Why? To be honest... I don't know for sure, baby brother. However, my love for you drives my actions. I want you to be happy and abandon your anger. You can still fix all this."

The music of Artemis' voice, full of affection, gave him pause. He looked at his sister in shock and disbelief. He never thought this was her plan to bring Daphne back into his life to stop him from his mission.

"This world needs to survive. Otherwise, all our work will be in vain."

She disappeared before he could ask any more questions, leaving him more troubled and assured. His nerve ending shocked him with understanding. People regarded him as a pawn for their schemes, but he refused to be exploited.

"Artemis, I'm growing weary of your recent habit of being cryptic," he muttered, annoyed.

However, his demeanor changed when the upstairs water shut off. A devilish debonaire smile crept over his handsome face.

Chapter 21

Tension in the Air

As Dafnie stepped out of the shower, a wave of exhaustion and confusion washed over her. Her day has been a relentless rollercoaster of emotions, leaving her drained—complete and utter exhaustion. The weight of her brutal and emotionally charged experiences weighed on her weary shoulders.

Every bit of adrenaline that propelled her throughout the day dissipated. Wiped out and depleted, she shuffled her feet, hating the all-too-consuming weakness. She longed for a proper night's rest, a moment to gather her thoughts and regain her strength. When she peered at the comfortable bed in the bedroom, she couldn't resist the temptation to climb in and allow sleep to claim her.

Accepting the eeriness in the air. Like a thick fog descended upon her. Hard to think freely. Like walking on eggshells, she tried not to upset the delicate balance of things. Apollo mentioned the creatures that appeared a few days prior. Any wrong move might set off a chain reaction with dire consequences for herself and her savior.

Have I been out cold for an entire week? She pondered, careful not to mumble her concerns like she always did.

She wished to analyze the situation, every rational cell in her body screaming to find an answer to her predicament. The weariness caused her brain to misfire as her concentration danced around in circles.

Maybe... she was overreacting—making a big deal out of nothing.

Dafnie shook her head and dried off hastily before using one of Apollo's plush towels. As she left the bathroom, she padded to the washing machine, her light footsteps muffled in the hallway—like an injured cat hesitating to move forward. Mrs. Lewis installed and upgraded many things in the house long ago. Most notable is the small laundry on the second floor, a pleasant addition —while alone with a stranger.

She sighed in relief when she glanced down the corridor and found it empty. Although she appreciated her savior's timing and help, she craved some alone time.

Still busy working in the kitchen, Apollo seemed oblivious to her presence. Tension thawing away, she let out a sigh. Instant calmness crashed over her consciousness. Her muscles wobbled as they lost their strength. The last thing she wanted was to walk about his house exposed, wearing only a towel. Her cheeks flushed with embarrassment at the thought.

After starting the machine, she hurried back to the bedroom, wondering what to put on while washing her dirty garments.

"Shit! I need something to wear. But what?!"

She mumbled, remembering the man in question and her primary source of concern.

His tall physique, broad shoulders, and athletic build awarded him the classic attractiveness desired by many. He exuded the quintessential image of a captivating model. Dafnie's hopes tanked at finding something that would fit her.

"Damn it! I know he's handsome, but I must be careful around him."

She nudged the door of the walking closet open, revealing neat stacks of folded piles of clothes and many elegant options. Her eyes scanned the impressive array of colors and patterns, searching for something to wear.

"It sounds like Mr. Dephoes loves being casual... And this shelving is to die for."

Once again, she defaulted to mumbling to find comfort as her eyes landed on a stack of casual shirts. She selected a simple black one and put it on. As expected, the garment was large for her small frame, but she had no choice but to wear it. She then moved to a bank of drawers and opened them until she found the drawer holding boxer briefs. Rolling it at the waist, she picked one to fit her slimmer midsection.

Before heading to the kitchen, a quick glance at the mirror revealed a confused and rumpled woman staring back at her. Her mind overflowed with questions about her day and her charitable neighbor.

"I guess I'm as ready as I can get. Now, it's time to get some answers. I hope I don't blackout from fatigue while eating. So tired."

The man who saved her from the nightmarish creatures gave off a troublesome aura. Like a blend of charm and danger rolled into one snug roll, confusing her to no end. Even after his aid, a nagging sensation throbbed at the back of her head, warning her to be careful.

The thought sent chills down her spine, and a sense of unease crept back in. Despite having just met the man, Dafnie felt an inexplicable familiarity, as if they crossed paths long ago.

She quietly made her way to the kitchen, her senses on high alert. He stood by the counter, boiling water and preparing a simple meal. He had his back to her but turned around as soon as she entered the room, almost as if he sensed her presence.

"Hello again!" A warm and charming smile graced the man's appearance. Without a doubt, he lived accustomed to having things go his way.

Dafnie breathed while covering her body and keeping her distance from Apollo. "Hi!"

"How are you feeling?" He walked over, reaching to flick away one of her many loose strands. It appeared to disturb him— as if her hair veiling her face was a crime.

Looking down at her feet, unease washed down her spine before she answered, "I'm fine... and thank you. I tried to get home, but those things blocked my way. I'll never forget what you did, risking your life. It's scary out there."

"I bet!"

The curt response cut like a knife, almost like he didn't want to hear her complain. "I'm sorry!"

"Sorry?!"

"Yes, I'll... I can climb your back fence and be out of your way."

Bewilderment marred his features. "Oh! Don't confuse my

brief responses with displeasure—far from that. I'm glad you're here. I just moved here and didn't want to uproot again."

"But... what about your safety?!"

"Are you hungry? I made dinner for us. I'm guessing you're famished."

Clear as day, he dogged her question. Worse! His eyes bore a strange, ravenous gleam—too provocative. She couldn't help but feel somewhat uncomfortable and vulnerable under his gaze.

"Yes... I appreciate it. It's been a rough day for me. I don't think I've eaten anything all day..." Nervousness compelled her to fidget with her fingers, grasping at strands of what to say next. "Sorry for the intrusion and going through your things. I had to go through your drawers to find something to wear. After washing my clothes, I'll take care of them."

"No worries, Dafnie. You can borrow whatever you need for as long as you want. I certainly don't mind," he said with a charming smile that disarmed her and crumbled her wall.

"Are you sure? I don't want to impose..."

"I'm very confident." Like a feline on the prowl, the man moved around the kitchen, putting together food-filled plates.

"Ummm... guess... no. I'm sorry I'm being a horrible guest. Thank you for your help!"

"You're welcome! Now, shall we?!"

Noticing how he kept inching closer to her. Before looking around for a chair, she stepped back on instinct, her body reacting to a neglected challenge. She found one opposite where he stood and sat, trying to keep some distance.

The tension became tangible in the air, pulsating with expectation. Outwardly, the man was nothing but a gentleman, yet his dubious demeanor gave her pause. His soothing words and gentle advances with an overwhelming hunger in his gaze.

"Amazing, isn't it?" Apollo asked, referring to the lavish spread he prepared for the supposed simple dinner, highlighting his cooking skills with a flourish of his hands.

Avoiding eye contact with the magnetic man bleeding danger, Dafnie fidgeted with her finger before answering. "It looks delicious."

"Well, anything for my lady."

Apollo's hypnotic movements enticed her to expect an unusual meal together. Excitement swelled within her, for no apparent reason, as he passed a dish overflowing with mouthwatering dishes.

His frigid tone sent chills all throughout her body, and goosebumps decorated her skin. With a stony expression, his desire-filled gaze drove her to uncomfortable heights. She tried to brush off these feelings, attributing them to her unsettling day, accepting the plate he offered, and trying hard to keep an air of composure.

She couldn't help but revel in the overbearing impression of being cornered as he sat beside her. His eyes fixed on her, raking over her form with an intensity that made her vulnerable.

His enthusiasm intensified, drumming like her ear-splitting heartbeat. He showed it with unabashed splendor. His actions juxtaposed the steel-clad, calm demeanor from early, now filled with agitation and restlessness. He peered at her, eyes pinning her. A feast to gulp and devour—not a needy neighbor.

The dinner became an obnoxious blur. She maintained polite conversation throughout the affair while avoiding physical contact with the man sitting close to her. At one point, her head spun, and a fire swallowed her body as his hands touched hers. Then...

"How's your tea? I used my homemade blend of herbs intended for the nerves. After tonight's distressing experience," he inquired, interest glowing in his eyes.

She hesitated for a moment before answering. "It's... quite good. I appreciate your kindness. Terrifying to think I was all alone and left behind."

Apollo's gaze became more intense. His glances lingered longer than they should have as his words took on a different, more hypnotic tone. His touch, accidental, sent shivers down her spine.

At that point, Dafnie encountered a forking change born from within her. An explicable attraction for Apollo sprouted from her core and spread throughout her frame like young laurel vines entangling close to her conscience. She couldn't resist the charming pull from his eyes as the limbs pulled her deeper into a void constructed of desire.

She knew something was off. Her body seemed to have a mind of its own, yearning for Apollo's heated attention but keeping her emotions in check.

He went to the modern wine rack in the dining room corner and selected an expensive-looking bottle. "I intended to use this delicious nectar of the blessed vineyard for another occasion, but tonight, I feel like merrymaking today," he said with a suggestive smile.

"I think you should save it for later. Please don't waste such an extravagant drink on a simpleton like me..."

"Oh! Celebration is in order. To another survivor in Phoebus Groove. However, I don't think you are a 'simpleton.' To me, you radiate like a solar queen."

Dafnie blushed as curiosity sent butterflies flying to the pit of her stomach at his comment. "I'm no 'solar queen.' I'm quite common. Why do you want to celebrate today of all days? Horrors lurk outside, praying on the innocent and unsuspecting."

Apollo leisurely got two wine glasses and a plate filled to the brim with various cheeses and palate cleansers. He poured the wine for both and held his glass up in a toast.

"To encounters!" Raising his glass, his stare turned lascivious as if he wanted to devour her.

She focused on her drink's rich color. It reminded her of Apollo's heated gaze, like a gazelle about to be eaten by a lion.

Shaking her head, she decided not to overthink his weird behavior. "To encounters!" She mouthed, hesitating for a brief second before sipping on her drink.

Like the man himself, the wine's warm and intoxicating flavor stirred her awareness, clouding her judgment. Her mind ran with images that seduced her steadfast resolve—like falling into a dangerous game hunter and prey.

Is he attempting to lure me into a snare? A promising yet alluring trap. I'm being cornered.

Her brain wandered for the rest of their dinner, and despite her best efforts, she seemed drawn in by his strong sexual pull. Out of the blue, he approached, nosing her throat and breathing in her scent. His generous lips traveled the column of her neck, leaving her breathless.

"W-What are you doing?"

A whisper escaped her mouth while a dense lump settled in her throat.

"Shhh… I'm imprinting your essence deep into my soul, my

darling. A part of my long and solitary existence," Apollo continued, sniffing and kissing her neck.

"My essence?" The fog grew thick as all traces of thought abandoned her.

"Yes, your essence, my dear naiad! My queen, my... world..." He trailed off as he caressed Dafnie's face and fed her a piece of fruit she didn't recognize.

A few seconds after receiving the little morsel, Dafnie's lightheadedness made her swoon with a tremendous thrill. With blazing, fierce eyes, he stared at her, his lustful desires clear in his fiery eyes. Infatuation consumed him.

"Can I kiss you, my precious nymph?"

"I have a very strict seven-date rule. No touching. Nor kissing. Or..." She couldn't comprehend why she reciprocated his advances, enraptured by passion and desire for the man who offered her refuge. "Yes..."

Even though she couldn't understand why she acted hastily with desire, she yearned for Apollo as much as he longed for her.

Chapter 22

Intoxicating Haze

As Apollo leaned in, a rush of mixed emotions bombarded Dafnie–hesitation, excitement, and an inexplicable passion that was hard to deny. His mouth met hers, a soft but insistent pressure, and her world spun. Heat exploded between them, consuming her awareness, and she responded to his kiss. His hand cradled her face, his thumb brushing her cheekbone, a gesture so intimate it made her shiver.

The overwhelming toxins of lusty appetite coming from his lips dragged her to the darkest depth of desire. The wine they shared mingled with the unique essence of him. He deepened their kiss, his tongue exploring her mouth, teasing her senses into overdrive. His other hand rested on her lower back, pulling her closer to him as much as their position allowed them, almost obliterating every inch of space between their bodies.

She sank in the intense yearning coursing through her, reducing their surroundings to nothing. Their impassioned confession of love drowned the nightmares from outside. Hardships were a distant memory. Lost in their passionate kiss, the world ceased to exist. Nothing mattered to them at that point.

The kiss seemed to go on forever. A dance of lips and tongues, and through it all, Apollo's fingers never eluded her, caressing her, anchoring her to him. He explored, memorizing every single inch of her face and body with his hands. A flash of a second of pure passion in which she succumbed to the overwhelming sensations he stirred within her.

With a sense of boldness, he parted from their kiss, disentangling from their fervent embrace. Left breathless, she longed for more. His lips traced a path down her delicate neck, where every tender kiss imprinted a scorching memory upon her supple skin. Mutual desire heightened the intensity of the moment. A hypnotizing dance unfurled between their arms, leaving them hungering for more.

The talented man explored her collarbone, his teeth nibbling at her sensitive flesh, eliciting a soft moan from Dafnie's lips. His hands cradled her waist, pulling her closer to him, emphasizing the heat radiating from their bodies.

He deepened the kiss, his hunger palpable. With urgency, he found the collar of her borrowed shirt and shredded the material as if it were flimsy paper. He pulled back to admire her exposed body.

"Such a beautiful view! A scene that will forever stay etched in my memories, my love."

With craving in his eyes and panting with lust, he lavished his stare on her naked bust. His heavy gaze traced the delicate contours of her small yet perky mounds. The marvel in his eye expressed enough.

Clear as day, abandon shone like the longest day of summer. But...

A hint of youthful affection pushed through the dense haze of lust.

***

She's perfect. My queen, you have always been perfect.

A sweet vision of her gentle curves and soft skin wetted his appetite and disrupted his faculties to think straight. The modest size of her bosom only added to the fascination, evoking guilelessness and unsullied charm. Time appeared to stand still as Apollo's thirst grew. His mouth turned dry as sand while his desire intensified with each passing second.

"I've been waiting for so long. Since the day I killed the python."

"The what?!"

"Shhh! What matters is that you're here with me."

The soft golden glow of the chandelier illuminated each subtle curve and swell of her breasts, casting mesmerizing shadows that danced and flickered, enticing his senses. The delicate interplay of light and shadow heightened the allure, eliciting a primal yearning deep within him.

With a gentle touch, his fingertips explored her velvety skin, tracing and discovering the exquisite contours. Her enthusiastic openness guided his performance. Apollo knew well that Dafnie's delicate and expressive lips rewarded his every caress with a delightful moan.

The provocative whimper sent ripples of desire through his body. Dafnie tilted her head back and pushed her chest toward him to allow the mighty Sun God the honor to explore to his heart's content. He marveled at how her soft mounds fit in his hands—not generous or small. A light touch was enough to make her nipples harden.

He lowered his head, brushing his lips against her heated flesh, the sweetness of her skin akin to a potion, intoxicating and addictive. Each gasp escaping Dafnie's lips was a sweet melody born of pleasure, intensifying his longing for her. His affection for her was profound, urging him to give in to his desires.

He couldn't take it any longer.

No more would he deny himself anymore.

He needed his beloved—ready to indulge.

Now...

Before her allure provoked him any further, Apollo scooped his lover in a possessive embrace. A frantic dash of passion ensued as he rushed them upstairs, slamming the door to his room and locking away the harsh reality of snooping on their rendezvous.

Dafnie's pulse quickened as his muscular arms cradled her close to his chest, her body pressed against him as he carried her across the room. His eyes, filled with a wild desire, stayed on her face, reading every flicker of her expression as he walked up the stairs and to his bedroom.

Once inside his room, he laid her on his plush bed. The room's faint light cast a dreamlike hue over her exposed chest. Dafnie was a chaste contradiction, looking virginal and tempting.

Apollo rose from the bed and slipped his shirt off his broad shoulders, revealing powerful muscles rippling his entire body. The silky fabric slipped over his well-toned abdominals, each ripple a testament to the relentless strength contained within. He was raw and perfect masculinity, shaped by some ancient god, complete with a look of pure ardor.

Every bit mesmerizing and refreshing as the dawn brings a new day.

Apollo's playful fingers crept to the waist of his jeans. A wicked smirk played on his luscious lips as he unbuckled his belt. The jeans, now loose, slid down his muscled thighs, revealing underwear was a commodity on his rippled body. His manhood stood proud, unabashed, and unrestrained on full display for her to admire.

She gasped in surprise at the sight of him. His glorious naked body carried the testament of unrivaled perfection. Unrivaled by anyone in the world's entire existence. His sculpted legs and his firm and well-rounded ass.

Every inch of him was flawlessly personified, a view of utter sexuality. The sight of him was enough to ignite an unimaginable, unexplainable desire within her. An intoxicating sexual energy that enveloped her in a shell of craving.

He moved toward her with the grace of a feral cat, each muscle rippling with effort. As he loomed over her, his silhouette dominated her field of view.

His gaze held hers as he reached out, his fingers tracing a delicate path along her arm, leaving her skin tingling in their wake. Their eyes locked as he leaned in, capturing her lips, and moved his hands to the waist of her boxer briefs and dragged them down her shapely legs.

His kisses enveloped her in a whirlwind of passion that left her breathless. Apollo's mouth continued its exploration all over her shape, leaving no part untouched. His hands roved over her entire body, each touch fanning the flame consuming her.

"You have captivated me, Dafnie. The gods themselves are incapable of resisting a beauty."

A dangerous whisper echoed in the room's silence as he kneeled between Dafnie's legs, giving him a full view of her delightful physique. "I'm planning to devour you."

She took a sharp breath, her mind a jumble of anticipation. She was eager for him to fulfill and make good on his promise. That made her bolder, and she explored his body with her hands, curious to feel if he was real.

As Apollo admired her boldness, a newfound desire sparked in his eyes, a yearning so potent it made her squirm with need.

His hot breath whispered against her ear, sending tingles through her senses. With ardent enthusiasm, he made it his point she understood she was his alone. "I will charm your heart, becoming the only one you desire, and your affection for others will pale in comparison as you direct your gaze just on me."

He turned his attention to a new goal for pleasure. He traced his lips down her neck, past her collarbone, to the soft valley between her breasts. His hot and ragged breath caused her skin to tingle in anticipation.

He took one breast in his hand, his thumb grazing the peak until it hardened. Letting out a breathy moan, her back arching off the bed to bring herself closer to him.

A wicked grin split Apollo's face, and without further delay, he lowered his mouth to the other breast. His lips closed around her nipple in a searing kiss. But his attention to Dafnie's breast was short-lived as he kissed down her body.

Apollo's hunger drove him to hunt for the delectable nectar found in only one place. As he took a deep sigh, the alluring scent of her arousal rewarded his efforts. His warm breath fanned across her tender folds, causing her to shiver in anticipation.

"Mmm... please..." she moaned, her voice shaking with need.

Her fingers tangled in his hair, guiding him closer to her. A coy smirk played on his lips, and he accepted her silent plea. As his tongue flicked her sensitive bud, a gasp escaped her lips, and her back arched off the bed. Dafnie's legs opened wider to allow him better access as waves of pleasure coursed through her body.

The unstoppable Mr. Delphoes continued his attentive ministrations. Each stroke of his tongue on her clit elicited a sweet moan from her. His fingers joined in the exploration, sliding first a finger into her with ease.

After inserting a second finger into her welcoming channel, his pace quickened, matching the rhythm of her hips as she moved against him. Seeking more enjoyment.

✳✳✳

Soon, the room filled with the sounds of their shared passion. The low hum of Apollo's admiration against her skin, the rustle of sheets tangling about their bodies. Dafnie's soft cries as she spiraled toward her climax. As she approached the edge of desire, he redoubled his efforts as if wishing to see her lose all restraints and bloom before his eyes.

With a final desperate cry, Dafnie tumbled over the verge into the abyss of pleasure. Her body convulsed as waves of ecstasy washed over her, leaving her breathless and sated. As the aftershocks subsided, he placed a delicate kiss on her inner thigh before ascending back up her body, his lips meeting hers in a soft kiss with the flavors of their nectar.

He lavished her with his absolute attention, alternating between soft kisses and gentle suckles that once again awakened her desire and left her panting and squirming beneath him. His other hand imitated his mouth's movements on her neglected breast, overwhelming her with delightful sensations.

As the intensity of their passion escalated, Apollo grabbed his engorged cock and positioned himself at her slick entrance. He gazed into Dafnie's eyes. Apollo's pupils were dark pools of desire. His hands cradled her face, his thumb tracing over her soft lips.

"May I?"

His panting caressed her cheeks as he hesitated, not knowing what to say. The fog of desire took her ability to think, so an answer escaped without reason. "I-I..."

"My beloved... I'm afraid if you deny me, I will not comply." His whisper echoed through the quiet room, nuzzling against her neck.

A satisfied smile played on Apollo's lips. His eyes filled with pure adoration for the woman in his arms. Content with the play of events when his precious nymph accepted him as a man.

✳✳✳

Dafnie nodded, lost for words and her heart pounding against her ribs with anticipation and nervousness. He sighed in relief as he pushed in. He entered her—slowly and carefully.

She gasped, her hands clutching onto his biceps. He stilled, allowing her to adjust to him before he moved again. His pace was slow and measured. She moaned as he filled her, her body stretching to accommodate him until he seated inside her—a snug fit that drained his insides.

Only after she adjusted to his full length did he move once again. His strokes were deep and steady. Each thrust sent waves of pleasure coursing through her. His gentle temperament hid a passionate intensity threatening to destroy any restraint. Feeling the adoration in each touch, all their kisses, and every thrust.

Apollo swayed with a caring akin to the mastery of a prodigious performer. His body intertwined with hers in a sensual dance. As they played their game of pleasure, she responded to his every thrust with a matching movement, losing herself in the encounter. Their bodies synchronized as they advanced towards their peak with each passing moment.

She became lost in bliss, moaning as he drove faster, grunting with absolute effort, untethered. It didn't take long before a cry escaped her lips. After a fulfilling zenith of satisfaction, her body trembled under the waves of bliss. Her lover followed right after, his climax ripping through him. He collapsed on top of her, their bodies still connected, their breaths mingling in the quiet room.

As they lay there, spent and sated, he stroked her hair as she drifted to sleep, inching closer to losing consciousness as her body relaxed.

"I cherish your existence and spirit. I want to have you by my side for eternity, to share every moment with you. Your presence brings me boundless joy. Let's be together and build more beautiful memories," he murmured into her ear, his voice loaded with raw emotion as flashbacks from the past resurfaced.

The handsome man wrapped his arms around her and pulled

her close to his chest. As their breathing slowed, silence packed the room packed with silence.

Chapter 23

The Morning

The gentle golden rays of the early morning streamed through the oversized bedroom windows, casting an incandescent glow on the wooden floor and furniture. As daybreak crept in, it illuminated every corner of the room, painting intricate patterns on the floors and walls through the sheer curtain.

Delicate dust particles suspended in the air played with the light like a joyous dance. The eagerness to craft a masterpiece, the sun shined with shimmering beams resembling ethereal fairies who came out and danced, conjuring a magical atmosphere that enveloped the entire space.

Soft rays stretched toward Dafnie, casting a warm and welcoming gleam. As she lay in bed, she exhaled. Her strange dream last night left her drained, but sleep eluded her despite her desire to carry on with her rest.

Her eyes fluttered open, her delicate lashes brushing against her skin as she adjusted to the gentle, golden glow of the morning light that seeped through the windows. In a brief, serene moment, she savored the undisturbed transition from slumber to wakefulness.

Dafnie's inherent early riser habit stirred within her. A gentle smile tugged at the corners of her lips, and a peaceful relaxation consumed her—and sated her presence. Sleep refused to release its hold on her, allowing nervous anticipation to wake her.

Her gaze swept across the room, taking in the foreign surroundings. Gilded sunbeams danced over the unfamiliar walls and furniture. The rays' playfulness teased her with secrets yet to be exposed.

Dafnie wondered how she made it into a stranger's bed. Sudden disorientation flustered her into a zigzagging dizziness as her head spun out of control. Her memories of the previous day were hazy at best. However, vivid details from the night before remained. Her skin prickled at the thought of their shared moment of passion, and anger grew from deep within her.

"Damn! I made a mistake staying here."

She tried to rise from the warm, comfortable bed when an abrupt unease crept through her body. As she attempted to move, the heaviness around her waist captured her attention. A vise-like grip pinned her down, making it impossible for her to leave undetected.

A strange, unsettling silence filled the room, only broken by her shallow breaths as she struggled against the weight of the man's arm. Every movement she produced seemed to intensify being trapped. At one point, he took a big breath and pulled her closer to him, tightening his grasp on her and snuggling her even more.

As Dafnie turned, cautious not to stir suspicion, her eyes met

Apollo's serene profile. His face softened by sleep, and his tousled blond hair, like a mantel, spread about his handsome face and pillow. Like shimmering golden threads in the early morning light, his luscious mane shone like beams of sun rays.

His breast rose and fell in a hypnotic cadence. The toned muscles beneath his alabaster skin rippled with each breath. A peaceful smile played on his lips, reflecting the tranquility of his dream. His undisturbed countenance was spellbinding.

Dafnie stared at Apollo, her heart pounding extra hard in her chest. The sight of the sleeping man captivated her, unlike the guy from last night, who viewed her as his prey.

In the morning light, his expression transformed, devoid of any lecherous intent. He looked like an angel, one that fell from the sky.

"He appears so young this way." Hesitation plagued her as she reached to brush a wayward strand spoiling his handsome face.

"I don't want to wake him."

She admired his golden stands, contrasting against the crisp white linen. The sunlight filtering through the curtains cast an ethereal glow on him.

His chiseled jaw was soft and stubble-free. His thick eyelashes, casting shadows over his sculpted cheekbones, and the sharp line of his nose and the fullness of his lips made him look charming. He looked like a statue, tempting her to explore some more.

However, she hesitated before doing anything rash. She didn't want to wake the man sprawled next to her. At that moment, her longing for solace led her to seek shelter in her sanctuary.

Holding her breath, she disentangled herself from Apollo's muscular arm. His peaceful face and steady breathing never faltered while her heart hammered like a drum. The morning air hit her bare skin as she slid out of bed. With laser focus, she aimed at her refuge, her home.

As Dafnie tiptoed to the closet, she couldn't help but wince, an unfamiliar soreness taking residence at the vee of her legs. The stark contrast between her petite frame and his rock-hard manhood reminded her of their night together. Although his gentle touch roused great pleasure in her, their differences in size revived the realization of his generous endowments.

She shook her head, pushing the memory of him rocking on top of her, pleasuring her in a way she never knew existed, and wrapped herself in one of Apollo's button-up shirts, too big for her.

The shirt hung from her slender form. The hem covered her thighs midway, and his musk permeated her senses. She tightened her grip on the fabric, a pitiful attempt to push away the heat that clawed at her.

Tiptoeing out of the room, she made her way downstairs, her bare feet not making a sound on the wooden floor. The eerie quietness of the house unsettled her frayed nerves, spiking her tremors to new heights. She found herself at the main window, looking outside, hoping no creatures lurked around.

Dafnie's heart fluttered as her eyes scanned the area. Her breath hitched, expectation catching in her throat. She searched for any sign of movement, making sure monsters didn't lurk in the shadows. Fortunately, Dafnie saw no creatures roaming around.

Concerned her to see the mutilated remains all over the place.

Her mind raced with ideas, and she tried to form a plan.

Motionless bodies littered the street, producing a haunting scene. But that didn't mean they wouldn't attack her once she stepped outside and closer to them. She took a deep inhale, steeling her nerves.

Time to leave!

A familiar cold seeping into his skin disturbed Apollo's peaceful slumber, contrasting with the warmth that lulled him to sleep last night. His heavy lids opened—a slow awakening to his fuzzy mind. The emptiness beside him disrupted the pleasant morning.

He hoped for nothing but snuggles, kisses, bodies tangled, and...

His heart pounded hard as he sat on the bed, the blood churning his head from the abrupt movement. His eyes darted around the room, searching for his precious nymph. The tousled sheets and lingering musk were the only remnants of their passionate encounter the previous evening.

His ears perked up at the faint ruffling sound from the first floor. In her efforts to find her house keys and bat, Dafnie stirred the house's unsettling silence. His heart flipped and somersaulted, realizing his lover left. Finding himself alone in bed stirred an illogical, burning anger within Apollo. Swiftly, he rose from his bed and slipped into his pajama pants. The thought of Dafnie leaving him invaded his mind, clouding his thoughts.

Not again... She cannot leave me again. Alone... I won't accept it this time. She'll stay by my side.

Anger forced its way into every single cell in his body as he fisted his hands to control his body.

The sound of the front door opening and closing reached his ears. A surge of adrenaline rushed through Apollo. Desperate, he sprinted down the stairs, the wooden floor creaking under his weight. Ignoring the cool morning air that enveloped him, giving him goosebumps, Apollo bolted after Dafnie, driven by a desperate need not to let her escape his grasp.

He caught up to her after their chase many millennia ago. She couldn't leave him now. He couldn't bear the thought of living without her again.

No! She's not allowed to leave me again. She's my queen... my heart... my... everything.

With desperation consuming his thoughts, he tried to soothe his distressing emotions—a hopeless act on his part.

As Apollo ran outside, about to catch her, his precious nymph stopped dead in her tracks. Petrification heaped her on the spot—unable to move. Dafnie dropped her bat and keys when an alarming realization smacked him hard.

The street grew silent, attracting unwanted attention from every direction. Dread dumped on his head as a nagging feeling crept to the back of his neck—the hair on his body stood on end. The impression of hungry eyes settled upon them, an oppressive hand seeking to drag them into a nightmarish chasm.

And by the looks of it, his precious lover's apparent trepidation whispered she unknowingly experienced the same.

She shook, the violent tremors crumbling her perception as

she looked around, taking in the chaos. A light sheen of sweat covered her entire body as she hyperventilated.

There's no escape from this. I'm stuck!

Before her, a horrific sight unfolded, like from a horror movie. A half-eaten creature with pus-filled welts oozing a putrid liquid. Apollo pulled her into a tight embrace, turning her away from the traumatic scene. He watched in panic as the stronger creatures tore into the weak or dead, their sharp teeth and claws ripping through flesh. The chilling picture reflected in his nightmares, a racket he wished to spare his beloved from ever hearing.

As he walked toward her house, she pushed forward with determination—and fear. She hesitated to venture deeper into unfamiliar territory.

"This is so fucked up. Shit!" Apollo shouted, moving closer.

Her body reacted and stepped back, smelling another kind of danger coming too close for comfort. "How is it possible that something like this happened this quick?" Dafnie found the will to ask for the one thing plaguing her mind.

"Daphne, darling! It's been two weeks since everything went to utter hellish shit... These fucking creatures appeared a week ago and..." Apollo clarified.

"Two weeks? But..." Grasping at the delicate tendrils of truth, she scanned her surroundings. "You said it's been a week?!"

"Not my intention to mislead you..."

"Mislead me. Y-you did something... and put me under a spell. A-and these..."

Dafnie shrunk in disgust as she glared at the dismembered creature.

"This recent development started a week ago? I've been asleep only one night, not two weeks."

Her head pounded with tension as her focus wavered. Confusion threatened to consume her if she didn't search for answers.

"And... who is this Daphne? You keep calling me by that name. My name is Dafnie... there is a difference."

"That's you... I know it's..." he implored.

"No! It's not me. My name is Dafnie Valencia. I'm not the person you believe I am. Please, stop, you're confused!"

She forced her voice to carry heavy and unwavering through the air as she bent to grab her key and bat and go to her house.

"Don't walk away from me."

"Why? What will you do? Uhh... Give me some other herb to dull my mind... like you did last night?! To take advantage of my weak mental state after going through a hell of a day?!" She shouted matter-of-factly, staring at him defiantly.

"I'll chase and hunt you down. Then I'll teach you to belong by my side. By the end, once I'm through with you, you'll beg me to stay and to love... often... hard... until you can't stand it any longer. A-and afterward, I will love you again until you succumb—concede that I'm the victor. And after, I will love you some more. This time around, I won't allow you to slip through my fingers. Not again. I'll go to great lengths to show you're mine," Apollo threatened, eyes unfocused as he disclosed his plans.

"B-beg... you to stay?"

"Yes! You'll beg for my touch after I'm done with you."

Fight or flight!

Terror consumed her mind as entrapment blanketed her

awareness, invariably paralyzed, making it hard to think coherently.

I can't think straight and decide. Why not choose both? Fight while sprinting to safety. I'll see how far I can get,

The preparation sensitized her, choosing defiance instead of compliance.

Pushing past her fear, Dafnie stood tall and faced Apollo with a steadfast look in her eyes. Her determined voice rang out, forcing her to declare a refusal for anyone to hear.

"I'll never beg. You can't control me."

Apollo's eyes gleamed with desire and challenge at the dare.

Fuck! Stupid of me to oppose him that way. I didn't think this through, damn it. She thought, conflict teasing after speaking her unhinged mind.

Unfortunately for her, the man moved like a hunter. Hellbent on catching his prey and bending her to his will this time. His wish to possess her and bend her to his will dripped like a busted pipe.

But first, he needed to catch her.

Chapter 24

A Hunter's Obsession

"B-beg... you to stay." Dafnie's body shook as she stammered her reply.

"Yes! You'll beg for my touch after I'm done with you." Apollo's vicious declaration came like a death sentence, wincing at his harsh reaction. His impulsivity ate at his entrails instead of showering adorations on the one lover he wanted to spend eternity with since his youth.

Apollo witnessed a devastating fear in her eyes, and it pained him to see that expression on her face. He tried to pull her into his embrace and protect her, but he made a big mistake. He pushed her way too much, past her comfort zone. Clear as day, she debated between fighting him or bolting as far away from him as soon as possible.

Fight or flight!

She expressed mixed emotions in her eyes, terror manifesting the most prominent.

Fuck! That was so stupid! Why did I say such a thing to her? I've corned her like an animal to be hunted down. I'm being a heartless prick with her, he thought. He chastised himself for his hasty choice of words.

She panicked at first, but a swift transformation in her demeanor followed like a storm to chaos. Dafnie looked determined to confront him with every ounce of strength within her petite body. She wanted her safety and freedom—she refused to be controlled like a pretty little doll.

Then...

"I'll never beg. You can't control me."

In a daring move, she made her escape to run far away from him. She rushed with all her might. However, to Dafnie's dismay, Apollo's deep-seated hunter instincts surfaced from the abyssal confines of his essence, overpowering other thoughts or considerations.

His gaze sharpened, fixated on his precious bird, determined to capture her this time without fail. The air seemed to thicken with anticipation as he prepared to unleash his full might upon her, ready to bend her resolve to his will.

A battle of wits and strength, a clash between predator and prey, fate hanging in the balance. Little did she know a formidable challenge awaited her. Dafnie made the mistake of running.

His obsessive predatory desire blinded him as he focused on seeing her delicate and beautiful face again in the throes of passion. While he pounced on her, bringing her toward newfound pleasure and erasing anyone's past attempts at wooing her. Apollo would make sure she would enjoy being with him.

But first, he needed to catch his nymph.

Apollo's heart pounded like a raging drum, the adrenaline

coursing through his veins, powering his pursuit. His gaze fixed on Dafnie as she darted through the debris-strewn street with her lithe form. Ardent lust coursed through him, making him unstoppable.

He admired and enjoyed the fearlessness and resiliency that radiated from her. The sight of her running, her hair cascading behind her, her body swaying rhythmically with each stride, stirred a primal desire within him, fueling his determination.

He found himself transported to the time when he chased Daphne. This time, though, things would be extraordinary. Determined beyond reasonable thought to catch her and have a different ending.

Apollo maneuvered through the remnants of a broken world, his supernatural agility serving him well in this high-stakes chase. A predator in his element, with Dafnie as his desired prey. With every breath he took, he feasted on the sweet scent of her anxiety and resolve. The irresistible combination made him want her even more. A tempting dance between the hunter and the hunted.

However, a whirlwind of conflicting emotions plagued her restless spirit. Fear, defiance, and an inexplicable desire rose from deep within her soul, questioning her sanity.

Weird to experience this exhilaration with this stranger?

The thrill of the chase drove her heart to pound to a frightening tempo, mimicking her pursuer's heavy footfall. The closer he came, the caress of his presence enveloping her, his aura emitting a seductive and dangerous charm that caused shivers to ripple down her spine. Terrified! Yet her body responded to his proximity in strange and confusing ways.

However, destiny had other plans. Turning sharply, she dashed into her house, slamming the door behind her. However, her fruitless attempts resulted in nothing. A dominant hand stopped the door from closing. He pushed it open, hulking into the room with a menacing sight.

He then slammed the door, cutting off any means of evasion for her. The loud sound echoed throughout the house, followed by silence. Their heavy breathing turned into the only harmony tickling through the room. They stared at each other, locked in a clash between a hunter and his prey.

He realized her frenzied thoughts fused with a single purpose—racing to devise an escape plan. Her chest heaved as she leaned against the wall. Her senses heightened as Apollo approached her with a predatory grace, much like a cat's walk.

His wild hair curtained his features in ringlets of gold, and his eyes shone with sexual intent. His keen eyes took in the sight of her sanctuary—Dafnie's last line of defense. He took a deep breath, his rib cage expanding as every muscle rippled with the effort, and marveled at her sweet scent permeating the house. It drove him mad with desire.

A wicked, dangerous smirk crept across his captivating face as he cornered her against the wall. He trapped her between his outstretched arms as he looked at her. He savored the sound of her breathing, her breaths quick and shallow. It fueled his hunger, his appetite for her. He longed, more than anything, to hear her panting with pleasure as he basked in the sweetness of his hard-won triumph.

"Your urge to evade me fans my passion... so careful, my dear huntress," he warned.

She gasped at the treat, head whipping around, seeking an escape.

"You look way too… tempting," he drawled, reaching for her arms. His iron-like grip against Dafnie's slender arm became a firm restraint that held her in place and threatened to shatter the barriers erected about her heart to keep her safe. His heated gaze pierced into hers, both frightening and enticing.

"Dafnie!"

As her name slipped from his lips, a whispered utterance layered with a profound and powerful plea. The intensity of his confession exploded as tremors coursed rampant with numbing vehemence. His chest rose and fell with his labored breaths. "Stop running away from me… please!" he begged. Apollo seemed to reign in his desire somewhat, but his hunting instincts still affected him.

"I'll never force you. Never!"

Apollo's solemn vow oozed with trust—and promise. His grip loosened as if to reassure her. But his voice had an undeniable desperation, a raw need beyond mere lust.

His remarks hung between them like a hard-to-ignore tangible declaration.

Patience… I must find the strength to remain calm around her. Understand her! She's just a scared fawn in search of sanctuary. A reassuring hand should suffice. She'll calm down.

He believed as he closed the distance between them.

Scented with his intoxicating aroma—a heady mix of sweat, musk, and an indescribably masculine fragrance distinctive of him. He cultivated a strange thrill shooting down her spine, her body reacting in alarming and exciting ways.

"But I'll fight. I'll battle for your adoration. I'll go to war for your love and what it can be..."

His words echoed in the silence, resonating with a truth that Dafnie found hard to ignore. Heat radiating from his broad frame, enveloping her in a comforting but dangerous cocoon of warmth. Their closeness, synchronized breaths, and tangible tension created an exhilarating mix that made Dafnie's head swirl and her heart race.

She became curious about how far he would go for his desires and what he wanted most in the world. She couldn't help but ask, her voice just above a defiant whisper. "What makes you think I'll bend to your will, Apollo?"

Apollo's fingers tightened around her wrist. The touch sent a jolt of electricity through her veins. "You drive me wild with want and yearning. And I guarantee... you'll beg, my precious love," he murmured, his tone husky with unspent passion. "Not out of fear or submission. Your passionate tunes shall be out of lust, hunger, and demand."

The promise in his words—as compelling as the man himself. Caught in a storm of emotions, Dafnie's mind turned into a battlefield of panic, desire, logic, and tenderness as his heated urge filtered into hers. One thing became plain. Despite not claiming to like it, she enjoyed their game. Her hunter and lover. And she loved Apollo's formidable pursuit.

He ran a hand through his unruly hair. His eyes locked on her. He leaned closer to her, his movements controlled yet full of raw power. "Dafnie... I know who you are, but please try to understand how all this started. I want you." He spoke with a husky voice filled with a blend of emotions.

His eyes softened, a stark contrast to the hard lines of his face, as he gently took her hand and placed tender kisses on her wrist. "Do you remember our precious escapade last night?"

He stared at the necklace hanging warm against her neck, his thumb tracing the back of her hand.

His gentle touch morphed into a counterpoint to his firm grip on her.

"Do you recall the way our bodies moved together? As my hands mold on your skin. Your breath hitching at my tickling gasp and your body trembling every time I touched you."

A stark contrast to his earlier predatory demeanor, his tone held a delicate and coaxing tenderness. He chose his words with deliberation to remind her of their shared passion from the previous night.

"I'm sorry!" His eyes reflected genuine regret as he nuzzled his lover's neck like a remorseful kitten. "For the way I acted when you were vulnerable and in danger. Without thinking about how it might affect you, I behaved pretty recklessly."

His hand glided up to cup her cheek, thumb brushing and grazing her lower lip. "But Dafnie."

His voice dropped to a husky whisper.

"I can't offer an apology for this attraction—I refuse to. I've been yearning for your love for sooo… long that my whole body recognizes when you are around. Even before we met."

His other hand moved to touch the necklace he gave her. His fingers brushed against the pendant, a silent question hanging in the air. "I got you this because I wanted to protect you," he told her, his gaze never straying from hers. "Even before our meeting, no doubt, a connection between us tied our spirit threads. And now that we're together, it's stronger than ever."

Apollo's grip on her tightened, a desperate plea for his actions. "I cannot and will not live without you, Dafnie."

The fire in his eyes burned with resolution. His words stayed firm and insistent, leaving no room for refusal. He leaned closer, a silent pledge of what might be and what he craved.

"Dafnie," he breathed, the word heavy with affection and promise. "I want you. I need you. Now... please... don't deny me!"

His confession hung in the air, a palpable force that drew her to him like a moth to a flame. Filled with intense desire, his eyes locked onto hers. Their connection grew stronger with each passing moment. His last words echoed in the silence and at her core.

"Why me?" she whispered.

"You've always made my heart beat faster. I've loved you from the instant I saw you," Apollo confessed, his voice raw with emotion.

"That isn't me... We just met..."

"No, this isn't our first encounter. I don't know the purpose of your existence, but I intend to find out. But trust me, I love you. Always have..."

Apollo's statement hung in the air, thick as honey and just as irresistible. His eyes brimmed with unparalleled intensity. Dafnie's heart thumped hard against her chest, the rhythmic pulsing a testament to the tumultuous emotions coursing through her veins.

"Let me show you, Dafnie, my love!"

A honeyed whisper, smooth and intoxicating. A timbre that weakened her legs to favor the swooning sensation of excitement. It stood as a vow, a seductive pledge as wicked as the man pledging. His thumb traced the contour of her mouth, his feathery contact igniting a spark within her.

His lips descended on hers, soft, lingering on an intentional lock of kisses as deliberate and slow as a ballad—filled with rich promises and amplified passion. Dafnie's heart pounded as she responded to his kiss, her body pressing closer to his. Her fingers moved up his bare chest, exploring every peak and valley of his well-defined pecks.

His hands were strong and sure as they held her, his fingers digging into her skin like he feared she would vanish. His caress evolved into a fiery brand on her soul, the heat seeping into her very bones and igniting a fire within her. Both intoxicating and pleasurable, yearning for more.

Apollo's kisses grew more passionate and demanding, each filled with breathless urgency. She sipped the desire on his lips, a heady concoction that left her craving for more. His digits traveled down her body. He touched her in ways that turned her into a gasping and wanton woman. She sensed his warmth even through the thin barrier of her shirt.

"Mmm…"

Dafnie's groan mutated into a feathered whisper against his mouth.

The heat of their passion engulfed her, causing her to lose herself. Her hands clung to Apollo, her fingers digging into his muscular arms as she surrendered to the emotions swirling within her.

This matured beyond a mere game of seduction. The thrill of the chase. The exciting pursuit became a negligible match of wits. It surpassed the exhilaration of pursuit and the joy of the chased. Giving up control, they succumbed to the raw, primal lust that drove them in this hunt. It evolved into a seductive dance, like a cat pursuing its elusive mouse.

With every breath and beat of her soul, she fell deeper into the whirlpool of eros, drawn by the temptation that Apollo ignited within her—a burning inferno, a passionate fire that consumed her from the inside out.

Their bodies moved against each other in a sensual waltz. A dance of fixation and passion, leaving them panting and gasping for breath. A beautiful spin—as well as dangerous—leaving them both yearning for more.

Chapter 25

Tiger and Doe

"Mmm!" Tears streamed down her plump cheeks, and her eyes lost their focus luster. "This is not right?!"

Apollo took in her alluring scent that drove him to the edge of his senses.

"Why?! To me, it's perfect, my love. Explain to me why this is wrong?"

"I-I'm... not sure... There's this pull, but you're a stranger. I'm so confused... and nothing makes sense."

She clung to him as if searching for reassurance about their illogical encounter.

"I love you, and nothing in this world will stop me. This sensation flows deep into my bones and tells me I'm home again. No matter what, I'm in Elysium by your side."

Her fingers grazed his scalp as she tangled them in his satiny mane, giving him access to the sensitive spot on her neck. "No one ever said such things to me. It feels... mmm..."

He marveled at the melodious moans that escaped her lips. Watching his beloved unshackle and surrender to the throes of mouth-watering passion. He lost control once she clung to him with wanton desire in her eyes. Dafnie's nails bit into his arms, leaving a searing sensation behind, inflaming his lust.

"Let me show you're the one. You better get used to my attention. I plan to shower you with it every single day."

He won his original game of conquest.

But she agreed to his advances.

A willing consent to play this round of allure with a welcoming embrace. The thrill of chasing after her. Nothing compared to having her in his clutches—at last, their chase of seduction evolved into a match of winning over.

He witnessed her surrender of self-control when she greeted the raw and primal hold of her desires. Her charms drew him in like a moth to a flame. It became a waltz of pure temptation. He turned into a hungry tiger, and she became his golden deer.

Each labored breath she took pushed him to desire her even more, deepening his kiss. He wanted more of her and consumed her. Their bodies moved against one another in a seductive dance, leaving them panting and gasping for air—both yearning for more.

The fire inside him raged, burning hot and bright. His lips claimed hers with a wild and untamed ardor forced out from every pore. His deep and demanding kisses, his tongue exploring the sweet recesses of her mouth. She abandoned her inhibitions to his passionate onslaught, giving herself to him unfettered.

Apollo's hands explored her body, tracing her curves and dips with expert finesse, sending tiny vibrations down her spine. His skillful fingers undid the buttons of her shirt, revealing her flawless, sun-kissed skin.

He savored the sight, taking in each inch of her beautiful form, before his fingertips once again found their way to her, teasing and tormenting her senses, evoking gasps of pure pleasure. He relished in her pants and her moans—etching her reaction deep into his memory.

"My huntress, my love!"

The last vestiges of Dafnie's resistance crumbled under his relentless seduction. His intoxicating touch, a potent mixture of gentleness and dominance that sent pin-pricked tickles all over her—sensitive nerves standing at attention.

Her body seemed aflame with desire. His tender caress revealed that their heart throbbed in her chest—a wild beating and losing control of its tempo. She was on fire. Her skin tingled wherever he touched her. Her breath hitched in her throat.

Apollo's breaths turned into ragged puffs of air, matching her moans. His hands wandered everywhere, touching, exploring, igniting. Their coaxing make-out session became heated as their bodies came together. Intending to leave no space between them as if wanting to fuse into one.

"Dafnie..." He growled, unable to contain his eagerness. His intonation booming with excitement, reminiscent of a predator claiming his prize. Tightening his grip, holding onto her—a lifeline to his lust. His kisses intensified—growing more demanding as he moved his attention to her neck. Passion swept over her, consuming her.

Why am I incapable of thinking when he's close to me?

She lacked the resistance against him, no temperance since he was dangerous—a rich devastation with the power to disarm her.

Suddenly, with a swift movement, he hoisted her up. On instinct, her legs wrapped around his waist and entangled her finger in his golden mane. His lips returned to hers—a profound game of their tongues where he played to win. With every kiss, their zeal intensified with an electrifying shock, setting her body ablaze with rapture.

Their forms fit like matching pieces, two halves of a whole. With each breath, their hearts beat like a synchronized symphony of devotion. Their breaths mingled as she continued their passionate kissing. His essence became an intoxicating substance, and his touch transmuted into an all-consuming and indescribable impression. Apollo's hands tightened around her, pulling her even closer. Their bodies pressed together as if wanting to fuse—their souls becoming one.

His hot, puffy panting caressed her neck. His firm grip on her solidified into a compelling reassurance of his presence, strength, and determination to claim her as his own.

"Let go, my precious nymph."

He coaxed, his voice a sultry whisper. His words sounded like a melody that wove a seductive spell, making her hum in anticipation. The comforting drumming of his heart against her chest put her in an erotic trance.

"I will only if you don't betray me."

"Never, my love! You're stuck with me."

His hands roved down her body until he reached her bare bottom, provoking her to gasp and moan in pleasure as he massaged her shapely globes with sensual, precocious fingers. Once again, his lips found hers. Her pent-up emotions exploded after the delicate touch. An instant and overwhelming rush of passion swept her away in a single kiss.

His honeyed mouth held a heady toxin. An intoxicating mixture of sweetness and spiciness, unique to Apollo, drowning her in a daze of fervor. The feel of her petite frame pressed against his muscular one. His steely shaft rubbed her exposed opening—a greedy demand—covering his erection with her sweet nectar. Apollo's thrusting movements, driven by raw possessiveness, a sensual assault, left her yearning for more.

In the clutches of their desire, his lover lost focus and all awareness of reasoning. With a finality that stole his breath, she took a leap of faith, letting go as he thrust his full length and distorted her surroundings. His conscious self altered into a distant memory, alone in their remote world. He sensed her resistance slip away, replaced by primal surrender.

He awakened a dark and delicious thirst within her, elating his ego. Apollo's brand-like triumphant smile seared her with the reality of their shared passion.

"I'm the victor of our game, my beloved."

His unbridled bound to her like a gentle hug. His voice filled with satisfaction beyond his wildest fantasies.

"Never in my dreams did I fathom the delights I find with you." With a swollen heart, the murmur escaped the confines of his chest.

He pulled her closer, his arms like steel bands around her, holding her against him, not letting go.

"I prevailed, and you are my prize, and I intend to keep you forever."

***

Anticipation hung in the air, a tangible invitation to cross over to the domain where carnal pleasure reigned supreme.

Apollo's bulging cap hovered at her entrance, hard and pulsing with need. Steeped with her juices, his precum drove her excitement to new heights. Her body ached in anticipation—her sensitive skin heated while her breath quickened.

He captured her mouth with his, silencing her gasps as he pushed inside her in a slow rhythm.

"Mmmmmm..." she moaned, unable to articulate or form coherent words.

"Uhn..."

The captivating man groaned, eyes glossy and unfocused. Lost in his carnal trance as he entered her. His hips dipped with a steady and confident cadence, feeling the walls of her cavernous channel tightening its grip on him.

"I can't believe my luck, my love!"

"Don't stop, it's amazing! I want more..."

In the grasp of sheer lust, she renounced all her inhibitions and embraced her inner diva.

The world seemed to spin as he nudged his length into her. Their bodies became one. A perfect union as he reclaimed her mouth in a hungry ardor—desperate to a degree. He groaned as his tongue lapped at the sweetness of her.

Overwhelming waves of bliss struck him as his shaft delved deep into her opening, enveloping him in a snug embrace. Pinned to the wall, he used his impressive strength to lift her higher—a comfortable position for greater satisfaction. He pushed his cap into her opening. His pulsating cock sending flutters to her stomach as he sheathed himself further.

She lost her hold on reality and let go.

Finally!

✳✳✳

At first, he lingered, letting her adjust to his size. He watched her as the pleasure and desire cleared in her eyes, heightening his arousal. As he thrust deeper, Dafnie's moans of abandon echoed in his ears. He kept a slow, torturous pace, driving them both to the edge.

The room filled with the sounds of their lovemaking. Their ragged panting and whispered words of excitement created a symphony just meant for them.

"Apollo... more... faster! I'm almost... there. Don't stop!" she moaned, her body arching toward him in response. Their bodies moved in perfect harmony.

At the confession, self-imposed, steel-clad control slipped as he increased his speed. His thrusts became more frantic. He turned into a man driven by his need to claim her.

"My nymph... my darling... you're mine! For eternity," he growled, his voice filled with raw euphoria.

As they rode together, sweat trickled down their skin, leaving them slick and damp. The spicy scent of their arousal and the sound of flesh joining with flesh permeated the room. She matched his pace, meeting every single lunge with one of her own. The pleasure was a shared symphony, their limbs harmonizing in their lustful dance.

Their passion turned into a fierce and unrelenting storm as

their bodies' movements became more needy and desperate. Consumed by desire, their souls appeared to ignite in a passionate blaze reflected through their heated gaze.

Apollo's hands played with her erect nipples with predatory starvation as he ferociously thrust into her with a focused determination that left her gasping. Dafnie's hands clawed at his back, her nails leaving trails of hunger on his skin.

"My sweetheart, you're too precious. I love it."

He hissed at the burning sensation of her nails gouging his skin. He marveled at the pain. It meant his beloved lapped up his relentless pounding, which drove him into a rutting frenzy.

"Ahhhh! Mmmmm! Please don't stop."

His sweet lover moaned with an unquenchable desire.

Her eyes glazed over. Her channel became hotter and wetter. Only a few thrusts away from her climax. Her impending release hovered close as Apollo doubled his efforts and rewarded her with a formidable pummeling of his own.

"Aaah!" Dafnie's guttural cry came as she arched her back in pure ecstasy. Her ability for coherent understanding disappeared seconds later.

Her fingernails dug even deeper into his back, leaving a trail of fire in their wake.

Blinding delirium!

Every thrust of his hips sent delicious shocks coursing through her, coaxing blissful sounds from her parted lips. Her shapely legs wrapped around his waist, pulling him tighter into her as she held in the uncontainable.

Her walls clenched his length, driving him mad with desperation. He focused his gaze on her face, savoring her ecstatic expression. Molten lava blazed through, pushing to the surface as he conquered her body with unrestrained intensity.

"Dafnie, you're mine, my muse, and my desire." His voice morphed into a low growl as he buried his head in the nook of her shoulder and bit her neck to give her a sensual love bite.

"Ahh!"

She cried as a second orgasm assaulted her, gripping him even tighter. "I-I…"

Her precious core rewarded his efforts, sumptuous spasm around his cock—rapid flutters of love—sending him over the edge only after one last thrust.

"Ugh... Uhhhh! My love! Fuck!"

The rumble that escaped his lips reverberated through the room as he found his own climax. His world shattered into a million pieces. Apollo's heart pounded in his chest, the echo of their mutual pleasure still coursing through his veins.

Their apex hit him like a tidal wave, their bodies trembling in shared bliss. Her slippery body brought out her flushed afterglow as she clung to him. A rich, alluring fragrance enveloped the room as their ecstasy peaked, producing a hedonistic atmosphere only matched by their lust. The cacophony of their heavy breathing stood as the only sound in the house.

At this moment, they existed only for each other, their arms entwined possessively. As the storm of their passion receded, holding her close, their forms still quivering from the aftershocks. Consumed in utter satisfaction reflected the magnitude of their lovemaking.

In a safe embrace, clutching Dafnie's well-spent and limp

body. His erect manhood nestled inside her wet and warm channel. Despite his desire to devour her again, he couldn't ignore the signs of her weakening state as he enfolded her in his arms. On the verge of fainting, her limber legs slid off his waist.

"That was incredible," Apollo's voice echoed in the silence as he leaned in for a tender whisper. "You're mine, Dafnie. Forever!"

"Mmmm... it was more than that, my darling."

Her simple response fluttered to his ear as she snuggled against his chest and took a deep breath.

"I feel sleepy... mmm... I love you."

The confession spilled from her lips as surprise settled from head to toe while he rejoiced. His elated heart did flips of victory.

At last, the beautiful nymph that slipped through his fingers was in her rightful place—by his side.

And...

He belonged to her—a part of her.

His throat tightened as wetness filtered down his cheeks.

"I love you, too... my dear!" He hesitated, his gasp catching in his chest as all else faded.

Their mingling essence trickled down his leg, leaving warmth and stickiness behind. Now, he couldn't help but marvel at the copious nectar that flowed from their union.

A smile tugged at his lips, recalling their precious bond.

Not wanting to be apart from his queen, he pulled out of her, unwilling, as more of their mingled release dripped from his groin, puddling on the floor and dirtying his pants. She swayed between the confines of his arms as she tried to find her balance. Her sweet honey left a sparkling trail down her legs.

"Look at us. We're a mess and in dire need of a shower..." he remarked with a beam as she nodded her agreement.

"I'm sorry... These scratches look angry. I-I ought to fetch the first aid kit."

She apologized—her tone shy as if confessing to a hideous crime.

"I take it you liked it."

He teased, his smile innocent yet wicket-painting his features.

"Was it good?" he asked at once, worried about his lover as he leaned in to lick her damp neck and sensing a shiver run through her delicate frame.

An affirmative nod rewarded his attempt. He beamed as he welcomed her in his arms, circling around her in a vice-like embrace.

"Why this hesitation?"

Chapter 26

"Look at us. We're in dire need of a shower..."

Apollo stared at their disheveled state with a smirk—pleased with the outcome.

Very amused!

They wrapped themselves in a cocoon of spent desire and delectable. Dafnie, his delicate nymph, lay nestled in his arms, her body limp and exhausted. He couldn't help but marvel at her. The sheen of sweat highlighted her skin's radiance, her form aglow in the aftermath of their passion.

She embraced him tighter, hiding her face, and nodded. "I'm sorry... I-I scratched you, and it looks bad. I don't understand what got into me?!"

Her apology came as a hum only meant for him.

"Did you like it? Is it good?"

His initial concern faded away as he received a reassuring nod of affirmation from his shy lover. Joy consumed him as his beloved nymph expressed her contentment.

"Then worry no more. Those will heal soon. I promise!"

He smiled and embraced his sweet naiad even tighter. His loving fingers traced the curve of her hip. His azure gaze softened as he looked at her. Her chest rose and fell with a slow and steady cadence and satiated breaths.

"Come, darling!" His voice reverberated with a deep, husky rumble.

He scooped her body to carry her up the stairs, cradling her against him and supporting her. His muscles rippled under her touch. The raw power of his godly form is distinct even in this tender moment. "Let's get cleaned up."

Her eyes fluttered open as she looked at him, her gaze heavy with exhaustion and satisfaction. She managed a weak smile, her fingers tracing the contour of his chiseled torso.

"The shower?"

Her whisper carried hesitation that drove him frantic with bliss.

He nodded, a mischievous twinkle in his eyes. "Yes, my nymph." His soft voice conveyed authority, honed after years of ruling his lands and its people.

He took her into the bathroom, a gentle hold to not blemish her skin further. It turned out that Dafnie's house was an identical copy of his own, down to the smallest details. Familiar with it all, he found the room in no time. He took in the sight of her room, the opposite of his own.

Many plants and flowers filled her room, decorating every surface and window with warmth and nature. He couldn't help but smile, realizing his Daphne was still the same as before. As untamed as she carried a unique wild energy that captivated him from the start—he couldn't have been more thrilled.

He took her to the bathroom, placed her on the marble countertop, and started the hot water in the tub.

She gasped when he turned, putting his back on full display towards her. In her candor, her blunt nails drugged deep into his skin, leaving their mark. Watching her lose control pleased him, and he accepted the innocent punishment. However, guilt shone in her eyes.

I don't feel a thing, but the welts must look terrible for her to reach that way.

He shifted to hold her hands as she reached out to touch his back. "Don't give me that sad look. Everything is fine!"

His words held a reassuring note.

"They sting only a tiny... bit. Trust me! After our shower, those marks will disappear without a trace. Right now, allow me to wear them like a badge of honor, a reminder of what we just did."

"Okay..." She averted her eyes as perplexity colored her cheeks. "Make sure that... they get treated? I can help. I'm used to treating knicks and cuts from climbing."

He caressed her cheek. "Yes, my dear. You see, we immortals can heal our own injuries. But I will enjoy these little tokens of your love for a while longer."

"Immortal?!" Her murmur rang louder than church bells announcing midday.

"Don't mind me. At times, I make silly comments." A glint of playfulness darkened his tone as his intentions took on a shiny glimmer. Diversion and changing the subject became his specialty long ago. He was a true master.

A steamy mist inundated the room, setting a soothing

atmosphere. The mirror showed all their emotions, hiding nothing.

Devotion.

Tenderness.

Passion.

And desire.

The ease with which his dear reincarnated naiad disarmed him left him in disbelief and beyond comprehension. A human is reducing the mighty sun god to smithereens. Dafnie, his precious and beautiful nymph, weakened him.

He planted a tender kiss as he nuzzled her cheek.

"Now, let's get you cleaned up."

While being careful, he picked her up and placed her in the steaming shower. The water's comforting embrace eased her muscles, prompting a quiet sigh to escape her lips.

He slipped in behind her and wrapped his arms around her, pulling her close against his chest. As a gentle lover, he rinsed away the sweat and all hints of their encounter, fondly caressing every inch of her soft skin with soapy hands. She closed her eyes and leaned into his touch, safe and content in his hold.

As the warm spray washed over them, washing away all traces of their amorous play, he showed his softer side, treating his beloved with delicate adoration and care. But in his eyes, the spark of desire still lingered. His loins, still ablaze with passion, tormented his mind, but he resorted to taking deep breaths to calm his raging appetite—all for the sake of the woman who so trusted him with her life.

Apollo reveled in Dafnie's silken skin beneath his fingertips. He took his time, tracing dainty paths along her mouthwatering figure, appreciating her softness. His firm hands massaged her tensed muscles.

Her peaceful breathing as she relaxed filled the room, intermingled with the soft moans escaping her lips sometimes. The steamy atmosphere heightened their senses, intensifying each contact.

"Are you enjoying this?"

He leaned in close and groaned into her ear.

She turned to face him in a shy yet bold move, her finger reaching out to explore his alabaster body. Her fingertips danced over his muscular chest, tracing the contours of his abs and exploring his brawny arms. Her touch, tentative at first, gained confidence as she explored him. As delicate as a feather, evoking emotions that tested his composure, he grappled to stay in control.

A soft gasp fell from Dafnie's lips as Apollo's cock hardened because of her attention. Her wild heartbeat galloped unrestrained as a blush spread across her cheeks. He tried to restrain himself, but his desire was too palpable.

It appeared to thrill her, this raw, uncontained longing he had for her. It encouraged her. Shifting tentatively, her fingers brushed against his erect manhood under the water. Her face burned brighter, but she did not retreat. Instead, she met his gaze, bliss mirrored in her deep eyes.

She then straddled his waist, a smile playing on her lips. His brain went haywire for a second before clouding over with lust.

"Ahhhhh!"

His beloved attention tore a moan from his chest. She gyrated her hips around his erection. Her breath hitched as she stimulated her clit with each careful grind. He savored the slight tremors that coursed through her as he dribbled his craving when he captured her mouth.

"You beautiful thing! You seem fearless now. What changed, because I'm loving it?"

Apollo's curiosity grabbed hold of his heart, pining to hear her response.

"Apollo..." she muttered, lost in her desire and unable to respond beyond his name. Her voice was a husky plea that echoed in the steam-filled room. Her motions became bolder, her body responding with an unfamiliar eagerness. A soft moan escaped her lips as she positioned her wanton entrance to his awaiting head, standing at attention.

He reached for her hips and pulled her down his length, coaxing a guttural growl from deep within him and guiding her movements, complementing her rhythm. His touch left behind a trail of goosebumps like a brand upon her skin, igniting an intoxicating need reflected in her eyes. And only he could satisfy.

The once quiet bathroom a few minutes ago was now filled with the music of their heavy breathing and gentle whimpers. The sound of the water lapping their entwined limbs made their exchange slow and intimate. As their motions became needier, their bodies entangled in the language of desire—a silent conversation of only caresses and gasps.

He, the mighty sun god, reveled in the shivers that ran through her and the soft sigh that escaped her luscious lips. He drank in the way her body moved up and down his length and responded to his touch.

He wanted to kiss her sensual lips, so he claimed her mouth. To disarm her with a heady kiss that left her disarmed. She leaned in for a hungry kiss and into his very being. As they lost their frenzied ardor, their movements pressed on with urgent appetite.

"Fuck, Dafnie! You're so fucking beautiful... mmmm! aaaaah!"

Apollo moaned as he threw his head back in pleasure. Her channel swelled, painfully tightening around his organ as she inched closer to release. His focus slipped away, consumed by the thought of their mutual euphoria.

Apollo's body tensed with primal need and groaned in response to Dafnie's wanton gestures, fracturing his composure. He relished the tantalizing friction against his throbbing length. Each grind to his loins was a sweet torment.

His hands, large and capable, roamed her body, tracing the curve of her hips and her waist, coming to rest on her breasts. He kneaded them gently as he pulled her down, pushing himself deeper inside her. Their moans merged in the steamy bath, a sinful symphony of pleasure.

"Incredible!"

The delicious tautness building in his lower abdomen as a sign of his impending release inched closer. His movements became erratic; his control slipped out of reach.

"Aaaaah! So... good... I want more!"

She breathed softly, embracing him as she rode him faster. Her head rested on his neck.

"Dafnie."

Unable to hold back his words of praise, Apollo's groan reverberated through the room.

"You're... I can't... hold back. So fucking good... my love."

His voice trailed off as sensations overwhelmed him. His grip on her tightened, his knuckles turning white.

Her body, on the brink of climax, gazed at him, her gaze hazy with desire. She felt her release building, a delicious pressure at the pit of her stomach, a sweet promise of great relief. She reached between them, stimulating her clit as she continued to ride him. A gasp escaped her lips as the first wave of her orgasm washed over her. Her channel trembling with intense pleasure clamping down on his cock.

He watched her with heavy-lidded eyes. His azure stare darkened with lust. The sight of her shuddering figure as she climbed over her peak pushed him over the edge. His hips jerked under her, his release exploding within her as he gritted his teeth and dug his fingers into her fleshy butt.

"Dafnie... Ahh!" Her name was a ragged whisper as he crossed over and found his climax. His body tensed and shuddered beneath hers.

Their climactic bliss washed over them, their breathing labored. Their bodies, entwined and sated, remained in the warm water, basking in the aftermath of their shared pleasure. Apollo cradled her in his arms, his fingers stroking her hair as he kissed her neck lovingly.

"I don't know what made me do something like that."

She confided, appearing shy and out of place.

"I just met you, and... I'm not like that!"

"Shhh! Don't do that to yourself. Just let it be."

His tender words poured out of his heart, still pounding furiously in his chest. A frenetic rhythm only she could incite.

As he enfolded her in a possessive hug, he sensed her body relaxing against him. Her eyelids grew heavy with exhaustion, looking depleted as she nodded off. He stepped back, creating an unwanted distance between them, and finished washing her.

Cradling her delicate form in his arms, he carried her away. He wrapped her in a plush towel, its soft fibers absorbing the droplets that clung to her skin.

The cool air in the room provided a stark contrast to the heated bath, causing her to shiver slightly. Pursuing solace from the chill, she nestled closer to him, seeking the warmth from his embrace. She sighed when she found comfort and closed her eyes.

With a strength contradicting his gentle demeanor, he effortlessly hoisted her in his arms, carrying her back to the bedroom. As he laid her down, the bed's soft sheets enveloped her in a soft shield.

As he slipped into bed beside her, his body radiated a comforting heat that encircled her. Pulling her close against his broad chest, his hand traced patterns on her skin idly, his fingertips dancing over the curve of her waist, down to the delicate swell of her hips.

He then remembered their lovemaking in the bath and how he tightened his grip on her hips. He moved the sheets aside to reveal some nasty bruises on her skin. Misery consumed him for being so harsh with his sweet nymph. He kissed her forehead as he willed his power to heal the ugly marks from her hips. "I'm sorry for treating you so rough. I'll keep my emotions in check so this doesn't happen again."

"You're fine. It's not like I hated it or I'm complaining."

She mumbled as she snuggled deeper into his embrace.

"I feel exhausted…"

"Just sleep. Everything will be okay—you're safe with me. I'll be right here for you." Apollo's tender sigh filled the air in the quiet room.

Each affectionate assurance sent a wave of tenderness over her exhaustion. His warm breath tickled her skin as he whispered into her ear, his voice a soft melody that lulled her into a peaceful rest.

"I vow to protect you against all evil. Dafnie, I promise to always be there for you." The echoes of his words floated around the room like a soothing lullaby.

His statement seemed to ease her weary mind and body into a serene slumber under the heaven of his embrace. Dafnie's breathing became calm and regular. Even though the day was still young, she showed overwhelming signs of exhaustion.

The weight of stress took its toll, and her eyes carried a dull sheen. Fatigue overcame her as her frame slumped in his arms. She needed rest, and he planned to let her sleep until she recovered.

Like a silent guarding, he stayed awake, watching over her. The musky scent of lovemaking lingered in the air alongside the fresh aroma of his beloved's floral fragrances.

Apollo remained mesmerized. His gaze tracked the curve of her peaceful face and the soft rise and fall of her chest as she breathed. He couldn't believe he caught up to her—having her in his warm embrace.

Dafnie's soothing sighs in her rest resonated within him, adding a sweet melody to the sensations he experienced. With a gentle touch, his fingers traced the delicate contours of her face, relishing the silkiness of her skin. The longer he stared at his loving nymph, the deeper the desire, affection, and protectiveness—a foreign experience.

"Fernhoof, show yourself. I have a job for you."

He called out, breaking the silence.

"Yes, Milord! What is the mighty... greatest... magnificent desires?!"

The faun boasted, leaning on a wall, looking graceful and impish.

"Thank you for your loyalty and sarcasm... but I want you to do something. I want you to ask my servants to clean my place and her house. The kitchen and my room are a mess. Here, the entrance and bathroom require some attention. Bring a few items from my closet, and as long as it's casual, I don't care what you pick. I'm planning to spend my nights here with my skittish queen."

"Yes, Milord! Consider it done."

The cheery faun received Apollo's off-handed orders in good humor as he sauntered off. The lesser immortal, used to his master's barrage of instructions, went to please him, the crown prince of Olympus.

Fernhoof's eyes shone with determination.

"Try to be quiet. I want my beloved to relax. I will join her. So, I want you to be at your utmost behavior. Am I clear? What you do reflects on me. I already have lots on my plate."

"I will do my best, my lord!"

"By the way... drop the formalities. You know I hate it."

He waved Fernhoof to leave, and he lay down to rest with his exhausted and very dear darling bride.

Chapter 27

Echoes

As the first rays of sunlight peeked through the window, casting a soft golden glow across the room, Dafnie's eyelids fluttered open. The gentle warmth of the morning sun danced in her eyes, prompting her to wake.

She shifted around, the comforting weight of Apollo's arm draped over her waist, anchoring her into place.

His bare chest pressed against her back, radiating a soothing coziness that seeped into her very essence. Reassuring gratefulness permeated from him to her. When Dafnie woke up after blacking out, a sense of loneliness flowed over her, leaving her with sensations of emptiness.

Now, Apollo gave her the pleasure of being cherished. This ritual became an essential aspect of her mornings, even though they had just met.

Companionship!

But different...

Indeed, she turned into a woman craving a relationship, lusting after his passionate attention. Taking comfort with someone kind in this messed-up world.

Better yet…

He marveled at giving and receiving warm-hearted care.

A mated lover!

With delicate care, she untangled herself from his embrace, her fingertips grazing his arm as she pulled away. Dafnie's heart beat faster. She feared waking him from his slumber as she gazed upon his peaceful sleeping face.

Apollo's serene and perfect features captivated her. A distraction only enhanced by the tranquility that enveloped him. A profound sentiment of gratitude for this rare and precious moment of stillness enclosed her in a caring hold.

In that quiet space, she couldn't help but feel a surge of emotions welling up within her. A strange warmth filled her core, a blend of affection, desire, and an overwhelming, genuine sense of being seen and cherished. A weird experience she had never experienced with a man before.

Lost in her thoughts, she leaned in, planting a feather-light kiss on Apollo's forehead, making sure not to disturb him, before slipping out of the room. Her mind buzzed with anticipation of what really transpired while unconscious.

Donning a loose shirt and comfortable shorts, she padded over to the small table where her tablet lay. It hummed to life as the screen's weak glow illuminated the sitting area.

When she woke up a few days ago, her head did a series of flips and spins at the thought she slipped into a strange coma for two weeks. She became worried about blacking out for no reason and at once wanted to know what happened in the world to devolve in a short amount of time.

She scrolled through various reports and updates. The outdated articles on her screen turned into a disappointing reminder the modern world was long gone. As he mentioned earlier, any updates stopped two weeks ahead of the chaos. It followed the new virus and its mutation until it all ended.

Then, a week ago, the news turned to the bizarre. Reports of odd occurrences, people showing unusual abilities, and sightings of monsters flooded the info outlets. Her brows furrowed as she read them, trying to understand what was happening.

After the bizarre sights, the info flow stopped, enveloping the planet in an unsettling stillness. Her eyes swept across the final broadcast news on her screen. Her heart throbbed with anticipation.

Without realizing it, she played with her pendant, caressing its intricate design. While staring at the necklace, the memories of that strange night resurfaced in her mind. She shook her head and shrugged off the thoughts. Instead, she focused on the current situation and what she needed to do.

Still, Dafnie's unease lingered for a bit longer—and hard to ignore. Her old home vanished into distant memory. She became agitated, thinking about living in a dangerous world. He forced her to live this new reality, but she needed to adapt.

However, a plan formed in her head to get him to clean up his wreck, regardless of his willingness to do so.

She looked at the elegant man, still sleeping, and felt a pang of fear in her chest. Her mind raced with questions about what happened, engrossed in Apollo's serene, sleeping state.

By the looks of it, Apollo preferred to sleep in, surrendering to leisure. "Not a morning person!" A view of divine slumbering masculinity taking most of the bed.

His long golden curls were a wild mess around his handsome face, shimmering in the faint light that trickled in through the window. The sheets clung to his bare form, covering his lithe backside.

His broad shoulders, chiseled with the finesse of a master sculptor, a rhythmical rise and fall, attuned to his breath. The dimpled curve at the small of his back was a tempting sight, which the blankets attempted to hide—in a cheap and lame effort.

She invited the imagination to complete the hidden portrait of perfection. Not that she needed to imagine much. Having seen all of him, she drank his image like water to her thirsty eye. His unforgettable body burned into her memory at this point.

Looking comfortable, his muscular arms folded under his head, used as a pillow for his serene rest. His skin, kissed by the sun, glowed with an ethereal luminescence.

Silence filled the room with the rhythmic lullaby of his soft breath, punctuated by the faint sigh that escaped his lips as the morning light danced over his form.

The setting unfolded as a divine display of sheer power. He appeared almost too flawless to be of this world, lounging in all his naked splendor, a captivating vision.

Wanting to distract herself from the sleeping man, she returned to her search and typed in 'Apollo.' The web came alive with articles and images of his commanding presence.

"These don't look like him at all. He's handsome in person."

Dafnie browsed through the information, trying to put together the pieces.

People depicted him in various ways, presenting different perspectives of his personality. Some showed him as ruthless and tyrannical, while others painted him as a benevolent deity. But the man next to her appeared strange from those immortalized in tales. He looked temperamental and mischievous.

Yes...

But he also seemed kind and caring. His eyes held a wealth of emotion, difficult to decipher. She wondered if the man sleeping on her bed pretended for her sake or if his attentiveness turned out to be genuine.

She became engrossed in her research as he stirred on the bed.

His quick but fluid actions startled her as he took a shocked breath and sat upright like a stiff board.

"Argh! Fuck! She's gone again... Cursed be my luck, damn it!"

Apollo's frustrated groan reverberated throughout the room— his tone heavy with sleep.

"Who's gone?"

His sudden agitation startled her, giving her pause.

✳✳✳

"Shit... I thought... Y-you left... trying to get as far away from me! Fucking hell, I'm sorry..." He had an impeccable physique accompanied by an articulate potty mouth.

"I couldn't sleep, so I grabbed my tablet to read the news and investigate," Dafnie explained as she put the table down.

"What were you researching?" Apollo portrayed his curious nature with a simple question about what was going through his nymph's mind.

She didn't know Apollo's reaction, so she hesitated longer before answering. "Greek mythology. I'm doing some research, acknowledging the relationship I'm in, don't you think?"

"Greek mythology? That's interesting, considering you can ask me anything you want to know—right from the source of truth. There's no need to read about it. Most of the time, it's incomplete or inaccurate. There is too much loose interpretation."

So, her hunch was true...

"It looks like you're no longer trying to hide who you are."

He was the volatile sun god in the flesh and the same one who both blessed and cursed many.

"I want to be honest with the person I care about the most."

He called her by another name earlier. Her hunger to understand her situation got the best of her—to understand the truth.

"You like to live among humans. And..." She returned to her reading to learn more about the enigmatic man. "Daphne... the naiad that tuned into a tree?!"

He swallowed hard before sighing. "That's... right."

After hearing his terse response, she hesitated to dig for more, opting to find her own answers. *A sore subject to inquire, I guess! Maybe I can prod him later?!*

With no other choice, he pieced together the information she sought.

He mentioned Daphne's essence lived within her—her reincarnation. It didn't take her long to look her up and read about her tragic story and how Apollo lost her because of his pride.

"I thought reading about you some more would be best and give me an insight into who you are," she admitted.

"Ah! I see. Then again, you can always come to me for any

information. There is no need to look online and in books. I'll answer any of your questions."

"People's perspectives, mortal or immortal, can be one-sided. Besides, chronicling your exploits according to your perspective is only convenient for you. Now, will you be truthful because the mischievous glint in your eyes tells me otherwise?"

Dafnie countered, quick to catch Apollo's slight emotional cues.

"Of course! Ask me anything, but first, come to bed and lie with me."

He lured in with an enticing tone. There was no mistaking his lascivious intentions, which clung to the air like a heady pheromone.

His seductive voice sent shivers down to Dafnie's core. She took a deep breath to calm her emotions. He tried to provoke her, and she was letting him affect her.

"I see you've had many lovers and children. Why me?"

She stood to move closer to him.

He sighed as his body relaxed before her eyes.

"As you can see, none of my love affairs have worked out. The only affair that somehow managed out was with Thalia, but I wouldn't consider that a flourishing relationship."

A sad mask replaced his handsome features as his eyes turned unfocused and thoughtful.

"We didn't have romantic feelings for each other. We both didn't understand how we always ended up having sex. Also, our children didn't bring us closer. Just... fuck friends, now that I think about it."

He pointed out as he patted a spot next to him. "Please sit by me?"

She thought for a few minutes, watching his reaction before making her way to bed and sitting beside him. He didn't waste any time encircling her waist with his powerful arms and pulling her to him.

"What are you doing?" She jumped—somewhat—at his sudden move, but the comforting feel of his arms around her eased her startle. She turned her head to meet his gaze, a soft smile on his lips.

"I'm quite fascinated by you, Dafnie. You're not like the Daphne from my past, but in other ways, you are like her. I can savor her essence in you, but you also have a different, more powerful scent that drives me fucking mad. So much so that I want to stop this conversation and take you over and over until we faint from exhaustion."

She gasped, blushing as she played the scene in her mind.

"Oh, you naughty woman! So, you want me to take you nonstop? I can make that happen... Mark my words," He whispered in Dafnie's ear, sending shivers through her body.

Apollo's hand slid along the smooth curve of her hip. His touch was skilled and practiced in the art of seduction, provoking her to respond to his appetite. She was powerless against the raw desire within her, leaving her wondering how she became this needy.

"Can you stop talking that way? It's making me uncomfortable."

"Are you certain, Dafnie?" He asked, the strain unmistakable in his voice. When she nodded, he let out a dejected sigh. "As you wish, my love."

His tone carried a seductive allure that put her in a trance.

With a sudden rush of boldness, she pulled herself out of

Apollo's tempting grasp and sat. She turned her gaze to him, her eyes glittering with hesitation and excitement.

"Apollo," she began, her tone soft yet firm, "I think we need to talk. I have too many questions, and you're trying to distract me. Please get dressed."

His brows furrowed at her demand. The hasty shift in her demeanor surprised him, and he tried to decipher the meaning behind her words. "But Dafnie..." he started before shutting his mouth.

The sun god sighed, finally conceding to her request. He rose from the bed, his figure casting a long, dark shadow across the room that amplified his imposing physique. He moved around the room to a bag she did not recognize to get something to wear.

The silence between them was thick. The sight of the immortal, wounded yet magnificent, stirred feelings in her. But for now, she held her ground, her mind steadfast.

Determined to have a serious conversation with the man who aided her and then devoured her—still enjoying a delicious ache of her pussy.

She took a moment to gather her thoughts as he dressed in a simple T-shirt and jeans. She realized she had never spoken to him.

When he moved in, she stayed away from him until now—only after an emergency. They only exchanged words through a note after the gift he sent her.

The necklace.

Shaking her head, she patted the spot next to her to break the awkward silence.

"Come and sit by me. I'm hoping you'll behave after putting

on some clothes. Although my expectations are not high as I try to have a serious conversation."

Without budging a single inch and giving him a square stare, she spoke her mind.

Apollo's momentary surprise caused him to comply as he moved beside her on the bed, hugging her waist and dragging her toward him. He looked expectantly at her, waiting for her to begin the exchange.

"I want to talk about the necklace you gifted me."

For some odd reason, her voice trembled.

Chapter 28

Necklace and Tattoo

Apollo's tension softened as he recalled the day he gave her the necklace.

"It's a symbol of love and protection, Dafnie," he explained. "I wanted you to have something that reminded you of me and my promise to keep you safe."

"Why must you protect me? Is it like a craving or something?!"

Her insatiable curiosity seemed to compel her to dig deeper to find the truth, and he loved it.

He hesitated for a brief moment, took a deep breath, and answered.

"I moved to Phoebus Groove to escape the city because I liked my peaceful life. But when I came here, this pull invaded my existence, leading me toward you. I couldn't explain it, but..."

His eyes fixed on Dafnie as he unraveled a fragmented and complex account.

"I've lived among mortals for decades. It's not that I dislike humans, but I must confess that they don't rank high on my list of favorite beings at this point. It's only because of the muses' diligent work here that they have outstanding talent in the arts, and that pleases me. I even started a successful business in the music industry, but..."

He paused for a quick breath before he continued. "I became cynical, I guess."

Her eyes betrayed her curiosity as if she wanted to discover what had really happened, like a puzzle that needed solving. However, she restrained herself from interrupting or rushing him. *You're still the same, my enchanting huntress—observant and cautious. I love you more for it.*

His sheepish smile appeared unannounced. "I felt empty, like something was missing, which led to..."

"Which led to what?"

"I'm regretting what I did. Deeply! I... don't want to talk about it right this moment."

His confession hung heavy in the room, his words echoing with a deep-set remorse.

"My sister Artemis had a plan, Dafnie," he started, his voice a thoughtful murmur.

"She used you and demands I make amends on the matter. You were merely a means to an end for her. But I'm wiser now. They'll have to go through me first."

He continued as his hand brushed against the soft skin of her cheek.

"From the minute I moved into the neighborhood, there was this pull, an unseen force that drew me to you. Fate binding us with a strong knot ties our destinies."

His eyes bore into hers, his gaze brimming with a raw intensity that made Dafnie blush, giving her an attractive, subtle flush. "Before we even met, for some weird reason, I yearned for you."

Apollo confessed—his voice a whisper.

"In my heart, I knew you were special. It's hard to describe, but this inexplicable instinct drove me to gift you with this necklace. I reached out to the jeweler with a last-minute request, which they accommodated. Like a spur-of-the-moment purchase, you know? I can't really explain why I went. Even though I have the gift of prophecy, I can't see your future. That's just how it's always been, even back in your old life... before you slipped from my grasp..."

"Why do you feel this way for Daphne... and me?"

"Crush! You were my first love, and Daphne never even knew it. I regretted my cowardice, always watching from afar, not speaking to her—to your past self."

He chuckled at his foolishness.

"But now that I found you again, we can be together in this life."

As Apollo smiled at her, his face lit up with a mixture of hope and longing, creating an atmosphere of anticipation.

Dafnie's face of surprise gave him pause as she gazed into his eyes. He couldn't help but grapple with this attraction for her. Everything fell right into place with her around.

"Still. Why me? Why did you choose me? I bet you had your pick of many available women. What's so special about me?"

Her voice, tinged with doubt and insecurity, unearthed the echoes of her past failures.

He needed to apologize and settle the differences among them.

"Because to me, you are dear and cherished, Dafnie. You are not a pawn in Artemis's plan or whoever is behind all this. You were... I don't know, other than you'll play an important part in my life. I'm sorry! As I mentioned, my foresight doesn't work when you're in it. I guess I'm not being honest and losing my powers because of it." His unwavering gaze never left hers.

He traced the contours of her face, his touch a comforting warmth against her skin.

"I'm certain Artemis is using you for her schemes. But to me... you're the queen I yearned for, the one who fascinates me and sparks a yearning unlike anything."

Apollo's voice trembled with an undercurrent of emotion. "And my love, my connection, it's only grown stronger these last two days. You're not just a piece of Artemis's plan. You're a part of my soul. And I want you to understand that and experience it. The pendant I sent you was a gesture of my affection and my desire to protect you."

"Before I blacked out, I felt the necklace grow warm against my skin." She looked around the room as if looking for a lifeline of understanding. "Like coming to life, comforting me, and reassuring me."

She played with the charm as she remembered the sensation.

"Do you think it's related to why I lost consciousness that long?"

"Maybe my will safeguard you affected your body. Other than guessing, I don't know what happened."

After a deep cleansing sigh, more confused than before, his confession slipped from his lips.

"Others may have meddled, but there's no proof."

He reflected, his fingers tracing patterns on her arm.

"But I can't be certain. My sister is involved in this, and she said as much the last time I saw her. I believe she put a spell on the pendant. Other gods have intervened and altered my magic. I can't tell for sure."

Tugging his hair back, he paced around the room, trying to make sense of everything. *Trapped! Caged! Damn it!* He paused for a bit to calm his nerves before turning to admire his beloved.

"To me, anyone is a suspect. The wearers of the other jewelry I gifted haven't had similar experiences. She did something," he explained.

Their conversation paused as her attention drifted to her stomach. A low growl disrupted their intimate exchange. Her cheeks glowed with embarrassment as a soft gasp fluttered from her generous lips.

"Are you hungry?"

Apollo's amusement burst with an excited crescendo, giving him a twinkle in his eyes.

✳✳✳

Dafnie nodded, a sheepish smile tugging at the corners of her lips.

"I haven't had breakfast in over two weeks, so I'm pretty hungry."

Apollo assisted her to her feet and led her to the kitchen. The room's layout bore a subtle resemblance to his.

"It seems like I'm cooking in my house. Why is that?"

He looked in her fridge and noted her fresh and unspoiled food. It seemed time stopped ticking, refusing to continue with their only task while she slept this entire time.

"Mrs. Lewis, the earlier owner of your house, helped remodel my home. I wonder if they're okay."

She mused about the couple who were like family to her.

"The Lewises are fine. Their house is away from crowds—secluded and protected. The same goes for that neighbor who used to come here all the time. Danielle. I believe that's her name. Her family is doing okay—I believe. And it looks like she is involved with the man who helps her parents. By now, they've learned to stay safe and that the creatures only come out at night."

He dismissed the situation, disinterested, as he searched for ingredients for their breakfast.

"How do you know all this?"

"The future of people is clear to me, except for yours. It's one of my many gifts. Now, do you have any preferences for what you want to eat? I promised I'm an excellent cook."

A mischievous grin crept on his lips as he gathered the cutting board, a knife, and a bowl.

"I'm not a picky eater as long as it's not drugged."

A teasing yet knowing smile displayed on her lips.

Looking a bit awkward around Dafnie, he cut some vegetables, trying to avoid her eyes. He regretted his actions.

"I promise I'll not use that cheap trick on you again. Yeah! I'm temperamental, spiteful, and a jerk, but you mean the world to me, and I respect your wishes. The moment I met you, shock haywire my brain... Something base and primal woke from within me that made me lose control. My desire to have you in my life led me to behave irrationally. I'm... sorry for doing that to you... Shit! I'm acting like a fool."

"Why would you say that? You've been nothing but kind and caring toward me. You even saved me the other night."

She drummed her fingers as she tsked her displeasure.

"Although your actions after that were less than honorable. I might reciprocate by my volition if you seduced me without your special blend of dubious herbs."

Her melodious chuckle permeated the room with light-heartedness.

"At first, I would play hard to get, but your unmistakable charm would have captured my heart in the end. Still, I'm afraid my resistance would have been walking in the park for you with your charming attitude and experience."

He chuckled with a hint of arrogance in his good humor.

"I'll keep that in mind for future reference, then. Now, let's cook and check if my non-spiked culinary skills can win you over."

He continued to prepare their breakfast as if nothing happened.

She sat on the kitchen island, captivated by his skillful movements. The sizzle of the eggs and vegetables filled the room with a comforting aroma, and she watched as he moved with ease, his muscles rippling under his shirt. The sight made her blush, as the memory of their fiery encounters was still fresh in her mind.

"Can you tell me about the tattoo on your arm? When we first met, it covered your entire arm, but now it seems to have shrunk. I sense power from it."

He toasted the bread on the pan, breaking the uncomfortable silence between them.

She peeked at her tattoo, still covering half of her forearm. This odd development disturbed her.

"I have no clue what's going on. This design is special to me. I got it after my parents died..."

Dafnie paused, a saddened look tarnishing her attractive features.

"I... got something to remember them by."

She started playing with a random, likely non-existent flint on the counter's surface.

"They used to own a bay tree farm. The company is a big supplier of spices to exclusive restaurants, but after their death, I couldn't run it alone. Since I was their only child, the entire business passed to me. So, I had no one to turn to for help. Left with no choice, I hired someone to manage the homestead."

A heavy lump seemed to settle on her shoulders as she slid through the lyrics of her memories.

"I'm still the owner, but the new CEO manages everything at the estate. Well, at least he used to... I don't know how they're doing now," she explained.

He became cautious before saying anything. The last thing he wanted was a misunderstanding between them.

"The vision is unclear, but they'll manage. Their survival is in fate's archives."

Reaching to her wrist, he traced the pattern that appeared to have a life of its own.

"It's a beautiful tattoo. The fact you are a keeper of the laurel tree is an honorable duty. It's my most precious and sacred plant. Your family's choosing to cultivate and protect it celebrates me... and you. Very pleasing, indeed!"

Apollo murmured, his voice full of emotion as he worked on the coffee next.

"I'm sure your parents would be proud of your

accomplishments. Now..." He turned to point at her arm. "That tattoo holds a strong protection spell."

Apollo's eyebrows furrowed, his thoughts navigating the rapids of his conflicts.

"Where did you get that?"

She froze, thinking for a moment before answering.

"I got it from a parlor run by a couple. They suggested this design after I told them about my parents. However, I wanted the design on the inside of my wrist. It hurt like hell to put it there, but..."

Dafnie paused for a minute, but as she was about to continue, an unexpected sound filled the kitchen. A whisper of the wind, followed by a bright flash, caused her to turn toward the source of the commotion.

Chapter 29

Ambrosia

Apollo turned to point at her arm. His eyebrows furrowed as he connected with the design's intricate enchantment.

"Someone imbued your tattoo with a protection spell. Where did you get it?"

Dafnie froze, taking a moment before answering. "I got it from a parlor run by a couple. They suggested this design after I told them about my parents. I wanted something small, on the inside of my wrist, to remember them by, but..."

She paused. As she was about to continue, an unexpected sound filled the kitchen. A whisper of the wind, followed by a bright flash, caused her to turn toward the source of the disturbance.

"Hebe?!"

His calm but unsettled tone took a menacing cadence as the Greek goddess of youth materialized out of thin air.

The cupbearer of the gods, in all her youthful divine beauty, held a golden goblet brimming with a radiant liquid. Her eyes bore a stern and commanding quality, stressing the idea her sudden visit carried great significance.

"Morning, sun god Apollo! I have your daily dose of ambrosia heavenly drink here, and it's from Father."

Her voice echoed authority and urgency. "He insists you imbibe this harvest."

Apollo's eyes narrowed, apprehensive. He was always suspicious when his father acted too kind.

"But why this vintage?"

His gaze shifted between Hebe and the chalice.

"You know I don't like how you or Father make the nectar and specifically ask for the fruit so I can brew it myself."

Hebe shrugged, her expression calm despite the serious undertone of the situation.

"It's not my place to question Father's orders, Apollo. You know that..."

The fleeting answer twirled around the air as she held the cup toward him.

"For now, I'm not allowed to supply you with the fruit. It's best if you drink this elixir. Our sovereign ruler, Zeus, made this especially for you. You must drink it."

The gravity of the circumstances sank in. He glanced at his beloved, who looked perplexed before he took the chalice from Hebe's hands—reluctance to be fucking damn.

"Is he trying to kill me?"

The room fell into an intense silence as he brought the goblet to his lips, hesitating, waiting for an answer.

"No! Our Great Father, Zeus, will never do such a thing to

his favorite son, even though he doesn't express it. He has his reasons for doing this."

Hebe's vehement reverence rang through the quiet room.

He stared at the rich golden nectar shimmering under the kitchen lights. He looked at Dafnie, concern and worry etched on her face. If someone meant him ill will, he would not go down—that was a given.

Despite his seething anger, he refrained from challenging the goddess's words.

"Fuck it! Fine!"

The moment the celestial drink touched his lips, his face softened, and an undeterred exhale escaped. Its tantalizing sweet aroma was heavenly. He drank the divine elixir in one big gulp, his Adam's apple bobbing with a seductive bounce with each swallow.

As soon as he did, his expression morphed into one of pure bliss and ecstasy. His eyes closed instinctively, realizing the only experience that surpassed this reaction was driving his cock hard and good into his precious huntress. He let out another sigh, this time of contentment.

"Only one thing can surpass the effects of Ambrosia."

"What?!"

Both his lover and Hebe asked at the same time, unaware of his blissful state.

"Don't mind me."

When he opened his azure eyes again, Dafnie stared at him. A faint mist clouded his vision. A shimmering golden hue, the exact color as the nectar he had just consumed, and looked like little suns filled with life.

Hebe smiled at him knowingly as she received her chalice. "My work here is done. I shall be on my way."

"Wait!" he snapped, stopping Hebe before she disappeared into thin air. "You mentioned Father has his reasons for making this vintage, especially for me. Could you... elaborate?"

Hebe hesitated for a moment prior to answering, choosing her words with the utmost care. "We've been watching you, Apollo. We know your hardships, and we're concerned for you. With this, our father is ensuring you and your lover are safe to fulfill what's required of you."

"How will this protect those I love?" he challenged.

"That he did not say, but there is a purpose for everything that he does," Hebe answered. Her cryptic statement was hard to decipher.

"I fucking hate it when you talk in riddles, my dear sister."

"And you need to learn to read between the lines."

"Fuck, again?! Fine, I will take none of your banter. Now, before you leave... I want you to pass on a message to our father. In the future, I'll drink Zeus's elixir only if I can have the fruit. I have a lifelong hunting companion that needs it. My hawk is special to me."

Apollo's demand, his voice firm, brought forth his undeniable status. He stood above Hebe, not the other way around.

"I will convey your desires to Father, who will consider your request. I will say my goodbyes now."

As quick as she appeared, Hebe disappeared in a swift flash, leaving him and Dafnie once again alone in the kitchen.

His eyes locked with Dafnie's. "Well, that was unexpected. My father can be really... unpredictable."

With a soothing murmur, he tried to regain the normalcy they enjoyed before Hebe's sudden intrusion.

"Now, where were we?"

A glint of undeniable mischief lit up his eyes as he returned to their unfinished breakfast. The aroma of coffee mingled with the fading divine fragrance of the heavenly food.

Only for a moment, life seemed almost normal.

Apollo approached Dafnie, his presence drawing her in as he stood facing her, his arms wrapping around her waist. "So where were we?"

The husky whispered into her ear and made her tremble, placing a light kiss on her soft lips.

Her heart fluttered under his touch when an inevitable smile graced her features. "We were talking about the tattoo," she replied, tilting her head to look at him.

"Hmm, yes. Let's continue with that... but later. I've found something much more delicious."

His intense and seductive tone seeped from his mouth as he trailed kisses toward her generous lips.

He leaned in, his gaze locked onto Dafnie's, and without a second thought, he captured her lips in a deep, passionate kiss. His hands traced the curves of her hour-shaped frame, one hand at her nape, the other resting low on her hip, pulling her closer.

His tongue delved into her mouth, tasting her. Their breaths mingled; their heartbeats echoed in the enclosed space. He groaned. The flavor of her lips, the feel of her body against his, the intoxicating scent of her skin. Everything shot up to overwhelming heights to the point of perfection.

His fingers moved, exploring, caressing. He felt Dafnie gasp as his hand slipped under her shirt, his fingers skimming the smooth skin of her abdomen. The flicker of electricity between them grew, the air encircling them thickening, buzzing with raw passion and desire. The sun god's kisses became more urgent and hungrier.

His hands wandered higher, his fingertips gliding over a waiting breast that reacted to his touch. Dafnie's sharp intake of breath was all the encouragement he needed to lose himself in her enchanting essence. He was losing his mind with just a kiss.

Apollo's hand teased the little nipple, inciting her to wrap her legs around his waist. Her hands traveled to his hair, her fingers tangling in his golden locks. Her hand on him sent an electric zap through his soul, bringing forth a delicious fog. The way her body shifted against his became an intoxicating mist. Apollo groaned, his brain spiraling into a haze of pleasure, his senses consumed by Dafnie.

The room's temperature reached its boiling point. Apollo's hand moved in search of Dafnie's breast, her soft gasps echoing in his ears. His head was a whirl of sensations, every nerve ending screaming her name. But just as he picked his love up from the counter to take her to her room, a sudden grumbling noise interrupted them. He pulled back, a puzzled look on his face.

"Huh!" He uttered in askance, the echo of the strange sound still lingering in his ears.

Her face turned an intense shade of red as embarrassment plastered across her cheeks. "I-I... umm... think that was my stomach..."

Her stutter came as a surprise, her voice a whisper as she tried to cover her face.

He blinked twice, processing what had just happened. A chuckle escaped his lips, the harmony rumbling deep in his chest. "You must be starving, love."

His azure eyes twinkling with amusement.

"Yes, I am," she mumbled, burying her face in his chest to hide her mortification.

He cupped her cheek, tilting her head up so she could look at him. "Well then, let's serve you your breakfast. We wouldn't want to starve, my little nymph, would we?"

He grinned, heart filled with affection, as he returned to being the dotting mate.

She slid off the counter, her cheeks flushed from their passionate kiss. With hesitation, she reached into the cupboard, fumbling for the smooth surface of the plates. The cold stoneware felt somewhat grounding, but Apollo's touch on her skin still sent shivers down her spine.

Suddenly, a comforting heat soaked over her back, making her skin prickle with expectation.

As she turned around, she saw Apollo leaning against the cabinet, his blue eyes trained on her. A small smile pulled at the corner of his lips, a glint of satisfaction in his eyes. He was aware of his effect on her. He moved to her side, his light chest igniting flames over her skin again.

Their eyes locked, a silent oath hanging heavy in the air. "Breakfast is ready!"

His fingers ran down her arm, leaving a trail of goosebumps in its wake. His touch was electricity, sparking an intense need that reflected in Dafnie's eyes. "And it's getting cold."

His hands found their way to her waist, taking the plates and pulling her against his hard body.

"I promise the food is delicious. Simple but tasty." He pressed his lips to her neck. His whisper sent shivers throughout her frame. Apollo's hands roamed lower, exploring the curves on her backside before turning away, moving toward the stove, and serving their morning meal for them.

She took a deep breath to calm her raging heart. "You're a tease. You're aware of that and like to use it as a weapon. Well... at least you know how to use it against me to disarm me."

Her voice trailed off by the end as she composed herself, her fingers brushing, grazing the tattoo on her wrist.

With their meal served, they made their way to the table. He pulled out a chair for his beloved, and as they settled down, their breakfast spread out before them like an Olympian feast. A bit more at ease with their comfortable intimacy, the shy lump lodged in her throat came loose. Apollo's intense gaze no longer carried its usual overwhelming imposition.

"So, about that design." His soft voice filled with intrigue as he pushed for more. "It possesses a protective spell. What do you think it means?"

She glanced at her wrist, hesitating, prior to speaking again.

"It started glowing and moving when I went to gather supplies. While in danger, it covered my entire arm, but once you rescued me, it shrunk to just my forearm. Still, it's not back to normal, though."

"How big was it?"

"At first, the pattern was just on the inside of my wrist—a small thing..." Her voice trailed off. He reached across the table, taking her hand in his. Tracing the outlines of her tattoo with his thumb, he studied its outline.

"I'm sensing a sudden shift in its energy—not a terrible change. I wonder what triggered it?"

He caressed a tender yet ticklish spot on Dafnie's wrist.

"I hope you like what I made."

As soon as he finished, he grabbed the fork and ate, flashing one of his disarming smiles.

She smiled before joining him. "Mmmm! This is delicious." Her eyes widened as she wolfed down the rest of her meal. He decided not to press on about her peculiar tattoo and enjoyed the moment in silence.

Little did Apollo realize his kiss held a drop of ambrosia. The weak stimulant in the elixir gave the sun god the urge to enjoy his beloved. When their lips met, she swallowed traces of the aphrodisiac, making her react with want and leading her to deepen their kiss and swallow the drop of nectar that seemed meant for her.

Unbeknownst to them, this was all part of Zeus's intricate plan—aside from everyone else's plans—to bend the Crown Prince to his will. His father wanted his son to obey, following his every command without hesitation or question.

"Fucking foolish desire to please your family!"

"Beg your pardon?!"

"Nothing, my love! You just gained a fucked up family. But now... I just want to throw you on a bed and have my way with you."

Chapter 30

Unsettling

"I've been awake for a week, and still no answers. I can't find any explanation for my weird coma. On top of that, time seemed to stop while I slept. That's so strange. Why's this happening to me?!"

An overabundance of possibilities flooded her mind as she gnawed on her thumb—another nasty childhood habit when nervous.

Despite his best efforts, Apollo couldn't uncover any solutions —at least not the ones that pleased him. He tried to read her necklace and tattoo but couldn't. He then resorted to asking one of his companions, Fernhoof, to investigate the matter.

When she first met the immortal, she couldn't believe her eyes. A handsome male, a cross between a goat and a man, barged into her life and treated her like...

Royalty.

A light blush colored her cheeks whenever he came by to help with her needs.

Fernhoof called her lady or sometimes addressed her as queen. The dotting guy always made her life comfortable despite the circumstances. She never expected to meet someone like Fernhoof—served with such devotion and respect.

Not in her wildest dreams.

And forever etched in her mind.

However, their relationship faced many hiccups when they first met, and it was anything but ideal. Their shocking first meeting turned disastrous. The male didn't enjoy being stared at, plus she asked the most outrageous questions—a momentary brain fart.

But worse, Apollo found their encounter hilarious.

But who could blame her?

Encountering the handsome mythical creature took her breath away and weakened her knees.

And loosened her tongue.

But the faun soon warmed up to her. The forest immortal's charming smile and appreciation captivated her. Soon, the faun appreciated her sincere attempts to appreciate him on a deeper level. Fernhoof showed her he sympathized with her, and their bond grew a little each day.

Then, the day came when the immortal opted for an agreeable attitude—a welcomed familiarity. An almost borderline fixation on Apollo's approval and Dafnie's comfort, which she liked. She valued the effort.

The magic in the stories of both immortals filled her with hope for an exciting life. The faun roamed the heavens and the mortal world easily and unnoticed, searching for information. To find answers about the added charm put on her necklace and the reason for the tattoo's power, their quest to find answers just started.

But Fernhoof always came back empty-handed.

The situation developed behind his back and unfolded an exciting turn of affairs. Everyone involved in altering the necklace's blessing and the strange enchantment of her tattoo disappeared or didn't want to explain their motives.

So, passive tension ran high at all times.

"Apollo seems to be in his element—used to accustomed doted upon."

Though her lover hid behind a lively demeanor, she sensed the underlying stress.

"When events don't go his way, or answers aren't forthcoming, it puts him in a mood. He becomes erratic during moments like these—so keep an eye on him."

"I will!"

He became frustrated, and his discontent grew into a palpable inconvenience. When things didn't go his way or when others messed with his affairs, he didn't like not remaining in control. His gentle and caring attention to her wishes put her front and center. But his displeasure was a challenge to ignore whenever Fernhoof returned with no news on the issue.

Guilt settled over her as she realized she rattled the faun's peace and put him in a disagreeable mood.

"I'm sorry this is happening because of me. I didn't mean any of this and for you to be irritated."

She looked at him with a heaviness in her heart, and her expression reflected in her eyes, mirroring her conflict.

He stopped playing his guitar and looked at her with a soft

gaze.

"It's not your fault, Dafnie. You didn't ask for any of this, and I promise I'll find the answers for you."

"For some reason…" Dafnie's words flowed with utmost care —hesitant not to disturb their relative peace. Her godly lover's mood sizzled like the celestial body he lorded after. "You're mad. Why?"

Her timeless lover sighed, putting his guitar down.

"I'm sorry if I've been short with Fernhoof or you. It's just that… this situation concerns me more than I want to admit. It bothers me that after I blessed your necklace, someone messed with it and altered my gift to fit their plans. That's what annoys me the most. It puts you in danger. They attacked you because of my carelessness."

He finished, moving closer and giving her a tender embrace.

She understood he tried his best to protect her. For convenience, he made sure both houses kept a shielding spell. He also put a protective enchantment on a trail that ran behind their homes and ended by the creek. She took a deep breath as she returned for a hug. A sense of peace washed over her like a soothing balm.

After a while, Apollo retraced his steps back to the sofa, a gentle smile on his face. He reached out for his guitar. Shortly after, his fingers danced across the strings, filling the room with calming melodies.

She sat beside him with silent reverence, her eyes gazing out the window, watching the still lingering chaos of the world outside. Her heart pounded in her chest as she saw a horrifying view.

Out in the bright, fresh morning, in the middle of the eerily quiet street. The disfigured body of a creature lay discarded on the floor in a contorted position—in a pool of putrid blood and pus.

Dafnie's stomach churned at the sight of the grotesque form. The body's torn flesh, the gashes revealing bones and guts, were a grim testament to a savage attack by another, much more powerful beast roaming their surroundings.

"I hate that damn disgusting scene."

Even though she rarely cussed, her shaking hands and tight chest led her to lose her stern control. The situation called for her anger.

"Oh, my dear nymph! Did my potty mouth fucking rub on you?"

His amusement, which made him look part taken aback, filled her with overwhelming warmth. Her tummy tightened up, and butterflies tickled her nervousness.

Apollo cares about me.

He dots on me.

A mighty god... risks everything for me—a mere human.

Her mind, inflated by the vestiges of love, floated in the clouds with passion. He learned early on that she minded everything she said.

Dafnie's breath hitched, and her fingers instinctively curled into fists. The twisted horror of the scene was appalling, yet she couldn't tear her gaze away.

She absorbed all the gruesome details, her thoughts twisting and turning with questions and dread. The memory of the creature's horrific injuries would haunt her dreams tonight.

"The mess we find every morning is revolting and sickening. It's been happening more often for the past three days. Sure... a week ago we learned they would eat their dead... but now it seems they're attacking each other."

A bitter hint of squeamishness trailed up to her throat before she turned away from the disgusting sight. Suddenly, a chilling realization swept over Dafnie.

"It makes me sick and concerned."

Putting his guitar away, he drifted to the window to better understand the events befalling on the street.

"The number of mutilated corpses keeps increasing per day..."

His gaze took on a glossy shine as his sharp stare followed the unfolding incident.

"While scouting, Fernhoof found many bodies scattered around the streets. Not even carrions would eat their flesh. He also mentioned that it's becoming more dangerous at night."

"Do you think we are safe here?"

Then she remembered Apollo was a powerful god—a hunter.

No matter what, he dodged danger and survived, defying and sidestepping death at every turn. Indeed, he was a resilient and mighty—yet imperfect—immortal who fell hard for her. His devotion meant he would give up everything just to be with her.

"W-would I be fine? I have no power and am at your mercy. I can't..."

The reverberating pause turned into an unsettling expectation that caused more stress than comfort.

"Other than street smarts and being a fast runner, I don't think I can do much."

She moved beside the god, looking out the window, and stood motionless. Worse! Her rigid frame, her gaze unblinking, imprisoned her to the dreadful point. The eerie sight of the creature's gnarled and mutilated body and the gruesome end it met was a stark reminder of the monstrous horrors lurking outside.

Amid the horror, she found herself consumed by a suffocating bleakness and dread. With each passing moment, her world seemed to spiral into a chilling nightmare, entrapping her within her soul. A paralyzing fear gripped her mind.

Panic attack!

Ever since the death of her parent in that fatal accident, she grappled with anxiety and confusion. Most of the time, meditation helped her control her stress, but now she fell into the grasp of uncertainty. In a flash, an invasive sensation shook as darkness crept through her consciousness. Her heart pounded in her chest, and her breath came in quick gasps.

"Dafnie... my nymph! Please look at me and try to calm down."

Apollo's concern became a palpable impression as his eyes measured her condition. He moved closer and picked her up in his powerful arms. Making his way to the sofa, he laid her on the soft pillows with the gentleness of an experienced sculptor molding raw clay. He placed a reassuring hand on her forehead, trying to ground her.

"I-I... c-can't... b-breathe..." she choked out between sobs. "T-too m-much... to think..."

After witnessing her distress, worry marred his features. His protective nature kicked into overdrive as he slumped into a less imposing stance.

"Hush! Shh… shh… shh… Look at me, Dafnie. Breathe… in and out, my love."

He stroked her hair, attempting to calm her.

"Focus on my voice… in and out…"

She closed her eyes, and when she opened them again, she focused on his heaven-like eyes. His eyes reminded her of when she used to climb and reach the crest many weeks prior. His eyes aroused the freedom she experienced every time she reached the summit and lay on the ground, admiring the sky while soaking in the sun.

The azure of his eyes

"In and out…" Apollo's lullaby-like tone put her at ease. She calmed down.

Attempting to center herself, she leaned into his embrace and focused on his tone and calming presence. She took deep breaths, sensing the tension and anxiety seeping out of her body. After a few minutes, she settled down and wiped away her tears.

"Am I going to live trapped in this house for the rest of my life? To spend my days fearing the day they will break in and kill us?"

She looked at him, her voice laced with pain.

"I'm scared! And I don't know how much more of this I can take. We ought to get out and do something."

Apollo's expression softened as he looked at her, his hand caressing her cheek.

"Shh… Dafnie, look at me."

His whisper, a balm to her troubles, harbored a sweet melody to Dafnie's ears.

"No, my dear nymph. You will not live caged like a little bird, my queen."

His palm cradled her face, protective and gentle. An affectionate thumb rubbed away the stray tears that escaped her eyes.

"Rest easy, my love! There is no need to worry because everything will turn out fine. Those who try to harm you will deal with me."

Apollo's intense gaze held a confidence that melted any uncertainty away.

Driven by impulsiveness, he revealed his desire to shield her from the horrors surrounding them. When he pressed his lips against hers, he poured his hope to bring solace for the two of them.

Since their fateful encounter a week ago, their bodies have united several times a day without fail, strengthening their bond and making it even more profound.

She savored the overwhelming satisfaction of finding his lover from his lips. And it became clear he didn't intend to stop their tight connection ever.

Never!

But at that point, his demeanor held a yearning to ease Dafnie's troubled mind with his touch and presence, erasing the haunting image and robbing her of hope.

Slowly, he bent down, his lips hovering over hers. He waited for a moment as if asking for her permission. Her eyes sparkled as she leaned up to close the distance. Their mouths met in a soft, slow caress of their tongues, tingling sensations spreading throughout their bodies.

His hands moved to the back of her neck, tugging her closer as he deepened the kiss, his tongue teasing her lips open to explore the sweetness only found within. Forgetting everything that oppressed her, Dafnie heightened the ardor of their exchange, eliciting a contented moan from him.

"Hmm! I believe my nymph is needy today," he teased.

She gasped, her fingers clutching his shirt, pulling him tighter in her desperate embrace.

"Stop being a wiseass, and don't stop kissing me. I desire the distraction. Please!" She begged as she redoubled their kiss.

As they embraced, her lover's body radiated a scorching heat, his wild heartbeat against her chest grounding her to the moment. His hands roamed her form, every stroke electrifying. He moved down, his lips trailing kisses down her neck, his teeth nipping and biting at her skin, drawing soft moans from her lips.

His gentle kiss revealed he would fight for her sake—that she wasn't alone in this nightmare. She found comfort and solace in Apollo's touch as his love delivered a lifeline to this horror.

Chapter 31

The sunset appeared on the horizon, casting a warm glow. The red and orange hue of dusk enveloped the room. Apollo slowly stirred from his short yet invigorating nap, tightening his embrace around Dafnie's waist.

He and his beloved remained intertwined in each other's arms, her face buried in his chest, basking in the tranquility of their shared rest.

She calmed down after her crisis—at last.

Now, he must show her the beauty lingering in the world and distract her from the pain. He wanted nothing more than to give her pleasure and have her focus on him instead. At the very least, he ached for a timid smile from her.

And create beautiful memories together.

He brushed away stray hairs from her pretty face with a tender touch. He loved his nymph so much that containing himself came with its challenges. Even before Eros's golden arrow afflicted him, he always treasured Daphne. Once he met her reincarnation, Dafnie, his intense love and lust for her resurfaced to torture him.

He thought her spirit disappeared after transforming into a laurel tree, but somehow, her spiritual energy survived. There was no other explanation—her parents must have done something. They saved her essence and kept it until now, just as he released a calamity and started the apocalypse and the end of times for mortals.

On that fateful evening after the attack, his heart filled with sorrow. His century-old willpower spiraled out of control as his mind unraveled. Disbelief rooted him on the spot when memories of the day he lost Daphne entrapped him in prison made of uncertainties. Despair turned his blood run cold. Rage colored his vision red when the creature chased after his beloved.

Her life was beyond valuable to him. If anyone meant her harm, they would deal with him first. He carried his fierce determination to safeguard his cherished huntress like a shield. And like armor, he would defend her without hesitation.

She became his sole focus and new purpose in life.

She is now and forever mine. Her laughter, her touch, her scent—all mine!

An animalistic instinct surged to the surface, shutting his eyes to rational thinking.

He adored Dafnie throughout the day, losing count of the times they reached their climax and stored to greater heights. But he only hoped to become Dafnie's balm for her battered spirit.

His determination to create a sanctuary—a cocoon of pure safety for his bewitching lover. An escape from the haunting terrors that loomed beyond her refuge. Their bodies still intertwined, pausing for a moment and savoring the delicious current cursing through them before continuing their passionate affair.

No matter what, he still wished for more.

His fingers slowly traced her contours, traveling from her soft curves to her delicate collarbone, wringing goosebumps on her skin. During his unhurried exploration, he teased with deliberation, trying to memorize each inch of her frame. His touch was a blend of tenderness and hungry devotion.

He couldn't get enough of her.

He still wanted more.

Apollo's breath hitched as her shy caress explored his chest, sending shockwaves straight to his groin. She awoke from her nap, and his desire for her doubled at her tender yet hesitant attention.

His hands were not roaming freely over Dafnie's body, tracing the hills and valleys with profound adoration. His fingers danced over her skin, igniting a fire trail wherever they touched. He ground his engorged cock against the vee of her legs, also stimulating her sensitive clit.

He reveled in her shivers, sensed the quickening of her breath, and heard the soft gasps she tried to stifle. Every little sound, each tiny movement, transformed into a beautiful song, and he delighted at the gift.

Her hands ran through Apollo's golden hair. She tugged and pulled his locks as if trying to anchor herself amidst the overwhelming surge of pleasure. She clung to him as her life depended on him. Her nails dug into his back, her body arching to meet his as she rubbed her damp slit against his steely erection. Their bodies moved in a passionate dance as they tried to find release.

"Hmph! Ahh… Fuck, Dafnie… If we keep this up, I will end up coming… You're too tempting." He groaned, burying his face in the crook of Dafnie's shoulder, nipping at the tender spot of her neck.

"Ahhhh! Apollo… d-don't stop… I-I'm close. Mmmahhh… please! You make me feel alive," she begged.

"As you wish, my love! As you wish."

Driven by a wave of protectiveness, he pressed his lips to hers with a rekindled passion.

Apollo's heart pounded against his chest, echoing the rhythm of their frantic movements. The sweet flavor of her lips became his new ambrosia, giving him a new purpose in life. He reveled in their shared warmth, the softness of her skin, and the sound of her gentle moans.

With his kisses, he aimed to intoxicate her and leave her longing for more. Their motions became demanding, their needy caresses more desperate, as they both inched closer to their impending pinnacle.

"Hmm! Apollo… Aahhh!"

She moaned as she climaxed. Her eyes glazed over as she found bliss.

"Unh… Ahh!"

He followed soon after, finding his release. His body shuddered and convulsed, ecstasy coursing through his veins. His precious nymph caused this intoxicating pleasure. He never imagined —or even dared dream—stumbling upon intense gratification as he rubbed against his lover.

Lying beneath him, she looked ethereal. Dafnie became flushed and bathed in the vibrant hues of the setting sun. She was the embodiment of his desire—a long-denied craving of lust. As their breaths slowed and heartbeats steadied, he caressed her cheek.

"Dafnie..." Her decadent name lingered like a whispered secret.

Greed consumed his determination as he wanted more. He longed to witness the intensity of Dafnie's passion-brimmed gaze once again. He kissed Dafnie's soft lips, claiming them as his, grabbing this elusive love for his own.

This time, he planned to be gentle and go slow. Apollo drove from Dafnie's neck to her breasts, his mouth pressing against his lover's heated skin, igniting a fire within her as he teased her perfect mounds.

Dafnie reacted fervently, her hands instinctively moving, tracing the contours of Apollo's sculpted torso. Her fingers traced the rugged outline of his abdomen and skimmed along his muscular biceps.

His warm and comforting touch put her into a trance as she moved, reveling in their connection. He bore the gift of paradise as he wrapped her in his arms.

He couldn't resist the allure of Dafnie's body any longer, the way it beckoned him with an intoxicating fascination. Her eyes, hooded with expectation, offered many promises. His attraction to his precious naiad became unbearable and hard to ignore. Drawn to the flame of passion, he couldn't endure being away from her.

With a deep, rumbling growl, he positioned himself at her entrance, brushing against her with the most teasing of touches. A surge of warmth shot through her, making her quiver with anticipation, engorging his desire. "Ready? I want you and can't take it any longer..."

His husky voice was but a whisper hovering over the shell of her ear.

"Yes... mmmm!" Her soft tone held the magic of devotion as her gaze locked onto his. "I want you, Apollo. I want you now!"

✳✳✳

He slowly pushed into her. Her body welcomed him with a warm, tight embrace. Spurring him to heights of pleasure he never experienced with anyone before. Almost as if her entire being knew what he liked.

No matter how often they joined to become one, her receptiveness received him with overwhelming candor. Her body's keen response teased his appetite while her moves radiated effortless grace and beauty every time they became one.

His life mate transformed into a sight of perfection under his watch. Period!

She gasped, her fingers clawing at his back as she adjusted to his plentiful size, filling her and sending a flutter of ecstasy through her core.

Apollo groaned at the tightness, the wet heat of her enveloping him, each thrust driving him deeper into her. He held off until she relaxed before picking up the speed.

He became greedy around her. Unable to get enough of her. But he needed to be gentle with her and curve his never-ending lust. His body moved in a rhythmic cadence designed to bring them both the utmost pleasure as she wrapped her arms and legs around him.

Their bodies danced in synchronized motion, lost in the throes of their passion. The room teemed with the sounds and echoes of their lovemaking. Their gasps, their moans, the sensual creek of the bed, the cadenced slap of their skin each time he delved deeper. Their desire saturated the air, a heady mix of sweat and release intoxicating their senses.

She met every thrust with a knowing swivel of her hips, encouraging him to take her harder. Her back arched into his as she looked for more of him. The pleasure built, an inferno raging within her, waiting to break free.

Dafnie looked needy, absorbed in her passion. She wanted more, and he willingly gave her what she craved.

"Mmm... More, I want more. Mmm... ahh!"

She gasped. Her half-lidded eyes contained so much satisfaction.

He complied, his body moving faster, driving into her with a fevered force. Their bodies moved at the same time, trying to reach that delicious release.

Her pussy clamped hard on his cock, followed by a delightful flutter. Her eyes lost their focus as her canal filled with her treasured dew.

Without warning, his climax crashed upon him as stars danced in his line of vision. The rewarding intensity shook him to his very core.

Her walls kept pulsating and weeping. Copious amounts of Dafnie's nectar joined with Apollo's seed. The wetness flowing from her pussy made it comfortable for him to pound her contracting canal. He surged once, then twice, before coming within her sweet confines.

"Mmm ahhhh!"

Apollo's incoherent cry came while claiming Dafnie's lips and collapsing on top of her.

Being a god full of virility allowed him to continue their wild mating for the rest of the day. Still, his sweetheart drifted into a deep slumber, a satisfied smile on her lips. He brushed a wet strand of hair from her face, his gaze softening.

Watching her sleep, he wondered about her recent changes in paranoia and the panic attack from the morning. He witnessed how his precious lover would stare out the window for hours every night before returning to bed, asking him to hold her tight. Her wistful expression told him she missed the outdoors.

His foolish actions took a toll on her. Only he waited a little longer… and met her before his impulsive acts. He reconsidered his plans to end the mortal world and pursue her, chasing her like a love-sick boy to win her heart. A persistent thought caressed his mind.

Why didn't I wait?

"By the powers passed on to me by my father Zeus, I declare a profound slumber upon you this evening. The gentle caress of divine essence shall guide you into a realm of dreams so you can find peace and clarity. Dafnie, the celestial realm's loving grace, shall embrace you, washing away the burdens of the mortal world tonight. May visions of serenity and solace accompany your sleep as the sun god guards your rest. With each breath, nuzzle the blessings of the heavens and awaken refreshed in the dawn's tender light."

He whispered into his beloved's ear as she sighed deeply and succumbed to the divine slumber.

"Fernhoof, please clean the room and put on fresh sheets. Please make sure they are comfortable. Also, spread some lavender and chamomile essence around the room for a calming effect."

He instructed as he picked Dafnie's limp body from the bed and into his arms and headed to the bathroom. "Bring my crossbow. We're going out hunting tonight." He finished with a stern expression.

He avoided her questions about the mutilated bodies of creatures found every morning in the area. Now, he set out to investigate the situation and sweep the site.

The number of monsters spiked in the past few days, making the nights more treacherous. The creatures' cunning and tactical attacks became a concern at night. He committed himself to defending their neighborhood, no matter the cost.

After bathing and dressing his darling in a simple oversized pullover, he laid her on the freshly made bed. Her angelic looks softened his heart. Thus, the weight of responsibility compelled him to own up to his mistakes and fix the world.

With the patience of a saint, Fernhoof waited with his weapon and clothes. Apollo donned a black T-shirt and a pair of jeans Fernhoof brought over, followed by lace-up combat boots.

Worried about their safety, he ought to ensure his companion prepared for their evening hunt. "Are you ready, Fernhoof?"

The faun complied without delay. "Yes, sir! I'm ready."

"I want you to stay alert. We need to find out what's going on. I started this, but I admit these complications were not part of my plan."

Apollo's concern about their safety played with his drive to make the world better again—after he destroyed it. His plan was not turning out as expected.

Both he and Fernhoof disappeared from the room. They materialized outside Dafnie's house with their weapons ready.

"We ought to be cautious when out and about. The creatures have tried to attack me in the past, sir."

Fernhoof's unease permeated his tone, worrying Apollo.

"From my observations, they also seem more aggressive."

Apollo's grim determination stood behind his words.

"My foresight revealed nothing. Either I lost my gift as a seer, and my current visions are pure shit, or fate planned something sinister for me. I'm guessing I cannot see the future that involves Dafnie because I'm too proud. Just sweet fucking punishment for the wish-washy god of whatever lengthy list of talents I'm supposed to have hanging above my head for me to take."

Fernhoof bounced with optimism. "Sir, do not worry. You will fix this and be victorious, right?"

"I'm not sure! Like my father, my impulsiveness and rashness brought too much suffering and destruction. I swore never to act like him, but here I…"

Something horrifying shattered Apollo's moment of introspection. A dreadful mutation turned their way.

"KYAH… KYAHHH… KYAHHHHHHH…"

A monster stopped before them. It used to be a neighbor, now afflicted by the virus and the spores he released. He at once pointed his crossbow at the beast, who, judging by her tattered clothing, was a professional woman at some point.

He trained his weapon on the creature as he assessed his surroundings. Fernhoof was ready with his short sword prepared to attack. He stared back at several beady eyes fixed on him, poised to strike.

"Fernhoof, be on high alert. These mutants have evolved and can kill immortals. Please do not allow them to hurt you, my dear companion."

He warned, hearing another screech.

"KYAH... KYAHHH... KYAHHHHHHH..."

The horde charged as he released his arrows on them, precisely hitting their intended target, while Fernhoof rushed toward the oncoming hoard.

"HIIISSSS... KYAHHCK..."

The creature's hiss sent chills down his spine, but his time to atone and rectify was running out. Apollo and Fernhoof dealt with those creatures nonstop that night, thinning out the mob for the rest of the night.

Chapter 32

God Next Door

The vivid horrors she witnessed earlier the previous day still played in the back of her mind. Yet, to her surprise, the gruesome images didn't affect her as much as she thought they would. Something stirred within her, unearthing a suppressed strength she never realized she possessed.

An exciting turn of events.

Following her exhausting day, Dafnie experienced an unexpected sense of calmness. Admittedly, she acknowledged her emotions were running high, and yesterday was her breaking point. After her parents' death, she worked hard to stay centered and busy. When young, her faculties would spiral out of control. Since then, her priority centered on Dafnie's well-being. She found solace in going out on runs and meditating in nature.

Further on, she reconnected with herself and escaped the pressures of daily life. But over a week ago, everything changed. Her life turned upside down, leaving behind ghosts of the past.

After waking to a destroyed world, her life took an exciting turn. She discovered that her mysterious neighbor was the sun god Apollo. A man with a massive crush on his old flame, Daphne.

The naiad huntress passed away because Eros wanted to teach Apollo a lesson—to suffer for being a smartass. Apollo insisted that she, Dafnie, was Daphne's reincarnation and possessed the nymph's life essence. Strangely enough, Dafnie experiences conflicting emotions of happiness, confusion, and apprehension.

Apollo fell in love with Daphne—besotted with his mortal nymph. His behavior left Dafnie questioning his feelings towards her. As a result, he became obsessed with Dafnie as well. Her gaze lingered on his face, wondering if he felt the same way—if his heart belonged to her. His emotions, like a knotted rope, were hard to comprehend.

Has he not been able to heal and overcome her loss? Will my existence make him lose touch with reality?

Her gaze followed his movement throughout the room, her mind in a trance of curiosity. The divine scent of fresh veggies and meat permeated the first floor as he worked on their meal.

Maybe Apollo's fascination must be driven by his yearning. His fruitless desire for a fulfilling relationship with Daphne. Is he seeing me as nothing more than a mere replacement for the lost nymph and nothing else?

Her thoughts metamorphosed into a constant and unstoppable storm of questions.

Would he stop loving me after the effects of Eros's golden arrow wore off, and would that ever happen?

The weirdness of the situation unsettled her. A whirlwind of apprehension and confusion raced through Dafnie's mind. Her doubts confined her to a shell that wasn't hers, and her mind bec-ame a trap of confusion. Leaving her wondering.

Should I turn into this other woman, trying to fill the void in Apollo's heart? Dafnie didn't want to be a stand-in for Apollo's love life. She wanted to be more.

What she yearned for the most was his unconditional love. She preferred Apollo focused on her, the simple mortal software engineer who had been his neighbor during apocalyptic times. To concentrate on her current self rather than dwelling on his long-lost lover—an echoed remembrance. Even though she had no recollection of her previous life, Dafnie was here to stay by him.

But she recognized his dilemma.

Certainly, clinging to the past was futile, but Dafnie underst-ood the struggles of holding onto cherished memories. Her parents' image was a constant presence in her life, and the weight of their importance still plagues her to this day. A heavy weight settled in her chest, a dull ache that whispered of the futility of clinging to a memory so painful.

Starting a relationship with Apollo would be a mistake if the mythical golden arrow still afflicted him. The arrow's powers mi-ght still plague his heart and force Apollo to love her. Yet, Apollo stepped in to help her cope with the stress when her defenses bec-ame too overwhelming.

Swiftly, a thought struck Dafnie with a debilitating force. Perhaps Apollo's affection was not temporary. He cared for her with genuine zeal, and Dafnie coped with her mixed emotions for Apollo. Maybe Dafnie was fussing and making a big deal out of nothing. Perhaps she needed to calm down and let things be, allowing them to run their course between them.

Everything was hazy. Dafnie noted his concern and love for her. Despite that, she questioned his feelings because of past trauma. Daphne, the nymph, was a seasoned and fearless hunter, willing to forsake her life for her beliefs. The nymph sounded daring.

However, Dafnie was always an odd girl, always judged for being different. She had no luck finding friends and even less luck having a boyfriend. Growing up, she was a loner, and until now, she had no life partner. A life of loneliness and disappointment followed her around like a dark shadow.

When Dafnie lost her parents, she felt empty and hopeless. Dafnie thought she would live and die alone—being no one special and not having anyone special in her life. Never in her wildest dreams had she imagined someone like Apollo would show any interest in her.

His handsome magnetism drew the masses. People like him ignored plain women like her. Then Dafnie realized something. The trivial things he did for her made her question her hesitation.

Monsters wandered around, sensing their presence. Going outside was too risky. Therefore, Apollo devised a plan to make her happy and less stressed. Dafnie understood that going outdoors was dangerous. She risked her life every time she ventured out of the house.

Careless outdoor freedom was out of the question.

Dafnie couldn't go out on long runs, including to her favorite spot by the river. Outdoor excursions were out of the question. Apollo showed his consideration. After days of passionate confinement, he secured a path for her to enjoy daily. However, there was one inconvenience: the trail was short.

Why such a small running trail? She wondered and asked many times.

Apollo's answer was always the same. He could not foresee Dafnie's future, predict her behavior, or guard against potential threats. Left with no choice, Apollo resorted to defending a small area close to their houses. He would send Fernhoof and Daedalion to watch and protect her while he did whatever godly duties he needed to take care of for that day.

And about Apollo's daily godly duties imposed by the one and only king of all gods, Zeus... They were a mystery to Apollo. Every day, the random tasks seemed unimportant.

Every day without fail, Hebe would show up and bring his ambrosia nectar with an added request from his father. The requests were random but necessary. It seemed like Zeus disciplined Apollo and demoted him to being an errand boy.

Apollo seemed doubtful about his father's demands. Some days, he didn't seem to mind his obligations, with no objections. But sometimes, the demands bothered him, putting him in a foul mood.

As Apollo's lips grazed hers, Dafnie fiddled with the bittersweet longing. A pang of sadness consumed her mind and numbed her sense. The knowledge that his kiss was a fleeting memory, like a whisper that would soon fade after his departure. To Dafnie, the moment was like a wilting flower in the setting sun, leaving the echoes of an intrusive ache.

Before leaving for the day, Apollo would passionately make love to Dafnie after drinking his nectar. His frenzied actions made her feel like a forbidden fruit—his sole sustenance or last feast. Dafnie often wondered if Zeus spiked the ambrosia nectar with an aphrodisiac crafted only for Apollo. Whenever he consu-

med the substance, his behavior took a strange turn. He appeared compelled by an insatiable desire for her.

A great possibility.

But his eyes told a different story whenever they shared a passionate kiss or made love. His eyes were always ablaze with desire,
love, and longing whenever he looked at her. Most importantly,
Apollo's eyes held no doubt.

Each morning, Apollo would disappear for about an hour.
He gave Dafnie plenty of time to go for a quick run in the protected area and recharge. After a shower, Dafnie read something
and waited for him to come home.

Every time Apollo returned from meeting his father, he was
in a bad mood. She could only guess that his father condemned
his impulsive actions, which pushed Dafnie to lose her center
and focus and made her eager to see him depressed. Apollo sensed her distress and did everything within him to distract her
with his body. Using his body to ease Dafnie's pain was second
nature to Apollo, almost like a reflexive response.

However, that was in the past. The present atmosphere became a palpable, stark contrast to the usual routine.

Dafnie couldn't quite put her finger on it, especially after exp-
eriencing a moment of weakness. Yet, she had newfound
courage. A spark of fortitude grew within her, ignited by the terror from outside.

Unlike her usual self, Dafnie lay in bed for a while longer and
enjoyed Apollo's embrace. Despite being unusual for her to sleep
in, she stretched beneath the warm covers, savoring the stillness
of the morning. Today, Dafnie wanted to stay home.

She wished to rest and wait for Apollo to return from whatever duty he needed tending for the day. She planned to wait for

him under the covers and naked. To lure him to take her the moment he was home. For some weird, uncharacteristic reason, Dafnie's libido was in overdrive, feeling a sexual fire that was intoxicating her.

"You may not know this, but your sweet scent calls to me. Do you need me to help you with that?" Apollo whispered in Dafnie's ear as he pulled her even closer to him, rubbing his erection against her backside. His hand ventured to her crotch in search of her tender bud. "Are you not planning to go out on your run today?" Apollo asked as he kissed the sensitive spot on her neck while teasing her clit and entrance.

"No... mmmm!" Dafnie replied. She would enjoy the good things when they presented themselves if forced to survive the apocalypse. "I've taken today off to snuggle with you," Dafnie emphasized her words. Then she reached over to Apollo's teasing hand to guide him further south and between her legs.

"Snuggle? I've got other things in mind, and snuggling isn't one of them." Apollo kissed Dafnie's neck and complied with her request.

"Oh, for the love of Olympus and its rulers, Apollo! I'm here to deliver your nectar," Hebe announced herself in a condescending tone. The gods' cupbearer came with the sunrise, disrupting Apollo and Dafnie's plans.

"Fuck, Hebe! It's too early for you to be here, interrupting my morning... Why are you here?" Apollo shouted, annoyed at the intrusion. His half-sister needed to be more discrete when he was busy. Dafnie gave a little cry and hid under the covers. She sounded embarrassed at being caught in the process of having sex.

With incredible tolerance, Hebe ignored what was going on between Dafnie and Apollo and continued. "Your father asked me to come, so here I am."

"Damn it! Cock-blocked by my father? That's grand coming from someone who doesn't know how to control his urges. He's the biggest philanderer in existence. How dare he interrupt his son when he is busy with his one and only lover?" The interruption grated on Apollo's nerves.

"This is not the first time I've seen a god or demigod having sex. I've brought your nectar in the past while in the throes of passion with some random woman. You didn't care," Hebe said, unfazed. She rolled her eyes at Apollo's dramatic outburst, her indifferent posture contrasting his heated reaction.

Sullenly, Apollo took the cup and downed its contents. "Is my father expecting me now?"

"He's not expecting you today. You can lazy away your day with your lover."

His blood boiled, the icy edge in Hebe's voice fueling a fire of resentment that threatened to consume him. With her duty complete, Hebe vanished when her task was complete. The tension in the room dissipated after the unexpected visitor took her leave. Apollo turned his attention back to Dafnie, who hid under the sheets to avoid being seen by strangers.

Apollo could not help but admire the perfect contours of her body as he pulled the sheets off her. He dragged the covers away from Dafnie's slight frame, worshipping her beauty and taking his time.

With the back of his knuckles, he grazed the tempting curve

of her waist and over her curvy hips. Dafnie's beauty was unrivaled by any of Apollo's lovers. She carried her unintentional allure with delicate care while his burning desire for her intensified with each breath.

He leaned over her, his muscular body cast a shadow on her petite figure. His touch was gentle as he traced the curve of her hips, eliciting a soft sigh from Dafnie. Apollo closed in on her. His movement was fluid and graceful. Then, he pressed his lips against hers passionately, leaving them both breathless.

"It sounds like your plans for today have changed. Let's have breakfast. We skipped dinner last night, and I'm hungry. There are a few veggies from my garden ready to pick," Dafnie chirped as she got out of bed and headed for the window.

"Absolutely! Perhaps we should have breakfast in bed. Yesterday, I bought a few things from the Olympian gardens. I think you'll like it," Apollo suggested. His husky voice held great promise as he admired Dafnie's action. With a lazy demeanor, he stretched out on the bed and enjoyed the view.

Then Apollo realized Dafnie froze in her tracks. As Dafnie peered outside, Apollo caught as her eyes grew wide with terror. He jumped out of bed to stand beside her and saw something unexpected.

In the gentle light of dawn, horror unfolded before them.

A creature that bore an uncanny resemblance to one of their neighbors ripped apart a body lying on the ground. Apollo's enchantment around the house's perimeter muffled the creatures' growling and cries of agony. However, the horrible muted noise still resonated through the morning air.

The grotesque sight was one of primal savagery as one monster devoured the other. Stained dark red, the aberration showed its sharp teeth. It fed recently, likely tearing through skin and muscle with undeniable brutality. The creature showed its capability for carnage.

The horror made Dafnie pale in fear as she clutched at her stomach. She appeared pale and about to throw up. The vein on her neck drummed uncontrollably, and sweat flowed down her brow. She seemed paralyzed, rooted to the spot in sheer shock.

Her breath hitched in her throat. She breathed fast, as if her lungs starved for air. The wild look on her face screamed hysteria as her lips turned purple. Her lips parted as if to scream, but nothing came out. Her entire body quivered as if it were reluctant to obey the instinct to flee and seek shelter.

Witnessing Dafnie's terror, Apollo wrapped his arms around her quaking figure. His grip was a steadying anchor amidst the chaos framing their window.

Chapter 33

Unnerving Realities

An eerie silence permeated the atmosphere, broken by the distant echoes of growls and howls.

An old neighbor, transformed into one of those despicable creatures, savagely ripped apart another. The sound of bones crunching and flesh tearing filled the early morning hours. As seconds ticked past, the attacks became more violent on its helpless victim. The fiends' torturous groans echoed through the muted air.

The grotesque sight was one of horrific carnage.

Stained dark red, the aberration showed its sharp teeth that looked like they tore through skin and muscle with brutality and slaughter.

Dafnie's heart pounded like a drum, rooting her in place as sheer terror consumed her. Paralysis took hold of her body and brain. Her breath hitched in her throat. The horror constricted her lungs and made it difficult to breathe. Her mind screamed at her to move, but her legs refused to comply.

Sensing Dafnie's shock, Apollo wrapped his arms around her trembling figure. His grip was a steadying anchor amidst the dismay framing their window.

He pressed her close to his chest, his heart a steady rhythm against her back. "Shhh, it's going to be okay..." Apollo lowered his voice to a soothing murmur—intended to ease. His hand rubbed her arms in a comforting yet assuring gesture. "I won't let anything harm you," Apollo promised.

His warm and reassuring scent cut through the terror that clouded her awareness. Something snapped within her. The anger that grew from deep inside Dafnie overpowered her senses.

With each passing day, she hated the deteriorating state of the world, which seemed to get worse. A wave of icy fear washed over her as she examined a mutated, soulless neighbor who became a ravenous monster.

The fiend's terrifying eyes glazed and locked on its rotten meal as it lunged forward, revealing fangs that glistened with danger. Dafnie's breath caught in her throat as her face flushed with rage. She wanted the world to return to normal.

Suddenly, Dafnie broke free from Apollo's embrace, her eyes blazing with anger. Her fists clenched and unclenched, a silent testament to her raging emotions. "I'm not watching this anymore. I'll not stand by and not do something!" Her words echoed around the room as she walked toward the door and down the stairs.

Apollo was close behind. Dafnie could feel Apollo's hot breath on the back of her neck. His heavy breathing came as a reminder of his pursuit. Dafnie couldn't let him catch her, or Apollo would stop her from ridding the world of the vermis. Dafnie's hand trembled as she gripped the crossbow. A hollow ache in her chest as the sound of the door slamming shut drew the creature's attention.

The weapon seemed bulky and comforting in Dafnie's hand as she loaded and aimed the crossbow at the creature in one fluid motion. As the beast ran at her, Dafnie pulled the trigger. The missile flew true to the mutant's left eye socket.

With a fierce determination burning in her eyes, Dafnie stood her ground as the fiend charged again. The arrow lodged in its head fueled its rage, its growls thunderous in the silent street. Flinching, Dafnie prepared another projectile, her slender fingers dancing deftly over the weapon with a surprising grace she never knew she had in her.

She fired again, but the dart went through the monster's nose, hitting its brainstem and stopping her target. Dafnie then walked over to the still screeching foul animal that was being devoured alive and shot a missile into its head to end its suffering.

Apollo drew near Dafnie, watching her fearsome stance against the monstrous creature, and picked up the arrows she used on his way. A surge of admiration for Dafnie filled Apollo, but he pondered what sparked her newfound strength. A shiver danced down her spine as a chilling energy sparked within her, leaving her both enthralled and alarmed. And Apollo loved Dafnie's emerging fiery spirit.

"KYAHHHHHHH!" A sudden screech came from the inside of a house.

Apollo conjured his shining bow with its infinite divine arrows. He noted as Dafnie moved toward the shrieking monster. He focused on the derelict house. The entrance was eerily quiet, putting him on high alert. Apollo's finger wrapped around the bowstring as he pulled it taught. Driven by adrenaline-fueled survival instincts, Apollo and Dafnie move into action.

Apollo's golden arrow flew true to its target as the creature appeared by the door. He regarded Dafnie standing her ground, her stance solid and defiant as another shriek came from another direction.

"KYAHHHHHHH! Snap! Snap!" Two monsters ran, crazed by mindless hunger.

Apollo's blue eyes glowed with his godly powers, sharpening his vision and hearing as he aimed with practiced aim. He downed the oncoming horde of creatures pouring from the house with his heightened senses while Dafnie picked on the one in the front.

"GRRAA! KYAH! KYAHHHHHHHH!" The terrifying noise came from the house next to them. The building's insides echoed with more bone-chilling shrieking that sent shivers down their spines.

Apollo steeled his pounding heart. More than anything, he worried for Dafnie's safety but needed to focus for her sake. Apollo spotted movement in the house's window and aimed his bow at it. These creatures ruined his relaxing morning with Dafnie, which pissed him off. Apollo was bloodthirsty and prepared to exterminate anything that dared to come out of the house.

Troubled by their current predicament, Dafnie turned toward the source of the screams. She was ready to defend herself but changed her mind. The shadows inside the house danced and flickered, their movements unsettling her.

Dafnie considered it best to stand by Apollo and help protect their position together as much as she could. Dafnie moved closer to Apollo hesitantly, ensuring she would not attract attention as the monsters roamed too close for comfort.

Suddenly, a creature stood by the window and stared at them with greedy intent. "GRRRAAA! KYAHHHHHHH!" The terrifying scream was the only warning Dafnie and Apollo got before they heard a stampede of creatures charging for the door. Their growls and screams grew louder and more desperate as they approached the door, running toward them, their bloodshot eyes reflecting their primal hunger.

✳✳✳

The horde's behavior did not surprise Apollo. The sight before him brought back memories of his previous encounters. Every night, he hunted these creatures. He experienced their mindless frenzy and insatiable hunger. Dafnie's breath hitched as the horde of grotesqueries spilled out of the house at once.

"Stay by my side. Do not make any sudden moves. It'll attract their attention, and when I say so, attack without mercy. I just enchanted the crossbow to reload on its own and will not run out of arrows. The arrows will also pierce through their bones more effectively. Aim true and do not think. Act like you did before."

Apollo warned, and not missing a beat, he let go of his grip on his arrow. A bolt of fire flew with lethal precision, exploding once it reached the door, killing several creatures in one fluid movement. However, it didn't stop the remaining beasts inside the house from trying to come out and devour them.

Without wasting a second, Dafnie raised her crossbow. Her projectile shot through the air until it found its mark, piercing through one of the monster's heads with satisfying precision. Apollo let loose another one of his arrows, aimed with great accuracy at another creature. The arrow exploded in the process and took down several fiends.

Apollo loved the way Dafnie's body moved. He felt captivated by the determined sparkle in her eyes and the deadly grace with which she held the crossbow. Despite the fear gnawing inside him at seeing her getting hurt, Apollo couldn't help but feel a stirring desire for the hunter that still lived inside her.

One by one, the monsters fell. Their ear-splitting shrieks echoed throughout the area. When they dealt with the creatures, the street once again fell silent. As Dafnie fired one last arrow at a twitching monster, Apollo came to stand by her side to check on her, concerned about her mental state.

Apollo's powerful arm wrapped around Dafnie's waist and guided her movements toward her house. "How are you feeling?" Apollo asked when they went inside their home. He worried about her sudden behavior change and wanted to know if she was okay.

Breathing heavily, Dafnie turned to face Apollo and pressed her body against his. Standing near him, she could not resist the alluring and musky scent that filled the air. Dafnie's eyes teared up as she let herself crumble into him, her voice a whisper.

"I'm scared! I thought today would be a good day, but... I-I... d-don't know what came over me. Something snapped in me after I saw that creature eating another in broad daylight. I wanted to have a relaxing day," Dafnie finished as tears streamed down her cheeks. Her chest heaved as small sobs racked through her fra,e.

Apollo enveloped her in his embrace, offering her comfort

and security. His presence, the warmth radiating from his body, and the rhythmic beat of his heart against her ear all served as her anchor. A flood of emotions washed over them as they stood in the foyer.

Apollo placed a light kiss on top of Dafnie's head in a protective and reassuring gesture as he murmured into her ear, "It's fine, my darling hunter. We're safe now. I know you wanted to make breakfast for us, but how about I treat you today only after a quick shower?" Apollo's hand moved in circles on her back, his fingers tracing the curves of her backside.

"That sounds perfect. Right now, all I want to do is sleep and for you to hold me," Dafnie whispered, hugging him even tighter.

Apollo closed his eyes, savoring their warm embrace as he hung on to Dafnie for a little while, enjoying the comfort of the simple act. She clung to Apollo as if he was her lifeline. Apollo sensed her exhaustion, knowing she needed to recover after the traumatic morning. He felt surprised by Dafnie's unusual calmness. Dafnie was no seasoned hunter like himself, but she coped with her shock well.

As he held Dafnie, he gave in to his weariness and relaxed. As his head cleared, he questioned his decision to unleash such a calamity. After meeting Dafnie, he often asked himself why starting the apocalypse in the mortal world would be a clever idea.

Damn it, Apollo! Don't shit where you eat, he thought as bitterness clouded his mind.

The mortal world was his home since he got in trouble, which resulted in getting kicked out of Olympus often.

Why do I always get into people's shitlist? Apollo thought, realizing his slip. *I needed to sort out my priorities and stop repeating my mistakes.*

"Certainly, you need to sort your affairs soon, or you will lose quite a lot, my dear baby brother. Did you like my present? I admit she was and still is my most talented and devoted disciple. Although, it's a shame she lost her virginity to you. Out of every, she chose you on her own. She could have been one of my maiden hunters. Despite this, Dafnie had another purpose in her lifelong set by the Fates," Artemis whispered in Apollo's ear, startling him.

Chapter 34

"Hey! Fucking hell, Artemis! Stop sneaking up on people," Apollo complained as he veered toward his sister. Suddenly, the blood drained from his face, and he glanced at Dafnie. His heart drumming drowned all sound when Dafnie's delicate features revealed the truth.

"Wait... hold on!" Apollo's hesitation weakened his familiar gallantry. "Was I the first person you were intimate with?" His surprise spoke volumes as the information sank in. He realized he only thought about himself when they first met.

"Yes!" Dafnie mumbled as she also nodded. "Never had a boyfriend. No one seemed interested in me, so I gave up pursuing a relationship. I thought I would live alone for the rest of my life."

"So sorry... I wasn't thinking about it back then. I should have more control over myself," Apollo apologized and kissed her forehead to prove his regret. "And... don't call me 'baby brother' ever again. I hate it, fuck." He turned toward his sister with a scowl, tightening his embrace around Dafnie. He hated it whenever Arthemis teased him for being the younger one—like an inexperienced lad.

"I will regard you however I want, my dear brother. Remember, I'm the older one and even helped our mother deliver you. Show more respect! It'll do you some good. You often get into trouble because you forget to think before you act. For instance, Dafnie experienced that firsthand."

Artemis smirked as she regarded her brother's indignant expression as he rolled his eyes. "But let's not focus on some silly disputes for now. I'm here because we need to talk."

"Are you here because someone sent you to bring some news?" Apollo asked as he turned away from his sister to face Dafnie, stunned by his sincerity and trying to process what was happening.

"My nymph, let me get you some calming tea. It has been quite an eventful morning, and I don't want you to have another breakdown like the other day." Apollo kissed Dafnie's head, bearing a radiant smile.

Dafnie was appreciative, nodding her thanks, struggling to deal with the fact that the woman who appeared in the foyer was no other than Artemis, Apollo's twin. Icy dread gripped Dafnie's chest as air squeezed from her lungs. She accepted Apollo as the infamous god of music from Greek mythology. Now, his sister was here to deliver a message—a lousy feeling formed in the pit of her stomach that consumed her.

"Please do so. Your companion looks baffled and put out. You seem to have the habit of bewildering your male and female lovers. It's best if you cared for them better, Apollo." Artemis' mischievous smirk came accompanied by a spiteful tongue. "Ahem! I would also like a cup if you don't mind." Her kind smile illuminated the room as she challenged Apollo's death stare.

"Be careful with what you wish for. My generous tea offering could give you a horrible retching spell," Apollo muttered as he let go of Dafnie. He then snagged her hand to lead her into the kitchen with him.

"For Mount Olympus' sake, my dear baby brother, if you do such a thing, you'll have no choice but to take care of me. Are you sure you want to do that?" Artemis's eyes gleamed with amusement. Yet, the moment her gaze studied how Apollo escorted the Dafnie around, her onrushing, cruel taunt froze.

Artemis couldn't help but feel jealous at seeing the reincarnation of one of Artemis' most devout maiden hunters in her brother's arms. The day Artemis had been called in before her father to discuss the rebirth of the deceased nymph, she became livid.

The nymph's tragic death raised an unsettling, silent question in Artemis' heart. *What purpose did Daphne's demise serve? To become Apollo's wife when at his lowest?! Or for Zeus to control my brother?* Artemis' mind raced with unanswered possibilities.

Daphne's choice, a selfless act of surrender to Artemis' wishes, turned into a beacon. Artemis felt honored by the nymph's unconditional devotion.

And sacrifice!

Soon after, Artemis' entourage vowed to be like the naiad after her passing. Daphne's noble deed inspired the other huntresses. The stories of the naiad's fearless spirit and selflessness lingered in the annals of Mount Olympus lore—enshrined for eternity.

From the instant his eyes fell upon Daphne, Apollo became smitten, his heart captivated by her beauty. Disposing of any 'male' competition, Apollo admired the warring nymph from afar. His obsession grew each day, consuming his thoughts and stealing his prudence. Thus, the crux of their tragedy—unequivocal love—ensued.

Aware the nymph was Artemis's apprentice, Apollo kept a respectful distance. Daphne's relationship with the goddess tempered his affection. Daphne's radiance was like a beacon, drawing Apollo in, and despite his best efforts to conceal his emotions, the intensity of his attraction was undeniable.

Therefore, the start of demise began.

Just because Artemis decided never to marry did not mean she was against marriage. The concept of being a man's wife didn't resonate with her—simple. Yet, Apollo was the opposite of her. Her baby brother yearned for a connection and often brought his feelings to the forefront of his personality.

At first, she thought her brother's behavior was adorable. Apollo acted like a charming, star-crossed child when in love. Artemis even allowed her brother to fantasize about Daphne without getting in his way. Tempted to give her brother immense joy, Artemis nudged and encouraged Apollo and Daphne's relationship. She realized they would be a loving couple. However, she would not rush things and wait for the perfect opportunity.

But then Eros, the bastard, intervened. He thought it clever to teach Apollo a lesson by utilizing Daphne against her brother. The god of lust set forth a plan to destroy both Artemis's apprentice and Apollo's presumptuous will.

After the tragedy that claimed Daphne, the goddess of the

hunt turned to revenge. Artemis had roared her frustration, cursing the god of love. When she found Eros boasting he bested cocky-dickhead Apollo in a game of wits, she lost it.

Her brother deserved his punishment for destroying the mortal world on a whim. He was one massive wild card and unpredictable. He deserved it, but using Daphne as a tool of revenge against Apollo for retribution was cruel.

Apollo was not the same after that. The loss fucked with his mind. Eros didn't help the situation either, as he kept messing with Apollo's devotion to life, leading her brother down a darker and sinister path where he lost his heart.

Artemis believed Eros's meddling in Apollo's love life made her brother heartless whenever he felt wronged. Eros might look handsome on the outside, but the little shit was rotten on the inside. The grudge he harbored against Apollo poisoned the tenderness in the sun god's heart.

Seeing Dafnie in Apollo's arms, happy and at ease, made Arthemis jealous but content. Artemis wanted to pick on her brother for the time being. Her eyes pursued Apollo's retreating figure as he retired to the kitchen. A wave of loneliness washed over Artemis as her young brother moved around to make them tea—unaware.

Dafnie followed behind as Apollo drew her to the dining area, looking like she was still reeling from the emotionally charged morning. By the looks of it, Apollo was needier than usual. He seemed to be in the mood to stay close to his lover and to feel connected to the one he cared about the most, Dafnie.

Father was right in picking her. My baby brother changed in a short amount of time. I'm interested in seeing how strong he becomes as they continue this relationship. He is in love. How sweet, Artemis thought as a mischievous smile played on her face. *I'm going to taunt him for a bit—just a little.*

Artemis wanted to tease her brother more than anything, but she needed to be careful. Apollo was an accomplished herbalist and was more than capable of fulfilling his earlier threat.

Her eyes followed Apollo as he guided Dafnie into the chair, his touch light and reassuring. Bitter jealousy gripped Artemis's heart, her stomach twisting with envy. His hunter training was always present as Apollo padded to the kitchen after kissing his lover, ensuring her comfort.

Once in the kitchen, he boiled water to make their herbal tea, which would help Dafnie relax after the traumatic morning. Artemis sat opposite Dafnie and waited. She acknowledged the mighty sun god was quite comfortable doing menial everyday tasks, something Artemis had not seen in a while.

Artemis caught when Apollo filled a kettle with water and set it on the stove. She smiled at his domesticity but kept quiet. He selected a porcelain teapot tastefully decorated with matching cups and fetched an infuser from the drawer.

Apollo reached for a jar packed with fragrant herbs and packed the silver bauble before setting it in the pot. A pleasant smile played on Apollo's lips while he waited for the water to boil and gathered a few things to eat.

"You are truly in love with her..." Artemis whispered, no longer in the mood to mock her brother. She lingered as Dafnie opened her eyes, and Apollo's face flushed bright red with embarrassment as he turned away.

"Artemis, please don't start. It's not a suitable time," he pleaded, surprising Artemis. "I know you're in the mood to torment, but I beg you... don't..." he finished as the water started boiling and the kettle whistled. Apollo shifted his attention back to what he was doing. He switched off the stove and got the pot.

He casually filled the teapot, allowing the herbs to steep for a few minutes before the tea was ready. Apollo's attentive actions reflect his desire to provide Dafnie with solace and relaxation.

"I was planning on teasing the two of you, but I changed my mind." Artemis' eyes sparkled with honesty. "I saw what happened this morning. It's not looking good out there, and it seems to get worse by the day..." She paused for a moment, plucking her words with care.

Apollo scrutinized her, almost warning her not to talk too much, but Artemis had a job to do. She could no longer delay her task. "I cannot delay this. I must deliver my warning. One would think you learned your lesson after being exiled many times. Yet here you are again, making more stupid mistakes, costing you your position. When are you going to learn that being impulsive and cocky will only bring you inconveniences?"

Artemis massaged her temples before continuing. Dafnie stared at her intently while Apollo gave her a deadly stare.

"Father sent me here to remind you to clean up your mess. I take it you were not expecting this to happen when you unleashed your calamity on the world."

"What did you say?" Dafnie's breath hitched as she sprang from her seat, eyes wide with alarm. "He's responsible for all this dilemma?"

Chapter 35

Enigma of Apollo

"Father sent me here to remind you to clean up your mess. I take it you were not expecting this to happen when you unleashed your calamity on the world."

Artemis spoke without thinking, failing to acknowledge her slip. Apollo kept Dafnie in the dark about his involvement in the apocalypse.

Until now!

"What did you say?" Dafnie's fists clenched as concern coursed through her. She surged from her chair back, her face flushed as her bewildered mind spun from the move. "He's responsible for all this?" With unsteady hands, she clung to her seat and avoided losing her balance in front of everyone.

Over the weeks, there was only one person she trusted the most. Apollo has been her pillar of light in this terrifying world.

It's all a lie! To find out that Apollo caused all this chaos and destruction. Why?

Dafnie's thoughts rushed with accusations. When faced with adversity, she always turned to Apollo for help. She welcomed the sun god into her home and her well-guarded heart. Dafnie suffered as the last bits of faith slipped through her finger.

How could he be so spiteful and cause this destruction? Why did he do it? What was his reason for doing such a thing? Why was Apollo so heartless?

Dafnie's heartbeat galloped as her body trembled with irritation. The tension in the air was thick, making it hard for Dafnie to breathe. A flood of questions about Apollo's actions assaulted her, giving her a headache. But keeping her in the dark gave her an even more painful ache in her heart.

"Dafnie... please try to calm down." Artemis' pleading eyes shone with intensity as she moved closer to Dafnie.

Dafnie pointedly stared at the goddess. "Did you know of his plans?"

"Yes, his friends and family knew of his schemes. Our father even warned him not to do it, that he would get exiled from Olympus..." Artemis folded her arms in a defiant stance.

"Artemis, NO!" Apollo's booming voice reverberated throughout the room as his breathing became labored.

Apollo's posture and tight jaw spoke volumes about his culpability. Despite sharing a space for a while, his emotions remained a mystery in her eyes. "You didn't stop him... WHY?"

Dafnie's tone exploded with urgency. The question hung in the air like a stone thrown into the void.

"He's your brother, and you were powerless to prevent this? Decide it's best to let him ruin people's lives. No wonder humans no longer worship you a lot. You're all selfish and heartless!" Dafnie's voice shook with anger and disappointment as she turned toward where Apollo stood, unmoving. "That includes you, Apollo. Why?"

Artemis appeared embarrassed—unable to meet Dafnie's accusing gaze. Apollo stepped forward, his eyes pleading for her to understand and forgive him. "I-I didn't know. I-I never expected the situation would spiral out of control. Too late did I realize what I'd done. A-and then you came, and it got more dangerous. I-I-I'm sorry!" Apollo stammered, his voice cracking with emotion and uncertainty. His eyes had a wet shine that was atypical of the confident sun god.

✳✳✳

Apollo's despair and longing were too familiar—too haunting. The heavy weight of his emotions surfaced. Written all over his face were the echoes of his countless heartbreaks.

The familiar hollowness in his gaze pierced Artemis's heart. A stark reminder of the weight of sorrow he carried at unfulfilled desires. Apollo wore the same look when he lost yet another lover who meant the world to him. Losing Daphne cut Apollo deep, leaving him in a state of profound sorrow.

After dealing with Eros, Artemis found her brother lying on the floor of his forest pavilion, caressing the laurel wreath as if he were playing with Daphne's hair. Looking disheveled and heartbroken, her brother became an errant wanderer.

Having defeated the python that haunted his family, the triumphant Apollo started his day, boastfully celebrating his victory. However, by the end of that day, he was a total wreck. On that day, long ago, his eyes lost their sparkle, and cynicism took root within him. Apollo turned into an echo far from the radiant deity he used to be when he was young.

Please, Apollo, not... again!

Artemis' thoughts raced in desperation as she realized her brother had withdrawn from the world—from life itself. Apollo stared at Dafnie like a hungry lion about to attack. His eyes looked fierce and cautious while she met his gaze with unrelenting defiance.

Apollo fell apart like a helpless man, and Artemis refused to see her brother crumble again. She had to protect both him and Dafnie. Disheartened, Artemis needed to calm Apollo and offer some advice to the couple. "Enough... Apollo, please! Calm down," she moved before Dafnie and placed a hand on Dafnie's shoulder. "Dafnie, please calm down. You need to calm down." Artemis urged her brother to stop before he did something rash. Her tone conveyed a desperate plea for her brother's well-being.

The situation unraveled, welcoming an ominous cloud of anguish in the room. Artemis made a mistake by sharing confidential information that wasn't hers to share. "Yes, we are gods, but we make mistakes too. We're not perfect. We'll never be perfect. But I can assure you we're trying to fix this."

"Why should I believe you?" Dafnie stepped aside to look at Apollo. "You don't care... we mortals are nothing to you."

Apollo's eyes widened in shock at the realization that Dafnie condemned his deeds and would not listen to his excuses. He needed to own up to his mistake and diffuse the situation. "I'm sorry for what I did. I'm sorry that I didn't tell you earlier... but..."

Apollo trailed off as his eyes softened. "Dafnie... listen to me. I'll fix this."

"This is all your fault. You had the itch to destroy the world because you felt wronged and justified. You needed to teach us a lesson! Life hasn't been fair or kind to me, either. Your actions are making us all suffer. Now I must live for the rest of my life in a nightmare, all because of you," Dafnie's accusing gaze turned reproachful and bitter.

"Please, Dafnie! Hear me out..." Apollo begged. "I'm going to make things right. Thrust me! I will make everything right."

"How? How are you going to make things right? You destroyed the world, and many people have lost their lives because of your thoughtlessness. Can you turn back time? What about the future? Will I be able to trust that you won't have one of your outbursts and try to destroy the world again?" Dafnie shot, willfully staring at Apollo, giving him one chance to explain his terrible actions.

Apollo's heart hammered against his ribs, desperate to undo the damage he saw mirrored in Dafnie's eyes. It never occurred to Apollo that he would hurt the one he loved most, nor consider how Dafnie would feel if she found out he wanted to destroy the world from someone else. Apollo appeared insistent on proving to Dafnie that he cared and would do whatever it took to fix his mistakes.

"I'll never!" Apollo's dangerous whisper held the force of a gut punch. "Not after my sister delivers my punishment, which will cost me my immortality. Not after I found you..." Apollo's explosive retort reverberated through the room. His breath labored with desperation, and his eyes shone with fear.

Artemis's eyes widened as she studied the tension between Dafnie and Apollo as they continued to build. She could not believe the situation was getting out of control this way. Apollo's eyes begged for his lover's approval while Dafnie looked dejected with a heavy heart.

The huntress now understood why her father, Zeus, wanted to use Dafnie as his trump card. The aloft ruler of all the Olympians knew his son best. Zeus, aware of Apollo's infatuation with Dafnie, realized his son would only heed the words of his beloved.

Artemis couldn't bear seeing her brother and Dafnie fight any longer. She went toward her brother and placed an assuring hand on his shoulder. "Apollo, please go to your house tonight and try to get some rest. You need to calm down and clear your mind. You're impulsive when you get agitated."

"But..." Apollo objected but then caught Artemis's expression. Her eyes pleaded with him to heed her advice.

"But nothing. I'll talk to Dafnie and then check on you later. Please… I'll watch over Dafnie tonight and make sure she's safe. Does that sound good?" Artemis examined her brother's reaction. When Apollo nodded, she gave him a reassuring smile before she continued in a calm voice. "Now let me handle this, okay?"

She stroked Apollo's arm with sisterly love and pleaded for cooperation. Apollo suspected leaving would harm his relationship with Dafnie. He was about to object, but his sister shook her head to prevent him from saying anything else. From the pit of his stomach, Apollo wanted to oppose but reconsidered at the last minute.

"Trust me," Artemis urged Apollo as he calmed. Her brother's erratic behavior always surprised Artemis. Apollo was a powerful god but often acted like a mortal man. He was impulsive, naïve, sometimes insecure, and insufferably cocky.

Apollo was a literal walking contradiction, both perfect and imperfect. Defeated, her brother disappeared in a flash of soft golden light, leaving Artemis and Dafnie alone to talk about anything.

"Now, Dafnie... I believe the tea Apollo made is ready. Judging by its sweet scent, it's his special blend to soothe one's nerves. It's also quite delicious." Artemis chose two mugs from the nearby dish rack and poured the warm tea.

✳✳✳

Dafnie looked on the verge of tears. Confusion messed with her head. Dafnie didn't mean to unleash her fury on Apollo, but his actions confused her. She had no choice but to listen to Artemis's advice.

"Artemis, I'm... confused," Dafnie started, but Artemis gently grabbed her hand and squeezed it. "Why would he do that?"

"Because Apollo follows his heart most of the time, even when misguided," Artemis wanted to say more but refrained from the idea. It was best to describe Apollo in simple terms.

Tears streaked down Dafnie's face, but she seemed to relax after a few sips of the tea. She then looked at Artemis. "What makes you believe he will make things right? How will he fix this mess when he can't even fix himself?"

"To be honest, I don't know the answer. My brother has always been unpredictable and free-spirited. Apollo always stood out and never allowed others to change his way of viewing life," Artemis reflected as she sipped her tea. "But one thing I'm certain —you've changed him. For the next few days, he's been going to face trial by our father and the other gods. Rather than avoiding this trial, as he had done in the past, he's facing the consequences of his crimes head-on."

"He did? But why didn't he tell me?" Dafnie's eyes held an unwavering challenge powered by her question.

"I'm not sure, but it's because he wanted to repent for your sake. He wronged wants to make amends." Arthemis paused, searching for a way to diffuse Dafnie's disappointment. "Besides, he gave you that necklace, right? A pull between you two existed before you met."

Dafnie's hand flew to her neck, seeking the familiar weight of her necklace when reaching for the object in question. The cold metal pressed against her skin, a heavy anchor against the oncoming flood of panic. "What happens now?" Dafnie pushed for more information.

"I came as the enforcer of the verdict. He'll face punishment for his actions," Artemis said, her statement without hesitation.

"Will he lose his godhood?" Dafnie blurted out without thinking.

Artemis's face turned grim. "Some of it but not all. He must atone through hardship," she finished with a sigh.

They sat at the table, lingering until every drop of tea and the choice of food disappeared—leaving them satiated. Artemis stood to take the dirty dishes to the sink while Dafnie sat at the table, emotionally drained.

"I have a thought. I plan to invite my grandmother, Phoebe, to visit you. She's wise and can guide you. But promise me you won't tell Apollo. I suspect he cannot see the future if you're in it. It's the enchantment on the tattoo."

Dafnie looked down at her tattoo, now covering half her forearm. As Apollo and Artemis obsessed about her tattoo, Dafnie wondered about its meaning. Still, she got no explanation about its real purpose.

"I suggest you shower and take a nap. Apollo's been keeping you up late. I know my brother well. He overindulges with his lovers." Artemis popped a piece of fruit in her mouth before she continued. "I've heard he has quite the stamina."

Dafnie stood from the table and made a beeline to her bedroom. The warmth of her blush, spreading from her neck to the tip of her ears, prompted her to move faster. Images of how often they made love until dawn fluttered in her mind. Dafnie couldn't deny that she missed Apollo. Still, she was mad at him. Only a little angry.

Chapter 36

Anxiety

"No, no, no... It can't be happening again." Apollo's voice boomed through the room as he paced back and forth in his living room. He looked like a caged animal trapped in his thoughts and fears.

Apollo, whose self-assurance became legendary, trembled as his confidence shattered. He couldn't bear the thought of losing Dafnie, his love, his everything...

He seethed with fury. Engulfed by a sense of resentment and deep desperation...

His head spun with dizzying confusion. The icy fingers of panic gripped his soul as his body became weightless.

"Shit, not again... Why does this keep happening to me?" Apollo slumped on the bench, his shoulders shaking with every harsh exhale. He stared at the shiny lacker of the instrument as his mind abandoned all rational thoughts.

Apollo caressed the piano keys, looking for comfort, but nothing seemed to soothe his troubled heart. He replayed the moments at Dafnie's house. Criticism shone in Dafnie's eyes, judging him with cutting harshness. Her piercing gaze lingered on his head, haunting him for many hours.

"Now I have to live for the rest of my life in a nightmare... All because of you!" Dafnie's accusation played with his emotions nonstop.

"I'm cursed..." Apollo's dejection cut through the air as he rested his head on the instrument's shelf.

Apollo kept repeating Dafnie's question over and over. "Will I be able to trust you won't have one of your outbursts and try to destroy the world again?"

Dafnie's eye-opening inquiry pierced through Apollo's defenses. After all, he committed an inexcusable act against all human beings. Apollo allowed bitterness to consume him and brought about the world's destruction. In doing so, he put Dafnie, his precious nymph, in grave danger. He unleashed a chain of events in which humans and animals mutated, causing great suffering and irreversible damage.

Dafnie was right. He had no one else to blame but himself. As that realization sank in, Apollo's chest hurt, and his eyes stung with unshed tears. He believed he was a lost cause, undeserving of being loved by someone as gentle as Dafnie.

"No! I can't let those fucking confuse me, or I will lose her for good." His self-chastising tone reverberated across the room.

Apollo needed to do something. He would not give up on Dafnie. He would fight for her, do anything to be a better man, and win her trust. Dafnie was his star, pulling him out of the bitter darkness inside him. She brought back the spark and joy he once had.

"How are you going to make things right?" Apollo froze in his tracks as he remembered Dafnie's most condemning remark. A knot formed in his throat, making it hard for him to breathe. Apollo looked down at the keys with longing, finding some comfort in the familiar feel under his fingertips while suffering a significant loss in his heart. He needed to make things better with Dafnie but wasn't sure how.

Apollo paused his grim thoughts, taking a deep breath as his fingers hovered over the keys. He closed his eyes and caressed the smooth surface, mimicking the gentle touch only meant for a lover.

He ought to fix things with his lover, and music was always his preferred outlet for apologizing and finding solace. He found a melody that fitted his current mood, helping him calm his nerves. Apollo picked a song that conveyed great love to the woman who held his heart. Otherwise, he would lose his mind.

He poured his regret into every note, hoping she would hear the sincerity through his playing and forgive him.

He settled on a simple yet emotional tune. Soon, the room filled with harmony. The song's simplicity helped him express his feelings of sadness and agony.

He started with an improvised introduction that added depth to the original melody. As he progressed with his performance, the song turned darker, mirroring his uneasiness and insecurities. Apollo's nimble fingers moved across the keyboard with gentleness, counting his music would reach Dafnie's ears.

As Apollo ended his improvisation, he hummed the song with his entire heart. Its delicate, introspective tune was like a balm to his tumultuous soul. He poured his being into every note. Wishing Dafnie appreciated his desires from afar as his fingers flew over the keyboard, intensifying the tune's nostalgia.

He sang in perfect intonation, skillfully expressing his inner longing. Each word carried the great love Apollo felt within as stray tears escaped from the confines of his closed eyes. He used his power to deliver the sound through the air to its intended recipient. The melody came from his heart, assuming Dafnie would forgive his foolishness.

Apollo was so consumed with his ache and playing that he overlooked Artemis sitting on an armchair. She listened to her brother's lament, allowing him to send his grieving love to Dafnie.

When Apollo finished singing, he opened his eyes. Artemis stood across the room, watching and waiting for him.

"Apollo, that was beautiful and heartwarming. I don't let doubt overcome you. Dafnie understands your heart. Your apology will not go unnoticed. I'm sure of that." Artemis' calm and reassuring tone drifted through the room. "By the way, Dafnie is calm and under my sleeping spell. She's had a rough day, so I ensured she gets plenty of rest. That way, she can think for a while. Alone!" Artemis pressed on when Apollo seemed on the verge of protesting.

"Thank you, Artemis." Apollo's grave and filled with emotion voice had a menacing, chilling quality.

"Concern painted her gaze when I mentioned your punishment." Artemis's smile didn't quite reach her eyes, a hint of wistfulness infusing her tone.

Apollo paused, dejected that he was losing control of the situation, before continuing. "Does she have any idea what it is?"

"No!" Artemis's sorrow-filled voice filled the air.

"I... want to see her..." Apollo's broken voice trailed off. "I should be with her, Artemis?"

"I wouldn't advise that. Dafnie's still mad at you because you were dishonest. Give her until tomorrow and approach her with care." Artemis's words hung heavy around them, cloaked with grief. "If you love her, you must be tender with her feelings."

At the warning, Apollo faced the piano to distract himself from the sudden pain in his heart. "It's just that I can't stop thinking about her. I want to make amends for not being honest and right my wrongs. I don't want to lose her." Apollo's soft tone filled the tense room.

"You're in love and fight fiercely for her. Tomorrow, you'll apologize, but consider how you do that. I will not allow you to make a fool of yourself. Remember, you are a powerful god, not a stupid lad tending cows." Artemis' tender voice somehow soothed and irritated Apollo.

"Hey! I resent that statement." Apollo took offense at Artemis's remark but chose not to engage in more conflict.

"Either way, you must think before you talk to her instead of being impulsive. That is all." Artemis' resignation colored her cheeks as a sigh escaped her generous lips.

"I want to restore everything... and make her happy." Apollo's brief pause unnerved him to the core, refusing to recognize his shortcomings. "I only want her to be happy with me." Artemis stared at him, not surprised at his sudden rant. "To be the only man for her. I-I will fix this... I-I-I will be her... everything..." Apollo's incoherence shrouded him in uncertainty, grasping for words.

"Of course! You want to do all that. But what if that does not make things right with Dafnie? The world needs saving, and I'll make sure you don't get in the way," Artemis' knowing words held a hint of caring cruelty. Still, Dafnie's existence had a purpose. Apollo needed to get his priorities straight and was on board with what the gods wanted.

Something was wrong. Noticing the sudden change in Artemis's mood, Apollo felt she hid something important. He stood from the piano and ambled toward Artemis with feline grace and predatory strides, cornering her on her chair. He would not allow Artemis to manipulate him by using Dafnie.

Apollo was no fool. He prided himself on a cunning god who understood his sister's warning. He was confident the gods needed a hero to save the mortal world. Apollo would take on that responsibility. Dafnie played a big part in picking Earth's savior and delivering his ultimate punishment. Without this, she found herself tasked with saving the world.

"I must know our father's plan with Dafnie and me." Apollo's demand echoed through the room as his sister's eyes widened with surprise. "Is Zeus using her against me? I won't hesitate to oppose him if he's using her. He can do whatever he wants with me, but not her," Apollo threatened.

"I do not believe Father wants to hurt or use you. He realizes you have been miserable for a long time. Zeus was the one who gathered Daphne's essence to bring her back for your sake. He asked the Moirai to look at your thread of fate and asked the oracle to reveal your future in private. No one is privy to what they discussed, but your fate is fluid and uncertain," Artemis reflected. "You're still unable to foretell, right?"

Apollo hesitated before answering, "No, I can't."

"Destiny weaved a complicated web for you and Dafnie. She is your fate, which is why you can't see it. From now on, you must base your choices on faith." Artemis's words trailed off as she explained.

"That can't be. Fates decide our lives before we come into this world. Time flows as planned by the Cosmos." Apollo's unwavering words carried the weight of his circumstance. A force he could not alter, ever.

"I'm not so sure about that, my dear brother." Artemis stared into Apollo's troubled gaze to find answers. Instead, she uncovered more questions.

"Why do you believe that?" Apollo moved toward a nearby window facing Dafnie's house, longing to be beside her.

"It seems your purpose far exceeds that of a mere god. You and Dafnie have a crucial role to play in this world..." Artemis analyzed the implications of what she was saying.

"What do you mean by that?" With a knot of worry in his stomach, Apollo's question revealed a vulnerable uncertainty and fear of the answer he'd receive.

"Something is going on in Mount Olympus. The place is a mess, and Zeus looks worried all the time. He's not acting normal and hiding something. No one has a clue what he's concealing." Artemis' voice, laced with concern, fluttered like a delicate bird.

"Mmm... I understand!" Apollo's eyes, dulled with sorrow, mirrored the emptiness he saw in Dafnie's darkened room. "I'm willing to do anything, even lose my life, to save the world for Dafnie's sake." Apollo sat across from Artemis, still looking out the window. Artemis remained quiet, her senses on high alert, waiting for him to finish mulling over his thoughts.

After contemplating the house next door for a few minutes, Apollo tuned toward Artemis. A serious look on his face. "About the gods' verdict and my punishment. Can I ask you to wait until tomorrow? I want to talk to Dafnie and make amends with her first. Is that okay?" Apollo asked, hopeful that soon his loneliness would be a distant memory.

Artemis sighed. "You know the gods are impatient. They want you to face your punishment at once..." Artemis considered for a minute. "But they didn't give me a timeline of when to deliver the punishment. I'll agree with your request and wait until tomorrow."

The twins seldom agreed with anything. Thus, today was a rare and precious occurrence. Apollo nodded in understanding as his heart filled with gratitude. "Thank you, Artemis."

"Don't thank me. You may not like what I say."

Apollo shrugged, not letting the implications of her comment affect him. "I would also like Dafnie's opinion and to weigh in on my punishment. I'm willing to accept any punishment coming from her. It breaks my heart to see her suffer, and I'll do anything to make it up to her," Apollo confessed, his fondness for Dafnie giving him the courage to face adversity.

"Is that what you want?"

"Yes." Apollo would not budge on this matter. He remained indifferent to the other gods' opinions. In his eyes and heart, only Dafnie's perspective mattered.

"Then I will let you be." Artemis stood from her chair and disappeared with a flash of light.

"Good night and..." Apollo whispered as he stared at Dafnie's window for a while longer. "Until tomorrow, my love." Apollo knew the day and night would be troublesome. Patience wasn't his strong suit, but this time, he would wait.

"Fernhoof!" Apollo called to his trusty companion.

"Yes, Apollo?"

"We are going on a hunt. Get ready!"

And with that, Apollo produced his golden bow and quiver and headed out the front door. Fernhoof dutifully followed behind.

Chapter 37

Secrets and Safety

The early morning rays filtered through the window as the soft light lingered, tickling Dafnie's face. Having recovered from the previous day's stress, she peered at her surroundings. She fell asleep right after talking to Artemis. She took a quick shower and plopped on her bed, drained. Dafnie's emotional exhaustion depleted her, so her body gave out for the day.

The only time she checked out from the world was when her parents died in that terrible accident many years ago.

"¡Pa', Ma', ayuda por favor! I need your advice," Dafnie whispered as she stretched. She looked for the comforting and warm body that had been present every morning for the past few weeks but found her room empty. She was alone and cold.

Dafnie longed for the familiar yet comforting presence during her morning walks. She missed the weighty arm wrapped around her waist and the distinctive spicy musk scent that belonged to Apollo. She missed the slow rise and fall of Apollo's breathing and the heat of his body.

Emptiness and coldness greeted her.

Dafnie replayed the events from the previous day. The images assaulted her full force as she lay among the sheets longer than usual. Her mind tried to make sense of everything but didn't know where to start. Dafnie needed some answers, and Artemis had them.

Recognizing the futility of staying in bed, she got up without a second to spare. Dafnie slept most of the previous day and itched to leave the house. She headed to the bathroom and took a quick shower. After finishing her morning routine, she headed to the closet to wear something comfortable. It looked like a nippy day, so she chose a thick pair of leggings and a warm hoodie to complete her attire for the day.

Dafnie stared at her reflection with vacancy in her eyes. Her gaze looked hollow, as if a piece of her soul was missing. Shaking her head, Dafnie had breakfast. She was starving and weak and needed to eat something before she sorted out her problems.

Upon her arrival, the clatter of pans and the cheerful hum of Fernhoof greeted Dafnie like a warm hug. Artemis made her way to the table, reading a fictional book Dafnie didn't remember purchasing.

"I admit… mortals can be creative. But I'm disappointed they forgot we help them thrive. Humans are ungrateful creatures," Artemis said, closing the book. She then directed her intense stare at Dafnie.

Dafnie, recognizing the challenge, stared back with equal intensity as she sat across from the goddess of the hunt and moon.

"The gods have done nothing to garner the admiration of

your people. We're too proud to bother with Earth. We only show up when we want something," Artemis paused before continuing. "However, my little brother is not above such things. He prefers to live life without the royal intrigues. He even acts like a mortal. It reminds me of the time he spent with Admetus," Artemis gave Dafnie a pointed look as if testing her. "Did you know Apollo was Admetus' lover?"

When Dafnie prodded her, she was unsure of Artemis's intentions. Still, she knew Apollo didn't shy away from having a passionate relationship with someone he loved. "Yes, from what I read."

"What's in the books is nothing compared to reality. Their relationship was intense, and Apollo was a dotting companion. He loved Admetus dearly. His heart melted for the king, and Apollo's carefree behavior irritated our mother, but he was happy. They understood each other and based their bond on mutual respect," Dafnie sensed Artemis's comment was catty but respectful, respecting her brother's feelings and actions. "Their relationship was quite the scandal around Mount Olympus—a powerful and cunning god subjecting to a mortal in such a way became the talk of the town. Some gods even made fun of his impulsive choice. I can still remember our mother's anger. But Apollo didn't care. Their opinions meant nothing to him."

"I read Apollo has had many male and female lovers. I suppose you're trying to make me think less of him and discourage me from seeing him favorably. Guess what? It won't work," Dafnie needed to be firm with her reply, trying to clarify her point. "I don't care about those sorts of things. I'm confident about his desire for me. It's quite palpable every time he is near me. Besides, his sexual experience will make our sex more interesting and enjoyable. For someone as inexperienced as myself, I'm looking forward to learning about my sexuality from him." Defiance showed in Dafnie's eyes as she finished.

"Really? What if he tires of you and moves on to another lover?"

"Then... he moves on to another lover. Many couples break up all the time. I can't control him—that would be selfish and arrogant."

"Are you sure about that?" Artemis inquired.

The question surprised Dafnie. Would she be able to get over Apollo if he found someone else to love? Probably not... but that was beside the point. "I think you're taking your prying way too far. Mind your business," Dafnie finished, uncomfortable with the intrusion.

Artemis's gaze darted to Fernhoof—her cheeks turning crimson. "Fernhoof! I believe breakfast is ready. We don't need your help. It's time for you to leave and tend to your master," Artemis commanded Fernhoof while glaring at Dafnie.

Fernhoof felt proud to be Apollo's friend and didn't like Artemis's remark. "Hey! I don't appreciate your comment, Artemis. Apollo is not my master. We're friends. Do not get those two mixed up."

"Judging by how you treat Fernhoof, you don't know your brother that well. I have been living with Apollo all this time and haven't seen your brother disrespect Fernhoof the way you did," Dafnie accused.

Artemis felt wronged by the retort. "What did you say?"

"You heard me." Dafnie would not allow Artemis to intimidate her with her veiled threats.

There was a sudden flash of light. A woman materialized in

the dining room, ending their conversation. "I made it just in time. Fernhoof looks like he's about to pass out, and the two of you look like you want to kill each other. Artemis, I recommend you behave and not antagonize my granddaughter-in-law," Phoebe said as she sat beside Artemis, looking annoyed. Artemis paled when she saw her grandmother. "Now I need to talk to Dafnie privately."

"But Grandmother, we haven't had breakfast," Artemis complained.

"I believe you can go to the backyard and enjoy your meal there," Phoebe dismissed her granddaughter with a wave.

Artemis was not in the mood to contradict the other woman. "Yes, Grandmother! I'll give you some privacy."

Artemis grabbed her breakfast and headed to the yard. Phoebe stood, picked a plate, and filled it with Fernhoof's delicious fare, handpicking her items. "I think you are famished, considering you didn't eat yesterday. You have a crucial decision to make and need your energy."

The Titaness placed a dish loaded with meats and fruits before Dafnie. Instantly, her mouth watered at the sight of such a delightful array of food. Dafnie played with a piece of meat before responding. "Thank you very much. This meal... looks... so good," she said between hefty bites. Dafnie wolfed down her food in minutes.

Delighted, Phoebe studied Dafnie's healthy appetite after a tough day. "I apologize that your life has been challenging. But... I must confess... your road ahead will be difficult and lonely."

Dafnie stopped eating at the mention of the word "lonely." Hesitation crept in as she wondered what the response would be. "Why will it be lonely? Will... Apollo leave?"

"I can't go into too much detail, but your threads and futures are inconclusive. Both you and Apollo have a unique fate. It's unprecedented. A path that's written but is malleable. Every time we try to read your futures, it changes, but a few things still are the same."

Phoebe elegantly moved to sit next to Dafnie, admiring her for a while before she continued. "I understand why my grandson is so smitten with you." Her feather-light touch made Dafnie's breath catch in her throat. "I'm forbidden to tell you anymore. I hope you will not mind my ambiguity, but here is what I can say. You will bear Apollo's twins, a boy and a girl. You will be happy about the news for a short while, but you will face great suffering and separation. It'll be up to you to figure out how to come together."

"Separation?" Dafnie asked, afraid to inquire for more.

"Yes! I want you to understand that neither of your journeys will be easy. So, you must have faith," Phoebe said, then kissed Dafnie's forehead. "I'm sorry, but I'm not allowed to tell you anymore. Also, I would appreciate it if you didn't mention this to Apollo. He has his trials to fulfill."

"I understand... but one more thing, if I may ask."

The Titaness showed her motherly disposition, making Dafnie feel at ease. "You may."

"I'm having a tough time understanding something. Why is our future so unclear? Why us?"

"Bigger things loom that I'm not allowed to discuss with you. Your actions will shape the mortal and immortal world," Phoebe finished before standing from the table and moving toward the living room. A golden portal opened out of thin air as she stared at Dafnie. "The Moirai decided your relationship with

Apollo is important and meant to happen. Fates decided your first encounter was to fail, but not this time. Even if your relationship isn't perfect, it's what we all need to keep going and survive. It's what the two of you need to be happy. But keep in mind that the road ahead will be harsh. Be ready for anything. And please do not mention any of this to Apollo. It's important he remains ignorant of this information," Phoebe said before disappearing through the portal.

Dafnie sat at the table, her heart pounding, leaving an ache in her chest. Her head swam with questions, and like water, the answer slipped through her fingers. Phoebe delivered both a prophecy and a warning. Apollo's calamity wasn't the only thing they needed to worry about. There was something else going on, but what was it?

Dafnie didn't spot Artemis returning from the backyard, too engrossed with her problems. "Dafnie? Are you alright?" Artemis sounded worried this time.

"I think so! The sinking feeling of Apollo's disaster is the least of our worries. Other issues keep gnawing at my gut," Dafnie said, massaging her temples as a headache developed.

Artemis approached the table and sat across from Dafnie. "I mentioned this to Apollo yesterday and will repeat it to you. Mount Olympus is in chaos, and the gods are playing sides. Zeus keeps quiet and isn't telling anyone what's happening." She reached for the dirty dishes and took them to the kitchen. "Just a word of caution. Be prepared for the worst. And do not trust anyone."

"Does that include you and Apollo?" With no time for games, Dafnie wanted to be direct with the huntress.

"Let me be clear—once more. We are the only ones you can trust. I'd be cautious of everyone else."

"Does that include your friends? Should I be cautious of your companions?"

"Yes! From a strategic standpoint, you can never be too careful. Yet, gods and humans will do anything that guarantees their survival. Everyone else is inconsequential."

At least Artemis was candid with her opinions, and Dafnie appreciated her straightforwardness. "If I am to trust you, then what's next?"

"Next? Mmmm. Well... You need to decide if Apollo's punishment is fair or too lenient. He values your opinion and seeks your sanction on the matter, even above that of the divine. He stands ready to accept any penalty you consider fit. Also, he's very anxious. He's been staring out the window all morning. It gave me all sorts of heebie-jeebies. That man is on the prowl."

"Really?" Dafnie asked, surprised.

"Yes! When he sees you again, be prepared for the man to lunge at you like a ravenous tiger," Artemis said in a warning tone. She turned to look at Dafnie and produced a ring out of thin air. "I know you think better in the outdoors. I want you to have this. It's dangerous out there, and food and water will be scarce. But with this ring, you can summon containers holding provisions. I also place a blessing to protect you from harm," she said, placing the ring on Dafnie's thumb.

They watched Dafnie's tattoo interact with the jewelry, emitting a soft glow that caught their attention.

"Mmmm. Interesting reaction. Your ability to handle yourself against those creatures impressed me," Artemis said, staring at Dafnie. "You were a talented hunter in your past life, but I didn't know if your talents would transfer to this life. I'm glad the skill is still with you."

Dafnie looked at the band, admiring the craftsmanship. "Thank you... I'm at a loss here."

"Say nothing. You need all the help you can get to survive this world."

"Right," Dafnie agreed. "I'll leave now and process this new dilemma. There's a place by the creek that I go to think."

Chapter 38

Wolf

The gnawing anxiety in Apollo's chest kept him from sleeping. Every tick of the grandfather clock echoed the unease consuming him since yesterday. He was a fucked-up mess. Being a god meant Apollo didn't need food or sleep to survive. His emotions ran high all night as he watched Dafnie's house, leaving him exhausted the next day.

Many concerns assaulted him in a single second without mercy or control. He felt anger, frustration, and, above all, desire. His heart and mind were in battle, each contradicting the other.

Fury raged within Apollo like a wildfire that threatened to consume him. How could he be so senseless as to not be forthcoming with his precious nymph? But sure, he had to be a pretentious asshole. Apollo realized hiding the truth from Dafnie was a mistake. That was true until he did not know any better, and the whole situation blew in his face and got out of control.

"So plain and fucking stupid." The air hung heavy with silence as Apollo muttered to the empty room.

Frustration was a close second on his list of emotional rollercoasters for the day. His arrogance frustrated him often, but he repeated his mistakes. He thought he was safeguarding his beloved, yet he unknowingly suffocated her with his actions.

When he left Dafnie's house, he realized he thought little of her. Somehow, Apollo believed Dafnie couldn't handle the truth. Dafnie's resentment toward him wasn't surprising, given his malicious acts. He could see it from her condemning stare.

"I'm a little piece of shit of a motherfucker!" A heavy sigh escaped Apollo's lips as he pushed the chair to the window. His shoulders slumped with an unbearable sorrow. "I'm a fucking dick!" He buried his face in the crook of his arm.

He had been too proud and arrogant, like always. And now he was a total asshole. A wave of worry washed over Apollo, but he wouldn't betray her trust again. He acted as if she meant nothing when Dafnie was his entire world.

And that gave way to the ultimate piece of resistance and the most fucked-up of all the emotions. An insatiable craving for Daphne flowed through Apollo's body. All day and night, he felt horny.

There was no other way to put it politely.

No matter the scene's gruesomeness, the primal hunger to mate with his huntress lover burned hotter than ever. Apollo couldn't figure out when his anger and frustration led to desire. Whenever he thought of Dafnie's angry and defiant eyes, he couldn't help but feel a surge of an all-consuming lust.

Temptation made him desperate. The previous night, he wanted to sneak into Dafnie's house and apologize like a bumbling fool, but his sister gained an advantage over him. Artemis had fucking placed a protection spell on Dafnie's house that prevented him from going inside her house.

She'd cock-blocked him on purpose.

Apollo raised his head to look out the window and saw Artemis coming out of Dafnie's house, muttering while kicking some imaginary rocks from under her foot. Apollo noticed his twin looked frustrated. "That fucking bitch! I ought to give her a good spanking. Her enchantment is why I can't get close to Dafnie," Apollo complained, unable to hold in his annoyance.

He stood so fast from his chair that it flew across the room. Apollo looked at his sister with desperate intent, compelling her to look his way. "You little shit, look at me," he grumbled, and almost as on cue, Artemis turned toward him and paled the moment she saw him. "That's right, I'm going to kick your ass."

As usual, Artemis recovered from her initial shock and made a rude gesture for his enjoyment. She topped off her display of affection with a smug grin that colored her cheeks. She even sent sweet kisses flying his way. Apollo viciously scowled as he balled his hands, digging his nails into the tender flesh and drawing blood from the little crescent-shaped wounds. He couldn't believe Artemis was mocking him and wasn't happy about it.

"Sir, are you okay?" Fernhoof's query fluttered from behind the kitchen counter—as far away from Apollo as he could manage.

Apollo's eyes widened in shock as his heart pounded in his chest. "Fucking hell, Fernhoof! When did you come? I told you to monitor Dafnie. That means to stay at her house." Apollo's annoyance permeated the air.

"I got kicked out." Fernhoof's voice quivered with hesitation as his eyes darted around the room.

"BY WHOM?" Apollo, sullen and cockblocked, was losing his temper. "I'M NOT HAVING A GOOD DAY AT ALL. SO BE QUICK!!!"

"Your grandmother..." Fernhoof hesitated, afraid that Apollo might smite him right where he stood.

"WHAT? Why?" Apollo complained, slumping, but this time on the floor, considering he lost his chair during his outburst and couldn't figure out where it landed.

"Apollo, could it be Phoebe has?"

"Yeah! She has a prophecy and is delivering it. Shit! Why is it that my foresight doesn't work with Dafnie? What am I supposed to do?"

He fixated on the house next door, his penetrating eyes pleading for his wife to return. After a while, Apollo noticed Artemis went inside after finishing her meal. Her eyes lingered on him, her gaze filled with mixed emotions. A beautiful yet concerned smile played his sister's plump lips this time. He calmed down quite a bit and waited.

Sure, they had moments of sibling rivalries, but overall, they cared and watched out for each other. Apollo accepted the need to listen to his sister and wait without resentment.

That was until Dafnie walked out the back door.

Apollo's hunter instinct went into overdrive as he stood from his spot and staked the window. Compulsively, he reached down to his crotch, feeling the bulge taking residence since the night before.

He wanted his precious nymph next to him. Apollo craved falling asleep with Dafnie snuggled in a tight embrace, his arms wrapped around her petite waist. He missed waking every morning to her warmth and floral-minty scent. He yearned to kiss her and make love to her. To see her eyes glazed with raw pleasure as her flushed body moved in synchronized to and from against his, swiveling her hips to meet each of his thrusts. Apollo thirsted for Dafnie's gentle caress. Her exploration was hesitant until boldness commanded her senses, pulling him closer for a needy kiss.

He adored complying with Dafnie's wavering requests to listen to her sexy moans. Apollo wanted to feel her legs wrapped around his waist, feeling her possessive claim, accepting him as he loved her with eager enthusiasm.

Apollo's chest burned with a fiery rage. His fists clenched as he realized the unnecessary pain his lies inflicted on Dafnie. Little did he know his dishonesty got him kicked out of her house, sending him into a frenzy. He jeopardized their relationship and now acted rashly. Apollo was impulsive, lacking his usual calm and methodical nature. "I'm fucking riling myself up and losing my mind. Being a mindless jerk is one of my glorious traits on most days. I need to talk to my beloved Dafnie. Why am I this unstable?" Apollo asked, mumbling to no one. He found some comfort in talking about his predicament.

"What was that, my lord?" Fernhoof asked, looking concerned and wanting to help.

"It's nothing, my friend. I'm sorry." Apollo acknowledged his friend's hurt feelings and admitted his injustice. "It's strange, trying to figure out what came over me. I have these sudden outbursts that I can't control. For my love, I'll make things right for everyone." Humbled, Apollo smiled at his friend.

"I understand, Apollo, but you must apologize. It looks like she's going on a walk—a suitable time to talk. If you catch her and explain yourself to her, you can patch up your relationship."

Apollo felt desperate and wanted to know if Dafnie hated him. "Do you think she wants to see me?"

"Sir, you are a charming god..." Fernhoof hesitated before continuing in a firm, confident voice. "You are the mighty sun god who killed the fearsome python. Founded the Phythian Games and stewarded the performing arts. You are the mentor and inspiration to the muses. Gods, mortals, men, and women adore you. I do not doubt that your sweet Dafnie will forgive you."

Apollo was at a crossroads regarding what to do next. "Yeah! You are right… wooing her is the best option. I'll win her trust and love her nice and good." He claimed with confidence and a crazed look.

Careful not to anger Apollo anymore, Fernhoof wondered if Apollo was in the right mental state or if he needed to be left alone. "Well, Apollo, you must be sure she forgives you before you chase her. She won't appreciate it if you force yourself on her. May I remind you of that first night you met?"

"I'm going to approach her as a wolf. I don't think she'll be into snakes. They have a nasty reputation nowadays, and transforming into an old lady is wrong, but a wolf?! Now, that's another different story. They're mighty and handsome. Women these days think werewolves are sexy. So, I would feed into that fantasy. Also, they're one of my sacred animals." Apollo's eyes darted around, his voice a frantic whisper as he ignored Fernhoof.

Fernhoof's pleas went unheard, leaving him frustrated. "Apollo? Listen! You need to clear your mind and think this through."

Apollo stopped what he was saying and looked at his friend. Confusion washed over Apollo as his hands trembled, trying to decide what to do next. "Fernhoof, why am I acting this way?"

"Because you love Dafnie and will do anything for her. But you need to calm down." Fernhoof moved closer as he slumped his shoulder in a submissive stance. "When you're desperate, you become irrational. Make sure a rational idea is going through your head before you go to her. But that's my opinion. Now, she's out in the forest. Didn't you tell me she loves nature?"

"Yes, I did... I also hunted for those creatures because I wanted her to be safe. She goes on walks in the mornings and thinks by the creek."

"Right now, she's out there distressing and enjoying the woods. You need to go to her and apologize and make her understand you are sorry for being a dolt," Fernhoof finished good-heartedly, trying to be encouraging and honest.

"You are good, my friend. I'm going after her and plead my case," Apollo said as he removed his shirt and pants. His underwear and the rest of his clothes followed right after.

"Woah! What are you doing there, Apollo? You cannot get naked like that," Fernhoof complained when he saw Apollo undress. The faun knew the Apollo was perfect in every way. With his superior genes, the sun god made anyone blush with embarrassment.

Apollo was the embodiment of perfection!

"Why? It's my house. What do you think I'm doing? I'm apologizing and getting my love back as a wolf. As I pointed out earlier, modern women seem enamored with stories of alpha werewolves. I'm going to capitalize on that trend. Besides, this is my favorite shirt, and I don't want to ruin it when I transform into my striking wolf form." Apollo finished.

Chapter 39

Fright

The forecast was just as Dafnie expected. A crispness filled the air, carrying the distinct scent of pine—a clear sign of the season changing from summer to fall. The trees surrounding her house changed color from rich greens to fading colors.

Against Dafnie's liking, the crisp morning clung to her warm body. As always, the day started with a confusing undertone. So, it began when cold and hot weather wanted to coexist—forcing each other's wills. Indeed, a fickle time when putting on too many clothes could prove too hot, and not putting on enough layers was cold. The sun's rays gave a gentle but comforting warmth, trying to compromise with the frigid wind. Time for the fall breeze to bite with sharp fags of coldness throughout the day.

Although, Dafnie loved the vibrancy of colors. The leaves were an adorable mix of greens, reds, and goldens, tearing a pleasant sigh from my breast. The aspens would soon change to yellow, while the maple trees in her backyard would turn red.

As Dafnie admired her surroundings, an unsettling sensation washed over her. A lurking, invisible danger made her uneasy. Every rustle of leaves sent a tremor through her body, twisting her stomach into unpleasant knots. The impression seemed ominous, and it scared her. Deep inside, she knew the one watching her was none other than Apollo.

Intimidated, Dafnie headed for the back gate, trying to avoid looking in Apollo's direction. Dafnie sensed Apollo scrutinizing her from his living room window. She needed more time to gather her thoughts before facing him. Still, a nervous knot stabbed at her chest, thinking of their time together.

Dafnie crossed past her property boundaries, taking the shortest route to the neighborhood's walking track. The vegetation-crowded trail became a short course that traversed behind many community homes—easy to navigate with several picnicking areas and playgrounds. It also led to a trailhead she hiked during her lunch breaks when she wanted to step away from work and think.

Thus, outside the protective barrier, Dafnie took extra care before proceeding. She scanned her surroundings as she turned into the forest way. The area seemed clear, and the animals behaved as usual. "That's a good sign." A tremor ran through her as she exhaled, and her racing pulse settled.

The trail was easy and enjoyable.

Surrounding the path were aspens peppered with pine trees here and there. The slender white trunk of the tree, with its mahogany brown scars, was a stark contrast to the deep green of the pines.

After a while, evergreens became prevalent as Dafnie ventured deeper into the hilly section of the forest—closest to the creek. As she moved closer to her destination, memories of her past resurfaced. Apollo looked both pissed and distraught. He seemed very human, very mortal. Dafnie had difficulty figuring him out and was at a loss for what to make of him as a man.

Apollo's deceit hung heavy in her mind, and the unspoken truth of his actions wept like a poisonous fog between them. Honesty was important to her, and Apollo hadn't been straightforward with her the entire time they'd been together.

Each confrontation chipped away at her spirit. Drained, the weight of responsibility turned into a heavy burden.

After an eventful morning the previous day, Dafnie found herself exhausted, wanting nothing more than to sleep away for the rest of the day. Overwhelmed by recent events, Dafnie lost her battle to find sleep.

Dafnie wondered if Artemis had done something to her. She wouldn't put it past Artemis to cast a sleeping spell to calm her down. After meeting Apollo and getting to know him, she wouldn't doubt the goddess could control her. Apollo and Artemis were indeed siblings and were not above playing tricks to get what they wanted.

Lost in her thoughts, Dafnie didn't register her arrival at the peaceful creek. Although smaller than the other brooks in the area, it still held a calming allure for her. The gurgling sounds of the water soothed her raging mind. The water's alluring movement was hypnotic.

When she calmed, Dafnie considered the events since meeting Apollo in a more level-headed way.

"Why hide this from me instead of being honest? Is he afraid he may lose yet another lover he cherishes?" Dafnie's voice cracked with hesitation—a feathery murmur revealing fragments of insecurities. "He's a popular god and Zeus's favorite son. Shit! Hera even admires his imposing charm and elegance." A dreamy haze settled over Dafnie as she reflected on their first encounter. The desperation in Apollo's gaze was a telltale sign of his failures at love. "He remained unmarried until this point. Why?!" Dafnie stared around in defeat. Dread gripped her heart as silence rang through the room while Artemis stood unfaced. "I won't judge him if that's what you fear. Sure! When we met, he was brutish and looked..." Dafnie's musings, dissecting everything she learned about Apollo, lead her to realization. "Apollo is quite the passionate, dotting lover who's also desperate."

Her habit of overanalyzing kicked into overdrive as every detail of Apollo manifested in her thoughts. Apollo's actions and temperament were erratic, and he showed no mercy toward his adversaries. Apollo's infatuation with Daphne resulted from being hit by Eros's problems. Before that terrible incident with Daphne, Apollo's life was on the rise. One other time, Apollo lost control of himself when Hyacinth died.

"It's tragic to lose two lovers. Tough on him and... his ego. Is there such a thing as a depressed god?" Dafnie considered, feeling silly she was talking to herself this much. She would keep her thoughts to herself, but today appeared to be an exception. "Why does he need to be complicated?"

It didn't help she was Daphne's reincarnation.

The nymph's life essence was coursing through her veins. Dafnie stared at her hands, wondering about her real purpose in this world. She was an ordinary woman. The tattoo on her wrist caught her attention.

"What does it all mean? Is this all connected?"

Her recollection of getting tattooed was unclear. The only thing she could remember after losing her parents was that she was a husk of her formal self. But afterward, something clicked within her. Was Apollo the same as when he lost Daphne?

It explained his lack of self-control when he was around her, and if that was true, Dafnie couldn't blame his possessiveness and desperate attempts to have her nearby. Apollo was clutching onto what was dear to him to the point of suffocation.

After finding reasons that raised even more questions, Dafnie returned her gaze to her laurel tattoo. Admittedly, the design was beautiful, with intricate and delicate details—a unique brand with unexpected qualities.

"Apollo mentioned my tattoo held an interesting magic. When in town, it reacted and became alive when those creatures appeared. Does it mean someone is protecting me?" Dafnie clenched her jaw, simmering concern burning at the lack of information.

Then, something on the tattoo seemed to catch her eye. The ink had a faint but hypnotic glow that moved—slightly. The longer she stared, the more its allure pulled her in. Her brain turned into a foggy mess as she heard distant voices.

"Daphne, come here..." A chorus called out, their tones sweet and exciting.

A flood of memories from her past life rushed back. Danie foresaw her old self running in the forest like a wild forest creature. Her hair trailed behind like a veil of silken strands as visions of thrilling hunting excursions filled her vision. Then Apollo appeared, his golden hair gleaming in the sunlight—a magnificent sight that captivated her heart.

Apollo! The thought fluttered into Dafnie's mind, acknowledging the sun god's presence.

The mighty hunter saunters around with a cocky, signature charm. His untamable beauty, coupled with his tall stature, made him stand out from everyone. He was glorious. Dafnie couldn't help but feel drawn to him when he joined his sister during their hunts. His playful teasing and friendly attitude were captivating. Everyone adored him. Everyone admired him.

Somehow, he looked different—livelier and more carefree. Then there were the fleeting yet sensual stares Apollo would give her past self. She would catch Apollo watching her with desire. A flicker of possessive jealousy, sharp and sudden as a viper's strike, oozed from Apollo. His gaze held a firm hold on Dafnie as another man tried to get close. Daphne would have felt shy because of his attention, but now, as Dafnie, she longed for his touch.

Her past life memories came and went in the blink of an eye, and just like that, they left for good. But her mind kept going at a quick pace. Soon, her thoughts took her down a different route. A shiver ran down Dafnie's spine as she remembered the prophecy from earlier.

"Apollo's... fraternal twins? Like him and his sister... is there a purpose behind this?" Dafnie mumbled. "But... I have an IUD... will it not work with him?" She panicked as the implications became clear. "I better get tested. I could be pregnant... Argh!" Dafnie whined as she made a mental note on the matter. "Okay, well... that one... I'm not going to over-analyze that for now. I can't tell Apollo... Phoebe mentioned we'll be happy until a forceful separation. We will go our separate ways as part of our journey at some point. She said we needed to figure out how to get together. Does that mean just me? Or does Apollo need to be on board with it?"

Dafnie's vision blurred with dizziness, and her head swooned with a dizzying spin. The developing headache throbbed like a drum, swelling to unleash its fury. With a stressed and confused mind, Dafnie attempted to process the torrent of information Phoebe thrust upon her, each detail puzzling.

"Shit! I need to be ready for anything. For a separation and... suffering! Not again! I will be alone again?" Dafnie heaved at the idea of losing Apollo.

Although she was mad at him, Apollo had weaseled himself into her heart with his caring yet cocky attitude. "Charm will not fix our problems, though," she muttered, shaking her head. "So... our imperfect relationship will help save the world, but only if we work together?" Dafnie kept on musing, disheartened. "I'm not looking forward to what's coming. We'll face nothing but problems. But... Phoebe mentioned we must have faith and that everything will work out in the end..."

Dafnie traced the pattern of her tattoo, this time with interest. "I better make sure I don't mention this to Apollo. I'm unsure why, but something bad will happen if I tell him. Saying anything seems risky, as if we will face punishment."

Suddenly, a branch snapped, followed by rustling around the bushes. Dafnie glanced at her tattoo, worried that one of those creatures crept up on her while she was distracted. The pattern looked normal. If anything, it had a soft golden glow. The gentle, reassuring shine cleared her mind to an extent. However, all that vanished when Dafnie realized what stalked her.

A giant white wolf sauntered to her with a hypnotizing, almost seductive gaze. Dafnie turned pale at the sight of the animal.

Her breath caught in her throat, leaving a burning sensation that spread all over her chest.

With surprising speed, the creature sprinted toward her. Its presence filled the air with tension. The wolf's long legs covered the distance between them. Its azure glower glared at her, sizing her. Dafnie hyperventilated as panic rose from the pit of her stomach. Her entire body shook and broke into a cold sweat.

Shit! A wolf will fucking have me for lunch today. Dafnie's mind went into panic overdrive. Her fight-or-flight response rooted her to the spot.

She closed her eyes, making herself less threatening to the animal, and stood still. Hoping the creature would move on and not see her as a threat, Dafnie stayed as still as possible as the beast came closer and sniffed her.

Dafnie waited, terrified out of her wits, as the wolf continued sniffing. Dread gripped her as the creature brushed her skin, and her body convulsed with a silent scream. *Maybe Phoebe was wrong. No need for me to have a purpose. Right? It happened before* Dafnie's mind continued its morbid thoughts like a mantra.

She froze the moment the wolf opened its mouth. *Fuck! I-I'm going to die today? It's fucking going to rip my throat...* Dafnie gave up all hope as she waited on her grim fate.

Will it hurt? The naïve thought consumed her mind when the warm breath tickled her skin. Then, to her surprise, a hot tongue licked the sensitive area on her neck. Dafnie's brain crashed when supple lips sweetly kissed her, and a human hand cupped her face.

"What?" Dafnie gasped.

Chapter 40

Prowl

Apollo ran through the woods in his magnificent wolf form, surrounding where Dafnie disappeared for her walk. Pleased, he picked the wolf to impress his innocent lover. In his opinion, he looked imposing and handsome. There was no doubt in his mind that Dafnie would love his wolf transformation.

Along the way, Apollo ran into some creatures aimlessly ambling about. Despite their frailty, they posed a lethal threat if he wasn't careful. Lately, they turned up to have strange behaviors, making them unpredictable.

With no time e to waste, Apollo disposed of the monsters lurking around. At first, it appeared ruthless to kill people who were once his neighbors. He had no other option but to deal with the situation. There was no cure for their condition, and once the virus and the contaminated pollen entered a mortal's body, the person's fate was to mutate and become a living monster.

After Apollo finished scouting the area, he went to the nearby creek to wash off the fetid blood, guts, and grime stuck to his plush and soft coat. Apollo stepped into the river, shivering as the frigid water rushed past his paws.

He had to look perfect for Dafnie. Apollo wanted to sway Dafnie and leave no doubt they belonged together. His eyes sparkled with excitement at the idea of seeing Dafnie again.

Two days were too long for him to be apart from Dafnie. His primary goal was to impress her. Despite the freezing temperature, he plunged into the stream. He rolled back and forth on his back like a playful pup playing with the flow during a sweltering summer day, making sure the soft river rocks exfoliated his fur clean so he would look presentable.

He emerged after his bath had met his godly standards. A satisfied sigh escaped his lips as every speck of filth rinsed away, leaving neat, snowy fur. Standing by the small, gravelly shore, he vigorously shook his thick fur, making it rain all around him.

Although Apollo's movements were primal and instinctual, he somehow looked elegant as he padded away from the bank, still shaking off the stubborn water that clung to him. Compelled by desire, Apollo pushed to show Dafnie how much she meant to him. The joyful scents of nature fueled Apollo's determined search for his nymph, making him feel right at home.

Doubt crept over Apollo's heart, clawing at his confidence. *I should have told her as soon as we met.*

Dismissing his negative thoughts, he became even more influenced to impress. *I'm sure everything will turn out just fine. Dafnie loves me.* He went in search of Dafnie. Apollo knew he was a charmer and trusted his abilities to have Dafnie back in no time. She would undoubtedly forgive Apollo for all his wrongdoings, especially for not telling her the truth on their first encounter.

The notion excited Apollo so much that he'd been restless since the previous day. The only thing on his mind was to pin Dafnie under him and devour her. He wanted her to feel pleasure as he worshiped her. Apollo craved to see her provocative eyes clouded with passion and desire reserved just for him. His sole desire was for her to experience pure ecstasy to the point they lost count.

He planned to show Dafnie he loved and valued her more than his life. Apollo hoped to sing love songs inspired by Dafnie's beauty, lie in bed, and enjoy each other's company every second of their lives.

Fuck! I need to calm down. The last thing I want to do is jump at her the moment I come close and lay my eyes on her. I want to talk to her and make her understand she means the world to me.

Momentarily, the mortal world no longer mattered. Apollo's guilt melted away as he basked in the warmth of Dafnie's happiness. He wanted his precious nymph back.

The sun god tilted his head back to sniff the air and find his lover's sweet, musky, floral scent. *She is close by,* Apollo thought as he approached her scent. The closer he got, the stronger her scent of gardenia and musk was. He was going nuts with desire.

Only a short distance separated them!

Apollo needed to get through a thicket of brushes, and he would be within reach, next to his precious Dafnie. He caught a glimpse of her from the gaps in the bushes and became excited looking at glimpses of her beautiful, tawny skin. Dafnie mumbled now and then, a behavior he found adorable when she debated on her own.

Dafnie always looked beautiful, even when she wore simple clothes, which amazed Apollo. His nymph had curves in all the right places, which ignited feverish passion from deep within him. He became desperate and wanted to be near her.

The thorny thickets mirrored the tangled mess of his heart—a culprit to his separation from Dafnie. Unavoidably, he needed to go around the area or through the brushes to be by Dafnie. Apollo did not care if he got scratched or dirty. He just wanted to be near her.

In his rush, a twig snapped under the weight of his foot, catching Dafnie's attention. Her beautiful sparkling brown eyes scanned the area for the source of the sound. Apollo cursed as he alerted her. *I need to be more careful.*

On high alert, Dafnie looked down at the tattoo on her wrist. Anxiety flickered across her expression. During their time together, he spotted the tattoo reacting to him whenever he was close to her. *Oh yes, her tattoo seems to glow whenever I'm around. Not fair! Just when I wanted to surprise her.* Apollo thought as he readied himself, making sure not to look threatening. He pushed through the brush until he was visible.

Dafnie froze as her breath caught in her throat. The world fell silent around them—only the rustling of leaves filled the air. He strolled toward her, noticing she was unmoving and swallowing hard. *Is she impressed? I can't believe it's working. It's... fucking... working!* Apollo celebrated his victory by puffing his chest and moving closer with sure steps.

Apollo was careful not to alarm her, avoiding being threatening. He stood before her, mouth drooling and eyes focused. Her scent drove Apollo into a passionate frenzy. He caught a whiff of her delicate scent as she tilted her head, revealing the vulnerable spot on her neck.

Apollo felt his sweet Dafnie shaking. *Is she shaking because she wants me, too? Is Dafnie burning with desire like I am?* Apollo thought, hoping she would soon wrap her arm around him and embrace him.

He couldn't contain himself any longer. Apollo would not deny himself or Dafnie anymore. He transformed back into his human form. Without hesitating, not able to contain himself, he licked and kissed Dafnie's neck while cupping her face with a gentle touch.

"What?" Dafnie shouted wide-eyed, with a sheen of sweat covering her entire body.

SLAP!

Apollo received a hard slap from his beloved without warning. He watched in horror as Dafnie's face morphed into one of anger. He touched his burning cheek, feeling the hand-shaped welt on his chiseled cheek.

Unrestrained, Dafnie's tears fell as she gasped for air. "You fucking scared me, Apollo... I-I thought I was going to die. Didn't you realize how panicked I was? You scared the shit out of me." Her judgmental stare sized him up and down, making him feel vulnerable.

Dumbfounded by Dafnie's reaction, Apollo felt wronged as he sat back, dejected and still massaging his throbbing cheek. "Wow! I... wasn't expecting that reaction... It all seemed different in my head... That was a hard slap, my sweet nymph. I hoped you'd jump into my arms and surrender to my every whim."

Drying her tears, Dafnie turned away, still angry at Apollo. "Not when I think I'm about to die, you oaf."

Apollo realized his screw-up and didn't consider the repercussions of his actions. "I'm sorry, my love. I didn't mean to frighten you, but I've been anxious since yesterday. My mind can grow into a scattered, nonsensical mess, and I didn't think straight. I'm horrible at making important decisions when I'm horny and angry. My stories and legends highlight that fact nicely. But... can you find it in you to forgive my foolish actions?"

Seeming calmer, Dafnie turned to Apollo and stared for a few minutes, considering his apology. "Don't you ever do that again..."

"I won't do it again. I wasn't thinking..." Apollo rushed his apology without waiting for Dafnie to finish.

"AND!" Dafnie interrupted, not wanting to hear any more excuses. "Now... can you wear something? I can't think when you're naked."

Apollo caught Dafnie's furious blush and used Dafnie's embarrassment to his advantage. She admired his nakedness, and he would not let that opportunity go. "Am I distracting you?" He puffed his chest in an alluring display of masculinity.

Dafnie sighed, aware of his intentions. "Apollo, please... I'm being serious."

"And I'm trying to tempt you. Can't you see I'm trying hard to impress you?"

"You're one cocky bastard. Instead of apologizing for not telling me the truth and scaring me to death, here you are, trying to seduce me with your looks. Who do you take me for, a teenage girl who will fall for the first pretty boy who gives her some attention?!"

"Well... I was hoping for something like that. I don't want to lose your love over my dishonesty."

At least Apollo was honest with his response. Dafnie, aware of his tendency to act impulsively, cut him slack for being blunt. Understanding Apollo's past struggles with impulsive decisions. For instance, when he made good on his threat to Marsyas and later lived to regret it—all because of some silly contest. "Who said you lost my love in the first place?"

"I believed you didn't want me anymore and wanted to win you back. Since yesterday, I've been on edge."

"I could sense your oppressive stare from afar." Dafnie sounded lost once she spotted Apollo's manhood standing at attention. "Could you please get dressed? I'm trying to have a serious conversation."

Unabashed, Apollo stretched to make his point that he didn't mind flaunting his desire for his nymph. "First, I'm not sorry about that. My desire for you runs deep. Second, my clothes are back home."

"It sounds like you're making excuses. You are a god. I take it you can make clothes magically appear for you to wear."

Irritated, Apollo sat and waved his hand in circular motions as he changed into jeans and a T-shirt. "Fine. I'll cover up, but I hope to undress soon."

Dafnie smiled at his irritation, lightening the mood between them. When dissatisfied, she guessed he looked cute, like a spoiled little youth. "Only after we talk." She picked a twig from Apollo's hair. "Where were you? You have twigs and leaves all over your hair."

"Well... I intended to look perfect. I even took a thorough bath by the river, but the fastest way to you was through those shrubs." Apollo said. He started grooming his hair and picking off pieces of the bush from his hair. Dafnie kneeled by him, helping him with the task. Struck by the gesture, Apollo wanted to make things better between them. He moved closer to Dafnie, reaching out to caress her face. "We started our relationship all wrong. I was selfish and a jerk to you. Instead of getting to know you, I forced you to be with me. Not once did I stop to consider your feelings, my nymph. I want to start over with you. I want our relationship to work and be happy. May I have your name, my sweet nymph?"

Chapter 41

Attraction of the Divine

Apollo's gaze became tender and passionate. Dafnie noted a change in his demeanor as she beamed at him. Still disheveled by trudging through the bushes to get to her quicker, the god looked honest and charming.

"I admit I was impulsive when we first met and made a horrible mistake. I was only thinking about myself and putting my feelings before yours." Apollo's voice turned soft with sincerity. Apollo pressed his forehead against Dafnie, closing his eyes, taking a deep breath, and breathing in her sweet scent, which gave him a sense of belonging.

Dafnie remained silent, only breaking it when she caught sight of Apollo's eager gaze. "Apology accepted. However, it was shitty of you to influence me the way you did after the day I had. I woke to a destroyed world after thinking I'd been asleep for one night. The whole thing was terrifying. To think everyone I knew is now gone..."

Apollo looked like he was about to fall apart and was trying to find the right words. He knew he couldn't take back his actions but couldn't bear to see Dafnie in pain. "I know. I'm a fucking jerk for doing that to the world and you. Can you forgive me? Just tell me what to do to make things right..."

The sincerity in Apollo's eyes—how he faltered and tried to mend his mistakes—grew palpable. With a slow inhale, Dafnie's frustration abandoned her. "It's important to accept the consequences of your actions and take responsibility for them."

"But... I'll do my best to fix things, to make amends," Apollo promised, laying his head on Dafnie's lap before exhaling sullenly. Dafnie felt him shudder as he struggled to calm himself. "I promise I'll make things better..."

"Mmm... I'm still trying to figure out if your intentions are good."

"My intentions are good, my nymph! Please... trust me." Apollo's voice strained with a pleading fervor as it trailed off.

Dafnie couldn't help but smile and petted his head, running her fingers through his messy hair and picking out stray twigs. Long ago, she gave Apollo the chance to show what he meant. "Okay... I'll believe you for now, but you must prove yourself through your actions."

Apollo looked relieved and grateful as he sat up to look her in the eye, pressing a soft kiss on Dafnie's hand. "Thank you... I promise you won't regret it."

"Now... you mentioned earlier you wanted to start over and get to know me better." Dafnie straightened, her breath gasping before speaking once more. "Well, my name is Dafnie Valencia, and I'm your next-door neighbor."

Dafnie extended her hand for a shake, catching Apollo by

surprise. He stood in place, stupefied for a few moments, before reacting. "It's a pleasure to meet you, Miss Valencia. Apollo Delphoes at your service." Apollo took Dafnie's hand and kissed it. Dafnie giggled at the formal gesture and appreciated the effort. "So now that introductions are out of the way, tell me about yourself. I want to know more about who you are."

"Well, I'm the software engineering lead for a tech company. In my free time, I love trail running, climbing, and gardening," Dafnie replied, her eyes sparkling with excitement as she talked about her passions.

Apollo beamed at her enthusiasm, allowing Dafnie to continue talking about herself. He suspected she rarely opened up to others, but he wanted to know everything about her. "I adore the sparkle in your eyes when discussing your interests. To me, you shine like the sun."

Dafnie blushed at the compliment but couldn't help feeling a warmth spread through her body at Apollo's words. "You're supposed to be the god of the sun."

"Sure! But you are the goddess of my heart," Apollo said with a smile as bright as sunrays. "You rule this mighty god, wrapping him around your little finger."

Dafnie couldn't help but laugh at his cheesy line. "Stop it! You are exaggerating. I have no such power."

Apollo chuckled, his eyes sparkling with mischief. "But it's true! I'm under your charm."

"Your attention makes me uncomfortable. You're acting dramatic."

A teasing remark escaped Dafnie's lips. The light laughter in her voice revealed her amusement at the situation. Apollo wanted to play along and cupped her face to show her he was serious. "I can't help it. You're too sexy. Besides, I'm not being dramatic, Dafnie. I mean every word I say."

Dafnie felt he was sincere and leaned into his touch, feeling her heart flutter at his words. "Are you sure about that? Something tells me I shouldn't trust you."

"Then that means I'm at your mercy and must work hard to gain your faith in me. I admit I've been a taker so far, but not anymore. Your happiness matters to me at this moment." Apollo's sheepish grin spread across his face—similar to the one he wore the first time they met. A flash of pearly white teeth and the cutest dimples imaginable appeared as he smiled. Giving him a bad-boy look that contrasted with his elegant features.

Dafnie gasped when Apollo laughed uncontrollably. His smirk made him even more irresistible, both lethal and disarming, leaving her stunned. "I think you are a smooth talker and do things purposefully. You aren't playing by the rules."

"What rules?" Apollo asked, his eyes glinting with a naughty sheen.

With a hint of resentment, Dafnie played her part. "Well, Mr. Delphoes, you mentioned you wanted to get to know me better a few minutes ago. Now you're deflecting and making good on your desire to get me undressed and under you." She paused and cleared her throat.

Dafnie heard Apollo's light chuckles. He was trying hard to hide. She ignored his slyness before continuing. "We started our relationship a little backward. Instead of meeting at the town Farmer's Market or a street party, it seems we skipped all the meet cute and went straight to sex. Worse! You took advantage of my vulnerable state and emotions the day we met. It was tough to wake up to that, and I lost my mind. Do you care to explain that?"

Apollo sighed, knowing well that he was a jerk that day. He had no excuse for his behavior other than he was a horny god who seized an opportunity. He acted no differently than his father would have. "I owe you an apology for taking advantage of the situation that day... and the morning after. I got carried away when I saw you... but I couldn't help myself, and I'm sorry for being a fool."

The sincerity in Apollo's eyes was unmistakable, but a deep sadness also shone through, hinting at a hidden grief. A gasp escaped him, a strangled sound that made Dafnie worry. His chest heaved as if breathing was painful. His eyes glazed over, losing their usual spark, and a wave of hopelessness washed over him. "Hey, Apollo! Please calm down. I'm not going anywhere. You're stuck with me. I hope you don't mind that."

Clarity crept back into Apollo's eyes. He took a deep breath, steadying himself and brushing away the regret and self-doubt that fogged his mind. "I'm relieved to hear that, my love. More than you could ever know," he said, his voice a whisper.

The flamboyant god faded, replaced by a vulnerable man. Dafnie reached to caress his face. But Apollo had other plans. He turned to kiss her palm, cherishing the warmth seeping into him from her flesh.

His eyes locked on hers, the bright beam playing with the red highlights of her chestnut brown hair, giving her an ethereal glow that he couldn't get enough of. Feeling this was the turning point in their relationship. "I promise you, Dafnie, my life will be yours from this moment on. Every word, every touch, will aim to honor you," he vowed, his voice seeping with passion and commitment. "From the beginning, your beauty enchanted me, and I couldn't resist."

Dafnie laughed, rolling her eyes, feeling giddy for the first time. "You are quite the charmer, Mr. Delphoes, but let's see if your sweet words can win my heart."

"Oh, my sweet love, I haven't won your precious heart?"

Dafnie paused before saying anything else. As the wait stretched on, Apollo's initial enthusiasm waned, replaced by a palpable gloom that hung in the air. "Yes! You have won my heart with your most peculiar personality," she admitted.

"Peculiar personality?"

"Yes! A peculiar and bigger-than-life personality."

Filled with hope, Apollo needed to make sure Dafnie forgave him without a doubt. "It sounds like you are... not that mad at me?"

"I already have forgiven you," Dafnie said with a big smile.

"I'm thankful for the chance to make things right and start over. You have my word that I'll consistently listen to you and honor your desires. I cannot imagine my life without you. Dafnie, will you be my forever love?"

"Yes, but you know I won't be around. I will grow old and..."

Apollo placed his fingers on her lips, cutting her off. "Shhh, my love!" He said in a soothing voice. "That will not happen. I won't allow it."

Stunned, Dafnie didn't know what to say about his confession. "Apollo, I won't let you use your powers to give me eternal life. What if you..." Dafnie exclaimed, shocked that he would go to great lengths to have her by his side forever. The thought of becoming immortal was enticing but terrifying.

"If I were to stay by your side for all eternity, I would feel I reached the Elysian Fields," Apollo answered her question without waiting for her to finish.

Their eyes locked before Apollo pulled Dafnie closer. His hand caressed her cheek while the other moved to rest on the small of her back. He leaned in, closing the distance between them before brushing his lips against her, coaxing them open before he deepened their kiss.

Their mouths met in a fiery, hungry appetite consuming them both, their breaths mingling. Their breaths hitched, hearts pounding like war drums in their chests. Dafnie wrapped her arms around Apollo's neck, bringing him even closer. Lost in the experience, she savored the feel of his lips on hers. His subtle, wild musk, mixed with the taste of his skin, provoked a haze clouding her judgment.

Dafnie felt intoxicated by their intimate moment, while Apollo, absorbed in their desire, became bolder. His hands explored her body, causing her to react with every touch. Emboldened, Dafnie traced his firm muscles, waiting for her exploration. His scent—a powerful and intoxicating aroma—filled her senses.

His attention moved to her neck, leaving a scalding sensation that made her skin tingle with anticipation. Dafnie could feel the hardness of him pressed against her leg, making her weak with lust. His mouth drifted over hers with a hunger that matched her own, their tongues dancing to their passion.

Apollo took his time kissing Dafnie, savoring the moment and worshiping her velvety lips. Their breaths turned ragged as their faces glowed with devotion. Apollo gazed deep into her eyes as if weighing her longing. Once again, he nuzzled her sensitive collar, planting soft kisses. She gasped as he nipped at her earlobe, sending a jolt of pleasure through her frame. She fisted his hair at the nape of his neck, making Apollo hiss with yearning.

Dafnie heaved, leaning into his touch, her body responding to his caresses. "Apollo! I'm not sure we…" she moaned, her voice filled with raw desire. Her plead was enough to push Apollo over the edge of reason.

Grinning, Apollo whispered in her ear, "I told you, Dafnie, you are the goddess of my soul. And I'll worship until the end of time."

Dafnie's heart pounded with unease, clouding her thoughts as she fought for clarity amidst the danger. "No, not that. We can't do this here. It's too risky. What if one of those monsters shows up?"

Dafnie's nervousness outweighed all other concerns, including her drinking another drop of Ambrosia without their knowledge.

Chapter 42

Attraction of the Earthborn

Apollo noticed the flicker of concern in Dafnie's eyes and smiled reassuringly. "No worries, my sweet nymph. I can take us back to my house to have more privacy."

Dafnie suspected Apollo didn't want to return to her house because of Artemis, but she wanted to confirm. "Why your house and not mine?" Dafnie snuggled into Apollo's warm embrace, feeling the steady beat of his heart.

"I want to spend time with you without Artemis lurking around. She can be quite nosy, and I wouldn't put it past her to walk in on us." With a wave of his hand, he conjured a shimmering golden portal. The surrounding air crackled with energy while orbs of light sparked in and out of existence. "Are you ready? The strange feeling will soon pass."

Apollo kissed Dafnie's luscious lips before they both walked through the gateway. One moment, they were by the creek, and the next, they were in Apollo's large living room. Other than feeling disoriented, Dafnie was fine.

Relieved to see his friend and Dafnie safe, Fernhoof stopped his frantic trotting. Burned wood scented the room alongside a sweet tang hanging in the air. "Apollo? That took a while. I take it you made things right with Dafnie." He stood taller, surveying his companion.

With a warm smile and a protective hand on Dafnie, Apollo welcomed his longtime ally with a sincere heart. "Fernhoof, thanks for being there for me. I appreciate your concern. Dafnie and I... will retire. We'll not receive anyone today."

Fernhoof's gaze softened as he looked at Dafnie, nuzzling against Apollo's chest. "No worries. No one will disturb you until you're ready." His tone was gentle and caring. Fernhoof took his leave, giving Apollo and Dafnie some privacy.

Apollo wrapped his powerful arms around Dafnie's waist and lifted her off her feet. Her legs tightened around him, and a hum filled with pure exhilaration echoed her joy. Dafni inhaled his intoxicating scent, sighing with pleasure.

"Fuck, Dafnie! You're driving me up the wall. I can't wait any longer. I want you so much," Apollo growled when she kissed his neck, fueling his desire.

He hugged Dafnie even tighter, a primal hunger pulsing through his soul. Their lips met again, this time with more urgency and passion. Apollo's hands fondled Dafnie's buns as she ground herself against his erection. The friction between their bodies sent waves of bliss coursing through them, driving them into a frenzy.

Overwhelmed by lust, Dafnie wondered what was taking Apollo so long. "Apollo, what are you waiting for?" she asked, arching against his body, nipping his neck, and encouraging him to move.

In a rush, fueled by an intoxicating primal urge, Apollo climbed the stairs with a single focus in mind. "No need for words, my nymph." His voice, a low rumble of anticipation, held sweet promises.

Apollo placed Dafnie on the spacious bed with loving care as they arrived in his bedroom. His eyes glowed with desire like two miniature molten suns. "Dafnie, my love," Apollo's voice was a growl, a blend of passion and reverence.

Dafnie outlined the ridges of his muscular frame, pulling at his shirt, eager to feel his skin. Without hesitating, Apollo complied, discarding his clothing and revealing his chiseled upper body. Dafnie's breath hitched as her eyes roamed over his form, consuming his divine physique.

Apollo's broad shoulders and carved stomach muscles were a testament to his strength, his skin smooth yet firm under her touch. She traced her fingers down his toned chest. He allowed her to feel every inch of his god-like build, her touch eliciting a low growl from him.

Dafnie noticed his blue eye burning with desire, giving him a predatory look that excited her as she stroked his lips. His lips captured her thumb and gently sucked on it—a promise of what Apollo had in store for her soon. The act made Dafnie wither with excitement as she arched her body against his, making him shudder.

Apollo reached for her temple, brushing aside a few strands of hair. Then his fingers continued tracing the dainty curves of her face before leaning in and capturing her lips in a lustful kiss.

Their hands explored their bodies with an enthusiasm that left them wanting more.

Admiring his lover, Apollo's calloused hand captured hers, their fingers intertwining and palms pressing together. Apollo loved the contrast of their skin, a beautiful blend of her golden-tanned skin against his alabaster one.

Driven by craving, Apollo took hold of the hem of Dafnie's hoodie, his fingers grazing the delicate skin of her stomach, revealing more of her enticing skin. His fingers lingered on her small breasts, still encased in her sports bra. Admiring her perfect mounds against his pale, ample palm.

Apollo's mouth went dry at the thought of sucking her dark nipples as he gasped at the edge of her bra, exposing her petite mounds. Dafnie held her breath, anticipation coursing through her veins as Apollo's hands played with her nipples. She watched his expression, a lustful fascination displayed as he played with her buds.

"My Dafnie, my sweet nymph, you look beautiful in the throes of passion." Apollo dipped his head to take in the soft nip of her breast into his mouth.

His warm mouth elicited a sharp intake of breath from Dafnie, a gasp filled with pleasure and surprise, as his tongue swirled around her sensitive peak. With a foggy mind, Dafnie struggled to remove her top clothes. Apollo stopped her, held her arms above her head, and further pushed her supple breast into his mouth.

Dafnie moaned her complaint as she pulled on the restraining fabric. "Apollo, I want to touch you." She wrapped her legs around his waist and ground herself against his bulge.

Apollo closed his eyes, enjoying the sensation and breathing deeply to control his appetite. "Not yet. I want to enjoy you some more." He ground his groin against the vee of her legs. "Patience, love. Let me take care of you." Apollo's voice came out rough.

Dafnie loudly moaned as she felt a wave of heat surge through her body as Apollo's cool fingers brushed against her bare arms. She pulled against her restraints. Grinning, Apollo licked the curve of her breast and her nipples, causing her skin to erupt in goosebumps.

Apollo found her reaction adorable, continuing trailing kisses toward her neck as he played and pinched her sensitive nipples, enjoying her writhing body.

"You're a remarkable woman. Your beauty is unmatched by anyone. Ever!" The weight of Apollo's confession lingered, filling the silence.

Doubting him, Dafnie turned her face away from him. "Stop if you won't be honest. It's embarrassing to think that I'm like that," she whispered.

Apollo paused, sensing a shift in her behavior. He stopped kissing his beloved and fixed his gaze upon her, realizing her withdrawal. Even after being reincarnated, his darling nymph stayed the same.

Most of the time, Daphne was alone. She preferred spending time on summits or trees, joining the other maidens for hunting, bathing, or learning. She cherished her lone days in the woods.

He remembered watching her from afar, admiring her grace and beauty. She was still like a woodland creature that charmed any man's heart. He loved her for all that she was and wasn't. Her shyness was one of the many reasons he fell for her, and he wanted her to understand that she was precious.

With a delicate touch, he propped her chin while tuning her to meet his gaze. His blue eyes conveyed sincerity and love for her. "I mean every word I say, Dafnie. The thought of losing you chills my soul as dread infests my mind with troubled thoughts. To me, you're more precious than my beloved forest. Your carefree spirit shines brighter than the sun." Apollo's voice brimming with sincerity as his fingers grazed her plump lips. "Don't just take my word for it. I want you to see it."

Apollo shifted their weight to kneeling and moved his hands over the curve of Dafnie's hips before twirling her around toward the full-length mirror at the corner of the room. Given his smooth and experienced actions, there was no doubt in her mind about Apollo's experience with plenty of lovers.

Dafnie caught her reflection, noticing the faint blush tainting her cheeks. The passion Apollo had for her was undeniable. Their skin glowed in the bright afternoon light. The contrast of their skin was breathtaking and captivating. Apollo's eyes shimmered with a primal desire as he pressed his head against her shoulder, voraciously kissing her. His hands, one caressing her breast and the other thrust inside her leggings, teasing her clit.

"Apollo..." her voice was a mere whisper as the pleasure built within her, leaving her breathless. She could not tear her gaze away from their reflection, a blush creeping up her cheeks as she took in their erotic display.

"Shh, my love," Apollo hushed her, his lips brushing her ear, causing her to shiver. "Look at you, Dafnie," he whispered, his breath hot against her skin, as he made eye contact with Dafnie through the mirror.

Apollo slowly withdrew his hand from between Dafnie's trembling thighs, his fingers glistening with her arousal. His heart pounded as he brought them to his mouth, tasting her excitement. His eyes darkened, never leaving hers, as he savored her. "You taste as beautiful as you look."

He then grazed his wet fingers over her lower lip. She opened her mouth, letting out a soft moan as the sweet flavor of her desire met her tongue and ground her rear against his erection.

"Fuck, Dafnie! You turn me on so much. You are beauty, hope, and strength incarnate. My dear wife, you're my everything." Apollo inhaled sharply, Dafnie's unique scent filling his lungs before claiming her lips.

She turned around to meet Apollo's fervent kiss as he laid her on the bed. Dafnie's heart pounded in her chest as his fingers traveled down her body, resting on the dip of her waist. He hooked his thumbs on the waist of her pants, leisurely pulling them down her legs. Apollo's touch was electrifying, causing a jolt of pleasure to course through her veins.

Apollo revealed the rest of Dafnie's body to his wanton gaze. He marveled at her tempting curves, valleys, and generous hips. Apollo's fingers traced a path down her abdomen, causing her to arch her back and moan. The sight of Dafnie in the throes of bliss was intoxicating, and Apollo was more than willing to drown in it as he committed Dafnie's seductive image to memory.

Dafnie bit her lips as she caressed one of her breasts while pinching her nipple and teasing her sensitive bundle of nerves. "Mi amor, are you just planning to stare?" She caught him by surprise.

"Oh my, my precious nymph, a pet name of my own? I was becoming impatient at not having one." Apollo's laugh filled the room with playfulness as his eyes twinkled with mischief. "We're getting impatient, are we?"

Chapter 43

Passion

If he wanted to play that game, Dafnie was ready for the challenge. She closed her eyes, caving in at the pleasure built within her. She inserted a slender finger inside her swollen channel. Still, she soon introduced a second one, which wasn't enough for her.

Apollo's mouth went dry, and for a moment, he lost his concentration as he managed a weak whisper. "Fuck me, that's sexy!"

Driven by lust, he moved into action and trailed light kisses until he reached her core. He let her fingers continue their intimate play as he licked her bundle of nerves, eliciting a sharp sigh from Dafnie.

Encouraged by her reaction, Apollo sucked on her clit while inserting his finger into her hot canal alongside her fingers.

"Hmmm! Apollo..." Dafnie sighed as her free hand, which played with her breast at some point, gripped the bedsheets. She withdrew her digits from her dewy slit, only to be stopped by Apollo. He devoured on her hand voraciously.

While he was busy sucking Dafnie's fingers, he angled his finger inside her, touching a spot within her that made her quake with want. His expert touch drove her wild as he continued his attention with his tongue. Heat spiraled outward from her core, becoming more intense with each passing moment.

"Ah! Mmm... Apollo... more," she begged, her breath hitching as he added another finger, stretching her further.

Apollo, ever the attentive lover, obliged her demands. His fingers, coated in her slick warmth, moved deeper, his tongue never relenting against her sensitive bud. Her fingers threaded through Apollo's golden strands, holding him in place as she approached her peak.

Apollo's eyes darted up to meet her gaze, raw desire burning in her eyes as she neared her release, and her inner walls twitched rhythmically. She looked stunning, writhing beneath him, her cheeks flushed with pleasure. Her body arched with a graceful curve, contrasting the tension in her muscles that came with her impending release. The quickening beat of her heart, a tangible thing beneath his touch. He knew she was close to the edge.

Through heavy-lidded eyes, he consumed her ethereal beauty like a starving animal. Soon, the room filled with the sound of her ragged breathing while his fingers persisted with their relentless assault on her core.

Her breath hitched, a gasp escaping her lips as her center clenched hard around him. He felt her body convulse in waves of lust, her grip on him tightening as she reached her climax. "Ahhh... Apollo!" Her cry echoed around the room as a violent shudder ran through her slight frame.

Her heart pounded in her chest. Apollo enjoyed as her inner walls spasmed around his fingers, the warm rush of her release coating them. Apollo stilled for a moment, watching Dafnie with a sense of satisfaction. He licked his wet lips, savoring the taste of her on his tongue.

After a moment, he withdrew his fingers, his gaze never leaving her as he kneeled between her legs. "Taste this, my sweet nymph." Apollo's voice turned husky with desire. He brought the glistening digits up to her lips, offering her a taste of her arousal. Dafnie opened her mouth, her tongue darting out to lick the sweet essence of his fingers.

The sight of her lapping at his fingers with breathtaking hunger sent a jolt of lust through him, and he couldn't resist any longer. He reached down to unfasten his pants, the fabric dropping from his slim hips and pooling around his knees. Apollo finished getting undressed, tossing his pants aside as his bulging erection sprung free, standing tall and stiff, throbbing with need. He looked down at Dafnie, her eyes brimming with anticipation as she stared at his manhood.

"Look at me, Dafnie, needy and desperate. You hold on me is your true strength." His voice turned thick with raw emotion. His gaze never left hers. He brushed back his hair while the other hand traced the hardened chest and stomach muscles. Before long, he reached his hardened length and stroked it with slow and intentional motions.

His body towering over hers and half-closed eyes was a sight that made Dafnie's mouth go dry. The firm strokes of Apollo's hand on his hardened length sent waves of lustful needs coursing through her.

Apollo moaned to provoke Dafnie while putting on a show

for her. "Nnnahhh!" he groaned as the sensation intensified. "Want to help me, my love?" he asked, his deep voice echoing in the room. The corners of his mouth lifted in a seductive smile, his gaze intense and inviting.

Dafnie shifted around and crawled toward him, her hands reaching out to replace him on his throbbing manhood. Her fingers wrapped around him, eliciting a low growl from Apollo as she slowly stroked him, matching their earlier rhythm.

Sensing his firm, throbbing presence within her grasp delivered a quake of euphoria. Her chest felt tight with nervousness and anticipation, making her stomach flutter. She pressed a soft kiss to his head, already seeping precum.

Encouraged by his response, Dafnie opened her mouth to take him in, running her tongue along his length as she welcomed him into her warm mouth. Apollo's eyes fluttered shut at the sensation, a low growl rumbling from his chest. Apollo's fingers grasped her hair, subtly directing her actions to his liking. With a gentle swirl of her tongue along his length, she glided up and down his firm flesh. Being deliberate in savoring the moment, she pleasured her lover as she raked her nails on his tights, leaving little red welts on his otherwise flawless skin.

Apollo's head fell back as a shudder ripped through him, enjoying Dafnie's delicate mouth on him. "Hmmm... my love." His moan grew louder as he increased his thrusting, careful not to be too rough with his wife.

His attention drove Dafnie wild, and his reaction suggested she affected him in the same way. Her movements became more purposeful as her tongue swirled around him, and her hand moved in tandem with her mouth. Dafnie felt like a ravishing enchanter capable of persuading the mighty sun god.

The room filled with Apollo's heavy breaths and moans, the tension between them reaching a fevered pitch of emotions. Once Apollo opened his eyes again, the sight of Dafnie lapping hungrily at his manhood sent a sudden jolt of thirst through him. He couldn't hold back any longer as his chest swelled with lustful hunger.

His deep voice, thick with pleasure, echoed throughout the room. "Dafnie... ah... I'm coming, my love. Mmm ahh!" His words tapered off into a groan as he reached his peak. His fingers tangled in her hair tightened, his hips lunged forward one last time, and with a deep, guttural growl, he spilled his release into her mouth.

The taste of him, musky and tangy Apollo, spread over her tongue. Dafnie took him, her lips sealing around him as she swallowed, her own body humming in response to his pleasure. The sight of her acceptance, her desire matching his, drew a low, satisfied sigh from Apollo's lips.

Dafnie watched as Apollo's chest heaved with excitement. As he came down from his ecstatic height, the messy golden tendrils of his hair fell over his sweaty forehead. Like a gift she always yearned for, a light flush on his cheeks that spread to his ears. His gaze held an unusual softness, a vulnerability only she recognized. Apollo looked beyond handsome.

Putting no thought to her actions, Dafnie placed a soft kiss on his sensitive length before moving up his body. Her lips left a trail of kisses in their wake. The aftershocks of his climax, still coursing through him, rocked her core, hazing her mind. His body shuddered beneath her feathered touch as she savored each tremor.

Dafnie kissed him with a fiery passion, her lips lingering on his. Their heated breaths mingled in a harmonious dance of gratifying exertion. Apollo's hands reached her waist, pulling her close to him. His hands, busy playing and making music, now traced the contours of her skin. Admired for his restraint, Apollo succumbed to the intoxicating appeal of a mortal with no divine powers.

Apollo couldn't resist any longer. There was no point denying his longing, as he was ready to go again. He pulled at Dafnie's hair with practiced gentleness and tilted her head back to kiss her plump lips before laying her on the bed. "I crave something more." To drive his point home, he positioned himself between her legs. Their eyes locked, and a wicked grin passed over his handsome face. "I want to be inside you."

Her answer was a desperate nod and a breathless plea. "Please, Apollo... I need you to..." That was all the invitation he needed. With a low growl, he thrust into her, burying himself to the hilt within her welcoming heat.

His girth stretched and filled Dafnie to the brink. Her body wiggled in reaction to Apollo's claim. Growing into a delicious mix of pleasure and pain that drove her frantic with love. "Apollo... Nah!" She let out a low, guttural moan. Her tender voice choked with pleasure as her climax washed over her—her body flushing bright red.

The muscles of her inner walls contracted around him in waves, and her ecstatic cry spurred him on. His thrusts continued even as she shuddered beneath him. The rhythm of his movements increased, making the wet sounds of their bodies slapping against each other fill the room. His eyes became darker with desire, almost consuming the azure of his eyes as he watched her face contort in pleasure.

Apollo admired Dafnie's flushed cheeks and how she bit her lip to hold her moans. He leaned down, kissing her with an intensity to steal her breath away. Her body accepted him, sending waves of pure satisfaction through him.

Then his lips moved from her mouth down her neck, trailing starved kisses and nips along her collarbone. She gasped as his hand found one of her breasts and pinched her nipple between his fingers.

The stimulation heightened Dafnie's lust as she wrapped herself around Apollo's imposing build. Their magnetic pull swayed into a frantic game of devotion as their souls came together. The golden rays kissed their bodies as the sun snuck into their room. Dazed, Apollo's wild heartbeat thundered in his chest as he basked in their shared moment of passion—the intoxicating scent of love while losing touch with reality. Apollo placed a hand on Dafnie's back whilst nestling the other in her hair. Pulling her close, he blurred the line between mortal and divine, submerged in the throes of their passion.

Each thrust drove them closer and closer to the edge. Apollo's lips found hers again, swallowing her sounds as he picked up his pace. She could feel her climax building, her body tightening around him as she clung to him.

When Apollo pushed into her, a prophecy came rushing like a tidal wave consuming her consciousness. The image of fraternal twins staring back with strength and sweet love. Her daughter inherited her delicate features, while her son possessed Apollo's legendary beauty. But something much deeper caught her attention.

The girl possessed Apollo's mesmerizing azure eyes, brilliant pools of blue that sparkled with an ethereal light. As for the boy, his sun-like golden-brown eyes mirrored the hazel in her own. Her precious babies from Phoebe's prophecy shone with power and grace, signaling onrushing change.

The vision didn't last long, as her body shook with the intensity of her orgasm. Apollo's renewed enthusiasm distracted her while he found his release.

Apollo didn't slow. His motions became more frantic as he chased his release. Dafnie's eyes glazed over as she gasped for air. Aftershocks of pleasure kept her senses heightened as her body came down from her height.

Apollo, not giving her a chance to recover, continued his urgent thrusting. "Oh, fuck!"

Dafnie felt him stiffen above her, his loud groans filling the room as he found his release. As they lay panting, Apollo touched his forehead against hers as his eyes closed, his hand stroking her hair. She snuggled into him, feeling his heartbeat calming against her chest. A silent, warm embrace filled her lightness while a burst of pure bliss exploded within her. Relief escaped the confines of her mouth while the idea brought peace to her heart.

Then, for a moment of clarity, Dafnie couldn't resist thinking of her future. *Is this how it happens? Is this how I get pregnant?* The thought triggered a tidal wave of concern.

Dafnie should keep her pregnancy a secret from Apollo until the right time. Besides, the situation was too new, and the evidence was too scant to be sure.

Chapter 44

Deep Connection

As the afterglow of their lovemaking faded, Apollo and Dafnie lay entangled in each other's arms. A sheen of sweat glistened on their satiated bodies, and their breaths were short and ragged gasps. Apollo ran his fingers through Dafnie's messy hair, admiring the carmine blush that started on her cheek and spread to her ears.

Apollo rolled onto his back with a soft sigh, drawing Dafnie close. Her body relaxed with satisfaction, the exhaustion melting away. Dafnie snuggled against Apollo, resting her head on his chest. Their eyes met. His gaze now held a deeper connection.

"I know I'm imperfect and a rebellious motherfucker, but despite my flaws, I wonder if... will you have me the way I am?" Apollo's vulnerability crept into his confident voice while his imposing frame slumped with dejection.

Dafnie could only nod, her throat tight with emotion. "I love the way you are. Your cheekiness grew on me already."

A profound silence enveloped them, filled with unspoken words that resonated deeply between them. Dafnie caressed his chest, but Apollo grabbed her hand and brought it to his lips. He placed a feathery kiss on her palm before setting it over his heart.

His thumb traced the tattoo's outline on her wrist and traced the intricate lines, his light touch tickling her. "This one holds great power. Love created it and bound it by fate. I've seen nothing like this." Mesmerized by the design's complex patterns and vibrant colors, Apollo's gaze held a dreamy sheen—transfixed.

A warm smile bloomed on Dafnie's face as she looked at him. Her hand brushed a few loose strands from her ponytail behind her ear, and she said something he couldn't discern. A static noise prevented him from hearing what she was telling him.

She walked on a busy sidewalk, pointing at something in a shopping district. Nothing was immune from her curious gaze. She turned to point at a toy store, a pretty dress in a boutique's display, or a delicious-looking treat at a bakery. Whenever she did, joy gleamed in her eyes.

Apollo's heart swelled with love for Dafnie—a beautiful and terrifying vision. *I've destroyed Earth, yet this world looks different. What does it mean?* Going deeper into the dream, he extended his hand to Dafnie.

The moment their hands touched, the image became blurry, and a flurry of bizarre images flooded his mind. The fleeting prophetical fragment manifested and soon disappeared, leaving Dafnie's smiling image engraved in his memory behind.

Disorientation and confusion overcame Apollo when he regained his senses. He examined his surroundings before settling on her. Dafnie stared at him with concern as Apollo studied her closely. He embraced her and offered her a comforting smile.

Dafnie appeared hesitant to speak up. She kissed his solid chest. "Are you okay? Is something the matter?"

Apollo hesitated to answer immediately. He wanted to tell her what he saw but refused to worry her. "Give me a moment. I saw something and must learn its meaning." With a sigh, he closed his eyes. A grin played on his lips as prophecy's soothing warmth flooded him.

The vision was still fresh in his mind. Apollo combed through the events shown to him. *The world seemed normal, and she seemed calm and happy. She looks... different.* The thought shrouded him with peace, watching the prophecy. He focused on Dafnie as she led the sight.

He then concentrated on Dafnie's hand, brushing her hair away from her face. Her tattoo looked different from the real one. The color shifted to a red-orange hue, while its design remained simple.

He couldn't gather anything else from the vision and continued to flow with the events as they played in his head. When their hands touched, the blurry images that followed baffled him. Apollo peered at his outstretched arm. Meanwhile, a heaviness settled on his chest. He sported the same style tattoo as his wife but with slight differences.

His and her tattoos had clean lines, yet subtle flaws were visible upon closer inspection. The pattern was forest green. He noticed no magic or anything special about the motif. It looked like its only purpose was ornamental. However, the tattoos held emotional value. They were devoid of power.

Opening his eyes, Apollo knew creating a spiritual link with her would be vital. Although the joyous vision filled with laughter, the weight of the challenges to come troubled his heart.

"Let us tie our fates and weave our strings of destiny as one, my sweet nymph," Apollo murmured, pressing his wrist into her tattoo. "Do you trust me?"

Dafnie hesitated for a moment. Her confidence surged when she noticed his concerned eyes, so she nodded. "Yes, I trust you. But what's going on?"

A glow emanated from their connected skins. Apollo was channeling his powers to form a bond between them. "Foreboding. I had a prophecy of many trials and tribulations, but we can overcome anything together." The weight of Apollo's confession brought an ominous silence to the room. His gaze turned intense, and golden freckles appeared on his irises, revealing the depth of his concern.

Suddenly, an exact copy of her tattoo appeared on his wrist, the fresh ink glowing with magical energy. There was no doubt his magic sealed their connection and held firm. He sensed their spiritual connection, intertwined in a way that transcended anything he had ever felt in the past. They had a strong bond now.

The energy pulsed through their bodies, sending waves of warmth and comfort. "Now we are one. We share the same fate and destiny." Apollo leaned in, his voice choking with intense emotions. He triggered the apocalypse out of misguided beliefs and subjected Dafnie to live a nightmare.

Looking into Apollo's eyes, Dafnie accepted whatever lay ahead. They needed to be ready for anything. But she wanted to know something first. "Why did you start all this? Immortals like you shouldn't bother about the human world."

"The human world is my domain. But I admit, dragging humanity into my messed up life was unjust," Apollo confessed with regret and a heavy voice. "I was reckless, thinking the solution to my problems was to drag everyone when I felt cynical and pessimistic. Now I know I was wrong. If only..."

Curious about what he would say next, Dafnie pressed on. She wouldn't let this one pass. "If only what, Apollo? Share your thoughts with me."

He stared at her for several minutes before answering, "I made a mistake not waiting for you to open your door on the day I left that necklace." He reached for the delicate pendant hanging from her neck and turned it in his hand to examine it more. "I should've spared the world—save you—from my calamity. Rather, I subjected you to my whims as I ignored Earth. Then my need to have you, to make you mine, without a care for anyone, consumed my mind. After our chance meeting, all I could think of was to charm you and have my way with you."

A shy giggle burst through Dafnie's lips while a sudden pang of desire filled Dafnie's heart, but she couldn't hold back her laughing spell. "Are you sure about that? Can you think of anything else besides sex?"

Apollo couldn't hold his deep, booming laugh. "Yes! I'm a proud and confident bastard. Besides... I'll do anything to stay with you. I would have gone into full seduction with you." He then turned to Dafnie and kissed her lips. "Mmmm! I want to seduce you right now." He whispered into her ear.

His fingers traced a path down to her waist, where he discovered a sensitive spot that elicited giggles from Dafnie.

Trying to catch her breath, Dafnie tried to wiggle away from the offending hand. "Hahaha... Apollo, please stop it. It tickles."

Being mischievous, Apollo took full advantage of this newfound knowledge. With each playful prod and tickle, he drew delightful giggles from her, an intoxicating sound. Her writhing and the blush on her cheeks were tempting.

Apollo chuckled as his fingers continued their playful onslaught against her sides. "It looks like I've found your weakness, my nymph." Apollo's voice was a husky tease mixed with his laughter.

Dafnie's helpless giggles filled the room, spurring Apollo on. Her infectious laughter captivated Apollo as her playful mood drew him in. He ceased tickling, leaving her breathless and flushed in his arms.

He watched her, feeling his chest swell with affection as he caressed a soft cheek. "You are beautiful, Dafnie. I'm an auspicious god—foolish but lucky." His sincere eyes held her captive, and a soft smile played on his lips as he leaned in, sealing his admission with a tender kiss.

At that moment, Dafnie nudged Apollo onto his back, taking control of their intimacy, and climbed on top of him, straddling his hips. Her dewy entrance came in direct contact with his engorged groin. She explored his abdominal muscles and chest, feeling every ridge of his hardened body. She took in his strength and virality, rich with a magnetic charm capable of captivating the masses.

Dafnie rubbed herself onto him, her movements slow and deliberate. As she increased her pace, both gasping in unison, Apollo gripped her waist, his touch gentle yet firm as he found himself short of breath. "You're playing with fire there, my sweet nymph. If you keep doing that, I will have you again."

"Who said you're in charge? This time, I'll take the lead."

Apollo wasn't expecting this wild side from Dafnie, but he loved it. He noticed the playfulness in her eyes and could only smirk as he lay back, giving her the reins. "By all means, my nymph, lead the way."

Dafnie flashed him an alluring smile as she leaned in for a kiss. Her hands explored his body with confidence as she guided his rock-hard length. "I'm the one who will be in control for tonight." Her defiant eyes filled with determination and desire.

Surprised yet intrigued, Apollo gave her a challenging smirk. "I look forward to seeing what you can do, my nymph."

Dafnie set an unhurried rhythm, savoring the feel of Apollo within her. His groans filled the room, spurring Dafnie to keep going and quicken her movements.

She leaned over him, pressing her lips into his. Apollo brought his hand between them and to her sensitive hooded pearl. His touch sent jolts of pleasure through her body as her rhythm faltered for a moment.

Dafnie buried her face into his neck as she whimpered. Her walls swelled around Apollo's cock as he held Dafnie in place and pounded against her. Dafnie gasped and clung to Apollo as the waves of pleasure washed over her. Lost in the throes of passion, Apollo peaked right after she came.

Dafnie slumped onto him, spent but satiated. He enveloped her in his muscular arms as he placed soft kisses on her head.

Dafnie giggled as she lay on top of Apollo, feeling sleepy. "I think I overdid it. For tonight, let's not leave this little sanctuary. Today, let's not trouble ourselves with anything."

"Don't worry. I don't want to leave this room either. We've got plenty of time." Apollo's words echoed through the room as he settled deeper into the embrace.

Thus, he closed his eyes for a quick nap.

Chapter 45

Loyalty Unwavering

By dusk, the sky turned a pink-orange hue, and the first stars appeared on the horizon. Moonlight filtered through the kitchen windows, and the antique mahogany grandfather clock in the foyer, which Apollo bought when he lived in England in the 1890s, announced the evening hours.

Fernhoof sighed as he assembled a charcuterie slab with various fruits, cheeses, and cold cuts. "Argh! Those two need to stop! I'm getting a lover for the night," he said, popping a grape in his mouth. His munching reflected his frustration. "And I will be extra loud, damn it! Apollo can be an asshole when he's feeling competitive or when he needs to prove himself. Like now..."

Thump! Crash!

Fernhoof jumped after the terrible commission upstairs but dismissed it as he heard Dafnie giggle right after. He shook his head, biting a piece of sharp cheese and washing it with a hearty gulp of red wine. "Those two and their ravenous appetites are getting to me. I wonder what they broke. I hope it wasn't expensive or invaluable, but I doubt he'd care," he said, his ears picking on their passionate cries. "Perhaps... I should take a walk. I need to get away from this madness. Maybe I'll stumble upon a lovely nymph or a male who might be interested in a simple faun," Fernhoof said as he brought the slab filled with food and a bottle of wine to the second floor.

The corners of his mouth turned up in a mischievous grin as he entertained potential lovers for the evening. Soon, he stood outside Apollo's room, trying to decide what to do next. He stared at the door for a while longer. He tried to figure out if he should interrupt his friend. Instead, he set the food on the table closest to the room. Fernhoof heard the faint sound of Apollo's firm tone. The sun god's affectionate whispers carried a tinge of amusement.

A playful giggle fluttered around the hallway like a hesitant bird testing its surroundings. "You're incorrigible! Mmmnnn! Apollo... aaahhh! That feels so... good." Dafnie's voice quivered with lust, revealing her innermost feelings for everyone to admire.

"Fuck, Dafnie! I can't get enough of you today." Apollo's loud groans echoed through the room, swelling the air with desire.

"Mi amor, please... faster..." Dafnie's desperate whisper sounded on the verge of release.

"My sweet nymph, you don't have to tell me twice," Apollo's tone sounding strained.

The creaking noise of furniture reverberated throughout the second floor as their lovemaking became louder and needier. Fernhoof blushed, hearing his friend's unabashed displays of devotion. Apollo's indifference to people's opinion of him, especially his activities with his lovers behind closed doors, didn't face him a bit. With an unapologetic spirit, Apollo projected his emotions openly, leaving an undeniable impression on those who crossed paths with him.

Crestfallen, Fernhoof returned to the kitchen to prepare dinner for himself. He planned to eat and drink like a god. Fernhoof went to the basement, where Apollo set up a cellar with gourmet food and a wine cellar to weather his calamity. The storage room contained an expansive selection Apollo had gathered over the years.

Despite his somewhat casual demeanor, he had a penchant for luxury. Apollo was a connoisseur who enjoyed life's finer things. His vast collection of fine wines and exotic ingredients in the basement was a testament to his expensive tastes. He loved to indulge in finery, and his fancies were as eclectic as his character.

Fernhoof found comfort in the cellar's woodsy aroma, salivating at the sight of perfectly arranged bottles. Apollo's wines boasted vintages dating back centuries. Only Dionysus, the god of wine, rivaled his selection. "Apollo sure likes the good life."

He selected a robust red wine, a gift from Dionysus from his collection, that would pair well with his meal for the night. Fernhoof chuckled with mischief, enjoying what he was about to do. "If he finds out I took this bottle, he'll be so pissed. But after his wild day with Dafnie, I don't think he'll mind. He will be quite content and sexed up when Apollo learns of my intrusion."

Apollo, unconcerned, wouldn't bat an eye if Fernhoof settled in and enjoy the god's hospitality. The Olympian would even urge Fernhoof to make himself at home—to enjoy his wares. Fernhoof always admired Apollo's personality, a proud and unapologetic individual who still cared for those loyal to him.

As he sat to open a bottle of Apollo's best vintage and a hearty cold dinner, Fernhoof noticed a flash of golden light coming from the house entrance. Fernhoof scrambled to his feet, aware of the new arrival by the familiar scent of pine and oiled leather.

"Fernhoof, where is Apollo?" Artemis asked, her voice sounding threatening but also held no threat.

"Upstairs?" Fernhoof said, hesitating for a moment but gaining the courage to continue. "Would you like to eat something? I found a treat I'm certain you'll enjoy."

Ignoring him, Artemis entered the dining room and looked up the stairs. "I tracked Dafnie here many hours ago. He's defiling my precious hunter—the one who vowed to stay chaste for me in her past life. She did this against her father's wishes. Apollo's corrupted appetite knows no bounds. I bet Peneus is ecstatic having Apollo, an Olympian, as a son-in-law." Despair shone in her eyes as the muffled sounds of Apollo and Dafnie's lovemaking came from the upper floor. Even the air had the intoxicating scent of their desire.

It amazed Fernhoof that those two still had the energy to continue their affair—borderline absurd. "Apollo is a beast in bed and his endurance is unbelievable. No doubt he takes after his father," Fernhoof muttered, feeling embarrassed that the two were still humping like a lion and a lioness in heat.

Artemis's fists clenched. Her anger was palpable. Fernhoof felt sympathy for the goddess. "Very typical of him to not care about others, even with the looming threat of enraging Zeus for ignoring his orders."

"You know... he was a complete mess last night after the fight. His aim was completely off. You, more than anyone else, know that is rare. He focus strayed because his emotions were awash in turmoil. He was restless and desperate. If you think I'm trying to justify his actions, then you're wrong. His heart ached, and today, he's making sure Dafnie knows she means the world to him."

"It's already late, and Apollo asked to postpone hearing our father's sentence until today. I need him ready," Artemis said more calmly.

"Uhhmmm... sorry, but he's busy and told me he doesn't want to be disturbed," Fernhoof apologized. "I made myself clear about his plans. If Zeus gets angry, we have no choice but to summon his wife."

"What do you mean by that?"

"Hera sent me a message to inform her when Zeus shows up. I have this gut feeling that she has her plans, and Zeus doesn't know about them. You know she's cunning and calculating."

Having no other choice after hearing Fernhoof's explanation, Artemis sighed and plopped on a chair by the dining table. "Well then, if that's the case, we'll have to wait. I hope Hera's plan is good because if it's not, I fear for things to come," she said, her voice filled with apprehension as she closed her eyes and took a deep breath.

Artemis stared at the ceiling. A disheartened look fleetingly appeared on her face. "He's head over heels for her... I know I'm acting jealous, and I'm aware of that. Just once, I wish for his happiness to last. I wish everything works out for them, but I'm concerned."

Fernhoof understood Artemis's point. Zeus was acting weird long before Apollo unleashed his calamity on the world. Something sinister was going on. He nodded in agreement, sensing it was the right time to lighten the mood.

Fernhoof stared at the bottle in front of him before saying anything else. "No one can control your brother, not even Zeus. All I can do is consume this fine wine and enjoy myself. Do you care to join me?" he asked, opening the bottle and preparing to enjoy his dinner.

He saw no point in worrying about Artemis causing a scene. "Can we delay this meeting? Would Zeus mind doing this tomorrow?"

"You know how he is. He only cares about himself and favors anything that accommodates his whims his whims. He is remorseless and intolerant if anyone disobeys. All he wants is to affirm his dominance over the other gods. I'm surprised he loves Apollo, but then again, my brother sometimes acts like our father."

Fernhoof opened the bottle, and the sweet aroma of the wine filled the room. He leaned back, a contented sigh escaping his lips as satisfaction tinted his face. The rich, earthy tones of the wine opposed the tense atmosphere, providing a strange sense of comfort amidst the impending chaos. He poured himself a glass, the dark liquid tempting and inviting. The inviting scent caught Artemis's attention.

"That horny dog! Did he convince Dionysus to part ways with one of his finest wines?" Artemis asked, her gaze locked onto the enticing glass. Fernhoof chuckled, glad for the slight reprieve in the tension.

"Apollo has his ways, and Dionysus has a soft spot for him. Considering Apollo provides the musical entrainment for Dionysus' soirees. He may have asked for these as payment. So... a bottle will go unnoticed while we wait around. Now come and let us enjoy ourselves!" He gestured toward the bottle, an invitation.

Artemis grabbed the glass Fernhoof had already poured and took a sip. The flavors were a rich blend of fruits and spices that teased her senses with its bold spices. She closed her eyes for a second to appreciate the taste. "That motherfucker knows how to make a superb wine."

"I know. That's why I snatched it."

The wine was as complex and appealing as Apollo himself, having an allure she couldn't deny. "Do you think Dio created this vintage for Apollo?"

"Probably, but who knows? I'll enjoy it with my dinner."

"Well, I'll leave you to your meal. I'll retire to my pavilion. Tell Apollo to be ready by tomorrow if you can. We cannot waste any more time," Artemis said, looking calm and collected.

"What if he's not ready?" Fernhoof wanted to antagonize the goddess before sipping from Artemis's glass. The goddess's visage was pure beauty. And his opportunity to steal a kiss from her, even if it wasn't a direct one.

"Oh, for goodness' fucking sake! That prick better be ready, Fernhoof. It can cost him if he pisses off the wrong person, and we've already made clear who that is," she said, turning toward the stairs where she could still hear the muffled sounds of sex. "I cannot believe his lustful appetite. He's defiling my precious hunter. It's unacceptable that he gets to have her. She was the best of all my maidens. THAT JACKASS!"

And saying nothing else, she disappeared, leaving Fernhoof alone. "I better finish my dinner and find a lover for the night. Artemis wouldn't allow anyone to interrupt or cause problems."

Chapter 46

Zeus appeared at Apollo's home early in the morning—uninvited and unexpected. The gentle light of dawn flooded the living room, and he looked around. He regarded the mess and clutter in the tiny dwelling. Then, Zeus spotted Fernhoof asleep on the sofa bed, and the firm yet sweet aroma of wine lingered about him.

Looking disgusted, Zeus didn't appreciate Apollo living like a peasant. "I can't believe my son allows this behavior from his subordinates. He's a fucking prince!" His eyes landed on the hawk perched on the pole, noticing how the sunlight glinted off the bird's dark, glossy feathers while it preened itself.

Zeus shook his head, displeased that his son, the prince of all gods, wasn't acting according to his station and status. Apollo had always been a rebel and untamable. Zeus hoped Apollo would change and outgrow his beastly character, but that had never

happened. Apollo remained as wild as the forest and unpredictable as a tempestuous storm.

"His heart, not his head, has always ruled Apollo's character. I need to control him and get him on my side," Zeus muttered as he bit his lips and drew blood. "He's also a passionate man. Using that nymph's life essence was the right choice. That should make that brat more compliant to agree to my plans."

As he took a deep breath, he caught the unmistakable scent of sex wafting in the air. Zeus could make out the overpowering masculine scent of Apollo mingled with the sweet fragrance of a woman. A smirk stretched across his lips as he thought of Apollo, his composure crumbling over a woman he brought to existence.

The feeling was intoxicating—a heady mix of excitement and greed.

"I can continue with my plan now that he's bound to that woman by desire. But... I admit Dafnie is beyond beautiful, even if she's oblivious to it. If she didn't have the purpose of making my son compliant with my wishes, I would've taken her as one of my lovers a long time ago. I must be careful and can't afford Apollo's wrath."

Zeus explored the plain house where his son lived in. Apollo had the habit of moving around often, looking for a place to call home. "He knows that Mount Olympus is his home. He's not focused on his responsibilities as a prince and needs to be more serious. When will he stop being a troublemaker? He needs to be ready to command his people whenever he needs them," he mulled as he continued to gauge the state of Apollo's home. Zeus noticed his son converted the living room into a luscious music room.

Disappointed, Zeus sighed before exploring the house to understand how Apollo lived among humans these days. He needed to ensure Apollo returned to Olympus after cleaning his mess in the mortal world. No matter what, Zeus needed Apollo under his control and to do his bidding.

Zeus considered the house beneath him, thinking the place was appalling and crude. He wanted to scold Apollo for living in a house like this, embracing a simple life. His son's astounding power and abundant wealth were all squandered in a bleak and forgotten position. "Apollo's a fucking prince, not a wretched peasant. His purpose was to aid me in governing, not to squander his time on trivial matters. He should live in his palace, commanding over others and his domains. He needs to be like me, Zeus, the mighty ruler of all the gods."

Zeus furrowed his brow in displeasure at the sight of Apollo's spartan home, setting off to find his son. The air hung heavy with undeclared tension. The sweet smell of sex told him his son was in his room with the nymph Dafnie. Apollo slept away his day from the lustful stupor of the previous day. Zeus had been watching his son as of late. His messengers monitored Apollo's every movement, ensuring Zeus was always aware of his son's whereabouts.

Yesterday afternoon, one of his spies informed him that Apollo locked himself away in his house and refused to see anyone. Zeus investigated the situation—personally. He refused to have any inconsistencies in his plans, and Apollo was a huge variable. Disguised as an innocent-looking finch, Zeus flew to the plain house to check on his dear firstborn son. But little did he know he would run into a scene that left him wanting.

There wasn't a doubt in Zeus' mind his son was a virile man driven by raw desire, peaking at his son's intimate affairs. He witnessed as Apollo rammed into Dafnie's wanton body. The lovely nymph looked beautiful as she accepted her lover's cock. The look on her face let him know she loved every second of her passionate dance with Apollo, digging her nails into the skin of his back as she cried out in pure ecstasy. "I should've taken her for myself," he murmured. The human nymph looked tempting, and at some point, Zeus had to resist the temptation to whisk her away to his chambers to claim her for his own. "If it weren't because I needed my son compliant and, on my side, I wouldn't have allowed him to have her."

Zeus turned toward a mirror by the base of the stairs. He stared at his image and reflected. Their physical similarities were uncanny. Apollo looked so much like his father. The connection was undeniable, unmistakable. Although a distinct color, their luscious manes had a halo-like radiance that both mortals and gods admired.

A wild, untamed fire blazed in Zeus and Apollo's eyes, compelling absolute obedience. Their bodies, sculpted by divine artistry, highlighted the strength and majesty of their lineage.

While similar in physical presence, father and son exhibited noticeable differences. Zeus's generous beard, which gave him a mature appearance, was the most notable difference between their similarly chiseled features. Zeus was the more rugged of the two. Apollo was taller and had refined mannerisms. The sun god moved with unique grace, while Zeus carried himself with a gruff disposition.

The time to act!

Zeus went up the stairs, straining his ears to listen for any signs of activity. Other than the deep breaths from sleep, the house was quiet. He entered the room with a determined expression, his furrowed brow highlighting his intent. Like bolts of lightning, his piercing eyes fixated on Apollo as he lay sleeping, his arm wrapped around Dafnie in a possessive hold.

Without a doubt, Apollo posed a message to those who dared intrude on his privacy. Dafnie was under his protection. Zeus needed to be careful not to mess with him about his lover.

"Good morning, Father," Apollo said as his eyes landed on Zeus. He waved his hand over Dafnie, golden tendrils shooting from his fingers and weaving their magic over Dafnie. "She'll not wake. I put her in a deep slumber. We can talk… freely."

"Good morning to you, my son. Did you have a great night?" Zeus asked. He found a comfortable chaise by the corner next to the window. His eyes lingered on the beautiful woman sleeping next to his son.

"Yes, I did. Although your mighty presence woke me when you stepped inside my house." Apollo said, eyeing his father. "May I add to stop gawking at my wife? I don't appreciate your lascivious intent with her. It's written all over your face that you want her, and I understand you don't care, but she is not a doll for you to play with. She's precious to me." Apollo's voice was a low growl, protective and unyielding.

Zeus and Apollo stared at each other with disdain. Their tension rose, becoming palpable. Rigid in posture, they were ready to attack at any provocation. Pride and stubborn determination shone in their eyes. Both of their piercing gaze held the intensity of a predator. A suffocating silence, rich with anticipation, pressed down, not a sound breaking the tension.

"Father," Apollo began with a tone sharpened by a blend of respect and defiance as he leaned forward, ensuring his wife was decent and well covered from his father's prying eyes. "Your sovereignty is legendary. I know I fucked up, and I must atone for my mistakes, but I don't take your intrusion kindly." Apollo's voice echoed throughout the room.

"Spoken like a true prince. Only you can get away with it. Your irritable nature, insufferable as it may be, still earns my respect."

"That's because I don't kiss your ass."

"True, but like me, you don't give a fuck about anything or anyone."

"You're wrong. I'm nothing like you. I care about others."

"Really! Now explain how it felt to take revenge on humans after being wronged?" Zeus teased, keeping eye contact with Apollo and gauging his reaction.

Apollo learned long ago that reacting to his father's baits was a dangerous game and remained calm before answering. "I apologize for being a prick and strive to avoid being a major asshole. However, I cannot say the same about you. You are a bastard all the fucking time." Apollo used his most threatening voice and stared with grave hostility.

Zeus stood from his chair with murderous intent, ready to kill his wayward son. A low hum vibrated through the room as the surrounding energy intensified, thickening the silence with a sense of power. His blue eyes lit up as energy orbs formed in his hands. Zeus' lightning energy manifested with a crackling noise, and he was ready to strike down his favorite son.

Unafraid and ready, Apollo jumped out of bed. Without a care in the world that he was naked, he got ready to defend Dafnie and his family. He summoned his pyrokinetic powers and pooled his powers within his chest. Intense heat emanated from his body as his eyes glowed an amber color.

Apollo flashed his father a sinister smile. The fire Apollo cont-ained inside his body gave him a demonic yet charming demeanor. "Old man! It's best to be careful with what you do from here on out. I'd hate to see you overexert yourself and break your hip." The menace in his words charged the room with a thr-eatening energy.

"You better learn your place, or I will smite you where you stand, but not before witnessing your wife turned to ash with my bolt."

Apollo's wrath was palpable, his stance unyielding against his father's formidable powers. "Your bolts can scar the heavens, but even with the power of thunder, you better not forget that heat and fire are my domain."

Without warning, Apollo and Zeus fell to their knees, clutch-ing their heads and grunting in pain. The destructive powers they summoned recoiled and soon extinguished from existence. A serene and beautiful woman materialized in the room, stand-ing between her husband and stepson. Her presence comman-ded immediate obedience, even from the king of gods.

She raised her delicate hand, and the hatred in the room diss-olved and replaced with calm. "Calm down and behave! Seriously, Zeus, you're complaining about your son being a lost case, but you're no different. I would even say you are far worse," Hera complained before turning to Apollo and releasing him from her mental cage. "Apollo, at least cover your lower body. You are sporting a massive hard-on. I don't wish to see my son's frantic emotions while he fights his father."

Apollo summoned a long sarong to cover himself. Breathless and shuddering from the mental assault, Apollo struggled to his feet, watching Hera move around the room with royal grace.

Hera's dominance over his father was undeniable—she easily manipulated him. Her invisible mental grip rendered his father helpless, still immobilized on the ground and gasping for air. Apollo darted next to his lover to embrace her.

Hera walked over to Dafnie, still under Apollo's sleeping spell and unaware of the surrounding upheaval. She caressed her face with maternal concern. "Zeus, you know Dafnie's under my protection. The moment you threatened her life, you became my problem and risked igniting a wrath far greater than the one you would unleash. I swear, if you harm her, you won't escape the maddening prison I will entrap you in. Ask Dionysus about his punishments."

"Fuck, Hera! Release me from this hell."

"Will you calm down? I released Apollo because he can be calm and collected when needed. He gets the message, but you are a different story." Hera observed Apollo cradling and kissing Dafnie.

Zeus took several deep breaths, doing his best to calm down, even though he was still in pain from Hera's mental assault. "Release me. I'm calm now."

"All right, but you must go next door and wait until they're ready to see us." Hera turned to stare at Apollo, who was possessively holding a sleeping Dafnie against his chest. "Look at him! You threaten his wife, and all he wants to do is comfort and protect her."

As soon as Hera released Zeus from her shackles, he disappeared.

"Thank you, my Queen."

"You can be less formal when we're talking in private, but I understand why you're doing it." Hera's eyes hardened with determination. "Dafnie, Apollo, I bless this union. The road that lies ahead of you won't be easy. Expect lots of suffering. Thus, your connection will transcend all challenges. You should never lose hope, especially in each other."

Hera turned toward Apollo and caressed his smooth face with maternal care. "You asked to delay your punishment until the next day. Yet that was yesterday. You ought to face the consequences of your actions. I'm buying you time to have a relaxing morning with your wife, but please do not deflect. We'll wait for you at Dafnie's house."

Chapter 47

Protective Embrace

Apollo's vulnerable gazed upon Dafnie's sleeping form. A wave of weakness washed over him, leaving him breathless. No amount of celestial power could make him feel any better. Apollo was unprepared for the turmoil that brewed inside him, feeling like shit.

His anger at his father was about to consume him and destroy the one person he held dear to his heart. Apollo knew his unhinged emotions would cost him dearly one of these days, but he never imagined the one he loved the most would pay the ultimate price.

At that moment, he replayed everything that transpired with his father. Things had never been great between them. Father and son rarely agreed on anything. Apollo had a knack for getting under his father's skin, and Zeus always annoyed his eldest prince. His father threatened the one person he couldn't bear to see in harm's way.

As delicate tendrils of sunlight crept through the room, playing on Dafnie's skin and casting a golden luster on her cheek, Apollo's emotions crumbled and succumbed to the inevitable as tears streamed down his face.

Many believed that gods were above profound human emotions, such as crying, but he didn't care what others thought of him. Dafnie was more than just his consort. She was his heart's true solace.

When Apollo released his sleeping spell on Dafnie, he made her a promise. "I'll make sure no harm comes to you from scheming gods. I will ensure you are well-trained and well-prepared. You will defend yourself with ease. I will not harm you—that I promise."

Apollo's teary eyes focused on her serene expression, contrasting his mood as she slowly awakened. Sighing in contentment, Dafnie stretched, looking relaxed and content. Apollo's heart swelled with love as he admired his lover's adorable way of waking. He reached out with the tenderest of touches, making her beam at his light touch.

Her eyelids fluttered open and met his troubled gaze. Dafnie's brow furrowed in worry as she noted Apollo's tear-stained face. His watery orbs spoke volumes of the unspoken concerns. "Something happened, didn't it?"

"Yes. My father came over, and like always, we fought. It got out of hand." Driven by an irresistible urge to be honest, Apollo blurted out the truth, his voice thick with grief. Leaning, Apollo's warm breath brushed against her skin as he kissed her forehead. Moving tenderly, he traced a path of soft kisses, caressing every inch of her face with affection before lingering on her neck, savoring the moment's intimacy.

Dafnie sighed, not knowing what to say. She closed her eyes and embraced Apollo, allowing him to continue kissing her. Apollo's tension was apparent in his body, leaving her to imagine the fears that plagued him.

Kissing Dafnie was a balm to his aching heart, but Apollo wanted more. "My dear wife, Hera, anointed our union this morning. Although I had already considered us married when we first met, Hera's blessing made it official in everyone's eyes. It will always be uncontested, not even by the gods," he said, moving between Dafnie's legs, removing his sarong, and claiming her lips in a fervent kiss.

She wrapped her arms and legs around him, drawing him nearer in a tender embrace. Apollo didn't need to utter any words for Dafnie to sense his desire to have her as close to him as possible. "Mi amor, I want you inside!"

"You don't need to tell me twice, my sweet nymph," Apollo said, entering her with a powerful thrust.

As pleasure surged over her, she dug her nails into Apollo's back. Her senses heightened as the fiery intensity of their connection intensified. The overwhelming rapture of the moment drove her into a frenzy. "Ever since we met, I'm whole. I love you so much," she declared, moaning and etching her unrestrained longing into his flesh.

He hissed at the burning sensation as her fingers traced a feverish pattern across his back. He laughed full-heartedly. "I don't want to discourage you, but your enthusiasm with your nails, though oddly enjoyable, is becoming painful."

He claimed Dafnie's lips before embarrassment consumed her because of his revelation. In her embrace, Apollo found his haven. He couldn't help but feel elated after Dafnie's confession.

He whispered his devotion as he increased his pace. "I love you, my sweet nymph. I will always be by your side."

After his tense morning with his father, Apollo only wanted to focus on Dafnie. The walls of her channel swell, squeezing and pulsating around his cock. Dafnie was close to coming.

"Ahh! Apollo, please don't stop. I'm... I'm coming!"

"Nah! You feel so good," Apollo said as Dafnie pulsated around this throbbing rod, and nectar flowed from her core before he closed his eyes, grunting with gusto as he, too, came with his beloved wife. "Fuck!"

Dafnie moaned in pleasure, embracing Apollo as he collapsed on top of her, careful not to crush her with his heavier build. "Ahhh!"

Their hearts beat fast, and their breathing was heavy with the aftermath of passion.

They took their time to enjoy their bliss in silence as they held each other. Dafnie's brown locks framed her head like an elaborate crown on the pillow, and her cheeks flushed in the afterglow. Apollo's light-golden hair strewn across Dafnie's chest like a silk blanket.

Apollo propped up to stare into Dafnie's eyes. Love and adoration greeted him from her lovely eyes, swelling his heart with foreign passion. "I can be a moody and imperfect god sometimes, but I'll always love you."

Apollo rolled off Dafnie and sat on the bed, pulling her to his lap. "Now we need to get ready. I'm not looking forward to seeing my father."

"I can see that. Let's take it one step at a time. I really... need a shower right now. I feel all gross," Dafnie said, puckering her lips, making her look adorable.

Apollo, finding her playful indignation adorable, laughed. "Well, I better take care of my sweet nymph's needs before she gets mad at me."

With lingering kisses, Apollo and Dafnie rose from the bed to shower. As soon as the shower was ready, they stepped into the welcoming waterfall of warm water. The relaxing stream washed the remnants of their wild coupling from the previous day. Apollo pulled Dafnie in for a kiss as his hands roamed her body with shameless deliberation.

Breathlessly, Dafnie nudged him against the shower wall. With a smile, she grabbed the soap and washed Apollo's muscled form. Her touch ignited sparks on his wet skin as she traced every contour and ridge on his body.

"You're playing with fire, love," Apollo said. He bent down to reach Dafnie's lips, her much smaller form only reaching his shoulders, and picked her up, allowing her to wrap her legs around his waist. Apollo, ever the attentive lover, took his time kissing her and exploring the soft curves of her body.

Before long, they found themselves once again lost in their passion as Apollo pressed Dafnie against the colder tiles, still engaged in their fiery kiss. "I want you again," he murmured against her lips.

"I would like that. We're together until our end," Dafnie breathed in response, arching into him, inviting him to claim the depths of her once more.

He entered her as they moved as one under the stream of water. Each cry of pleasure and slap of wet skin reverberated against the walls, amplifying the sounds of their union. Their movements became urgent, their need to climax driving them to completion. Panting and sated, they came back to themselves.

They stayed still, letting the water run over them, basking in the afterglow. Dafnie's hands rested on Apollo's chest, tracing the water droplets that zigzagged down his form. "With you, I find peace," she whispered, snuggling against his chest.

"And in you, I find home," Apollo said as he put his lover down.

They washed the residues of their love before stepping out of the shower. Apollo cared for Dafnie's needs, wrapped her in a soft towel, and brushed her hair. Dafnie giggled as he concentrated on untangling her hair. "Is your hair always this tangled?"

"It happens all the time! Don't you have that problem?"

"Sweet nymph! I'm a god. My hair is always perfect, and I never have to struggle with tangled hair."

Dafnie looked at him askance, and his hair was indeed splendid. "Do you even brush your hair?"

"Nope! It will remain silky and smooth, regardless. Do you want me to make your hair perfect like mine?" Apollo asked as he finished brushing her hair.

Dafnie looked at Apollo. "No, I like my hair this way better," she said, feigning displeasure. She flashed him a smile before strolling toward the walk-in closet.

She perused Apollo's wardrobe and picked a button-up shirt and boxer briefs to make herself presentable. Her clothes from the previous day were dirty, and she didn't want to wear them. Apollo followed suit and donned a simple T-shirt and jeans before following Dafnie to the kitchen.

For the first time, he acknowledged the way Dafnie swayed her hips. The movement was slight but still noticeable. A bemused smile graced his features before he caught up to her and hugged her from behind. "I must admit... my clothes look divine on you. Far better than it will ever do on me." He picked her up, his chuckle filled with pure delight, making Dafnie laugh full-heartedly before running down the stairs to the kitchen.

After placing Dafnie on the counter, he went about his kitchen to gather the ingredients for their breakfast. With the ability of someone well-versed in cooking, he mixed and cut the ingredients for their breakfast with well honed skills. Though he didn't need substance like mortals, he loved to eat. After their intense night together, he could only guess that Dafnie was famished. "You must be starving, so I'm giving you lots of carbs and sugars," he said with a chuckle as he winked. "My dear, I'm about to concoct a divine breakfast that will make you fall in love with me again."

Dafnie giggled at his bombastic display but knew he was not telling her everything. "You're not acting your normal self, mi amor. Don't get me wrong... I love the attention. I get you are excited that we're now married. However, I don't need any blessings, as I feel deep in my heart that our union took place long ago. Can you tell me what happened earlier today?"

Apollo pressed the button on his espresso machine, trying to buy some time. "I promised you to be honest... The argument this morning was bad. My father threatened to kill you. I lost it and tried to kill him. I almost lost control."

Dafnie climbed down from the counter and approached Apollo. She touched his face with a gentle caress. He struggled to avoid her gaze, trying to avoid his attention elsewhere. Just as she was about to speak, Fernhoof appeared and interrupted her. He cleared his throat, announcing his presence to Apollo and Dafnie.

"Moring, Fernhoof!" Apollo said, looking uncomfortable but

recovering fast. "Danie needs a change of clothes. I can collect them, but my father is at her house, and I don't wish to see him."

"I heard what he said, and I'm sorry, my friend. Let me get those for you."

Dafnie waited for Fernhoof to leave before saying anything else. "I won't push to reveal anything, but I need to know if you're okay."

"I'm fine, but I want to focus on us and not think of my problems. You're my priority, meaning I need to feed you right now. It's been a while since you've eaten anything."

Apollo returned to making their breakfast, skillfully flipping pancakes. Dafnie marveled at his effortless poise and how his muscles flexed under the thin fabric of his shirt, a sight that made her heart flutter with desire. The aroma of rich butter and fried batter made her mouth water. She grabbed two cups from the cupboard and moved toward the automatic espresso machine. She added a bit of honey and vanilla to the cups before putting them under the machine's spout. The room became infused with the comforting scent as the coffee machine brewed.

They maneuvered around in the kitchen. Apollo plated the pancakes, drizzled with maple syrup and berries. They sat across from each other, enjoying their breakfast in silence. Apollo followed her movements as she enjoyed every morsel of the delicious meal. His eyes never left hers as she brought a forkful of the fluffy treat to her lips. Just like any other day, Hebe delivered his nectar later that morning.

On that morning, he examined the thick liquid, but against his better judgment, he gulped the substance down. "I don't think he's trying to kill me, but he's up to something," Apollo said as he turned toward Dafnie. "Be careful around my father. He may not harm you, but he likes to play perverse games with others. He's cunning and poisonous as fuck."

Chapter 48

Calm

While Dafnie changed, Apollo tidied his place. He started in the kitchen and quickly finished his chores. When he moved to clean the living room, he realized Fernhoof had rummaged through his cellar and had helped himself to his most expensive wine and provisions. The sight made him chuckle. Apollo braced himself for his friend's sharp tongue over being forced to listen to him and Dafnie. Apollo only guessed Fernhoof seemed frustrated and teased him. "I take it you had a nice dinner?"

Feeling defiant, Fernhoof spoke his mind, looking Apollo straight in his eyes. "Your escapade last night was infuriating. It was torture having to listen to the two of you having wild sex all fucking night! I don't mind, but I had to stay behind to protect your domain while you were… busy."

Apollo laughed at his friend's sassy attitude. He appreciated Fernhoof's company. "I was just asking, and I'm glad you enjoyed yourself. I hope you found a lover for the evening after my sister left."

"Thank you for asking and for your concern. Yep! I found two lovers to keep me company for the night—a nymph and a beautiful fellow. They were delightful. I came home somewhat late, but the commotion upstairs woke me," Fernhoof said, careful not to anger Apollo. "Your father can be a complete scumbag... I heard his threat. Are you okay?"

Apollo did not answer, distracting himself by picking up the mess his friend had made the previous evening. Although he felt hurt that his father had threatened his wife, Apollo was honest with his friend. Their bond, forged through past hardships, relied on their mutual honesty.

"After my morning scare, I'm calmer, but he crossed the line this time. I've never interfered with his affairs. Never! In the past few years, his erratic behavior has worsened over the centuries. He's been giving me mixed signals this whole damn time that a hard reset was necessary for the gods to regain their dominion. He mentioned restoring the ancient ways and how we should rule this world. My mistake to assume... to misread him. Having too much free time on my hands didn't help either. Like a fool, I overanalyzed his cryptic messages and acted alone, thinking what my father wanted was what I did. I should've ignored him like in the past."

Apollo sat on the sofa as he dumped his trash in Fernhoof's trash bag. He closed his eyes, trying to remember his conversations with his father about restoring Mount Olympus' authority on Earth. Instead, his mind was on his father, threatening to end Dafnie's life on repeat.

Fernhoof smiled, a sad glint shining in his eyes. "If it makes you feel any better, I could have stopped you, but I didn't. I should've seen you needed a friend, but I ignored the signs. Zeus is an insufferable manipulator who always gets his way and gets others to do his bidding. Did he say that to trick you into doing his dirty work?"

"Maybe, I wonder..." Apollo looked out the window, noticing the destruction his impulse behavior to please his father had caused. "Dafnie is about to come downstairs. Can you please finish cleaning the house?" He turned to look at his friend and smiled. "We need to make sure the house is ready for our departure. We'll leave in the next few days. I was hoping you could talk to one of my palace servants to take care of our houses while we are gone. Once I fix this mess, I want to return to Phoebus Groove, away from Mount Olympus, and start a family with Dafnie. I plan to make her immortal so we can be together—forever. I have a gut feeling that turning her will be successful with the blessings she has."

"Are you talking about her tattoo?"

"Yes! After copying the design onto my body, I better understand its intent. Someone other than my father is trying to use her for a greater purpose. He's unaware of that. Otherwise, he wouldn't have threatened her the way he did. She's coming, but I will talk to her about everything before we go face Zeus," he said, walking toward Dafnie, who came down the stairs.

She looked at Apollo with a big, beautiful smile that disarmed him and took his breath away. Her eyes sparkled with joy and peace, and her lips curled into a radiant smile that made him weak in the knees. She looked stunning even in a simple white hoodie that hugged her frame and jeans.

"Wow! You sure can take my breath away... I feel like a lad

with a crush. A crush on a certain nymph, who turned to a tree and broke my heart."

Finally, closing the distance between them, Dafnie kissed his cheek. "I'm curious about who this nymph is that you had a crush on."

Apollo wrapped his arms around Dafnie, bending down to kiss her neck. "That nymph? Why? None compared to you, my dearest, not even her."

Dafnie's laughter echoed throughout the room. "What a charmer. I better be careful with you. I see how you get your way. You're a people charmer," she said.

Dafnie's gaze held a playful spark but remained guarded. She had been getting ready when she overheard Apollo's conversation. At the last minute, she changed her mind about mentioning it to Apollo. She'd give him some time to confess whenever he was ready. Apollo was a master politician and confident tactician. He was the only one to navigate the treacherous currents of authority. Their time together had taught her that Apollo was calculating and methodical with his plans. Nothing escaped his meticulous deliberations, and he was not above using his seductive appeal to get people to obey his bidding.

His experience as a ruler among the gods gave Apollo the edge in commanding and persuading others. The only exception was Zeus. Despite their similar behaviors, Apollo and his father constantly clashed—their tension intensified with time. They seldom spoke to one another. When they did, emotions ran high, landing Apollo in trouble because of his impulsive actions. The shocking revelation of Zeus's part in the apocalypse made Dafnie's mind reel with mistrust. An icy dread gripped her heart as they got closer to her house. Indeed, their relationship was a delicate balancing act.

Apollo leaned in close as if about to kiss her. "Mmmm! My nymph gets my secrets. I can tell something is troubling you," he said, kissing her cheek. "I was thinking of taking a short stroll before heading to your house. We have much to talk about."

Grabbing onto his arm, Dafnie leaned on his shoulder and sighed in relief as she was at peace by his side. "I'd love that."

As soon as they walked outside, Dafnie took a deep breath. The crisp morning air felt invigorating after spending almost an entire day indoors. Apollo guided them to the trail that ran behind their homes. They walked awhile, listening to the birds chirping and the leaves rustling in the gentle breeze. Soon, they found a bench and settled onto it to enjoy their morning.

"I'm guessing you overheard my conversation this morning. How are you feeling? Do you think less of me after everything?"

Dafnie took her time answering. It seemed Apollo was in no rush to hear her answer, either. "I don't think less of you. You're Zeus's son, and it makes sense you can lead others. It looks like you're as powerful as Zeus. You even dared to confront him as equals. Although you seem frustrated because another governs you, and you're uncomfortable with that dynamic. You cannot control their plans, and that puts you on edge. I think I understand now." She paused, looking at him with a depth of understanding. "Now let's confront your father and show him we are not his pawns. We're prepared to tackle any challenges that come our way," Dafnie said with determination.

"Then let's get this over with. I plan to leave for New York City in a few days. We'll then travel to the other locations."

"Other locations?"

"Yes… Fuck, I was stupid. I sowed the plant in various locations. Destroying them will stop the spread of the pollen. Or…"

"Or what?"

"I can alter the plant to release a different pollen to help eradicate the virus. It won't help the infected, though. Their change is irreversible."

"Okay! At least those unaffected will have a better chance of surviving." She tried to understand the implications of Apollo's statement. "Does that mean…"

"It means the gods will rule over the mortal world again, which is bad. Deities show indifference towards humans, including myself, often taking their lives for granted. We're a self-centered and self-serving bunch. As for my plans, I intend to protect as many humans as possible. I'm the founder of cities and law."

"You didn't protect humans this time, however. You mindlessly followed your father's desires without questioning his motives. Why are you yearning for his approval? Why now?" Dafnie asked with reproach.

Apollo, saddened by Dafnie's reprimand, couldn't argue. She was right. "I… don't know. I guess I'm jealous of humans' brief lives. They get to feel more because of their short lifespan. My life has no stakes, so I have nothing to lose. Life becomes boring after a while. It's common for immortals to lose touch with reality. My father is no exception. He's become disconnected from mortals and no longer shows concern for the world."

Dafnie stood, pulling Apollo and leading the way toward her house. "Then let's raise those stakes for you. We cannot change what you did, and sitting around will not fix this problem. It's time to tidy up this chaos, but I have one stipulation. I want to come along."

"No, Dafnie. It's too dangerous…"

She turned and gave Apollo a hard stare that gave him pause. "I won't accept that. What do you want me to do?! Can I sit around until you return? That won't happen. I'm coming along to help, and that is final."

Apollo pulled her to face him, caressing her face, catching Dafnie by surprise. "You don't need to come. It's dangerous…"

"I decided! I'm coming, and that's final." She turned to walk away before calling out to him. "Are you coming? I'd like you to hold my hand," she said, admitting she felt vulnerable. "I'm scared and hate feeling this way."

"Hey! Don't feel that way. We'll do this together, I promise." Apollo kissed her forehead before grabbing her hand and placing it over his heart, trying to convey that he cared about her. He walked her to her house, saying nothing else. Words were unnecessary. Apollo understood better than anyone. Dafnie had decided, and he couldn't sway her not to come otherwise. His priority was to train her as a hunter.

As they approached Dafnie's home, the bright sunlight couldn't erase the ominous reminder of Apollo's argument with Zeus—a fresh storm clouding his mind. Apollo's heart was a battlefield of dread and defiance. He needed to keep his emotions in check for Dafnie's sake. He would gladly bite his tongue so as not to rise to his father's goading. The thought of Dafnie's safety gave him the strength to face his father's cruelty.

Apollo's steps slowed as they approached the back door of the house. "I don't want to do this, but I must." His chest felt constricted.

"I don't have any powers. I'm not strong, but I'm here with you."

Apollo took a deep breath before opening the door and putting up his political mask. His sister and mother greeted him as they came in. "Please don't tell me you are in trouble because of me."

"No, my dear son, I'm here because I'm with you. Your father has done nothing for us other than make demands. He celebrated your birth as his firstborn son, but that's where his adoration ended. I'm here to ensure he doesn't take advantage of the situation," Leto said, approaching and kissing her son's forehead. She turned toward Dafnie and kissed her cheek before addressing her. "You're more beautiful than I expected. The rumors were finally true. I now see why my son fell for you in your past life."

Dafnie didn't know what to say. Nervously, she gazed at Leto, a captivating woman radiating immense charm and grace. Dafnie felt intimidated by such regality. She then caught sight of Leto's light blue eyes rivaling Apollo's remarkable orbs.

"I can see you're not used to our kind. We're different, humans and immortals. We're majestic, and everyone wants to be us. My son is so handsome. I'm glad he has my eyes and personality," Leto said with overflowing love. "I'm very proud of him despite being troublesome."

"Nice to meet you, ma'am."

"Oh, shush! Call me Mother," Leto said as she pried Dafnie off Apollo's hold, leaned in, and whispered to her. "The mother of my future grandchildren should call me Mother, right? I can tell they will be strong and beautiful babies."

"You know about it?"

"Oh, my mother doesn't keep any secrets concerning my children from me."

"Mother, what are you scheming?" Apollo asked, sounding vexed.

Leto turned toward her son and slashed her most innocent smile. "Oh, nothing, my son. I hope you're ready to face your father. He's quite irritable this morning, and it's annoying me."

They found Zeus and Hera sitting by the fireplace when they entered the living room. Hera looked calm, while Zeus seethed with anger. Artemis moved to stand between Zeus and Dafnie, trying to protect her from her father's wrath. Apollo stood on Dafnie's side, opposite his mother, and clutched her hand. He straightened his back and took a deep breath before moving to the sofa across from his father.

Sensing the growing tension in the room, Hera spoke first, ensuring no problems would arise between her husband and stepson. "Considering the events from this morning, I created a barrier in this room for Dafnie's protection. If anyone dares harm a single hair on her, you'll experience great suffering. Now we can begin."

The god-king was not in the mood to waste his time. He hated engaging in frivolities and wanted to leave as soon as possible. "Apollo, your transgression has not only unleashed chaos upon the mortal world but also has challenged the order of the gods. As such, your punishment must be instructive and transformative." Zeus' booming voice filled the expanse.

And so, Apollo's judgment started.

Chapter 49

Edict of Mortality

Wronged and vexed by his father's intrusion in the morning, Apollo was not in the mood to be civil with his father. "Well... hello to you too, father. Considering that you tried to kill Dafnie and me earlier this morning, I believe we're off to a great start," he growled, expressing his tone. "Nothing better than some healthy family dispute in the morning."

The meeting was not starting well, and Hera intervened. "I believe we're getting off track here. At this time, it's best to get to the point. This conversation is getting tiresome," Hera said, turning to Apollo to address him. "Your father is aware not to intrude in your affairs just to provoke you."

Turning to the great Zeus, Hera expressed her thoughts and feelings without hesitation.

"You knew better than to barge into your son's domains like a peasant to deliver the news of your arrival. You could have ordered Fernhoof to summon Apollo for you. He's a lesser immortal and is bound to do your bidding. Didn't it occur to you that your son needs his privacy? He would have been more agreeable if you just waited for him downstairs. But patience is not your strong suit, I reckon."

"Downstairs was a mess. Besides, these places are not fit for the king and the first prince," Zeus objected, his face red from anger.

"You don't have a say where your son lives. You should have instructed the faun to clean if it bothered you. Make the place suitable for the king."

Apollo couldn't believe his eyes, seeing Zeus and Hera fight in front of others. "I think that's enough. I'm not here to discuss how I'll live my life. Also, do not boss around my friends."

There was a brief pause before everyone settled down. Apollo sat, pulling Dafnie to sit next to him and to be at eye level with the monarchs. Leto and Artemis stood in place, prepared to defend their family in case anything unexpected occurred. Apollo waited until the tension dissipated before saying anything. Aware of Dafnie's tense muscles, he massaged her thigh, trying to calm her.

"I don't want to waste anyone's time. The sooner we go our separate ways, the better. I have much to do and plan. I want to return to my life," Apollo said. He sighed, trying to calm down. He wanted his father out of his house. "And please, Father, I respectfully ask that you refrain from looking at her that way." Apollo caught his father's lecherous gaze—focused on Dafnie.

Zeus growled before expressing his discontent. "I will stare at whomever I please. No one can stop me."

Exasperated and displeased by their childish behavior, Hera got pissed and had enough of Zeus's and Apollo's bickering.

"No, you will not. You'll respect your son's wishes when they concern his family. Now, let's not waste time. My time is precious. I have more important matters to attend to."

A staring match of willfulness lasted minutes. Father and son didn't blink. Both were too stubborn to budge. Dafnie sensed Apollo's inner turmoil since he transferred her tattoo onto him. Apollo disliked his father more than ever, but as the minutes ticked, the tension decreased between them.

Before long, the king of gods addressed the sun god. "Apollo, you must face trials that test your humility, wisdom, and compassion. You may not return to Mount Olympus until you reverse the damage you caused on Earth. You will be a servant to humankind, aiding in their rebuilding without the help of your divine powers."

"No, you can't take away my son's power. How will he rebuild this world if he doesn't have his powers?" Leto moved to beg her ruler, only to be stopped by her daughter.

"Mother, please, let him finish. I'm willing to take his punishment, so do not interfere."

"But Apollo..."

"No, Mother! I ask you not to interfere with my affairs with my father. I wish to never return to Mount Olympus and to live among humans from now on. Trust me, I want this," Apollo said forcefully.

Zeus's wicked smile didn't hide his joy at hearing that his son didn't want to return to Olympus. "It's your choice if you want to return, but I'm happy to hear you plan to stay."

"The feeling is mutual. I couldn't be happier. I wish to be far from there."

"The two of you, stop it. Hera, please, do something?" Leto

asked, but when she saw the queen shaking her head, the Titaness became desperate and turned toward her ex-husband. "Zeus, when did you stop loving your son?"

"He needs to learn his place as you need to learn yours," Zeus commanded to a stunned Leto.

"I'd appreciate it if you treat my mother with respect," Apollo's disdain oozed from his tone.

Worried, Dafnie looked around, trying to find an opportunity to defuse the situation. Seeing they were getting nowhere with their conversation, Dafnie stared at Hera, the only person who acted calmly during the altercation. The queen goddess ignored everyone except her. Dafnie felt a dizzying and confusing pull from Hera. Her ears rang, and then a sweet voice invaded her head. Come on, stop this nonsense. You can do this, my dear Dafnie. You have the power to make Zeus speechless. He'll get pissed but not move against you. Come on and see what happens!

"STOP IT! JUST SHUT UP AND STOP IT!" Dafnie screamed without realizing what she had done. Hera smiled at her, and the others stared at her, dumbfounded.

Apollo turned to look at his lover. He reached for her hand, trying to understand the unfolding events. He followed Dafnie's vision, only to land on Hera as he understood what was happening. Hera was performing one of her mind tricks on Dafnie when she spoke up again.

"Can we get this over? I want you all gone. The only exceptions are Artemis and Leto. They're my guests," Dafnie turned toward Zeus. "I'm sorry, but you intruded into my home with hostility. I don't trust you. So, the sooner you leave my house, the better."

"You insolent..."

Dafnie had enough of Zeus's attitude when she lost her temper. Unafraid of the other man, she spoke her mind and wanted him gone. "I'm insolent! So what? How about respecting my house? I'm the host, not you."

A fleeting glance at Hera revealed the goddess no longer hid her wicked smile, making it clear to everyone that she was behind Dafnie's outburst. No one, not even Zeus, dared to mention anything else. There was no other choice. They had to overcome their disagreements and continued the meeting to decide Apollo's banishment.

"Agreed. The sooner my father finishes his affairs here, the better. And like she said, you are in her house. You owe her the respect she deserves as our host."

Apollo was not above taking advantage of the situation and trying to play his cards in his favor. Hera remained quiet and vigilant, nodding at him in approval. When he stared at his mother, she looked amused.

"Fine. I want to leave this hellhole you named after yourself, son," Zeus said, refusing to look at Dafnie. "Apollo, I'll strip you of your divine powers until you can rectify the chaos you've unleashed," Zeus said, announcing his decision. "He cannot communicate with other gods. I want him disconnected from his allies, including his family. I'm the exception. No excuses! If any god interferes with Apollo's mission, he'll regain his powers, but I will punish the offending god." He stared at Leto and Artemis to make his point. "Lesser immortals, like his companion Fernhoof, are the only ones that can help you from now on. His limitations will be identical to his master's. This compulsory service as a guardian to the mortals will teach him empathy and consequences outside the divine realm."

Dafnie's shoulders slumped, looking overwhelmed and at a crossroads. The punishment was severe enough, and adding more hardship to the complicated situation didn't feel right. She was about to stand when Apollo held her in place, offering her some support.

"Dafnie has a say on this, too. I wronged her world and jeopardized her way of life. It's only fair she gets to have a say on this. Her opinion matters to me."

"Is my punishment not good enough?! Is that what you're trying to say?"

"Zeus, the king of Mount Olympus, should know better than this. Don't twist my words, father. I never said such a thing. For her sake, I seek only atonement—nothing more. The weight of my wrongdoings compels me to do nothing less. By the way, I'm not doing this for you."

Sensing another argument about to bubble up, Dafnie spoke up to deliver a piece of her mind. "Can the two of you stop this, now?! Considering you can't agree most of the time, I'm speaking up again. Let's see if you'll listen this time around. I'm coming along, and that's final. Apollo, I'm not waiting at home for your return," she asserted, holding her hand in Apollo's to remain quiet. "Apollo needs to be more like me, a mortal, and understand that humans suffer from hunger and tiredness. He won't understand the gravity of his actions without being vulnerable first."

She heard Apollo sigh loudly from the corner of her eye as he facepalmed himself. As for Zeus, the god looked surprised. She didn't even bother to look at Hera. A warm glow of the goddess's approval radiated through her. *Good girl!* She was the only one who could hear Hera through their mental link.

Zeus contemplated for a moment, his eyes narrowing. "Very well. Apollo will experience the frailty of mortals. Dafnie, through your influence, you'll go with him, leading him through the challenges of mortal life."

With a snap of his fingers, the god-king delivered his punishment. In an instant, Apollo collapsed to the floor, withering and groaning in agony. Dafnie, having borne witness to such a display of power, became concerned. Before she could approach her husband, Hera steered her away from him.

"We need to talk in private," Hera said as she moved to the kitchen area, with Zeus following behind.

"But Apollo is suffering."

"He's used to this—it's not his first time. However, his punishment was extra painful this time around. Your defiance angered me greatly, Apollo."

"ARGH! YOU FUCKING DICK! MAKE IT GO AWAY... NOW." Apollo shouted from the living room as his mother and sister helped him to the sofa. "WHY DO YOU CRAVE TO PROVE YOU'RE A FUCKING ASSHOLE?"

"Not this time, Apollo. I'm enjoying seeing you scream in pain when you're a disobedient brat."

Dafnie couldn't believe what was happening and that she was the root cause of Apollo's pain. Leto and Artemis rushed to help him back onto the sofa. When she glimpsed his face, he looked in so much pain that it shattered her heart.

"Please, don't mind my husband. He's vicious and likes to get back at you for defying him. By the way... my dear husband, I compelled her to defy you—to stand against you. Do not take it out on her."

"Knowing how you are, I figured as much," he said to his

wife as he turned toward Dafnie. "I take it Phoebe visited you. I hope you understand its meaning. If you fail, you'll experience my wrath, and your children will be on the hook to continue Apollo's punishment."

Dafnie's blunt tone left no room for misjudgment beyond frustration with these political games. "Understood! No need to tell me again. I got the message the first time when Phoebe delivered her message."

Zeus nodded before walking away toward his son.

"Here—a few presents," Hera said, producing two pouches. "This pouch has a silver bracelet. It can summon a special crossbow with the truest of aims. It also has a quiver that will never run out of arrows. Also, the bracelet will allow you to communicate with me and give you access to one of Apollo's pavilions outside Mount Olympus. It's between Olympus and the mortal world, so he can visit the place without disobeying his father. There's another bracelet for you that you can give to whomever you want. I gathered all of Apollo's weapons within the golden bracelet, enabling anyone wearing it to summon them at will. Take note, these are powerful artifacts. Now, this other pouch holds special stones. Show them to Apollo—he'll know what they are. If anyone interferes with your mission, you can use these to compel them to help you."

"Compel? That sounds menacing. I'm not too fond of the idea. They make me uncomfortable."

Hera approached Dafnie and whispered as she handed over the pouch. "It's ominous, but you may need them. Zeus ordered not to help Apollo, but he mentioned nothing about helping you. Don't hesitate. Use the bracelet to summon me when in need."

Dafnie considered the implications of the message. Curious, she wanted to know more. "What's your plan... this power scheme you seem to play?"

Hera smiled, looking satisfied in Dafnie's quick wits and picking up one of her warnings. "To answer your question, I always have a plan. Let me make myself and my intentions clear. I implanted thoughts of your reincarnation in Zeus's head and... made him think it was his idea. You have a vital role in my plan. You're safe with me, not him. Currently, Zeus relies on you getting pregnant with Apollo's offspring. Like me, he always has a backup plan—your children are his collateral. Mark my words! He will cast you aside once you no longer serve his needs."

Shock washed over Dafnie. Was it wise to trust Hera? She felt there was no other choice. Dafnie needed to trust her. She asked about another pressing issue Hera brought up during their conversation. "Who do you think may interfere with our efforts? I need to make sure we succeed."

"That's my girl! I now feel justified in influencing my husband to gather your essence. To bring you back to support Apollo with his destiny. I have someone in mind. This god has a grudge against Apollo. He's been scurrying around Olympus and asking about Apollo and you. Ask Apollo about it. I'm certain he'll tell you more about it. My only advice is to be careful."

Dafnie looked around toward the living room. Apollo lay prostrate on the couch, breathing hard and in pain. Zeus sat next to him and muttered something. She approached the duo, allowing them time to finish their conversation.

Apollo couldn't believe his ears. His father was once again spewing nonsense. With undeniable confidence, Zeus dispatched Phoebe to deliver a thinly veiled threat to Dafnie. Failure would lead to their deaths, he suspected. He looked at Dafnie, approaching as he extended his hand to her. She smiled at him, filling his heart with so much love at seeing her smile. I will not fail you, my love. He thought as he remembered the carefree Dafnie smiling at him from his prophetic vision.

He felt bitter about his father's selfish actions. "I understand what I need to do. There's no point wasting your time any longer, especially with those you consider lower and insignificant."

"I will take my leave," Zeus said. He then turned to the other gods to issue his last command. "No one may help Apollo. Am I clear?"

"Yes, your Majesty!" Like a well-trained choir ensemble, everyone replied at once.

They disappeared in a flash of light, leaving Dafnie and Apollo alone in the living room.

Chapter 50

Godly Journey

After the gods left, Dafnie headed to the kitchen and snagged an apple from the fruit basket Fernhoof bought from one of Apollo's palaces. She then went to the fridge to grab some meat cured by Fernhoof earlier that week. She grabbed a cutting board to slice the fruit and aged venison. Picking a plate, she arranged Apollo's light snack in seconds. Her hands moved about the motions with practiced ease.

He looked so frail!

The thought weighed on her mind as her fingers fidgeted with an almond before popping it into her mouth. Dafnie sighed, wishing they had some old amenities, like electricity, which had been out for weeks.

I should have installed those solar panels when I had the chance—at least enough to run the fridge. I miss having a cold drink.

She looked at the plate, thinking about their situation.

Apollo's powers made life easier, but his punishment would make venturing into their new world challenging.

I worry about Apollo's lack of energy. I hope he gets better after this light snack. He looked in pain when he received his father's trial.

The rhythmic sound of Apollo's troubled breathing interrupted the otherwise silent living room. Dafnie strained her neck to get a good look at her husband. His weakened state kept him lying motionless on the sofa. She spotted a sweat trail across Apollo's brows as he stared at the ceiling. It looked like he would pass out at any moment. She became concerned about his health. Helping him recover his strength was the only thing she could think of.

The clink of dishes set aside to dry was the only sound that interrupted the silence. As she navigated the kitchen, a persistent thought lingered in her mind, unwilling to leave her alone.

Toying with the idea floating in her mind, she smiled at the beautiful idea.

Apollo... my husband! We didn't have a ceremony or a reception. But... it feels good to be Mrs. Valencia-Delphoes. Now, I must find out if I'm expecting. That vision came out of nowhere!

She thought about being part of Apollo's life. A sense of joy washed over her as images of their time together washed over her mind. Delight painted her heart with hope.

There had been many sudden changes. Not only was Dafnie married to an exiled god, but life had also taken an unexpected turn towards rusticity, thanks to Apollo's lack of consideration.

Argh! I cannot see into the future, but I'm not looking forward to cold showers. The thought of filth made her shudder. "Yuck, gross! I have been dirty, but I'll manage."

Not considering the consequences of his actions, their existence now hinged on resourcefulness and the bounties of nature. They gathered whatever they could find relying on their wits for survival. Frequently, Apollo and Fernhoof hunted for game to preserve for later—adapt to a life of self-reliance. During the preceding weeks, she learned the ins and outs of gathering to survive. Thanks to her parents' farming business, Dafnie was already decent at gardening. Still, she needed to learn to live in the wild.

She looked down at the snack before her, deciding it needed some nuts to add healthy fats to help her love recover. She grabbed some almonds and placed them on the plate. Content with her selection, she walked into the living room. Apollo remained sprawled on the couch, emitting low groans while trying to find a more comfortable position.

"I'm sorry you're in pain, mi amor. I didn't mean to cause you such distress. How're you holding up?"

Apollo sighed in relief before answering. "Ugh! My sweet nymph, I'm okay. Do not worry. I'm better, but that jackass was being extra spiteful today. Trust me, you did nothing wrong. He's the one who took it too far. I believe seeing my dick this morning made him jealous. Compared to him, I'm well endowed." Apollo busted out, laughing at his joke. After noticing Dafnie's horror, he quickly apologized for making fun of his father. "I'm sorry, my love. I'm snappy and cannot move. My body hurts so much."

"Can you sit? I'll bring you something to eat. It's best to regain your strength soon. As a mortal, you'll feel very vulnerable. You need to take great care and remember not to push yourself." She sat beside him, picking up a slice of apple with venison and feeding it to him.

Apollo sat with significant effort and opened his mouth, hoping Dafnie would feed him. She laughed, seeing the mix of neediness and helplessness written all over his face. "You're hopeless and need to understand that you're not invincible. It's easy to get hurt. Be prudent in all your plans. Recklessness is risky and endangers lives. My life is in your hands now. Just remember that."

"I apologize you're involved in this mess. I hate that you're forcing yourself to help me fix my mistakes. You deserve a quiet life, to be treated like a queen, and to live in luxury." Apollo reached out to caress Dafnie's face, admiring her beauty and strength. Her ability to handle herself before his father surprised and impressed him. "One more thing! It's reckless to defy my father the way you did. I could've lost you if he felt he needed to end your life for challenging him."

"It's all in the past. We need to make travel plans. Where are we going first?"

Apollo considered his physical state, still suffering the aftereffects of his painful transformation. Because of his weakness, he didn't want to risk the lives of Dafnie and Fernhoof. "We're going to New York City first. I asked Fernhoof to prepare for our trip and ask one of my servants to guard our homes. Since I no longer have my powers, we must go on foot. However, let me warn you that the trek ahead will be difficult and have its fair share of dangers."

"When are we planning to leave?" Dafnie asked, offering another piece of fruit with meat, but Apollo dragged her to sit on his lap instead. "I take it you're gaining some of your strength?"

"I feel much better now that you're here with me—couldn't ask for anything else."

"My handsome husband, I want to be prepared, even if you don't fear the king of gods. What dangers should we expect?"

"First, wasn't it you who told my father that he was just a mere guest? I must admit that was brave and stupid but sexy as hell." Apollo flashed a devilish smile. "Second, I've been preparing and planning for weeks. My exile this time will be brutal. I can't afford any loose ends."

He then placed his head on her chest and breathed in her scent. Soon, Apollo hesitated, not admitting his grave mistake. Acknowledgment of the disastrous consequences of his screwed-up plan shone in his eyes. A weight that pressed him down on his typical, easy-going character—skin looking clammy.

"I'm concerned about my plant's effects on animals and humans. Its pollen became unstable, causing some concerning mutations to nature."

Dafnie gave him a stern look, expressing great concern—and determination. Her eyes fixed on him as she gently pulled away from his arms. Desperate to keep her in place, Apollo grasped her shoulders and caressed her face, unwilling to let her go. However, his attempts to bring her into his embrace only seemed to intensify her resistance as she pushed against him with greater force. Conflict shone through her eyes as she battled her desire to stay close to him and her need for personal space.

Seeing her reaction as Apollo felt even weaker than his heart shattered into pieces was shocking. Apollo wanted nothing more than to erase her expression. "Please! Don't look at me like that. Not only does my body hurt, but not my heart aches with the fear of losing you." His voice trembled with vulnerability.

Dafnie pushed a few tangled strands of hair off Apollo's forehead.

"I know you worry about the world. Still, I'm a little upset with you." She noted Apollo was getting some of his skin color back, and his cheeks looked flush.

She sighed before continuing to clarify her concerns. "I'm upset because I'm confused about your relationship with your father. You dislike Zeus but want his approval. Why do you let your father plant such sinister thoughts in your mind? It looks like you like to bait each other like two kids. What gets me the most is seeing you getting hurt because you lost your cool. However, I apologize because I wasn't better when I lost it with Zeus. I have to say, Hera is cunning. I must be careful around her." She leaned down and kissed his forehead. The warmth of his skin against her lips was a comforting caress. "How are you feeling?"

"My body is still in pain, but I love your attention." Apollo enjoyed his wife's delicate kisses and fleeting touches. But concern sank in his mind. "I wonder if I will get my nectar? If prepared correctly, you can use ambrosia to make a tonic capable of enhancing a mortal's stamina and endurance. I know how to prepare for it, but I lack resources. You can only find them on Olympus. I'm no longer welcome there."

He remembered their earlier meeting, which he promised never to repeat. The unpleasant encounter, marked by heated words, left him resentful. His mood darkened at the mention of Zeus' pretentious attitude.

"We'll manage with what we have." Dafnie pretended to be annoyed by the situation. She picked an almond and pressed it against Apollo's lips to feed the helpless god.

In a better mood, Apollo took the little morsel and kissed her fingers. After his horrible experience, he felt like indulging in the comforting embrace of Dafnie's arms, enjoying her sweet lips.

"Right at this moment, going out doesn't concern me. I'm in too much pain to think straight. Our journey outside Phoebus Groove will be uncertain and dangerous, so I want to enjoy this peaceful time with you."

Fernhoof barged into the house from the backdoor. He looked furious, distraught, and human. "Fuck, Apollo! What did you do? I lost my beautiful appearance. My luscious fur and my beautiful horns are all gone," he screamed, looking around for someone.

"They're all gone. It's nice to see you in this form, Keith!"

"Shit! Noooo! It took me centuries to grow those horns to perfection. Perfection! Now... I look... HIDEOUS."

Fernhoof stood before them, looking both elegant and pissed. Dafnie's jaw dropped, and her eyes widened in disbelief. The tall man with bronzed skin wore a black shirt, leather pants, and dress shoes. His lustrous black hair cascaded down his broad and chiseled shoulders. Thick eyebrows and a well-groomed goatee framed his handsome face, coupled with generous lips. Dafnie had always known their friend was attractive, but she never imagined Fernhoof was this captivating. "Wait—you called him Keith. Why?"

"That's the name I use as a human," Fernhoof said as he turned to Apollo. "This is not glamour. This transformation is the 'real deal,' man. Am I being punished, too?"

"Yes... and no. If you want to go with me, you must become human. You are the most affected because you have pledged your loyalty to me long ago and never left my side." A wave of sadness washed over Apollo as he realized his friend was now involved. "Do you still have your powers?"

"I still have some powers, but I can feel death creeping into this body. It's creepy and uncomfortable."

"I understand, my friend. Just bear it for a while longer. I promise I'll reward you handsomely."

"You'd better because this is disturbing. When are we planning to leave?"

"Dafnie is coming along. We plan to leave soon rather than later. Did you get everything ready?"

"Almost, but Dafnie needs a backpack with supplies. I hope you don't get mad at me for this, but I can't find your weapons. Have you summoned and moved them? They seem to be nowhere. I looked everywhere."

"What?"

Standing up from the sofa, Dafnie headed to the kitchen to fetch the pouches Hera gave her. "Wait—I know where they are. Hera gave me a few things before leaving." She retrieved the bags from the kitchen island and settled next to Apollo to show him their gifts. "She gave me these."

"Keith, can you get everything ready? I'd like us to leave tomorrow morning."

"Sure. Two of your servants will move here tomorrow to protect your estate. I take it you'll stay here."

"Yes!" Apollo said as he took the pouches Dafnie held.

Keith turned to finish their preparation. "Then I'm using your bed tonight. I'm not sleeping on that bed in the guest room. It's hard as rocks." Keith's curt remark stunned Apollo—but didn't shock him.

"Enjoy!" Apollo dismissed offhandedly, distracted by the velvet bags. The first pouch held two bracelets. One was silver, the other golden. Dafnie reached over to the golden one and slipped the jewelry on his wrist. He mimicked her and fastened the silver bracelet around her wrist.

"Hera told me I could give this cuff to anyone that would use it well."

"The 'Queen' has always been a cunning woman. Are my weapons here?"

"Yes! Hera mentioned all your favorite weapons are inside your cuff." Dafnie caressed the intricate design on Apollo's cuff. "She then gave me this other pouch, and I'm concerned about it."

"Why are you concerned?" Apollo asked as he took the smaller sack from her hand. When he peeked inside the bag, he understood why she worried their situation would worsen in time. "Why did she give you this?"

"She said if anyone interferes, we can use these against them," she said, hesitating and trying to avoid revealing too much of her conversation. "Is it right to keep a secret? I shouldn't say more about our safety."

"Whatever information Hera and my grandmother told you, keep it sealed within yourself. I understand now you need to carry the burden of secrecy."

"I'm sorry..."

"You don't have to be sorry, my love. Embrace it and use that information for power," he said as he kissed her tenderly. "Now about those stones..." He closed his eyes and produced a small sharp knife.

"How did you do that?"

"I concentrated on the object I wanted. If you close your eyes and concentrate, it'll reveal its secrets. Before we leave, I'll teach you how. Now..." Apollo said as he pricked his finger. "You need your blood to bind the pebbles and make them work. When they are white, it means they're inactive. See?"

He showed her as the rocks turned from white to gold as he rubbed his blood on them. The tiny round pebbles looked like precious stones with their soft glow. "Now, these are bound to me. And with your blood..."

He took Dafnie's hand and pricked one of her fingers. He then rubbed her blood over the stones, and they changed color. Streaks of forest green swirled around the golden color, creating a fascinating pattern on the rocks. "Pretty! The color is befitting of you."

Apollo placed the small pebbles back into the pouch, his stern gaze fixed on Dafnie with a solemn expression. "You need to be careful with these. After the person fulfills their purpose, the stone will dissolve and disappear. You use them by expressing a clear intent and placing the stone over the target's heart. The process is painful, and it could even kill them if they disobey."

"Understood. But why would she give me something this harmful?"

"Hera's always several steps ahead with her schemes, and her knowledge is vast. We shouldn't use them—they're dangerous," Apollo warned, throwing the pouch on the coffee table. He couldn't focus on anything else, captivated by Dafnie's alluring movements against his crotch. "Now, my love, you have been sitting on my lap, and your involuntary movements excite me very much."

He kissed Dafnie's neck, sending shivers down her spine. His lips were heaven on her skin, and she reacted with goosebumps all over her body. Apollo trailed kisses to her lips as Dafnie received him with loving eagerness, and their breaths mingled.

They wasted no time. Dafnie wanted her sun god, and Apollo enjoyed his forest nymph. Without further delay, they removed their clothes, Dafnie making a display as she undressed. Standing exposed before him, Apollo admired her hourglass shape.

Her irresistible charm drew him in so much he couldn't resist the urge to reach out and guide her back onto his lap. She straddled his hips as he grabbed the base of his cock and positioned himself at her warm entrance.

It seemed she was as desperate as he was as she impaled herself onto his rod. Their breaths hitched at their sudden union. Dafnie never averted her gaze from Apollo's as she moved up and down his cock. Their bodies united with great zeal as they moved faster into completion—a race to prove their love emerged from their desperate yet fulfilling lovemaking.

Their breathing and moans grew louder, moving closer to their satisfactory end. Once they reached their pinnacle, they moaned in unison as they each found their release. Their fluids mixed and became one. Apollo kissed her breasts before sighing with satisfaction.

"Fuck, why am I so drained after one go?" Apollo asked as he tried to catch his laborious breath.

"Welcome to mortality, mi amor. But don't worry. We have the entire day to heal."

Chapter 51

Celestial Gambit

Apollo's house was alive and active the following day. The last details of their plans fell into place. Two of Apollo's trusted servants, Xenia and Kyros, who had been with him for many millennia, were going about the house, making proper arrangements for Apollo's and Dafnie's departure.

The couple meticulously inspected every nook and cranny, ensuring everything was in perfect order. Afterward, Kyros went through the backpacks and equipment their lord and lady needed for their journey. In the kitchen, Fernhoof secured their provisions for the next week. While Apollo talked to his subordinate, Dafnie packed a few essentials, just in case.

Dafnie expected Apollo and Fernhoof to survive on their wits alone, but not her. She ought to prepare for anything that awaited them in the open. Securing the basics was paramount in her priorities. After scribbling down a quick list of items, she stashed the paper in her pocket. Ready, she left the bedroom to join the others in the living room. Once she reached the bottom of the stairs, she found Apollo and Fernhoof discussing their plans, and she listened in secret.

"We need to take a straightforward route to New York. Roads and highways will be our best options," Fernhoof argued.

"We won't have cover. It's fine if it's just us, but I fear for Dafnie's safety. Her skills as a skilled hunter remain buried in her mind. During tough times, she can summon her abilities. She showed me her hunting talents a few days ago, but that was an exception. We train her to manifest her skills at will. We must act cautiously, Fernhoof," Apollo said as he finished packing. "I know you hate being called Keith, but we have no choice. Have you considered a last name?"

"Yeah, I was going to use Fernhoff."

"Nice! No one will suspect if we call you Fernhoof by accident."

"Exactly," Fernhoof replied, storing the sleeping bags and tents away.

Dafnie peered around the corner as a smile played on her lips, revealing she listened to their conversation. "I'm ready."

"How long were you planning to stay hidden?" Apollo asked, smirking knowingly. "It's unbecoming to spy on people."

"Well, I didn't want to interrupt your chat. It seemed important." Dafnie noticed Apollo's and Fernhoof's pouches looking empty. "Is that everything you'll bring?"

"Yes. Let me check your bag. Xenia and Kyros brought a few items we can use." Apollo's face broke into a grin, in good spirits, as he rummaged through her stuff.

Dafnie was glad she hid her list in her pocket—away from prying eyes. With his mind preoccupied, she chose not to burden

Apollo with her potential pregnancy concerns. She didn't want to stay behind and wait. "What are these?"

"Sleeping bags! They're thin but comfortable." The Sun God showed her a tiny square of folded bed sheets. He then picked up a small package and stuffed it in her bag. "Now, this is a tent. As you can see, it barely takes up any space. And this other sack has several changes of clothes, although it's in the style and trends typical in Olympus."

Dafnie felt everyone acted tense, which livened the mood. "You mean tunics and whatnot?"

"Yeah—tunics, sarongs, and whatnots," Apollo walked to her to kiss her before continuing his instructions. "Now, do you remember the hand signals I taught you last night?"

"Sure do."

"You must learn to signal—communication is vital. Now... stay close and pay attention to our surroundings. Watch out for the party members and what they're trying to communicate. How should you alert me when I'm distracted or unresponsive?"

"Because I lack whistling skills like you and Fernhoof, I'll tsk twice until you answer."

Apollo grabbed a utility belt with a pouch and a small hunting knife. He inspected the weapon before handing the belt to Danie. With Apollo's help, she secured the belt around her waist and leg.

"You know how to summon your crossbow and other weapons. Concentrate on what you need, like we practiced. I want you to arm yourself when we walk out that door. Even though Fernhoof and I swept the area, we should always expect danger on every corner. Unknown things live in the shadows. I want you always to be ready to defend with all you have." He then held her face to get her full attention. "If you're feeling tired, let us know. We've loaded most of our supplies into our bracelets, but they have their limit. I ensured your bracelet has enough space for your bag if needed, but only carrying the essentials is best."

"Apollo, I'll be fine. Compared to you, I'm inexperienced but not weak. Lead climbing and running strenuous trails are my thing. I know it's not much, but I'll manage. Trust me, I'm a quick learner."

"All right, my love." Apollo kissed her forehead in understanding. Next, he pinned his trusty faun companion with a discerning gaze as they walked out of the safety of their home. "If we are ready... Fernhoof! We'll follow your plan, but be on the lookout. We need to be on high alert. I'm counting on your instincts, my friend," Apollo said, patting Fernhoof on the back.

Keith finished adjusting his equipment before he grabbed his gear from the table. "Understood! Should we get this party going? We must leave as soon as possible and find a safe place by nightfall. The creatures are most active at night," he said, fidgeting with his bag.

"We need to be vigilant. The monsters roam the day as well."

"Agree..."

"I understand your concern about the attacks. But have you considered the journey? It'll be long and tiresome. We'll get tired and hungry, and we can get hurt and sick. Have you thought of that?" Dafnie asked the group.

Puzzled, Fernhoof and Apollo exchanged looks.

"She's right, Apollo. We need ambrosia tonics. We're not used to being mortals."

Daedalion rushed into the kitchen from the open window as

if on cue. The bird dropped a pack on Dafnie's hands and flew to its perch, waiting for a treat. Apollo walked over to his companion to reward him for the message. "Hey, Daedalion! I'm sorry I don't have your favorite snack, my dear friend. Are you coming with us? You would be of immense help."

The bird screeched its agreement while Apollo petted its chest with a light touch. Dafnie saw a brief, dreamy, boyish smile on her husband's face before it disappeared. She opened the pouch and discovered a note with three vials. "Apollo, I think you need to see this," she called out, pulling out the bag's contents.

Apollo ignored the vials, took the paper from her, and read its content aloud. "You know what this is. Every day, you'll receive a vial for each party member. Don't fuck things up for me. ~ Zeus."

Apollo closed his eyes and sighed, looking torn and disappointed. "That was a waste of scribble. My father should've known better. Dafnie, drink your tonic now, as it will give you a boost. Xenia and Kyros, we're on our way out," Apollo instructed as he swung his bag over his shoulder and took a vial from Dafnie's hand. He opened the container and brought it to his lips. He tilted his head back and down the liquid in one swift motion. Without looking back, Apollo summoned his crossbow and hip quiver from his bracelet and went outside to scope the area.

Feeling confused, Dafnie hoisted her backpack and hesitantly drank her tonic while staring at Apollo's back. Once she finished, the container vanished from Dafnie's hand, catching her by surprise. In an instant, a sense of rejuvenation washed over her, leaving her invigorated and revitalized. The fatigue she felt before dissipated as vigor coursed through her veins. "Amazing! I feel great."

Taking the last vial, Fernhoof gave her a knowing smile. "This is some incredible stuff. I'm glad we are getting these. Otherwise, it would be rough." Fernhoof gulped the contents of his vial and headed outside to meet with Apollo.

"Xenia and Kyros, I entrust our homes to you. Please be safe." Dafnie walked toward the house's entrance before turning around. "One last thing! Please take care of my garden. My garden is dear and special to me. It makes me feel connected to my parents."

"Of course, my lady," Xenia answered. "No worries. We'll take good care of your home. We were thinking of moving to help Prince Apollo with his new life here with you."

"Prince?"

"Yes. Apollo's an Olympian royalty—firstborn son with lots of influence. His mother was one of Zeus's consorts. His status is above everyone else except Zeus himself."

"Yeah, right? I'm not sure why I forgot Apollo was the son of a king," Dafnie said, trying to internalize the information.

"Don't fret, my lady. He doesn't enjoy being a prince," Kyros answered. "He prefers to live a simple life rather than being bothered by schemes and politics."

"Dafnie, we need to go. We have a long day ahead before we stop for the night." Fernhoof's cry broke through Dafnie's thoughts as Apollo, now ready, gestured for them to move.

"Right. I'm coming." Dafnie smiled at Apollo as she turned to Xenia and Kyros. She lowered her voice to hide her intentions. "Can you do me a favor and prepare a nursery for twins? I'll tell Apollo in time, but I can share the news with you."

"My lady, are you expecting?" Xenia looked excited.

Dafnie turned to meet with Apollo and Fernhoof, nervousness knotting her gut. "I'm not sure yet, but it will happen."

"What will happen?" Apollo asked, curious about their conversation.

"In due time, mi amor." Dafnie kissed him as they met on the street and summoned her weapon. She attached the quiver to her belt and nodded, ready to start their journey.

Apollo pouted, feigning disappointment at being excluded from the information loop. "I disapprove of secrets, but you have reasons to keep them, and I can trust you."

"Don't worry about it. I'm confirming Xenia and Kyros are ready for our return, nothing else."

Apollo kissed her passionately before signaling they needed to move. He took the lead, walking slower, so Dafnie remained close to him, under his watchful eye and protection. Taking the rear, Fernhoof ensured there were no threats behind.

Dafnie became uneasy when they approached the town center. Its remnants sent chills down her spine as memories flooded back of being chased by monsters. The once bustling streets lay in ruin. The state of the buildings surprised her. Apollo's eyes narrowed, assessing the damage. Dafnie's hand tightened around the foregrip of her weapon, her senses on high alert. The pharmacy, her destination, came to sight the deeper they went into town.

"Tsk, tsk!" Dafnie alerted the group.

Alerted, Apollo turned to examine his lover. Dafnie smiled at him, trying to show him that everything was fine. "I must stop at the pharmacy to get some feminine products."

"Oh, sure." Apollo caressed her cheek. He leaned down for a

private chat while Fernhoof looked around for any danger. "I'm wondering if I should grab some condoms. I'm surprised that you haven't become pregnant yet," Apollo said, kissing her neck, sending shivers all over her body.

Dafnie blushed, the color running to her ears, which made Apollo chuckle. "A year ago, I got an IUD."

"I should've known. But…" Apollo rubbed the back of his neck to ease some tension. "My foresight doesn't work when it involves you. I'm still having problems seeing our future. Although it's exciting to live without knowing what comes next." He chuckled at her cute expression. "You know… IUDs are quite effective with immortals. I want to enjoy our relationship for as long as we can manage," he whispered seductively.

"You two cut it off. We're not even out of town yet, and you want to have sex already? At this rate, we'll never finish this mission. Please save it for the evening."

Apollo's vanity oozed out of him as bits of his pompousness surfaced. "Right! We need to hurry. Is that okay, Dafnie?"

"Sure! It shouldn't take long."

Apollo nodded as he headed straight to the front of the store and opened the door, his crossbow braced and ready in case of an attack. The shop was messy, showing signs of a quick evacuation. He wanted to ensure safety before letting Dafnie inside. Having checked the shop and confirmed it was clear, he motioned for Dafnie to enter while he waited near the door. "Hurry, we have little time."

"I'll be quick." Dafnie rushed inside the store and to the wellness section. She gathered a handful of pregnancy kits and discreetly stuffed them into the bottom of her bag. After getting her secret cargo, she headed to the feminine hygiene aisle, absentmindedly selecting a few items without considering her choices. She didn't want to add too much weight to her bag, but she felt she needed to hide the purpose of her stop. With her belongings in hand, she moved to the entrance and signaled her readiness to the group.

They hurriedly passed the town's boundary, leaving behind the once-familiar structures of Phoebus Groove. Once again, Apollo took the lead, securing the road before them. Out of nowhere, a thick fog surrounded the group, hiding them from any creature lurking around.

✳✳✳

"When I suggested the world needed to start over to Apollo, I didn't mean to unleash the apocalypse. People must worship me again. I didn't ask for the apocalypse."

Zeus strolled out of the city hall, watching the group disappear. Not in the mood to play games, Zeus wanted to be upfront with his cunning wife. "Hera, show yourself, NOW!" There was no response. "Damn it, Hera! I said come out. NOW!"

"What is your problem, Zeus? I'm not at your disposal. I have matters to attend to." Hera sauntered from the vacant store. She watched from the shadows as the reborn nymph displayed prodigious strength. Dafnie's awakening inched near. Hera just needed to exercise patience.

"I swear if you tempt me..."

"If I tempt you... what, Zeus? What are you planning to do? Kill me? We both know you don't have that power over me anymore. I have the power to bend you to my will."

"What is your plan?"

"The details of my plan don't concern you, but know that Nyx, Gaia, and Peneus support me. Also, Artemis supports me. She's my right hand."

"Fuck, Hera! Even my daughter? Earth is mine. Don't you interfere with what is rightfully mine!"

"Only if you don't hinder my plans. I need Apollo and his family." Hera brushed away an errant curl as she stared out into the distance. "They're mine."

Zeus wanted his ancient glory back and would stop at nothing to make it happen. "Not before Apollo uses his powers to fix this planet. If he fails, his twins are mine. They'll help me rebuild the world their father destroyed."

His growl filled the air with hostility as he turned to leave the uncivilized town. The young mortal woman he captured waited for him, wanton and ready for him to feast on. Zeus' monstrous appetite gnawed at him like a vicious predator, thinking of his prey. "Make sure Apollo's wife delivers healthy babies." He vanished without waiting for a response.

"Of course, Zeus. Dafnie will deliver strong demigods." Hera's radiant smile clogged her surroundings with hope and optimism. When Zeus disappeared, she continued her discourse. "I will ensure Apollo's family becomes the cause of your downfall, my dear husband. Your son will fulfill his prophecy that you've been too ignorant to recognize."

Be the first to discover new releases, exclusive content, and behind-the-scenes insights into the magical worlds of romantasy and diverse romance. Sign up to our newsletter at yfvalentine.com for more stories and news.

Y.F. Valentine

Y.F. Valentine is a Puerto Rican indie author who loves writing romance and championing diversity and representation. Her favorite genre, romantasy, weaves tales of love, magic, and passion, featuring dynamic and relatable diverse couples that resonate with readers.

Born and raised in Puerto Rico, Y.F. Valentine began her artistic journey as a cellist, performing music that continues to inspire her creative process.

Y.F. Valentine combines her analytical mindset with her artistic spirit, crafting deeply engaging characters and rich, imaginative worlds. Her work celebrates love in all forms, creating stories that captivate and inspire. She lives with her mixed-race family of five with an overly protective little dog.

You can find Y.F. Valentine on: Instagram @https://

www.instagram.com/y.f.valentine, Twitter @https://x.com/
y_f_valentine, and at https://yfvalentine.com/.